DEC 21 2017

W9-BXU-687

SIGNAL LOSS

Also by Garry Disher

SIGNAL LOSS

Garry Disher

Copyright © 2016 by Garry Disher
First published by The Text Publishing Co. Australia

First edition published in the United States in 2017 by
Soho Press, Inc.
853 Broadway
New York, NY 10003

Library of Congress Cataloging-in-Publication Data

Disher, Garry.
Signal loss / Garry Disher.
Series: A Hal Challis investigation ; 7

ISBN 978-1-61695-859-6
eISBN 978-1-61695-860-2

1. Challis, Hal (Fictitious character)—Fiction. 2. Destry, Ellen
(Fictitious character)—Fiction. 3. Police—Australia—
Melbourne Region (Vic.)—Fiction. I. Title
PR9619.3.D56 S55 2017   823'.914—dc23   2017021392

Printed in the United States of America

10 9 8 7 6 5 4 3 2 1

for Ann and Peter

1

LOVELOCK AND PYM. THEY sounded like some kind of show-business duo—magicians, maybe; folk singers.

In fact they worked for Hector Kaye, who used to run with the Finks out of Kings Cross. That was before he set up as a legitimate businessman and started importing crystal meth from China. They didn't come cheap, Lovelock and Pym. Kaye paid them well and he'd bought them each a house and a car in the past year.

Their next project was to knock off a guy named Owen Valentine down in Victoria. Fifty grand plus a thousand a day each for expenses. Four days minimum, two days on the road from Sydney, two days back. The coast route, not the Hume: fewer cops. There was no reason why they couldn't fly down on fake IDs, they had plenty to choose from, but neither of them had ever seen the south coast. They'd be renting a Mercedes with one of the fake IDs, a big sedan with room in the boot for a body.

That was the basic set-up. Now Hector moved on to the finer detail: "Grab this Valentine prick as soon as his girl-friend and kids have left the house, pack up his clothes and toiletries and shit so it looks like he's done a runner, whack him, disappear the body."

The three of them were on Hector's deck overlooking Double Bay, sitting around a glass and stainless steel outdoor setting, sipping margaritas. Lovelock, a literal-minded man who despised fag drinks like margaritas, said, "Whack him at his house, or take him somewhere first?"

"Not at his fucking house, genius. He's done a *runner*, right? No blood."

"Then disappear him," Lovelock repeated flatly.

"Bury him," Kaye specified. "Deep. You'll need a shovel."

Lovelock had never been to Victoria. "Where?"

"Here," said Kaye, tapping a map. He had the long, clean forefingers of a businessman. No grease, scars or swollen knuckles. Only with his sleeves rolled back you could see a scroll of black ink: *Respect Few, Fear None.*

Lovelock and Pym studied the map dubiously. It was a bad fax, or more likely a scan, showing a twenty-kilometer-square detail of the Mornington Peninsula south-east of Melbourne. Kaye had used pink highlighter to mark a coastal town, Moonta, and an inland track named Lintermans Lane.

"Grab the guy in Moonta, bury him in Lintermans Lane. Got it," said Lovelock.

Meanwhile Pym was examining the other paperwork on the table: head-and-shoulders shots of their victim, typed information, a mobile number. A slight, nervy man who liked to query and quibble, he stared at Kaye. "You're sending us to the dark side of the moon, boss."

"It's not the fucking Simpson Desert, it's an hour from Melbourne," said Kaye. "If you don't want the job, I'll send someone else."

"Can't you use a local guy?"

"It's a *favor* for a local guy, all right? He doesn't want anything to come back on him. You go in, do it, get out. Jesus, you're getting paid enough."

Sea birds wheeled above the water, blindingly blue under

the early summer sun. A solitary cloud above. Pym ignored all that. Curious to know how far he could push, he said, "What's your cut?"

"The satisfaction of doing a favor for an associate," Kaye snarled, "all right?"

Pym saluted him. "You're the boss."

"That I am."

So Lovelock and Pym took the coast road, the ocean only occasionally visible. Stopped Wednesday night at Bega, where they fitted the Mercedes with plates from a Victorian car, and then down through Gippsland to the tip of Westernport Bay. After ascertaining that Moonta was no more than a bunch of beach houses with a single shop, they drove another ten minutes to the town of Waterloo, which had a motel. Pym went for a run as soon as they checked in, then drove to the Bunnings on the edge of town and bought a shovel and tarp. Paid cash, the visor of his John Deere cap low on his brow. Lovelock stayed in, sinking a six-pack of Victoria Bitter as he watched the T20 game on Fox. Over dinner—chicken salad for Pym, meat-lovers pizza for Lovelock—they studied the paperwork again.

Lovelock chewed, swallowed, burped. "Guy looks like a meth head."

Pym nodded. In photographs, Owen Valentine had a narrow, bruised, hunted-looking face under a firebreak haircut, his parted dry lips revealing mossy teeth.

Lovelock snatched another bite and ruminated. "You ever ask yourself what we're doing?"

Christ, thought Pym, hating it when Lovelock got philosophical. "No."

Lovelock waved his pizza slice, tumbling a lump of greyish

meat onto the nasty bedspread. "I mean, all we ever do is what we're told. You ever thought of going independent?"

"No," Pym said, without much hope it would shut Lovelock up.

"Okay, so ask yourself: here's a meth head, and we're getting fifty grand to waste him. Makes you think, right? All that money?"

"Think what?"

"Whatever this Valentine character did to piss off Hector's mate, it must have been big. I mean, fifty grand."

"So?"

"So he knows something, stole a shitload of drugs, something."

"So?"

"So yeah, we top him, bury him. But why not ask a few questions first?" Lovelock said, getting out his cigarettes.

Pym made him take his filthy habit outside, Pym who didn't touch steroids, ice, nicotine, alcohol. He was a killer these days, but quite a bit of the old Pym lingered from before. Clean, straight. Good job as an aide to a Liberal Party MP, before a small misstep in the form of a Facebook post. A few frank thoughts on immigrants and Muslims that prompted a swift change of careers.

He made Lovelock take his filthy habit outside, but still kissed him goodnight.

ON FRIDAY MORNING—AFTER PYM'S run and Lovelock's sleep-in—they drove back up to Moonta. Through farmland that backed onto the mudflats and mangroves, along small, tight roads to the little township. It was no more than a collection of short, sandy streets settled with beach houses of various kinds, some costly, others renovated cottages, with a few wood and plaster kit homes of the kind pictured in brochures with names like "The Inlander" or "The Californian."

The house where Owen Valentine lived with his girlfriend and their kids was a shabby fibro structure set amid ti trees on a narrow dirt track unobservantly named Banksia Court. Pulling the Mercedes under a nearby tree, Lovelock and Pym watched and waited, and presently a rusty white Corolla pulled out of the car shed at the side of the house, a woman and one child aboard.

"So far so good," Pym said.

"There's supposed to be two kids. Where's the other one?"

"Maybe it's too tiny to see," said Pym, irritated. "How the fuck would I know?"

"I'm just saying."

They stared at the house gloomily, wondering if they'd have to factor in a second killing. It would mean more work.

"Okay, time to rock and roll," Pym said.

THEY ENTERED BY THE CAR shed and a connecting door to the kitchen. Found Owen Valentine asleep on a sofa in the sitting room. Pym was disgusted. Takeaway food containers, wine bottles, overflowing ashtrays, a greasy meth pipe on the coffee table. And the place stank. Drugs, garbage, pine sap from a miserable Christmas tree in the corner, dog shit.

"Hey there, cutie," murmured Lovelock, bending to a tiny black toilet brush of a dog. Dogs loved him, and this one licked his hand.

"Leave it," snapped Pym.

He kicked the sleeping man's leg. Valentine snorted, a skinny, ice-ravaged creature dressed in shorts and a T-shirt. Gummy eyes, when they finally opened. Three or four days' worth of whiskers, grubby feet with a yellow talon at the end of each toe.

"Get up, arsehole," Pym said. To get the message across, he scraped the blade of his boning knife along the ridges and whorls of his left thumb.

"Who the fuck are you?" croaked Valentine.

"Your worst nightmare," Lovelock said, grabbing Valentine by the shirt, lifting him out of the chair, driving his fist into the skinny belly.

The dog yapped, appreciating the game.

"Careful," said Pym. "No blood, no signs of disturbance."

So they moved to the car shed, shut the street door and duct-taped Valentine to a cobwebby green plastic garden chair. Lovelock scooped up the dog and tickled its ears as he looked around. Old paint tins, packaged screws and nails on a work bench, various edged tools hanging from the walls. Engine oil in the air; a hint of brine from the nearby beach.

And sweat. It was hot in the shed, getting hotter, the early December sun beating hard upon the roofing iron. Pissed pants now, too. Valentine bewildered and afraid, his eyes bugging out.

"You've been a naughty boy, Owen," Lovelock said, aiming at the general, not the specific, hoping Valentine would spill some information they could profit from. "Haven't you, eh? A liability. Some unhappy people."

A look of resignation passed over Valentine's face, chased by fear and ice twitches. He thrashed about in his chair and opened his mouth to yell. Lovelock slammed his fists left and right at Valentine's head and stomach, and Valentine, reduced to skin and bone, rattled and jerked in the chair, not riding the blows at all.

Pym, fastidious, stood clear of the flying blood, sweat and mucus. Presently he said, "That'll do." The two of them paused for a moment, regarding the miserable figure in the chair.

Valentine did nothing, said nothing, his head lolling. It made Lovelock mad. And his fists hurt.

He moved in again, screaming, "Where the *fuck* is it, you piece of shit?"

Valentine lifted his misshapen head. His eyes were reduced to puffy slits. He whispered, "I'm sorry," working his tongue and lips to moisten the rotting mouth.

"My turn," Pym said, nudging Lovelock aside. He drew a line of blood beads along Valentine's forearm with the tip of his knife. "You're holding out on us, Owen."

Valentine's eyes rolled back and his chin dropped to his chest. Blood dripped from his arm, bloody drool gathered on his chin, a poor glistening thread of it stretching, finally reaching his lap.

"Faking it," Lovelock said.

He leaned in, jetted smoke into Valentine's face and shouted, "Where the fuck is it?"

Valentine tried to lift his head and failed.

"What's that?" said Lovelock comically. "Can't hear you, mate. Work those tonsils."

Valentine's chin fell to his chest but he was conscious, his eyes open. Lovelock said to Pym, "You have another go."

Pym, gagging at the smell, flicked his blade tip at Valentine's nostrils, earlobes, eyebrows. Fluids leaked, pooling around the chair, darkening the cement floor, and Valentine shuddered, his eyes fluttering, his head tipping to his shoulder.

Lovelock's impatience grew. This shouldn't be taking so long. Elbowing Pym away, he delivering another flurry of punches, left and right. "*Wake up, bozo.*"

Nothing. He tapped the bruised cheeks, lifted the mashed eyelids, felt for a pulse.

Found a pulse. Muttered, "Not dead, then," and slapped

Valentine's face. "Come on buddy, wake up. Don't piss us about."

Still nothing.

He stood back. "I'm not buying it, Owen," he said critically. "Wake the fuck up."

"Can I try?" said Pym, his voice a whispery rasp, almost indistinguishable from the sound of the hot wind outside, leafy branches scraping the nearby walls, fences and rooftops.

"Go for your life."

Pym used his fingers this time, pinching and flicking, darting in like a wasp. Finding pleasure where, for Lovelock, administering a beating was merely work.

No response. Pym stood back and Lovelock took his place again. "Maybe he's unconscious."

"Oh, do you think?" said Pym. "You did hit him quite hard."

Lovelock flushed.

He pulled out one of his phones, tapped the screen with a blunt forefinger.

Three taps, Pym noted. Appalled, he said, "Who the fuck are you calling?"

"Triple zero."

"You mad?"

Lovelock waved his free hand irritably, a shut-up gesture, and said pleasantly, "Ambulance service, please."

Pym blinked, checked the exits. There were two: the connecting door to Valentine's kitchen, currently open, and the roller door to the street, currently closed.

"No," Lovelock was saying, "I don't actually need an ambulance, not yet, but could you give me a couple of tips on how to revive a mate who—?"

He listened, nodded, said, "No, he just fainted. The heat, I think."

Listened again, said, "No, an ambulance would be over-kill, I just need . . . On drugs? I don't think so," he added, glancing at Valentine as if to confirm the diagnosis. Listened a bit more, frustration growing. "Look, should I pump his chest? Throw cold water on him? What? No, no, don't put me through to—"

He stabbed the off button. Stripped away the battery cover, removed battery and sim card, ground the whole phone into the concrete with his boot, put the pieces in his pocket.

"The mind boggles," said Pym.

"She was going to put me through to the cops," Lovelock said, sounding surprised.

"Jesus Christ. Look, let's just finish him off and get out of here."

"Fine," said Lovelock, smarting. "Wait."

He leaned his heavy face toward Valentine, peeled up the eyelids, felt for a pulse. "Oh well. Mission accomplished."

Pym checked, confirmed, sighed. "I'll get the car. You grab his clothes and toilet bag."

LIFTING THE ROLLER DOOR, PYM glanced both ways along the street, jogged to the Mercedes and reversed it into the car shed, almost forgetting—until the sensor set up a frantic beeping—that Valentine was back there, strapped to a chair, blood pooling. He braked, switched off, got out, opened the boot and spread the tarp over the carpeted interior. Satisfied, he yelled for Lovelock: "Give us a hand."

Lovelock wandered in from the house with a gym bag of shoes and clothing in one hand, an aluminum gun case in the other. "Check this out."

Pym shook his head. "Put it back."

"You kidding? Not this beauty."

He flipped open the lid to reveal an elegant wood and blued-steel rifle fitted with a scope.

"Mate, please," Pym said.

"Just for the rest of the day, okay?"

"Fat chance. If we get pulled over . . ."

"I'll ditch it before we head back to Sydney, okay?"

With that, Lovelock opened a rear door of the Mercedes and stowed the gun case behind the front seats, concealed under a shirt and a pair of jeans from the gym bag.

Washing his palms together in satisfaction he said, "Now for our host."

Pym sliced the body free of the tape, shoved the chair under a workbench and with a *one, two, three*, helped Lovelock toss Valentine into the boot before he noticed a police car pulling into the curb. Blocking the driveway.

Without missing a beat, Pym shut the boot, crossed to the stack of paint tins and levered the lid from a liter of white undercoat. He poured the paint liberally over the blood- and mucus-stained concrete, splashed a little on his hands, trousers and shoes, and dropped the tin amid the muck.

Just as a uniformed cop stepped into the car shed. "Gentlemen." He paused for his eyes to adjust before edging down along the driver's side of the Mercedes.

Pym nodded, working a harassed look onto his face. He'd often felt harassed, so it was no great stretch. Lovelock, the idiot, merely looked alarmed.

"Constable Tankard, Waterloo police," announced the cop. He was a pink, beefy, damp-looking guy, his flesh pushing hard against his waistband and collar. "We had a complaint, a disturbance at this address."

"Disturbance?" said Pym, frowning.

"Raised voices and so forth."

Pym tried a rueful look. He'd never felt rueful in his life, only betrayed or let down, and struggled to get it right. "No disturbance," he said. "As you can see, I just spilled paint everywhere. Probably people heard me swearing."

The cop's heavy face took that in and he turned to Lovelock. Looked him up and down, paying attention to his knuckles. "Hurt yourself, sir?"

Pym tensed but Lovelock handled it well. Scrutinizing his hands, then his arms and knees, he said, "The wife's always going off at me, can't drive a nail in without drawing blood." He gave a little head shake. "Sorry, we've both been in the wars this morning, sorry if we gave offense."

The cop chuckled and had another look at the Mercedes, perhaps thinking, *Rich city blokes, hopelessly impractical,* and said with a grin, "Okay, boys, I'll leave you to it."

He returned to his car. Lovelock and Pym watched and waited through all of the cop stuff, the radio confirmation, time check and notebook record, followed by the mirror adjustment, the fastening of the seatbelt, the turning of the ignition key. Finally, he was gone.

"Let's get the fuck out of here," Lovelock said.

Pym couldn't have put it better himself.

FOLLOWING THE DIRECTIONS ON Hector's fax, they headed inland, into a hinterland area of dirt roads that serviced orchards and farms. Many were prosperous-looking places, shaved and combed, set back on hillsides far from the road. But closer to, faded by the sun and the roiling dust of passing vehicles, were one or two weatherboard hovels, abandoned or rented by the kinds of depressed, raw-faced men and women who wash up in rural areas to work with animals and machines.

Pym, slumped in the passenger seat, hated it. He was a city boy. Yeah, the coast was nearby, Melbourne no more than an hour away, but here, today, it was all dryness and hot dust tossed about by a dirty wind. Small stones pinged under the chassis.

And then Owen Valentine's dog jumped between the seats, made a few circles of his lap, and settled down to sleep.

Pym was aghast. Holding his hands away from his body, he shouted, "What the fuck?"

Lovelock grinned. "Mate, he just jumped in."

"Bullshit. You put him in, you cunt."

"Hey! Watch the tone."

"I don't want a fucking dog in the car," Pym said.

"Put him in the back if he bothers you."

Cringing, Pym did that, then wiped his palms on his pants. He felt soiled. "Filthy creature."

"Yeah? Fuck you," Lovelock said, driving with one hand, his elbow hanging on the sill of his open window, a negligent cigarette in his other hand. He drew hungrily on it, the tip flaring, flicked the ash into their slipstream, steered the car over the corrugations, drew smoke again.

"Bushfire weather," warned Pym.

"Mate, summer's barely started."

Pym folded his arms, stared glumly ahead. Lovelock finished his cigarette. Gave Pym a certain look, and flicked the butt into the ditch.

Pym remembered: he was supposed to text the client. He took a cheap disposable phone from his pocket and saw that he had no signal bars. When the signal returned he got halfway through the message; lost signal again. The fucking place was full of dead zones. Finally, message sent. No "Dear Bill" or "Fred" or "Susan." Hector Kaye hadn't told them who'd contracted the job. Just: *It's done.*

Then he removed and snapped the sim card and tossed it

with the phone, battery cover and battery out of the window. He settled back. Peered at the map and said, "Slow down, we turn just up here."

They came to a T-intersection. "Hang a left."

Lovelock made the turn. The road, still dirt, was flat for the first half-kilometer, later climbing through grassy, heavily treed farmland and over a rise to more of the same. Just ahead of them huddled a large weatherboard house, a pretty place—garden beds, rosebushes and small native trees—but unfortunately sited too close to the road. On the grassy verge was a blackboard and a white chalked message: DUST, PLEASE SLOW DOWN.

Lovelock, grinning, said, "Watch this," and accelerated, flinging stones, raising an angry cloud. Pym glanced at the house as they passed. An elderly woman was in the garden, weeding. Enclosed in dust, a hazy shape, she flung a futile arm across her face and tucked her head, a picture of misery.

Pym shook his head. "Yeah, good one."

The wind was gusting all about, and it gusted over Lovelock's discarded cigarette.

Otherwise, the burning coal tip might have winked out eventually, but, revived by the wind, it glowed, red hot, finding nourishment in a dead stalk of grass. That stalk ignited another, which ignited a paper scrap. Flames spread, mere flickers at first, licking at the grass.

LOVELOCK AND PYM, SOME kilometers away, had found the track marked on the map, Lintermans Lane. It arrowed through paddocks and stands of eucalypts to a disused reservoir where you might profitably bury a body. Except that local landowners and shire environment protection officers, fed up with the degradation left by trail bikes and four-wheel drives, had bolted a sturdy, lockable tubular metal gate across the entrance. There was a narrow gap for bushwalkers and a set of rails for horse riders but, without a key, Lovelock and Pym in the Merc were fucked.

"We're fucked," said Pym.

"I could ram it."

"I don't think so," Pym said, taking in the solid posts, the rigid iron. Not to mention the damage to the car.

"Shit."

"Don't sweat it," Pym said. "We'll carry him in."

Lovelock glanced around uneasily. No traffic, no nearby houses, only dust, trees whipping in the wind, a hint of distant smoke. "We could just dump him."

"Weren't you listening? No body. It has to look like he did a runner."

"Yeah, yeah," Lovelock said. He strapped on his combat knife, ninety-nine dollars on eBay from somewhere in Texas, and slung Owen Valentine's rifle across his back. "Let's do it."

"Oh for God's sake," Pym snarled, grabbing the shovel. "We're not going to war."

"You never know," Lovelock said, feeling a martial impulse deep inside him. He fitted his Ray-Bans, checked his image in the smoky glass of the Merc.

"When you're quite ready," Pym said.

"You crack me up, mate," Lovelock said, unconcerned. He reached into the car and heaved. In one continuous motion he had Valentine's body over his shoulder and was striding through the pedestrian gap and along the laneway.

SOON, TREES CROWDING ON either side, the track became a dim tunnel, the ground a mat of pine needles and dead grass, little sign that any vehicles had been along here in the recent past. Vigorous blackberry canes reached for them, the berries still clenched tight and green. A magpie watched them pass, a butterfly, a bull the size of a Volkswagen in an adjacent paddock. Lovelock and Pym were alone in the world but for a vapor trail high above. Pym tried to gauge the direction. Melbourne to Hobart? Meanwhile, the wind came marauding through every gap in the tree line and Pym blinked to rid his eyes of grit. And he could smell smoke. He wished this was over with.

They walked for a kilometer, stopping where the laneway stopped, at a locked farm gate in a fence choked with blackberries and bracken. A faded sign said DEVILBEND RESERVOIR NO ADMITTANCE. Lovelock merely tumbled the dead man over the gate to the forbidden side and climbed over.

Pym followed. He was hot and wind-lashed, vegetation cuts on his hands and forearms. He considered he was earning his share of the fifty grand.

Fifty grand to kill a man and hide the body. What was that about? Too late now, Valentine was taking his secrets to his grave.

They walked, reaching a marshy cove, where the water lapped at reeds and mud. They started digging.

MEANWHILE A MAN NAMED Colin Hauser was walking toward the laneway. He generally walked at daybreak, but this morning he'd had to hang around and take delivery of two ride-on mowers and a little Kubota tractor, and the driver was late, so it was ten before he could shower, have breakfast. Then he fixed a broken pump before taking a call from his lawyer, who'd been talking to his wife's lawyer about a late alimony payment. By then it was late morning.

He almost didn't walk. It felt out of kilter, walking just before lunch instead of at dawn. Plus the heat, the dust and the wind. But he did walk, out along his driveway, onto the dirt road and up and over the hill, passing Mrs. Broderick's place, her dust-warning sign covered in dust, and finally to the road that would take him to the top of Lintermans Lane. The wind whipped his jeans and plastered his shirt to his back and in the air there was a trace of smoke. He glanced around uneasily: a hot northerly. A bad fire day, even if it was barely summer.

A Mercedes was parked at the barrier to the lane. Just beyond it, apparently returning from a stroll, were two men: Thick and Thin, he thought. Large and Small. The little guy stiffened to see Hauser's approach, a kind of feral alertness appearing on his face—*As though I've got no right to be here*, Hauser thought. He wanted to say, "*I* walk here every day; who the fuck are you?"

By now he was ten meters from the gate. The big guy had some kind of hunting knife strapped to his thigh and was carrying a rifle—and not just any rifle but Arnold Coxhell's AR16. The only social intercourse Colin Hauser got these days was taking deliveries in the dark hours and hanging out at the Westernport Sporting Shooters firing range, where he'd become mates with Coxhell. He remembered the guy showing off his Colt one day. Semi-auto, the non-military version of a US Army rifle, accurate up to a thousand meters in the right conditions with a rapid fire capability and negligible kick. Fitted with a Redfield variable-power scope for low-light conditions.

And two weeks ago, Arnold mentioned he'd been burgled. They'd forced his gun cabinet and disappeared with his shotgun and his Colt.

"A lot of that going around," Hauser had said. He personally knew of an orchardist and a poultry farmer who'd lost rifles to thieves in the past six months.

And here was the Colt. Had to be Arnold's. Couldn't be another one like it on the Peninsula, fitted with that scope.

Disguising his interest, Hauser reached the gate, did some hamstring stretches against a rail, nodded hello and walked back the way he'd come, as if he did this every day, every day turned back when he reached the gate, every day saw strangers in the lane. He made mental notes as he walked back past Mrs. Broderick's and up and over the hill: date, time, location, description of the men, their vehicle, the rifle, the shovel. Repeated it like a mantra, all the way home.

As soon as the guy had disappeared into the nearby side road, Pym said, "He saw us."

Well, that was obvious. "He totally did," Lovelock said.

"Well?"

"Well what?"

Pym said, a tight vibration in his voice, "Well ask yourself what we look like."

"No big deal. Just a couple of guys out walking. Like him."

"You want to wake up to yourself," said Pym, "with that stupid fucking knife and that gun, me with a muddy shovel. He'll go home and he'll start thinking about what he's just seen and in a couple of days or even a couple of hours he'll think maybe he should report it."

Lovelock chewed his lip, thinking. Finally he slipped the rifle strap from his shoulder, smacked the stock into his left palm. "Better safe than sorry, right?"

They climbed into the Mercedes and followed the man. Past the old woman's house to the top of the rise, where they paused to sneak a look. The guy was halfway down the slope, turning into a driveway. Pym narrowed his gaze:

there was a house back there, a hundred meters in, concealed with several sheds and a windmill behind a stand of pine trees.

"All right then."

THE SMOKE HEAVIER NOW, a boiling cloud of it over in the east, Hauser hurried past his dogs in their kennels, through the garden gate and indoors. Straight to his study, where he wrote it all down on a blank sheet of printer paper before he forgot.

An explosion of barking outside.

THE BIG CAR PURRED downhill and into the driveway. Just inside it was a small clearing where the guy evidently stowed his garbage and recycle bins rather than wheel them to and fro on collection day. Lovelock steered into the clearing, sending both bins flying, stopped, grabbed the rifle and they got out.

Coming to the house, the sheds spread out on a slope beyond it, they were startled by barking, a pair of dogs lunging at them, caught short by chains. Slow learners, the dogs lunged again. "Jesus Christ," muttered Pym.

"Good doggies," said Lovelock.

They paused at the garden gate. The house was small, an unloved 1970s brick veneer. Rosebushes grew wild around it, the lawn was knee high in drying grass, stiff dead plants sat in terracotta pots on the veranda. They stepped through the gate and onto the veranda. The front door was locked and smeared in a layer of pollen and dust, proof that it was never used. The kitchen door was unlocked and opened smoothly with barely a squeak.

The kitchen was a hovel, almost bereft of natural light, smelling of cooked meat, dust balls and greasy plates. The hallway was no better, a dingy tunnel offering a couple of half-open doors. An armchair before a giant TV in one room, an unmade bed in another. Old odors: stale air, unwashed clothes, unwashed armpits.

Finally, at the end, a small study, more loved than the other rooms: desk, shelves, computer and printer, phone, filing cabinets. And the man from the laneway gate, standing behind his desk.

HAUSER FOLDED THE PAPER in two and had slipped it between the pages of his desk diary when the voice warned, "Don't touch the phone."

Not that it mattered. Lovelock fired the Colt a millisecond later.

A huge sound, shocking, and the dogs, momentarily silenced, started up again, a different note this time, as if they were stricken with grief.

Lovelock stepped around the desk and fired again, straight down into Hauser's skull.

A KIND OF SILENCE settled.

Then Pym took charge. "Don't touch anything."

"Mate, I'm not fucking stupid."

"Pick up the cartridges."

"Why? I never touched them. The cops will pin it on who-ever's prints are on them."

Pym opened his mouth to speak, reconsidered. "Fair enough. Robbery gone wrong."

"If you say so," said Lovelock doubtfully, not seeing any-thing of value in the place.

"Pull out a few drawers, make a mess, grab small stuff."

While Lovelock was doing that, Pym checked the desk phone, a handkerchief masking his fingers. The last number called was not the police but a mobile, a couple of hours earlier.

He knelt at the body, searched the pockets. A Swiss Army knife, a battered wallet containing cards and a five dollar note, which he took.

Lovelock returned, carrying an iPad, an old Nokia, a Ziploc bag of marijuana. "Look what I found in the freezer," he said, waving the weed.

"Good for you," snapped Pym. "Come on, let's get out of here."

"You're a bundle of laughs."

"What, you think we should throw a party? We've just killed two men. We're a long way from home."

Rolling his eyes, Lovelock followed Pym out of the house. Past the dogs, which seemed to cower this time, reading the men accurately, and down the driveway to the Mercedes.

Pym sniffed the air. "Smoke."

He turned full circle but the pines towered thickly, offering only a washed-out patch of noonday sky. What did he know about fires? Didn't want to be caught among pine trees, though.

Same as before, Lovelock drove, Pym rode shotgun, and Owen Valentine's toilet-brush dog lay curled asleep on the back seat. They passed the dust-warning sign and Lovelock accelerated again, but his heart wasn't in it this time.

A SERIES OF LEFT and right turns, then they were east of the reservoir, approaching a sealed road. A police car was parked at the intersection, lights flashing, and the skyline over near the town they'd stayed in last night was thick with smoke, a nasty boiling heap of it.

Lovelock braked. "He's seen us."

Pym floated a hand from his lap and wrapped his fingers

around Lovelock's meaty forearm, reassuring. What he always did when Lovelock lost it. "Calm down. He's not after us."

"How do you know?"

"Ask yourself what he's doing there, okay? It's the fire. He's warning traffic."

"If you say so."

"I say so. Just drive up normally, wind your window down, see what he says. If you U-turn now, he *will* remember us, especially if it turns out the fire was deliberately lit."

Lovelock swallowed, his heavy features beaded with sweat, but accelerated slowly toward the intersection. The policeman, a young uniformed constable in wraparound sunglasses, turned to watch them. At the last moment an irritated expression crossed his face, as if to say here was another moron too stupid to be out on the roads. He gestured at Lovelock: turn left, away from the fire.

Lovelock saluted, complied. "Didn't even bother to talk to us," he said, glancing at the rear-view mirror.

Then: "Fuck, he's on his radio."

"Settle down. He's been told to keep tabs on the traffic, that's all," Pym said, craning his head around to peer back along the road. He couldn't see anything now, the road full of bends, the roadside trees.

"What if he calls in the plates?"

"Ah. Trouble."

"So keep fucking watching," said Lovelock tensely.

A half-minute, a minute, and the road behind them remained clear. "Nothing," Pym said.

"But what about *ahead* of us, did you think about that?"

"You're being paranoid."

"There's a good reason for that," Lovelock said, his hands white-knuckled on the steering wheel. He swung into the nearest side road. "Soon as it's safe, I'm switching the plates again."

"And ditch the fucking rifle," Pym said.

"Yeah, yeah."

Pym glanced around uneasily. The road—a narrow graveled track through lightly timbered farmland—was heading in the right direction to meet the highway to Gippsland, but there were kilo-meters to go before that and now the smoke was a wall ahead of them.

His voice a tense squeak, he said, "We need to go back."

He'd seen a lick of flame in the smoke, sparks streaming on the wind. And the smoke was closing in suddenly. Not kilometers away after all. The treetops were thrashing, twigs and branches and a twist of roofing iron flying past the windscreen.

"Fuck."

Embers were thick around them, touching off new fires, and now Pym was afraid. He clutched Lovelock's forearm for reassurance. "Mate . . ."

Lovelock slowed the car. Brought it to a stop, gauging the width of the road. Too narrow for an easy turn, Pym could see that at a glance, and the ditches on either side were a mystery. Deep? Would they get stuck? He couldn't tell.

The engine stalled. Lovelock ground the starter motor as the heat smacked into them. Paint blistering, you never saw anything like it, felt heat like it or heard anything like the snarling fury. It came in hard. You couldn't speak, do anything.

2

THAT WAS FRIDAY.

People talked about the fire and the burnt-out car all weekend, and on Monday morning it was still uppermost in Hal Challis's mind as he showered, a bucket at his feet.

The first rule of rural or regional policing being *Don't live where your "clients" live*, the CIU inspector resided in an old farmhouse on a dirt road several kilometers inland of the Waterloo police station. The fruitcakes, wingnuts and homicidal maniacs could still find him if they tried hard enough, but that would require effort, and even if they applied effort, most of them would lose their nerve out where the streetlights ended.

So, a rural address—but right now rural meant tinder-dry grass and highly inflammable pines and eucalypts. There'd been no rain for months. Dams were dry, rainwater tanks emptying fast. No mains water where Challis lived, so his showers were brief and he bucketed the sudsy run-off onto his roses. Not his pot plants: Ellen Destry, staying the night with him recently, had caught him pouring shower water onto the potted lavender she'd given him, and gone mildly ballistic. "You want to kill it?" she demanded, her hands on her hips. "Put it on the roses, nothing will kill them."

Challis had nodded, agreeable. When it came to relationships, he was a cultivator—otherwise he'd be no good at catching killers and thieves—but he was no cultivator of trees, shrubs or seedlings. His mode, other than slashing and burning, was mostly absent-minded neglect.

Challis toweled off, fretting. Last night he'd ordered a tanker-load of water for the underground house tank. But should he use it to fight a fire, if it came to that? More to the point, could he? He hadn't started his portable pump, a petrol Honda, since last summer. He tried to remember the steps involved. Fasten the hoses, prime the pump, switch on petrol flow, apply the choke, pull the starter rope . . . Or should he cut and run if a bushfire threatened? Grab wallet, keys, phone, photos and documents and head for the beach?

He didn't want to perish in flames like the two men caught on a dirt road near Waterloo last Friday. No ID yet, and stolen plates.

He shaved, the towel around his middle. It was 7:05 A.M. The water tanker was due at 7:30.

Twenty minutes later, dressed in chinos and a thin linen jacket over an untucked short-sleeved shirt, coffee and muesli under his belt, he heard a belching stutter down on the road, a truck decelerating, and stepped outside to guide the driver. Another hot, wind-storming day, and with his hooked face, his hair and jacket wings flying, Challis looked as if he'd summoned the wind and would ride it to the finish. He sniffed it. No smoke. Just dust, and now diesel fumes, as the water carrier ground up his driveway.

Challis signaled, pointed, beckoned; finally held up his hand in the universal STOP gesture. The driver got out. They shook hands.

"That her?" the driver said, glancing at the concrete lid of the underground tank a few meters from Challis's back wall.

"Yep."

The driver unrolled a heavy-duty black hose fitted with a bulky metal nozzle and dragged it to the tank, levered off the meter-square concrete lid, and fed the hose into the tank. Then he returned to the truck, got the water flowing, and the two men chatted about this and that. Friday's bushfire, the heat, the dryness; the water guy saying he'd been run off his feet.

BY EIGHT O'CLOCK CHALLIS had paid the man and was heading for the fire zone. He poked about for an hour on the perimeter. By Australian standards it had been a small fire—grassland, fences, trees and one hayshed—but fierce. Two men dead and a new Waterloo housing estate in the path of the flames. Heading along the dirt road where the men had died, he found smoldering gum trees monitored by a mop-up crew of firefighters, a crime-scene technician supervising the loading of the burnt-out Mercedes onto a flat-bed truck. Challis said a brief hello, turned around, headed back to Coolart Road.

Looking east from the road's low hilltops, he could see irregular black patches amid the dead and dying grasses, together with charred stands of trees, and, in the far distance, blackness to the very edge of Waterloo. He tried and failed to imagine what the dead men had hoped to achieve by heading *toward* the flames. Then again, a fire is a confusing mess of smoke and noise. Perhaps they didn't know where the flames were until it was too late.

Before heading for the town, he turned back and made for the Westernport Incident Control Center at the Moorooduc fire station. Here the incident controller showed him a set of Google Earth images on a large flat screen. "Started here." North-west of Waterloo. "Spread quickly in this direction."

Moving south-east. Challis tried to make sense of the paler strips across the blackness. "What road's this, and this?"

The man named them.

"What time Friday?"

"About eleven in the morning."

"No reports of incinerators, chainsaws, mowers . . . ?"

"None."

"Your thoughts?"

"Cigarette," the incident controller said.

CHALLIS HEADED FOR WATERLOO, knowing they'd never find the culprit. An unplanned act by an ordinary civilian? It wasn't like going after a criminal. The standard method—trace, interview and eliminate—wouldn't work here. And as for the intuitive side of investigation, how do you think your way into the mind of an otherwise blameless man or woman who would fling a lit cigarette out of a car window on a hot, windy day? No way of sniffing out this person's desires or fears; no blurring of the line between hunter and hunted. No infiltrating the underground community of cigarette butt-flickers, looking for the embittered, the jealous, the weak or treacherous.

The fire wasn't his headache anyway. The epidemic of ice crimes was, and firefighters mopping up yesterday had found an abandoned drug lab on the Belair Close estate.

BELAIR CLOSE WAS A first-home-buyers dream estate, according to the billboards, but right now it was no more than a handful of bare slabs knitted together by culs-de-sac and short, doubling-back streets. Not a straight line in sight. One house—the drug lab—had been completed to lockup stage, three others were wooden frames and the rest was a dustbowl. The prevailing colors were brown, grey and black:

the broken soil, the concrete slabs, the new roads and the burnt grass around the margins. There were odd yellow highlights in the abandoned earthmoving equipment.

Challis steered toward the drug lab. It was small, cheaply modern, but fire and smoke damaged now, and tucked away in the back corner of the desolate building site, meters from the edge of the fire. Police cars, a crime-scene van and, where Belair Close abutted another estate, a staggered line of trainee constables deployed to keep out gawkers from the other estates.

When Challis had taken up the post of Inspector, Westernport Region Crime Investigation Unit a few years ago, all of this area had been farmland. The old Peninsula towns of Rosebud, Mornington and Waterloo had doubled in size since then, which according to the politicians indicated a healthy economy. The police and the various social services knew this progress had also brought social distress and criminality, as funding for schools, public transport, police staffing levels and welfare services lagged behind.

Challis parked, got out, signed the attendance log maintained by John Tankard, a senior constable at Waterloo. "Pam Murphy here?"

"Somewhere."

"Who from the crime-scene unit?"

"Scobie Sutton, a couple of others."

Challis nodded his thanks and approached the house, pausing as two men and a woman dressed in hazard suits and breathing apparatus carted out scorched and melted lab gear—beakers, glass and rubber tubing. He watched them place the material on the ground away from the house. They went back inside, the men returning with smoke-stained bottled chemicals and a few five-liter drums, the woman with two trays of kitty litter, used by speed and ice cooks to absorb chemical fumes. One of the men, tall, gaunt, looked like Scobie Sutton.

Then Pam Murphy was grinning at him. "Boss."

"What have we got?"

A good detective, Pam. Sharp, agile, trim; perspiring now in her protective suit. Swiping the back of her wrist across her forehead, she said, "When you say 'What have we got?' I'm never too sure if you mean it or you've watched too much *CSI*. Or it's an ironic commentary on the clichéd situations in which you so often find yourself."

"Or all three," Challis said.

"And if *you*—a highly decorated and greatly esteemed senior detective—don't know the answer, where does that leave a lowly detective like me?"

"Detecting, I hope."

They stood together watching the forensic team come and go from the house. The front, side and rear doors had been opened to ventilate the building. Challis could smell the fumes. Couldn't really see in: the cooks had draped heavy blackout curtains over all the windows.

"Do we know how long it was in operation?"

"Not long. The builder says they got the house to lockup two weeks ago."

Challis stared at the place morosely. A hydroponic marijuana operation might stay put for weeks or even months, but ice manufacturers tended to cook for no more than three or four days before moving on. He hated ice. It was cheap, easy to get, easy to make. A dirty drug, and probably behind a rash of local crimes. Some apparently planned—drive-by shootings, the firebombing of houses and cars. Many random, unpredictable—road-rage attacks, unprovoked stabbings, paranoid meltdowns, an upsurge in domestic assaults . . .

On any evening of the week, the Waterloo police station

lockup housed men, women and teenagers coming off an ice high, screaming, head-banging, kicking the walls.

"Who found it?"

"An emergency services volunteer, first, except he didn't know it was a lab." Murphy pointed. "He was over on the Seaview Estate, doing the evacuation door-knock, saw a van outside this place, came over and got bashed by a couple of men who then took off."

Challis tensed. "The men caught in the fire?"

Except they'd been heading toward Waterloo, not away . . .

Murphy shook her head. "They were in a car, right? The emergency services guy is positive it was a van here."

"Plate number?"

"He didn't get it."

"Descriptions?"

Murphy checked her notes. "One young and scruffy, the other heavier looking. Tatts, muscles. He didn't get a good look."

"Students?" Bikie gangs were known to use kids who had a bit of chemistry and lab knowledge.

"Possibly," Murphy said. "Anyway, he filed it at the back of his mind and kept going door-to-door. Then when the fire threatened the back veranda here, a couple of fire trucks doused the place. No one checked again until yesterday, when the guy remembered and reported it. One of the uniforms came around for a closer look."

She paused. "The thing is, there's evidence a child spent time here. We found clothes—pink and yellow T-shirts and shorts and underpants."

"The volunteer didn't see her?"

Murphy shook her head. "She could have been in the van already. The fire had reached the back fence so they might have been getting ready to leave."

A sudden wind flurry came from the burnt fringe of woodland, carrying soot. Unnoticed by Challis, a particle eddied, dipped, alighted on his earlobe. Pam Murphy reached out, a tissue very white in her sun-browned hand, and swiped it away.

"Ash," she explained, showing him the evidence.

An intimate gesture. Signifying, in this case, nothing. If pinned down, Challis might say he found Pam Murphy attractive, but in general he admired the look of the runner, the gymnast, the effortless tennis player—women like Pam. Like Ellen Destry. In any case, she'd already forgotten cleaning the soot from his ear and was watching the house, almost quivering with unexpressed or thwarted tension. He knew she hated the standing-around aspect of police work. She was on the hunt. She was always on the hunt.

He stared gloomily across the desolate tract of house slabs, scaffolding, dusty earthmoving equipment to the abutting Seaview Estate, which had been occupied for fifteen years. The residents, kept back by the line of trainee constables, were watching the police operation from footpaths, driveways, front yards and back fences. They'd been evacuated on Friday, but now they were safe at home again, watching a new drama. There were one or two dealers on the estate, a handful of users, but mostly struggling families lived there in threadbare, generally law-abiding decency. A vicious crime family had once controlled the estate but was in tatters now, its members dead or in jail, or fucking up some other township.

One of the crime-scene technicians emerged from the house. A scarecrow figure, he dragged off his breathing gear and headed straight for them, the hazard suit baggy on his bony frame.

"Inspector. Pam," he said. Acknowledging them both.

"Scobie."

Until a year ago, Scobie Sutton had been a CIU detective. Sensitive, a chronic worrier, too straight to handle the lies, evasions, ambiguities and unfairness of normal policing, he was better suited to gathering and interpreting evidence. He held up a couple of evidence bags. Pills of various shapes, colors and sizes in one, whitish granules in the other.

"Ice, for sure," he said. "Don't know about the pills until I test them."

"Prints?"

Sutton glanced back at the house and grimaced. "A lot of smoke and water damage. And anything still intact seems to have been wiped down. But with a fire at the back door . . . maybe they rushed it and we'll get lucky."

"You found evidence a child had been there?" said Challis.

Sutton had a daughter, and the thought of a child in peril would get to him. He closed his eyes, swayed a little. "I have no idea where she fits in. Meanwhile, as soon as I finish here I have to process the car from Friday's fire."

Then he was gone, taking the drugs to an evidence-logging officer and re-entering the house.

Murphy said, "Boss, this doesn't seem like the hub of an ice empire."

"Agreed." Challis nodded glumly. "Too small, too haphazard."

But there was an ice empire somewhere nearby. The fallout was all around them. "Maybe we'll learn something at the drug-squad briefing."

3

THE DRUG-SQUAD BRIEFING . . .
The Melbourne-based squad had recently mounted a series of operations in rural Victoria. The aim was both to investigate ice manufacture and distribution and to educate local police. It was Westernport's turn, beginning after lunch with a series of talks: a drug-squad senior sergeant, an ex-addict and dealer, and a parent of addicts. Challis saw the sense of the operation, but it would tie up the station all afternoon and he had work to do.

Returning to his car, he steered out of the estate and onto a winding road that took him to Frankston-Flinders Road and Waterloo. Soon he was passing tire outfitters, car repairers, a BP service station, Waterloo Mowers, Waterloo Bait and Tackle, a motel, a broad stretch of parkland at the edge of a mangrove belt and the tricky Westernport tidal flats, and finally he was on High Street. Banks, pharmacies, cafes, other small businesses. Then the roundabout at the top where, it seemed to Challis, two of the main industries of Waterloo faced each other: the police station and the McDonald's.

Parking in the potholed yard at the rear of the police station, he entered through a side door. Waterloo was a training station. Provisional constables were sent here to work alongside uniformed police, CIU detectives and civilian staff for a few months, then sent elsewhere. They were a blur to Challis. He talked to them at crime scenes, gave them the benefit of his experience, but he didn't try to befriend them. They always moved on—and some of them were obliged to move on to other careers.

He cultivated relations with the civilian staff, however. They knew everything and everyone in the station. You'd ask them for more stationery, the key to a cabinet, IT advice, phone numbers, Constable X's whereabouts. Needing to know that all was ready for the drug-squad briefing, he stepped into the general office, a nerve center of filing cabinets, desks and civilian clerks at the rear of the building.

Damn. Lunchtime, so the room was deserted—or so Challis believed until the door to an inner office opened and Janine Quine emerged. Startled, she said, "I was just answering Annette's phone."

Challis nodded. Annette Tranh, the office manager, was away on sick leave. "We all set for this afternoon's briefing?"

Quine was an angular woman, mid-thirties, strain and privation in her face. Prim and efficient, not given to trading insults or gossip with the police or her colleagues, she was also virtually unknowable. Which suited the Waterloo senior officers, like Challis, who managed small teams and often needed clerical and other support. Challis called her Jan, she called him Inspector. The talk was she had a no-hoper husband at home. Alcoholic, gambler; something like that.

And now she flashed him a jumpy smile and smoothed her palms down the front of her thighs. Bony hands, one tiny engagement ring, one thin wedding band.

With those hands smoothing, smoothing her thighs, she said, "I've put in extra chairs, carafes of water, cups." She stared at the ceiling for further inspiration and added, "An urn, biscuits, tea and coffee."

"The monitor?"

"In place."

"Wi-fi?"

"Good to go."

She worked her mouth anxiously, as if the technology might fail between now and then.

"That's great, Jan, many thanks."

"Pens," she said in a rush, her face reddening, "pads, spare memory sticks."

"Excellent," Challis said, wanting to edge away.

She was looking at him, bursting with powerful feelings. "Friends of ours were asking . . ."

Challis lifted an eyebrow. "Asking?"

In a rush she said, "They live on a bush block and with all these mower and tractor thefts they wondered if the police were any nearer to catching anybody."

Bemused by the implied criticism, Challis said, "The main thing your friends should think about is insurance cover and good locks. They shouldn't store vehicles and equipment unsecured."

She continued to look troubled, so he gave her a smile. It was intended to reassure but Challis's smiles were sometimes sharkish, the smiles of a hunter. Quine paled and looked away before collapsing into the chair behind her desk.

"Thanks again," Challis said, feeling uneasily that he'd offered no help or comfort.

BUT MENTION OF THE thefts—his second main headache after the ice epidemic—prompted him to check if Pam Murphy had returned to the station.

He found her in the CIU office, a small, open-plan room with desks, filing cabinets, phones and computers, the walls fluttering with paper: cartoons, memoranda, posters, photographs. His own office was a poky sub-room in one corner. Murphy had the landline to her ear, face twisted in perplexity. Her expression cleared when she spotted Challis. She said goodbye, cradled the handset.

"I could have waited," he told her.

Pam shrugged. "Just my mother."

"How is she?"

"I'm not sure," Murphy said, frowning. She coughed. "Boss, can I have Sunday off?"

Challis checked the impulse to say okay; spent a moment mentally sifting through the caseload, the work rosters. He didn't want to say yes and later discover solid reasons why he should have refused.

"Fine by me," he said eventually. "Everything okay?"

Faintly embarrassed, Murphy said, "Just that my mother wants to go on a little road trip around the Peninsula before the weather gets too hot. She grew up here."

"Sure," Challis said.

The notion of overtime pay and set hours was laughable if you were a CIU detective. Murphy had worked long hours, weekends and weekdays, for months now. He was happy to make allowances. No whiner or malingerer, she deserved some time off. And he knew that her mother, now a widow, had recently moved to an aged-care home in Malvern.

He looked at his watch. The briefing was not for another hour. "Can I take you to lunch?"

"Cafe Laconic?"

The Laconic had gone too gluten-free for Challis's liking, but he said, "Sure," again, and they walked down High Street, nodding hello here and there.

Seated at a window seat, where the air was cool, he said, "Mini briefing."

Murphy unfolded her napkin, used to his ways. "You're the boss."

"According to the log, another hobby-farm tractor was stolen on the weekend."

Murphy sipped at her glass of water, put it down, ran her fingers up and down the condensation. "Is this a cunning or even clumsy way to keep me working next Sunday instead of spending time with my dear old mother?"

Challis grinned. One of the town's bank managers walked by and they exchanged waves through the glass. He returned his attention to Murphy. "A tractor stolen now and then, sure, *but five in the past two months*? Together with spraying equipment, trailers, ride-on mowers . . . Who's taking them? How are they transported? Where are they stored?"

"Not to mention the rifles," Murphy said.

"Not to mention the rifles," Challis agreed.

He brooded. "Several of these places were on the register."

Waterloo police station held a register of homes left unoccupied while their owners holidayed or traveled on business. Some were rural, and with limited resources and personnel, the police could only manage an occasional drive-past. Burglars had taken advantage of that to break into four such houses in recent weeks.

"Luck," said Murphy, "or good intel."

Their muck arrived, arranged on white plates.

BACK AT THE STATION, they were told the drug-squad team had arrived.

"Settling in upstairs, sir," the desk sergeant said.

Challis nodded his thanks, punched in the security code and entered the main corridor with Murphy. Telling her he'd see her at the briefing, he made his way to the first-floor corridor and the small conference room assigned to the drug squad. Knocked and said, "Senior Sergeant Coolidge?"

Two men and two women were setting up laptops and files on two tables. They all looked up and one, an attractive woman with canny features and shoulder-length auburn hair, stalked across the room to him, her hand extended. "Inspector Challis."

Challis had read Coolidge's bio: late thirties, a master's in criminology, but she'd also spent years on the street, including undercover work. Married, no children. Given the weather, she wore a sleeveless white cotton top, a knee-length blue skirt, sandals. Like Pam Murphy she seemed full of suppressed drive.

They traded a few names and war stories, and Challis asked how she wanted to run the briefing.

"I'll say a few words, then we'll hear from our guest speakers"—she inclined her head to the far corner of the room, where two women were perched on the edge of plastic chairs, talking animatedly—"and I'll finish with a more police-oriented slant."

Challis grew aware of a warm scrutiny from Coolidge, her green eyes searching his face. Almost without appearing to move, she was suddenly very close. "I hear," she murmured, "that you found an ice lab on one of the housing estates."

Faintly rattled, surprised by a desire to touch her upper arm, he said, "Abandoned. Crime-scene people are going through it."

Her scent was subtle. Under the professional veneer she was soft, round, and performing a kind of carnal fathoming of him. Still murmuring, she said, "Typically, a lab like that would be here today, gone tomorrow." She cocked her head at him; he had the impression of her body saying one thing, her words another. "What concerns my team is the probable

presence of an organized *syndicate* on the Peninsula. Whoever's behind it is *importing* ice, not making it."

Challis felt faintly rebuked. Then Coolidge shot him a
broad smile. "How about a drink after work? You can show
me the sights."

4

PAM MURPHY SHUT DOWN her computer, locked her desk and headed along the upstairs corridor to the main briefing room. She paused in the doorway; the space was full. A mix of uniformed and plain-clothed officers sat around the long table, others lined the walls. She spotted a seat beside John Tankard, nodded hello, got out her notebook.

The room, stuffy in the early summer heat, would be putrid by the end of the briefing. Murphy shifted her bones to get comfortable, stared out of the window. Up here, away from the glass, she couldn't see much, just the roof of the McDonald's on the other side of the road, treetops, street-lights hung with pre-Christmas tinsel. A wispy cloud or two.

She turned her attention back to the room. Pads, pens, disposable cups and laptops distributed along the table, a whiteboard and a screen at the front of the room, a small corner table set with an urn, teabags, instant coffee, plastic cups and a tin biscuit box, almost empty. She fanned her face with her notebook. Challis caught her eye and grinned. As usual, he was propping up a wall.

Then a disturbance of the air. A woman who exuded a confidence both sexual and professional loped the length of the room, drawing everyone's attention. She stopped at the front. Clapped her hands: "If I could have your attention . . ."

The room subsided.

"My name is Senior Sergeant Coolidge and I'm attached to the ice unit of the Major Drug Investigation Division, based in Melbourne. You may have noticed that we've commandeered one of your conference rooms"—she bared her teeth, simulating a smile—"for a small operation we're mounting in the area. Just go about your business and we won't get in your way. Hopefully we can help one another in the days to come."

Another smile. Murphy sensed that no one returned it. She glanced at Challis, who was expressionless. He rolled his shoulders slightly, as if to relieve pressure.

Coolidge got down to business.

"We're facing an ice epidemic." She stopped, scowled. "I'm not sure why some of you are rolling your eyes. You can't be bored already; perhaps you don't like being lectured. Perhaps you think drug dealers and users are scum who should be left to wipe themselves out."

Her gaze ranged the room interrogatively. "You're free to leave, but I will say this: ice use, ice crime, has become a nightmare in rural and regional areas like this one. And if you're sitting there bored and resentful, just consider this: you could be the next one stabbed by a kid high on ice. Or you shoot this kid and spend the next few years being counseled or sued. Or your girlfriend or daughter or brother is an addict, or about to become one. Or your wife, driving home from school with the kids in the back, is beaten to death with a tire iron because some guy thought she looked at him the wrong way at a stop sign. Or your blameless next-door neighbor is firebombed because his nephew happens to owe a dealer money. Or you find yourself forking out tens of thousands of dollars on lawyers, counselors and rehab when your sister or daughter falls to ice. Or you older ones find yourselves raising your grand-kids because your kids are addicts."

She had them now. No one wanted to be seen as the officer who didn't give a shit.

"You must have an inkling of all this," Coolidge said. "You'd be deaf, dumb and blind not to. Here are some figures. There has been a 165 per cent increase in magis-trates' court convictions related to methamphetamine use in the past three years. Ice counts for 90 per cent of all drug arrests in many regional areas. Almost half the instances of domestic violence in the last few years are due to ice. Deaths where ice has been a factor—accidental or deliberate—have tripled."

She paused, intense.

"We're under-resourced, under-funded and under-appreciated"—that roused a murmur—"but that doesn't mean we roll over and let it happen. This is an informa-tion session. Some of you have come here not knowing or caring in particular about the uses or effects of ice, but if we're going to be effective, proud of what we do, we need to be prepared. I will speak about policing matters later. Right now I'll introduce the first of two guest speakers, Anne Talbot."

The woman who entered was about forty, plain-looking, worn-out, a little anxious. She smiled tightly and launched into her address: "I have three teenage sons. The youngest is thirteen and scared. He's scared he'll go the way of his older brothers, who started taking ice in about Year 10. One of them died of it. The other is in prison for aggravated bur-glary while high on ice."

It was a flat, bleak delivery.

"My son Jamie," Talbot said. "He was a lovely boy. Sweet, loved his footy, not bad at his studies. But his dad left us when Jamie was ten, and I worked two jobs to put a roof over our heads so I wasn't always there for him. Yeah, I know, an old story and a guilt trip. But it happens more than you think. Jamie smoked a little marijuana, like most kids, but then he smoked some ice and that was it. By the end—he's the one who died—he had a thousand-dollars-a-day habit. *He's a kid.* He beat me up several times, he stripped the house of valuables and drained my bank account. He stole from other users and pushers.

"Along the way, he became an enforcer. You know, he'd torch someone's car because they owed money. One day he phoned me, paranoid, saying someone was going to kill him. By now I was broke, and I was over the whole thing. I hung up on him. That night, the police came to tell me he'd been stabbed to death. So, on that occasion, it wasn't paranoia, someone *was* out to get him."

She gave them a wry smile; they shifted in their seats.

"It turns out he'd stolen from another pusher, who'd tracked him down and killed him. That's the police theory. I have no reason to doubt it.

"By now I was living with my two younger boys in a granny flat at the back of my brother's house. I'd had to sell our home, but there was such a high mortgage on it I was left with only a few thousand dollars. We stayed there for about four months, and then my second son, David, got hooked on ice and became so agitated and aggressive that my brother asked us to move out. He had his own family to worry about.

"We're in a caravan now, me and Andrew, my youngest. It's okay; not great. David was a problem: violent, delusional. His teeth were a mess, he looked like a skeleton, he stank of chemicals, his face and arms were covered in sores where he'd picked at his skin. He jumped off a building, broke his leg, and then attacked the ambulance crew who tried to help him. While he was in hospital the police arrested him. Apparently he'd been with Jamie on a couple of home invasions."

Talbot stood there, looking around in some defiance. "That's my story. It's being repeated in every town and suburb. I don't know what to do. I don't know where to go. I'm holding on by a thread."

She clasped her hands together, stared at the floor.

WITH ANNE TALBOT FAREWELLED and placed in a taxi, a woman named Mandy Reeve was called to the front of the room. To Pam Murphy's eyes, Reeve was expensively dressed, and she wondered if that had been a wise decision; it was bound to get everyone's backs up. But then she thought the clothing, flashy jewelry, bright nail polish, discreet shoulder tattoo and vivacity might prove a point: that dealers and users weren't necessarily all bogans and povos.

"I grew up in Camberwell," Reeve announced. "Upper-middle-class family, private school education, good at sport, passed Year 12 with good marks. I went to university, got an economics degree, started work in a bank and before long I was middle management on a six-figure annual salary."

She paused to meet their gaze, as if aware that she was not a sympathetic figure. "I started smoking ice on special occasions," she went on. "Someone's birthday, Grand Final day, New Year's Eve. It was a social scene. I'd go to a friend's house and the pipe would be passed around. I'm talking lawyer friends, senior public servants, business managers, commodities traders . . . Some of these friends had been taking ice on weekends for two or three years without health problems or police attention. If you've got an addictive personality, you're not going to be so lucky. The thing is, ice makes you feel great. Some of you here can probably attest to that."

She stared. The room was still.

"Ice makes you sharp, alert, able to concentrate for hours. Everything seems like fun. You don't need sleep; sex is great, no inhibitions, you can go for hours."

She grinned crookedly.

"Soon I was taking ice every weekend, and I'd be a wreck at work on Monday because I'd had virtually no sleep since Thursday or Friday. I'd smoke pot to try and come down.

"No one knew, though. Not my family, not my colleagues. I dressed well, I didn't stuff up at work, I functioned normally in social situations. But soon I needed ice every day. I spent all my money on it, partly because I felt so crap the day after that I had to take it again to feel all right. Nothing else in my life made me feel so good. Normal things like going for a swim, out to a movie with friends, just didn't measure up. In fact, stuff like that got in the way.

"Soon I was smoking *ten thousand dollars' worth each week*. I'd stop the car three or four times on the way to work, just to take a hit, keep the buzz.

"You'd think it would be obvious to people, but it wasn't. One of my mates at work said one Friday would I like to try a pipe after the pub. He didn't know I'd been using for a year. I didn't know *he'd* been using for three years.

"I didn't look like one of those poster children for the war on drugs, you know, rotting teeth, sunken cheeks, scabby skin. I looked fit and healthy.

"But I wasn't earning enough to maintain a ten-grand-a-week habit. So I started a life of crime."

She grinned at the room challengingly. Some grinned back, most scowled.

Unfazed, Reeve said, "I started dealing. I had access to a great product at a keen price, and a client base willing to pay for it. Good money, and I got ambitious for more of it. I employed runners; I'd send them to these little towns all over the Western District. They'd make contact with the local dealers who were selling crap weed or heavily cut coke or heroin or dicey pills, and give them free samples. Competitive prices for a reliable supply of quality product."

Reeve glanced out of the window, at the roof of the McDonald's. "Towns like this one. Not much in the way of entertainment, but lots of young tradesmen and unemployed school leavers. Even if they don't have much money, they've got enough to buy small amounts frequently, and *ice is cheap*."

Murphy stared at Reeve, stared at Coolidge, who was seated to one side. Thought: Coolidge reckons there's a similar network in place here.

Reeve was saying, "You'll want to know where I got the gear. Did I go into production, pay a few science students to cook meth in a shut-up house somewhere? A place like the one you guys found here in Waterloo this weekend? No, I was buying from a syndicate operating out of Tasmania. Bikies. They used to bring the gear up on the ferry."

She stopped, a flicker of pain crossing her face. "Then I was arrested with a carload of ice. A fine and a suspended sentence, but I lost my job. My family tried to help me; I turned my back on them. Got arrested again. Both times, I was held in a lockup after arrest and went through withdrawal, and it was hell. My whole body shaking, couldn't get comfortable, everything ached. And I was tired, so tired. I smelled revolting.

"So . . . another jail sentence, suspended for two years, and this time I let my family help me, God bless them. I went into rehab. I've been clean for over a year. But you know, maybe my neurochemistry's fucked, and I'll never be able to hold down a job or raise a child or maintain a relationship. I look okay. I'm not."

MURPHY, WATCHING, THOUGHT THE pain, fervor and regret were real, but a part of her was skeptical. Maybe Reeve would keep working at putting her life back together. Maybe she'd never use again, never reoffend. Murphy hoped so. She hoped Reeve would continue to educate short-sighted and lazy police officers. But a corner of her wondered about the itch inside Reeve, the longing in the dark hours.

And she wondered what Reeve *hadn't* told the police. She'd run a network of runners and dealers; Murphy knew what that entailed. Presumably she'd dealt out her share of rewards, threats and punishments. Had she paid for these crimes? Would she ever?

REEVE LEFT AND COOLIDGE claimed the room again.

"The takeaway is: open your eyes. As you go about your daily duties, think beyond what's immediately apparent, and pass your suspicions and observations on to your superiors. Ice could be behind that road-rage incident, head-on car smash or pub brawl you attend. That house fire: maybe the place had been rewired by an electrician high on ice. That mouthy kid outside a nightclub, that punch-up in a car park, that stabbing of a shopkeeper . . . Was it ice?"

Coolidge's gaze ranged around the room. "You've heard how ice makes users feel great. But with regular use—and some people are hooked very quickly—it causes aggression, anxiety, rage, paranoia, delusions and psychotic episodes. You've all had experience of trying to control someone like that. It can take six police officers to control one man. He'll be unstoppable. Capsicum spray? Forget it."

Everyone nodded. They knew. They'd seen it, experienced it.

"Who picks up the pieces?" said Coolidge. "You do.

"In addition to seeing ice at the root of random accidents, punch-ups and unprovoked violence, I want you to be aware that it could be at the root of certain criminal acts. A guy's car is torched. Vandals? Or did the guy owe money to the wrong people? Or had he been skimming, or had he wanted to quit working for a dealer, or did someone think he was informing? That home invasion: burglars? Or did the homeowner's granddaughter owe money to a syndicate?

"Think. Ask probing questions. Don't take anything at face value.

"I understand from Inspector Challis that you've had a rash of farm break-ins where rifles and shotguns have been stolen. Wouldn't surprise me if the guns are finding their way to an ice syndicate. Think, look, listen. Let's say you're working the front desk and a couple of teenagers come in and say they're worried about a friend, he's out of control. Don't dismiss it, don't just write it up and ignore it. Get a name. Get an address. Go and look. What if this kid needs help? You could intervene at just the right time—before he puts his mother in hospital with a crushed skull or dies of an overdose. Warn, advise, collate the kid's name against known dealers and users.

"Talk to hardware stores, pharmacists and specialist stores. Ask who's been buying large quantities of lab equipment, protective clothing and breathing apparatus, air-monitoring and decontamination equipment. As you've heard, some dealers, like Ms. Reeve, buy their supplies from a syndicate, but there are plenty of home-grown meth labs around.

"Speak to real estate agents and property managers. They'll have their suspicions: houses that are always heavily curtained, or where the tenants are never seen, or there's been suspicious comings and goings, or a certain smell hangs around all the time. The lab found here in Waterloo is a classic example.

"Talk to power companies about properties that show a sudden or prolonged spike in electricity usage.

"That'll help identify local sources, but it's probable that the ice in the Westernport region is also coming in from outside. The suppliers may be in competition with each other, hence some of the arson attacks and shootings we're seeing.

"Any questions?"

She didn't stop for questions but placed a shoebox on the table and pulled out a sealed Ziploc bag and a glass pipe.

"This," she said, waving the bag, "is ice. Crystalized methamphetamine. It's often smoked in a pipe like this one."

The ice went one way around the room, the pipe the other. The bag, when it came to Murphy, revealed opaque lumps resembling dirty crushed ice. The glass pipe was small, blackened, a smeared deposit inside the bulb.

"Some users inject," Coolidge said. "Their bodies fall apart much more quickly." She paused. "There might be in this room someone who has smoked ice and others who will be offered it. Consider this, please. With regular use your ability to produce dopamine—the pleasure chemical—is reduced. Your saliva glands will dry out, your teeth will rot. Psychoses will set in. You'll use up your savings. You'll cut corners at work, put your lives and the lives of your colleagues at risk. Please rethink what you're doing. Any questions?"

Again she didn't stop. "Facebook. Twitter. Monitor these sites. If you arrest someone, question someone, suspect someone, even help a messed-up user, check their social media postings. We're not talking geniuses here. Someone will brag about using, or a crime they've committed while flying on ice or getting the funds to buy it. Names and photos will be posted: dealers, suppliers, fellow users. A guy shows off a couple of firearms on his Facebook page: maybe he's your rifle thief.

"Any questions?"

WHEN THE ROOM WAS clear and Coolidge had returned to her temporary headquarters along the corridor, Pam Murphy helped Janine Quine wipe the table, clear away the plastic cups, vacuum the floor, clean the whiteboard. Quine was a wordless presence in the room, and Pam wondered what it was like for her, a civilian employee. Most people had infrequent yet uneasy contact with the police. They welcomed them during an emergency—rested easier knowing that such a concept as a police force existed—but what would it be like for a civilian working alongside the police day by day?

We all cheat and lie, Murphy thought. Mostly it's small stuff, harmless. Mostly we don't deserve a millisecond of police attention. She wanted to reassure Quine, tell her, "I'm flesh and blood just like you." She sensed this would make the poor woman even more tense, so she got out of there as soon as she could. Off to fight crime.

5

FIRST UP ON HER crime-fighting agenda, ask the Moonta Moth why he no longer wanted to press charges against Owen Valentine.

Tony Slatter was a retired public servant and a genial drunk. Married, divorced—more than once—he was not exactly a sad sack but not entirely understood or appreciated by everyone in Moonta, either; like a moth, he was drawn to house lights on balmy evenings. He'd wake at lunchtime, drink all afternoon and then, after dark, wander the dim streets of the little coastal town, blearily cheerful, a sloppy smile on his face. Spotting a porch light, he'd aim straight for it. Knock on the door, say hello, maybe plant a boozy kiss or wrap someone in his arms; step inside for a chat or another drink. The Moth. He'd been at it for years, tolerated by the locals, hated by the newcomers, the Melbourne weekender people.

And a week and a half ago he'd knocked on the wrong door. Owen Valentine, paranoid, flying on ice, had kicked, punched and head butted Slatter, putting him in hospital. Uniforms attended, statements were taken. But before CIU could follow through, Slatter had changed his mind about pressing charges.

PAM HEADED NORTHEAST OF Waterloo to the strip of ti tree, sand and huddled beach houses that was Moonta. Slatter lived in a timber house set in a cottage garden along a short, overhung laneway a hundred meters from the beach.

She knocked and presently he came to the door. Four o'clock and he'd been drinking, she could smell it. But he seemed clear-eyed, not addled. His arm was in a sling, fading bruises darkened eye and temple, and one ear was scabbed, the other still bandaged. He wore a white business shirt over grey board shorts, revealing knobby knees and old Nike runners.

"Mr. Slatter? Detective Constable Murphy, Waterloo CIU."

He rocked back and blinked. "Something wrong?"

"I understand you no longer wish to press charges against Owen Valentine?"

"That's correct."

"May I ask why? It was a serious assault."

"Look, it's all sorted."

Pam sharpened her voice. "Has he threatened you, Mr. Slatter?"

"What? No, nothing like that."

"If he has, we'll come down hard on him."

For a brief moment, Slatter was not a fool or a drunk but the canny bureaucrat he'd once been. "Nothing like that, and I'm sure you're busy with other cases. Meanwhile, I have a dental appointment."

"Are you intending to drive, Mr. Slatter?"

He smiled, a nasty little smile. "Taxi."

EVEN SO, IT WAS worth whispering a hard word in Owen Valentine's ear.

Murphy drove two streets to his house, a small, unloved shack behind a couple of straggly ti trees. Attached to one wall was a car shed, empty, the door up. A rusting Corolla was parked in the driveway, a little Nissan behind it. Pam called in the plates: the Nissan belonged to Irene Penford, aged fifty-nine, the Corolla to Christine Penford, aged twenty-eight.

Mother and daughter? Pam knocked on the front door, a cheap, hollow veneer panel, dog-scratched and rotting away at the bottom. Nothing. She knocked again, and a third time, and a woman answered.

"Yes?"

"Christine?"

"Who wants to know?"

Penford looked closer to forty than twenty-eight. A gaunt face, bad teeth and meth twitches. She carried a little boy in the crook of one arm. He gazed solemnly at Murphy, who winked, whereupon he gave her a transforming smile, ducking his head into his mother's scrawny neck.

"Police, Christine."

"I done nothing."

"I'd like to speak to Owen if I could. Is he home?"

"Nup."

"But he does live here?"

Tears filled the woman's eyes. "He run off on me."

"When?"

"Last Friday. I just got home and all his stuff was gone. Clothes, razor, Cluedo."

"Cluedo?"

"Our dog. Owen's dog."

"Did he leave a note?"

"Nup."

"Had you been arguing?"

"Nup."

"Could he be staying with a friend? Family?"

"We're his friends and family. What do you want him for?"

"Did Mr. Slatter visit him by any chance?"

"Who?"

"May I come in?" Pam asked, stepping up, giving the action a little push, so that Penford stepped aside.

There were stale druggie smells in the house, familiar to Murphy from dozens of visits to domestic disturbances and warrant servings over the years. At first glance, the front room was tidy, albeit grubby, but an ice pipe peeped out from beneath a clutter of magazines and toys on the coffee table. As though Penford had spotted the arrival of the unmarked CIU sedan and swept away the evidence.

"I told you, Owen's not here. He run off on me."

"Let's sit in the kitchen, Christine."

The older woman was there, washing dishes, and Pam had a sudden and complete image of a little domestic heartache. The mother knows her daughter and her daughter's partner are addicts, and visits often to see that they're more or less okay and not neglecting her grandson.

Pam reached out a hand to shake but Irene Penford said apologetically, "I'm all sudsy. Tea?"

"Mum, she won't be staying."

"I'd love a cup of tea," Pam said.

When it was poured and delivered the older woman said, "Is it about the bike?"

"Mum! Please! Just drop it."

"Bike, Mrs. Penford?"

"I gave Clover a bike for her birthday and the next thing I know, it's in the front window of the Barn."

The Bargain Barn, an auction house and secondhand dealership on Frankston-Flinders Road, between Waterloo Mowers and Peninsula Pumps.

"Clover?"

"My granddaughter," Irene Penford said. She was pinch-mouthed with worry.

Pam looked around as if the child might be hiding. "Perhaps Clover sold it because she needed money."

"*She's six.*"

"Mum, please," Christine Penford said.

Pam Murphy said, "Perhaps I could speak to Clover about it."

"She's not here," Christine said mulishly. "She's at a friend's."

"She's never here," the grandmother told Pam. "Haven't seen her for ages." She paused. "No prizes for guessing what happened."

No. Owen, or Christine, had sold the child's bike to buy drugs. But this was getting off topic. Pam said, "Christine, did Owen say anything to indicate he intended to leave you?"

"Not a thing."

"Good riddance," Irene Penford said.

"Mum, shut it."

Pam went on grimly, "Had there been anything off in his behavior the last week or two? Or any visitors or phone calls that didn't seem right to you?"

Christine shrugged. The boy squirmed in her arms, so she set him on the floor. He sat, patted the sticky linoleum, crawled across the room. Then he was at a dog's food bowl, caked and crusted, and his grandmother sighed, swept the bowl out from under him and clattered it into the sink. Outraged, he bawled.

His mother screeched, "Shut it Troy!"

"Christine, please."

"You shut it too, Mum."

Troy pulled a sulky face and crawled for the doorway.

There were times Murphy hated her job. She glanced around the room. Neat, but with little sense of domestic or family life. One lonely drawing, an elaborate scene involving unicorns, fairies and a misty castle, caught her eye. Fastened by a fridge magnet, it was vivid and animated.

Clearly the work of the older child. "Is Owen the father of both your children, Christine?"

"What's it to you?"

Pam had to get out of there. Rapidly she went on, "Christine, were you here when Owen punched and kicked a man named Slatter a few days ago?"

"Not his fault. That man just thought he could waltz in and—"

"So you were here."

"Said I was, didn't I?"

"I need to speak to Owen about it, Christine."

"Told you, he run off on me." Misery suffused Penford's face. "What am I supposed to do now?"

Taking a risk, Pam said, "Did Owen also take your stash, Christine?"

The eyes slid away. "What stash?"

Christine Penford was trying to moisten her mouth. She scratched at her face absently.

"Christine, we found no vehicle registered in Owen's name. How does he get around? There's no bus service to Moonta."

Penford jerked her head, indicating the Corolla in the driveway. "We share."

"But you take it to work each day."

"Yeah, so?"

"So how does he get around when you're not here? If he ran off on you, how did he do it?"

Penford shrugged. "How would I know? Bastard."

On her way out, Pam asked, "Do you have a recent photo of Owen I could use?"

"How come?"

"To show people. The neighbors."

Penford was alarmed now. "What do you mean?"

Pam said smoothly, "Standard procedure, Christine."

Penford took out a cracked-screen iPhone, tapped and swiped. She showed Pam a head-and-shoulders shot of a man who could have been her clone. Dark where she was fair, he was slight, gaunt, feral. Holding a dog.

"Text it to me," Pam said.

SHE WENT OUTSIDE WHERE the air was gusting and hot, but clean after the miserable Penford–Valentine hovel. Before heading for the CIU car she stepped into the car shed, half expecting to find stolen gear. Nothing. Dust, cobwebs, rusty tools, old paint tins. On the concrete floor a pool of white paint, dry but fresh-looking. What it meant, she didn't know or care.

It was irrelevant that Slatter no longer wanted to press charges, the attack had been severe and now the assailant was missing, so Pam knocked on a few doors. Of the remaining ten houses in the street, six were weekenders owned by Melbourne families. They hadn't been occupied on the evening Valentine attacked the Moth. The other four householders had been at home, and could attest to Slatter's propensity for knocking on doors expectantly, half-tanked and ready to chat and drink on. "Irritating but harmless," she was told.

As for Valentine? He kept to himself mostly. Rarely went out. Seemed suspicious of the world. They hadn't seen him for a few days. Didn't know where he was.

MURPHY DROVE OUT OF the choked collection of small houses on sandy lanes and back to the police station car park in Waterloo.

Four-thirty P.M. and John Tankard was climbing out of the CREST car. CREST: Community Response, Engagement, and Social Tasking, which boiled down to a uniformed constable targeting parents who flouted road and parking rules outside schools at drop-off and pick-up times. Of the handful of schools in the Waterloo catchment area, two were cramped and poorly sited for car access. Frustrated parents competed for parking spots, the losers parking haphazardly and illegally. Some of them abused or attacked other parents and sometimes teachers.

To Pam it was a cruel irony that John Tankard was ever given CREST duty. He had little if any sense of community, engagement or responsibility.

He leaned his ample rump on the car, half-closing his eyes against a flurry of dust. "Murph."

"How's it going, John?"

He began shaking his head. "They say kids are monsters, but it's the parents."

He was a large man, damp and hot; a man who stared at your breasts, and he was doing it now. Murphy retreated a little. "Yeah?"

"Jan Quine's husband."

"What about him?"

"The Quine kids take the bus to school, right?"

"Yeah, so?"

"So this morning he gets it into his head that the driver goes too fast over the speed bumps."

"He followed the bus?"

"Got it in one."

Pam shook her head, not interested; not really surprised by anything she heard in this job. "Huh."

"Yep. I had the traffic moving nice and smooth and he gets out of his car and starts abusing the bus driver. I'm trying to calm him down and the bus is trying to turn around and the other parents are tooting and swearing at each other. Fucking nightmare."

With a grunt he uncoiled from the car and they walked together to the back door of the station. Pam had heard the rumors about Janine Quine's husband being a closet gambler. Janine struggling to pay off his debts and keep food on the table, working a thankless job in the Waterloo cop shop.

Upstairs in CIU, she was told that Challis had gone out for a drink with the drug-squad senior sergeant. But he'd left a note on her desk. Roslyn Wreidt, address in Tyabb. She'd come home to find her house had been burgled.

Back downstairs, Pam signed out the CIU car again.

OUT ALONG FRANKSTON-FLINDERS ROAD, newish housing estates on her left, businesses and occasional houses on her right. These days her gaze went automatically to FOR SALE and FOR RENT signs, houses with removalists parked outside. Her current house, backing onto farmland behind Penzance Beach, had been sold, the new owner due to take residence after Christmas. She had no idea where to go; had been too busy and too paralyzed to look. And who moved house at this time of year?

Seeing nothing, she gently accelerated, slowing again when Traffic's beefy unmarked station wagon came into view, grille lights flashing red and blue, the driver booking a kid in a hot little Subaru. She waved. He didn't notice her.

The grass around her was dead and dying. Out in the east was a corner of burnt-out farmland. Canvas blinds were drawn over the eyes of the houses close to the road, fighting the heat. Death and decay hovered today. The Peninsula was normally green—fatly, moistly green—but this was the third drought year in a row. Straw and dirt prevailed now.

Right up to the black fringe where the fire had prowled. And so the ghost bicycle was a shock. Starkly white, angular; chained to a gum tree to mark the site of a road fatality.

She stopped for a crew patching potholes and clearing a fallen pine tree. Drummed her fingers on the wheel as she waited. Searched the AM and FM bands for some decent music, found only ads and mindless banter. She switched off and thought of her mother.

Harriet Murphy had tried staying on in the sprawling family home after her husband died. Eventually she'd found the place unmanageable, and now she was in a retirement village.

Hated it.

Vagaries of the job permitting, Pam made the drive up to the city via EastLink to see her mother about once a week. They would sit together in the tiny cottage or out in the sun if one of the garden benches wasn't occupied. None of it felt quite right. They both missed the old place, the airy rooms. and leafy backyard.

Pam pondered this morning's phone conversation. "I want to see the Peninsula before the place is crawling with holidaymakers," her mother had said.

"Your old stomping ground."

"Exactly. Are you free on Sunday?"

Well, Challis had okayed it, and Pam thought she might even enjoy touring around with her mother. But it was yet another reminder that she was the only one of the Murphy children who ever saw Harriet. Harriet excused them: they had families, lived busy lives. And Pam's life wasn't busy?

She thought about her brothers Liam and Daniel. She liked the women they'd married, and adored her nieces and nephews, but her brothers were academics—PhDs, both of them—and keenly aware that most people weren't.

What this meant, she was frequently reminded—often during Christmas lunch—was that a PhD didn't mean mastery of just one field, but of all. Her brothers knew everything. They could speak authoritatively on issues of law and order, for example. Civil liberties. Prisons. The police service. The police and race relations. The police and the right of peaceful protest. The police as political servants or political tools. The police and excessive use of violence. The police and their love of cars, guns and gadgets.

One lectured in economics, the other in linguistics . . .

Perhaps they thought they knew everything because they spent most of their time with twenty-year-olds who knew nothing at all.

Pam wondered how they'd cope if they encountered a minority who didn't fit one of their stereotypes. Like—to take a random example—a sharp female police officer.

She turned left, over the railway line in Tyabb, then left again before the airfield, and found where Roslyn Wreidt lived.

A SMALL BLOCK OF flats of a type common in city suburbs and country towns: about forty years old, grey stucco external wall, flat roof. Tiny apartments with aluminum-framed windows, low ceilings and an archway between sitting room and kitchen.

She walked around to the ground-floor rear apartment and knocked on a door in a dim entryway, almost dark; she could not at first form a clear impression of the woman who answered. A moment later she was shown to a room filled with pale Ikea fabrics and wood, the air stale.

"Please sit," Roslyn Wreidt whispered. "Tea? Coffee? Juice or water?"

"Water," Murphy said, realizing she was parched.

Wreidt hovered briefly, as if processing the answer and the actions it necessitated. She was small-framed, with bowed shoulders, dipped chin and whispery voice; she looked defeated by life. Or the burglary. Late twenties, Pam guessed. Dressed in jeans, runners, socks and a long-sleeved, high-necked top despite the heat. Eventually she tried a smile and made her way through to the kitchen stiffly, slowly, as if wading through chest-high seas. The fridge door hissed, a jug landed on a benchtop, a glass rattled, water gurgled.

Pam Murphy didn't discount the victim response to being burgled. Victims came home to broken glass, upturned or slashed furniture, missing valuables, turds on the bed, semen on their underwear. It was a violation, and victims grew vigilant and nervy. Some of them bought expensive security systems or moved house; some never stepped outside again. Then again, she'd seen plenty of householders who mentally rubbed their hands together and lied their way down the list of stolen valuables they intended to claim insurance on.

Wreidt returned with a dewy glass, so full the water level spilled over her fingers. She placed it on a coaster, jerked back, stared at her wet hand as if it were alien. She made to wipe it on her top, then her thigh, and finally dug a damp tissue from her sleeve.

She's been weeping, Murphy thought. Tread gently.

"Tell me about the break-in," she said. "You came home . . ."

In a whispery rush, Wreidt said, "I work part-time at the child-care place. I got home at lunchtime and there was this smell and I saw the mess on the floor and I was too scared to go in so I called the police."

Pam smiled. She was on the sofa, Wreidt in an armchair, perched on the edge as if to flee. "Let's go back a bit. You arrived home at lunchtime . . . Did you see anyone in the street? Strangers? Strange cars?"

"No."

"A normal day."

"Yes."

"You opened the front door."

"Yes."

"With your key? It was locked?"

Wreidt's eyes darted. "Yes."

"You smelled something. What, exactly?" Not wanting to lead Wreidt, but knowing this could take forever, she said, "Cigarette smell? Petrol? Perfume or aftershave?"

"A really rank smell."

"Body odor?"

Wreidt grimaced. She opened and closed her mouth, worked her tongue, as if tasting the air. "Like BO."

The drug-squad briefing still vivid in her memory, Pam thought: *ice addict?* "You saw things scattered around the floor. In this room? Your bedroom?"

"Here," whispered Wreidt. She pointed to a cabinet. "CDs and DVDs and some photos."

"The TV's still here."

Wreidt snorted, a little color now in both face and voice. "Too small, too cheap, too old. Took my HD recorder, though. All my shows taped on it."

"And your bedroom?"

The eyes were wild again, looking for a way out. "Nothing."

Ah. Roslyn Wreidt had been assaulted, maybe raped. A man had been in here waiting for her. Or she knew him. "You went outside immediately and called the police?"

"Yes."

"On your mobile?"

"Neighbor," Wreidt said, staring at the carpet.

Came home at lunchtime but didn't call the police until mid-afternoon. And her mobile was stolen.

Murphy didn't know where to go with this. She didn't know what questions to ask or how to ask them. But she did know that Roslyn Wreidt would have to be handled gently, by an expert like Ellen Destry. She stepped around the coffee table and knelt at the woman's knee and took the damp hands in hers. Felt resistance and then a massive unloading as Wreidt registered what Murphy said to her.

"He hurt you, didn't he, Ros?"

6

ELLEN DESTRY MIGHT HAVE responded promptly to Pam Murphy's text, but it sat in the server for a few hours. She was busy anyway, trying to break Albie Rofe.

The Westernport region's new sex-crimes unit was housed in a decrepit Californian bungalow two streets away from the police station. The house, owned by the shire, had sat unsold and empty for two years before being donated to Victoria Police. It needed painting, restumping and a new roof, but the interior was sound, if basic. Computers, phones, desks and filing cabinets crammed the largest room, another was the interview room, a third, fitted out with carpets, armchairs, a TV and a box of toys and children's books, was for traumatized victims and their families, a fourth was a briefing room. The last, a tiny box, was Ellen's office.

She was in the interview room with Rofe. The house, uninsulated, baked in the early summer sun, and Ellen felt grimy. Rofe, a soft mass of damp, loose flesh, looked not much better, and he scowled when Ellen remarked, "Beautiful weather we're having, Albie."

"Wouldn't know."

"Warm, sunny—beach weather. You hadn't noticed?"

Rofe examined his hands, pudgy hands viewed by eyes in a pudgy face. He was twenty-two years old, poorly put together and in need of fresh clothes, shower, shave and haircut. He shrugged massively.

"You like the outdoors, Albie? The beach?"

Rofe began to look hunted. He knew why he was there. He hadn't asked for a lawyer and had looked blank when offered one.

"Merricks Beach, Penzance Beach, Somers—you get around, Albie. A real lover of the outdoors."

Maybe his palms were wet. He rubbed them on his thighs. The interview room, the size of a medium bathroom, was close and stale. Full of Rofe's anxiety and pathetic nastiness now, five minutes into the interview. One window, but the kind that wound out from the bottom with only a small gap. It hindered rather than encouraged airflow. Who the hell had designed such a window? Ellen asked herself crankily. She got up, opened the door to let in warm, stale air. Picked up the manila folder that sat on the plastic table. Rofe was looking at it when he wasn't looking at his stumpy fingers. Ellen he hadn't looked at yet.

She opened the folder. Rofe flinched.

"Is this you, Albie?"

In the photograph, Rofe—wearing the same arse-crack tracksuit pants and baggy T-shirt he was wearing now—was casting a frightened glance at the camera from behind a ti tree. A hint of the vivid sea and the ruins of a little jetty in the background.

"Here's you," Ellen said, "enjoying the sea air at Balnarring Beach."

Rofe said nothing.

Another photo: "Here's your little Hyundai Excel. Close-up of your rear plate, in fact."

Rofe was transfixed, as if caught in a spotlight.

"I wonder why anyone would go to the trouble of taking such photos . . . Any ideas, Albie?"

"No," he whispered.

"Yes, it's a hard question. I'll answer it for you. A young woman was on the beach one day recently, minding her own business, sunbathing on her towel, reading a book and listening to her iPod, when a man came and sat beside her. Plenty of room on the beach, but he sat right next to her—and do you know what he did? He began to masturbate. She picked up her things and left.

"But what do you know, when she told her friends, some of them had had similar experiences, or had heard of similar experiences: a guy lurking, perving on topless bathers, flashing his poor excuse for a penis at a couple of young girls, sitting too close to women sunbathing alone, et cetera. Know anything about that, Albie?"

He said nothing. Ellen said, "So the first woman I mentioned decided to do something about it. She came back several days in a row until she saw you again, and she took your photo, along with a photo of your number plate."

Ellen watched him. She said, "We needed to be sure, Albie, so we got the registered owner's license photo and showed it around. And guess what? Several women have identified that person as the person who shook his willie at them and perved on them and sat too close to them. And that person is you."

Silence, the stillness deepening.

"I'm sorry," gasped Rofe. "It won't happen again."

Rofe's victims thought he was more pathetic than threatening, and none wanted to go the route of a trial, but Rofe didn't know that. "Oh, you think you can just say sorry and that's that? You just walk out of here and go home?"

He looked terrified. "I never touched them! I wouldn't!"

"I spoke to your mother . . ."

"Please!"

"She's at her wits' end with you. Scared you'll molest your little sister, scared you'll start looking in the neighbors' windows. Scared you'll start touching instead of looking."

"Please, I never would."

Ellen felt grimy: the heat, Albie Rofe. "You do know what jail would mean, don't you, Albie? You'd be eaten alive in there. Meanwhile you'd be on the sex offenders register for life, your name all over the newspapers. Your poor family would be forced to move to another town."

He was weeping, hot, splashing tears.

"So here's the thing, Albie. You start seeing a therapist. Your mother has agreed to that, and you have to as well. I'll monitor your progress. If you miss a session without good reason, I'll chase you down, understood?"

He whispered it: "Understood."

"And that would mean jail time, Albie."

The air was close and stinking and Ellen washed her hands of Albie Rofe as she watched him slink out. Hoping she'd done the right thing.

THE SEX-CRIMES UNIT WAS small: Ellen Destry (sergeant), Ian Judd (senior constable) and two constables, Lois Katsoulas and Jared Rykert. Rykert was finger-stabbing his keyboard, face clenched, when Ellen walked in from the interview room.

"How did it go?"

He'd been in court all day. "The fu—bloody magistrate," he said, turning his attention to Ellen.

"I can cope with the occasional four-letter word, Jared."

Rykert's eyes were moist—fury and something else.

Humiliation? "The prick got off with a warning," he said. "I spent weeks on it, Sarge."

Graham Tovey had assaulted four women in and around Waterloo in a three-week period, grabbing one on a service road behind a timber yard, another on the tidal flats board-walk and two near the foreshore skate park. He'd followed them, brought them to the ground with an arm around the neck, then digitally penetrated them before running off with their purses.

"A warning," echoed Ellen, shaking her head. Robbery and assault with intent to rape. The result should have been a sentence of up to ten years.

"No priors, he pleaded on the purse snatching, and denied the sexual assault. The magistrate bought it."

The magistrate, Lewis Deere, was notoriously skeptical of sexual assault claims. Especially if there were no independent witnesses and the claimant was, or had been, in a relationship with the accused, or had been drunk or high or not, in his view, appropriately dressed. He'd never been warned or investigated by the Bar Council, his language was too careful for that, but the police hated it when he was rostered on to one of their prosecutions.

Ellen pulled a chair up close to Rykert. He was young, athletic; looked more like a footballer or a brickie than a detective. He wore suit pants and a white shirt, the tie at half-mast, his ID on a blue lanyard around his neck. Strong, shapely fingers. He was almost handsome . . . but young, unformed, still easily wounded by setbacks.

"Look," she said, gently but with a no-nonsense edge to her voice. "Shit happens. Especially shit like Lewis Deere. It's disappointing, it's sometimes outrageous and it will continue to happen."

He snorted. "Good to know, Sarge."

"Listen to me," she said, some steel in her now. "Your only responsibility is to carry out the best investigation you can, and present the best case you can. After that, it's in the hands of lawyers, judges, magistrates and juries. Did you do the best job possible? Did you honor the victims?"

"Hundred per cent, Sarge."

"Then don't take it personally. Hold your head high."

"But there was no justice for those women."

"I know. It's heartbreaking. But if it's going to break you, you'd better leave the job right now, because you won't function well enough to get justice for the next victim who comes along."

"Sarge."

"Tovey will stuff up again."

"Sarge."

"Do you want to stay on?"

"Sarge."

"Good. Briefing in five."

ELLEN OPENED WINDOWS, TURNED on the electric fans, and stood at the head of the briefing room. She was new to this game, briefing a team. Under Hal Challis's command in the old days, she'd admired the calm, genial way he ran things, the way he propped up the wall with his right shoulder and quizzed the team and let them speak and allotted tasks at the end of it. He always provided tea, coffee and pastries, but Ellen wasn't going to do that at five o'clock on a hot afternoon, when all anyone wanted was a beer, a swim, somewhere cool to wind down. This briefing would be brief.

Everyone seated, she outlined a couple of upcoming operations, including a foreshore playground stake-out in Mornington early the following week.

"A man seen approaching and photographing children,"

she said, "and the locals have requested our help." Allocating Rykert and Katsoulas, she went on to ask for a recap of ongoing cases, occasionally jotting notes as each member of her team spoke. Asking questions, encouraging comments and suggestions.

Then she turned to Lois Katsoulas. "I now call on our social-media queen."

Katsoulas grinned. She was Rykert's age but cannier, tougher, a slight woman in a thin, sleeveless dress and white running shoes. Dark hair and eyes, a face full of quick expressions and snap comprehensions. She seemed to spend her days glued to her digital devices, playing, texting, touching base like any young woman, but it was nearly always work-related. Her fingers flashed on her laptop keys now and she turned the screen until everyone could see it.

"Here's the assault on the Stony Point line, soon after the train left Bittern station."

She tapped a key, starting a video clip. The quality was grainy, tones of black, white and grey, showing the interior of a railway carriage, a bench seat under a window, where a young man in a hoodie sat beside a young woman wearing a dress and headphones. He edged closer, bunched tight against her, and licked her neck. She froze. His hand went to her knee, edged up under the hem of her skirt; his fingers moved. There were other people there, other heads and shoulders in profile, but no one noticed, no one acted. There was only this dedicated, soundless assault.

Ellen watched intently. In the old days, the police had tended to look at the specifics of a sexual assault—who put what where, more or less—and laid charges if the case was strong enough. Her job still entailed that, but nowadays it was also important to understand the context, the power dynamics, the relationship between offender and victim.

Watching the young woman freeze, Ellen reflected that she'd been like most people in the old days, unable to understand why sexual assault victims didn't just scream, scratch, kick, punch, shout the house down. No one wanted that story. People wanted a revenge story, with victim and bystanders taking charge, brave, noble, as they wrestled the culprit to the ground and called the police.

But now, and especially in this new job, she understood that most victims did freeze, especially if they were in a public place. They didn't want to die or be hurt. Some felt shame. All felt a kind of paralyzed disbelief and shock—like the young woman on the Stony Point train.

And the offender was counting on that. He'd probably done this before, and got away with it. In his mind, his victims were giving him permission to continue. They weren't saying no, so they must be saying yes. They weren't pushing him away, they weren't objecting, they were cooperating.

And so Ellen made sure her team paid attention to how rapists manipulated their victims. *How* something happened had become as important as *what* had happened. "It's up on Facebook?"

"I posted it last night," Lois said.

"Not the whole clip?"

Lois shook her head. "Edited highlights, concentrating on the guy entering and leaving the carriage."

Facebook had become a useful crime-fighting tool. Officers like Katsoulas posted CCTV clips and images of assaults, criminal damage, petrol drive-aways, rubbish dumping, vandalism, shoplifting, hoon driving, theft from cars and graffiti acts. The wider community—witnesses, concerned citizens, law-and-order types as well as cop-haters and grievance-bearers—were able to post comments and encouraged to pass information on to the police.

Katsoulas spent a lot of time removing abusive and legally problematic responses, or bantering with the wits and the ratbags; but she'd also gleaned information that had led to arrests and deeper investigations. A snowdropper had been identified after a rash of thefts of underwear from the clotheslines of elderly women in Waterloo. Four Bandidos had been arrested after advertising the sale of tasers, pistols, swords and pit-bull terriers on a Facebook page. Two teen boys were in juvenile detention after showing clips of themselves doing burnouts in, and later torching, a stolen Audi.

Ellen straightened her back, stretched the kinks. "And?"

"Result, Sarge," Katsoulas said. "Four people gave us a name: Leo Hart, lives in Crib Point."

"Pick him up tomorrow."

Ian Judd scowled. "Why not now?"

Ellen's second-in-command was about fifty with sparse, greying hair and glasses, a tightly knotted tie at his throat. He was a hard worker but basically, she thought, a plodder. Years of experience but unimaginative; rarely given to insights or able to empathize readily with victims. He saw the world in terms of crime and punishment. A crime was committed, he investigated it. He would probably make an arrest, but the human factor was always irrelevant, even baffling. He was humorless, sometimes disapproving. The Facebook initiative was beyond his comprehension. It was words and images on a screen. It wasn't real.

Ellen stared at him, her mind racing. She was new to this, but was already aware that if she were to be a good boss, if she wanted the team to cohere around her while also being capable of independent thought and action, then she needed to know how to coax, and assist, and be firm, and neutral, and partial, and a host of other contradictions.

"Tomorrow morning," she said, "because a guy like him sleeps till noon. This late in the afternoon, he could be any-where." She smiled disarmingly at Judd. "I'll come with you, but it will be your arrest."

He grunted, apparently mollified.

7

ELLEN TEXTED HAL, *be there in 20,* and took the long way home, directly across the Peninsula to Port Phillip Bay and down the coast road to Dromana. The sea, glistening at her elbow in the setting sun, cleansed and calmed her. Windows open, an Emmylou Harris CD in the slot, she kept one eye ready for kids on skateboards, dozy tourists, after-work shoppers braking for parking spots, and the other eye on the bay. Distant ships, one or two windsurfers.

At the Dromana shops she turned left, upslope to a patchwork of small houses. Her own house, a bit paint-peeling and lived-in, was on a quiet dirt track screened by bush. The best feature, a broad wooden deck that offered a view of the water between the downhill neighbor's trees, was where she expected Hal to be.

And so he was. Except that her sister was there, too, drinking wine with him. Ellen parked, gathered her bag and her files, and locked the car, delaying her next moves. She hadn't spent time with Hal for days, but she always had to steel herself for an encounter with Allie.

She clomped up the wooden steps, around the corner of the house, to the deck, the outdoor table where her lover sat with her sister. The former sprawled a little in his chair, fatigued, but uncoiling easily when she appeared, a smile transforming his hawkish features. He grabbed her tightly and planted a kiss. She returned it, touching her palm to his cheek. "This is a pleasant surprise."

She meant Challis, but craned her head around to smile at Allie as she said it. Allie, perched like a bird, gave a weak smile in return.

Ellen gave her attention back to Challis. "Hey there."

"Hello."

"First things first: are you remembering to water the pot plants?"

"And piss on the lemon tree," Challis said.

"Good work."

He pulled away, grabbed the wine bottle, a Flying Duck shiraz. "Drink?"

"Just let me get out of my things . . ."

She slid open the glass door to the house, across the polished floorboards to her bedroom. A quick toilet stop, a scoop of cold water over her face, patted dry with the hand towel, and all the time thinking . . . But the water felt so good. She stripped off her work clothes, took a one-minute shower, and pulled on shorts and a T-shirt.

Punishing her hair with a brush at the bathroom mirror, Ellen continued to think. Allie wants something, she thought. A favor. Approval for some mad thing she wants to do.

A visit from Allie was never just a visit.

"Just a visit," said Allie tensely a minute later. "Aren't I allowed to visit my big sister?"

Ellen smiled brightly at her, smiled also at Challis, communicating one imperative: *Whatever it is, I'll need to deal with it. Best if you don't stay.*

Damn it.

He took a minute or two, chatting, glancing at his watch,

draining his wine. "A stolen moment to keep me going," he said, rising from his chair, then bent to kiss each sister. "I have someone to meet in"—he glanced at his watch again—"twenty minutes."

Then he was gone and Ellen was watching her sister.

"What?"

"Nothing."

"You gave me that look."

"What look?"

"Disapproving."

"Allie, I've been married and divorced, and twenty years in a job where I've seen everything. I don't do disapproval."

Allie liked to see Ellen as the sensible one and herself as the loveable screwball: disorganized, but bright, intuitive and creative. An irresistible Annie Hall figure. Today she was wearing a hectic assemblage of thin, bright, sheer fabrics, with clanking bracelets, scarlet lips and dramatic eye shadow. She'd have been working hard on Challis—and he would have been impervious to it.

It was all an act. Allie was in fact deeply conservative, craving order and acceptance even as she fought against both. She might have thought she'd found what she wanted in her first marriage, to a surgeon, but it transpired that he didn't see anything wrong in his parents having a key to the house and letting themselves in on Sunday mornings. ('They'd come straight to our bedroom, Ells!") When the surgeon started calling her "Mother," turning into his own father, she walked out. With almost a million dollars, which she had the nous not to fritter away on Indian ashrams, struggling artists or grow-your-wealth spruikers. Instead she spotted the wallet potential in a middle-aged real estate agent named Steve, who died leaving her with another million. The unifying theme of that marriage had been raunchy sex, and the loving couple never let you forget it. Ellen had called it the Allie and Steve Show. Steve's death, from a massive coronary, had come to her as a guilty relief.

She smiled at her sister. "You look well."

"You look tired," Allie said.

Ellen took a nourishing mouthful of wine and closed her eyes. Tilted her face to the dying sun.

"I've met this great guy," Allie said.

Ellen opened one eye. Allie had her profile on several dating websites. Ellen had nothing against that; she'd met plenty of people who'd formed happy and lasting attachments that way. But she knew Allie was chronically incapable of discrimination or caution when it came to meeting men, so, feeling just a little guilty, she'd peeked one day at Allie's EliteMatch profile:

> *I am a vibrant, happy person, fit and healthy, and enjoy romantic dinners with a glass of quality wine (not a beer drinker), picnics, walks on the beach, sensitive, intimate but energetic love-making (my days of one night stands are long over), soul-searching conversations, great art, music and literature, films that move me emotionally and intellectually, and overseas travel (I'm an old hand at that!).*
>
> *The person I am looking for is my soul mate, a best friend, a confidant, a life partner, not just a lover. I want a man I can laugh with, talk with, make merry mischief with, grow old with.*

In other words, I have money and I'm looking for sex, Ellen had thought.

She smiled, "On the net?"

"Actually, no," beamed Allie. She didn't elaborate.

Ellen said, "I look forward to meeting him."

"You will soon. I haven't told him you're with the police."

Ellen's antennae quivered in a familiar way. "Is that a problem?"

"Of course not."

Ellen sipped her wine. There will be something off about him, she thought. Allie senses but can't articulate it; meanwhile, she's smitten, yearning for happiness and needing to convince herself she's found the right one at last.

"What does he do?"

Allie leaned over the table and lowered her voice. "It's a bit hush-hush."

"What, he's a spy?"

Allie laughed uncomfortably. "Don't laugh. He's an officer, military intelligence or something. He can't really talk about what he does."

"Okay."

Ellen poured more wine and said roguishly over the rim of her glass, "Good in bed?"

Allie seemed to shut down. She shifted uncomfortably. That was the conservative core of her: uncomfortable with sex talk sister-to-sister; fully capable of raucous innuendo in mixed company. Then she surprised Ellen.

"Actually, we haven't really . . ."

Ellen felt embarrassed. She didn't want to pry. "Sorry, none of my business. What's his name?"

"Clive."

Blushing, Allie passed her iPhone across the table. "This is him."

The screen showed a burly upper torso, a solid head, hair cropped militarily short. Forties, Ellen guessed. A lived-in face, wary eyes above a hesitant smile. Bushy eyebrows, ears that stuck out a little. Not handsome, but not ugly either.

As if paging through more photographs, Ellen concealed

the screen from Allie and found the messages in-box. Dozens, hundreds of messages from this Clive. He's love-bombing her, she thought. She looked at times and dates: several times an hour.

She pressed the home button, passed back the phone. "I'll invite you both to dinner in a few days' time."

"Unless your work gets in the way," Allie said, her tone a little sour, as if to say Ellen's work had got in the way before, and would again; that she was the type to put it ahead of the needs of her little sister.

8

ELLEN SLEPT POORLY. THINKING of Allie, of her daughter away at university, of Challis, who'd not spend the night owing to Allie's visit, and her sex-crimes team and the victims they tried to help. At 2 A.M. she was at her window, looking out at the deep black stillness of the bay and feeling unsettled, sensing the night depths sounding maritime dangers, animals and men on the prowl. In bed she tossed and turned again and unbidden to her half-dreaming state came the image of her sister's heavy-set boyfriend.

He hadn't wanted to be photographed, she realized.

Thoroughly awake now, 4 A.M., Ellen checked her phone. A missed call from Pam Murphy, 4:45 yesterday, followed by a text that hadn't come through until hours later. Ellen shook her head, reminded of Challis's admonition, back when she was on his CIU team: If it's important, call. Don't send a text or an email. You won't even know if a text is received, let alone read, understood or acted on.

I had my phone off, Ellen thought, and then I drove home and got embroiled with Allie's drama.

Murphy's text was brief, but clear. A burglary victim had eventually admitted to being raped. Name, address and phone number followed. "She's close-mouthed, Sarge."

Ellen collapsed back on her pillow, turned out the light, closed her eyes.

And then it was dawn, birds quarreling outside her window. Feeling a fog behind her eyes, her bones aching with tiredness, Ellen dragged herself through a jog down to the beach and back. Shower, muesli and coffee, and by the time she was in Crib Point with Senior Constable Judd, arresting Leo Hart, her old sharpness had returned.

BACK AT THE STATION, she called Pam Murphy for more information on the probable rape of Ros Wreidt in Tyabb. "Probable?"

"She's reluctant, Sarge. I went in expecting a burglary, and only gradually realized she'd also been assaulted in some way. It took me ages to tease out her story, and there are lots of gaps in it."

Ellen thanked her and drove to Tyabb and knocked on the door of Wreidt's flat.

"I've already told the police everything," Wreidt said. "She had no right to tell the world about it."

"Constable Murphy is a very perceptive and sympathetic officer," Ellen said.

They moved to the kitchen, Wreidt still in a dressing-gown, baggy cotton pajamas and fluffy slippers. Comfort dress, Ellen thought, watching Wreidt sit with painful movements and close the gown at her throat.

"Not going to work today?"

"Calling in sick."

"Have you seen a doctor yet?"

"No need."

And so it proceeded, Wreidt tentative, non-responsive, veering into tepid resistance if Ellen pushed. Then a glazier arrived, followed by the landlord, and an insurance assessor to check on the job, and it all boiled down to a crime scene trampled upon and handled by a host of strangers . . .

That was odd. "Ms. Wreidt, when were you robbed?"

Wreidt looked away. "Friday."

"Just to be clear, Friday of last week, four days ago?"

"Yes," she whispered.

"You led Constable Murphy to believe it happened yesterday afternoon."

"I reported it to the police yesterday afternoon. The insurance company said I had to."

Many showers and shampoos and laundered sheets and vacuumed carpets since then, Ellen thought.

"But everything else is as you described it to Constable Murphy? You came home from work and encountered a man who sexually assaulted you and stole some of your belongings?"

"Yes."

The story emerged haltingly. A man had been waiting for Wreidt (it transpired that he'd broken a laundry window to gain entry). He grabbed her from behind, tied her up with her own tights, and raped her. He used a condom and made her shower afterward and tried to chat as he patted her dry and toweled her hair. When he left, together with her iPad, phone and the cash in her wallet, he told her to count to a hundred.

He wore a balaclava. He stank.

"Body odor?"

"I don't know, just this really awful smell."

THESE TWO FACTS—A bad smell, count to a hundred—took Ellen to a cube of four small townhouses in Somerville. The FOR SALE sign outside the end unit, next to a laneway, was new, and she felt bleak to see it there, hammered into the lawn.

Marilyn Sligo answered her knock on the door, a slim woman of thirty, dressed in cargo pants and a damp T-shirt. She held up oily hands. "I won't shake or hug."

Ellen smiled, followed her into the kitchen, a warm, steamy region of benchtops, hanging copper-bottomed pots, serious knives in a wooden block, a shelf of cookbooks, one open to a slab of text and a luscious photograph.

"Something smells good."

"Just a slow-cooking goulash thing, Don's favorite," Marilyn said, giving Ellen a sad, intent look.

Ellen nodded. The husband still wasn't coping. According to Marilyn, he wasn't bewildered, angry or accusatory, and he didn't think of her as sullied. But he was tiptoeing around her, as if fearful of bruising her with his maleness. All Marilyn wanted was to return to her old life. Not deny the rape, pretend it hadn't happened, life was all roses; just be her old self again. "How else am I going to come through this?" she'd said, on Ellen's last visit.

They chatted for a while, Ellen saying bluntly, "Sorry you feel you have to move."

Marilyn closed then opened her eyes. "Isn't human nature wonderful? This is a side street, right?" she asked, gesturing toward the front of the house. "Not very busy? So explain the extra traffic."

Ellen didn't need to. Sightseers. But how had they known a rape victim lived here?

"They slow down and point," Marilyn said. "Losers."

With a look of profound cynicism she added, "And do you know what happened in Target a couple of weeks ago? I was buying work pants for Don, and ran into this woman I work with. I don't know her very well, but she came over, full of false concern, and just dying to hear all the gory details. She said, 'Well, you are pretty sexy, you know,' as if to say I should be thankful a stranger found me attractive enough to rape." She shook her head.

Ellen grabbed her hand across the table and reworked

a line from her favorite film, *Love, Actually*: "Tell me who this woman is. Trained police snipers are only a phone call away."

Marilyn laughed tiredly. "I wish."

Ellen released her hand. "Sorry to go over old ground, and I know it was three months ago, but you told me the man who raped you gave off a bad smell."

Marilyn shuddered. "God, yes."

"Body odor or something else?"

"More like halitosis. Really rank breath, with an undercurrent of some other delightful stink."

"He helped you clean up afterward and tried to chat."

"Yes," Marilyn said, before giving Ellen a hard, searching look. "He's done it again."

"Yes."

Marilyn said, "Oh, God," and closed her eyes.

Then Ellen saw her rub her wrist unconsciously, and remembered that Marilyn had been wearing a bracelet the day of the attack. A Pandora. Given to her by her husband, it was hung with six of the most expensive charms in the range.

Ellen said, "Don was away, right?"

The eyes snapped open. "You can't believe Don raped me?"

"No, no. But you were alone for two weeks . . ."

Don Sligo was a fly-in, fly-out geologist working on a mining exploration lease in the Western Australian desert. Two weeks on, two off.

Marilyn finished Ellen's train of thought. "The guy watched me for a few days. He thought I was single."

"Possibly."

"Is your other victim single?"

Ellen probably should have trotted out the company line about her inability to comment on an ongoing case. She said, "Yes."

"And she said he tried to talk to her afterward?"

Ellen nodded.

Marilyn snorted. "He barely said anything to me during the rape, but afterward he was all pally. Advised me the healthy thing to do was quickly put it all behind me."

"Anything else?"

"Told me not to do or say anything for a while. Count to a hundred, he said."

ELLEN WALKED THROUGH THE hallucinatory noontime glare to her car, baking hot inside. She lowered all of the windows for a couple of minutes, the air conditioner blasting. Early summer, and already hot and dry, a droughty, bushfire summer stretching ahead.

She returned to Waterloo, parked under a scrap of shade and called a briefing.

"IF IT IS THE same man," Rykert said, "that hardly makes it a serial, Sarge."

"But we need to be sure," Ellen said. Running through the Wreidt and Sligo similarities again, she said, "Best-case scenario, we could have the beginnings of one, and we'll catch him soon. But I think there's a strong likelihood there are other victims. Ms. Wreidt didn't admit at first that she had been raped, and we've encountered that before. She reported it as a burglary, some days later. There might be other single women out there who reported burglaries and break-ins that were also in fact sexual assaults or rapes or incidents that had that potential—the guy was interrupted, for example, or got cold feet, or couldn't function. I want you to look at anything and everything. Reports of strangers lurking, women followed to their homes.

"Talk to CIU detectives in Waterloo, Mornington, Rosebud,

Dromana, Rye and Sorrento, and draw up a list of single female burglary victims going back three months. Don't approach these women yet: sound out responding police. Did the victim seem to be hiding anything? Did there seem to be more to the story? Were the circumstances odd in some way? You know the drill."

Lois shook her head. "Boss, the uniformed guys are always in a rush, and some of them have the emotional intelligence of a block of wood."

Ellen shrugged tiredly. "Do your best. If you do happen to uncover other instances, we'll go in gently, Jared with me, Lois with Ian."

"What if one of us is in court and we can't go in as pairs?" Judd asked.

"If it can't be helped, it can't be helped," Ellen said. "But if any of you find yourselves alone with a potential victim or witness, or transporting them back here, keep meticulous records of every minute of your time alone with them. I want you to note times—leaving, arriving, interview duration. I want meticulous vehicle logs—start and finish odometer readings, kilometers travelled, times, dates, everything. I don't want any of you facing malicious claims of sexual harassment, coercion or anything else."

Didn't want credible claims, either. Last month Judd had taken a witness statement from a sixteen-year-old girl who, with a friend, had been sexually assaulted by a team of teenage footballers at an eighteenth birthday party. A day after driving her home, he found himself accused of taking her to a deserted car park at Merricks Beach and touching her inappropriately. She later recanted, which threw her case against the footballers into doubt, but Ellen wondered. Had the girl felt waves of judgment or disapproval flowing from Ian Judd? Ellen had worked with him long enough to know he wasn't judgmental, but his demeanor was so contained and remote that he wasn't always the best person to interview victims.

If he'd been able to provide travel times and distances last month, he'd have saved himself a headache.

Saved her a headache. Being a boss wasn't all roses.

9

AFTER IT ALL WENT wrong for him—after the death, the arrest and the acquittal—Michael Traill faded from public view. His first impulse had been to head for Andamooka, Lightning Ridge or some other outback mining town, those havens for anyone wanting to hide and forget. But the distance, the heat. And his parents—cowed, then destroyed, by the publicity—were getting on. They needed him as he'd needed them, back when it all fell apart.

So he ran, but only a short distance. Seventy kilometers, less than an hour by car. Still a long way from his old life, his inner-Melbourne bachelor pad and his turbo Golf and his job as head of security at an upmarket Docklands pub. A long way down to a rusty, listing caravan in the backyard of an egg producer, for which he paid a peppercorn rent in exchange for yard maintenance. A long way down to the graveyard shift at the BP petrol station on the Moorooduc Highway, sitting behind the cash register from 10 P.M. until 6 A.M., looking out at the night, the occasional headlights passing by.

So here he was at 6:10 Wednesday morning, driving home. Taking a short cut east around the reservoir. Dawn light was leaking into the sky but the world would remain dim, blurred with shadows, for a while longer yet. Dawn, and the kangaroos were feeding, misty wraiths watching him from deep in the paddocks on either side of the road, and a kilometer down the road a small mob was crossing. He braked, skidded, his heart hammering. When the road was clear, he planted his foot, impatient now.

Then a huge buck kangaroo was in front of him, out of nowhere, and he hit it with a bony smack, the roo flipping up over the nose of the car, starring the windscreen and banging over the roof and into the ditch. Traill, blinded, jerked the wheel as if that might bring clarity, and slammed into a tree.

He sat, stunned.

Was that petrol he could smell? He climbed out, rocky on his feet. The roo was dying: a feeble kick or two and he was still. Traill's head hurt. He felt bruised, body and soul.

Crap car anyway, but on a good morning it got him home. On a morning when it hadn't been totaled by a kangaroo and a gum tree.

Traill had the nous then, all of his senses returning, to fish out his mobile phone and call for help.

Call who, exactly? The police? Animal welfare? His boss? A taxi? Tow truck?

Not his loving parents. He'd used up all the help they could give him. Used up their savings, their health. Almost their love and good will.

No signal bars anyway. "The Peninsula's full of dead zones, mate," his landlord told him, the first day on the job. "No signal bars, the power goes off if a leaf falls, and if we're not in the middle of a drought we're slogging around in mud."

A bit of a grouch, his landlord. Maybe smelling chicken shit all day did that to you. Fending off health and animal welfare inspectors, complaints from the neighbors. But grouch or not, Michael Traill couldn't call him for help because his phone showed not one signal bar.

He stood, and thought, told himself it could be ages before a car came along, and began to walk. After five minutes, he came to a driveway entrance, the name C. HAUSER on the letterbox and a row of agapanthus and pine trees. What was it with the rural properties on the Peninsula, their pine trees and agapanthus? He walked in, his thoughts turning to farm dogs and nervous shotguns. But what choice did he have?

Dogs, a quivering pair surging on their chains. They leapt, choked, made tight, demented circles and lunged again.

Their water bowls were dry, poor things. Traill glanced at the house, a miserable place that never saw the sun but crouched in the shade of more pines. No lights, no signs of life.

He turned to the dogs, stood there quietly, and began to sing. He was sweetly melodious, careful not to look directly into the eyes of either dog but at the ground. He approached. As he neared them he crouched, reducing his size. It all took five minutes and by now the dogs were alternating between yips and brief, bitten-off growls. They were not fearsome anymore but desperate. When he was very close he proffered his hand to one dog, then the other. They slobbered over him. They couldn't get enough of his hands knuckling their skulls, his fingers scratching behind their ears. He unclipped their collars, stood again, and watched them.

They knew something was wrong. They pressed hard against his legs, and when he carried their bowls to a water tank, stuck close to him. He filled the bowls, watched them drink, noisy and desperate.

There was nothing for it now but to approach the house. The moment he turned, the dogs were with him, all the way to the veranda, where they stopped, whimpered and dropped to their bellies. That was as far as they intended to go, and Traill was frightened now.

He didn't want to go in. Shouldn't he check the sheds first? The dogs watched him go, their faith with the house.

Nothing, only locked doors, dim shapes within. No farmer, dead or alive.

And so Michael Traill returned to the little house and smelled death on the air the moment he stepped in.

10

UNIFORMS ATTENDED FIRST, CONFIRMED Traill's story, and notified Waterloo CIU. Challis took the call. He'd been listing and scratching out possible Christmas presents for Ellen Destry, so the call came at the right time.

He met Pam Murphy in the car park, tossed her the keys to the CIU Holden. "You drive."

The car hadn't been washed in weeks. Baked by the sun, windows up, the interior reeked of superheated plastics and stale humanity. Murphy wound down all of the windows and cranked up the air-conditioning. They sat like that for a couple of minutes before she sealed them off from the world again and drove out of the station yard. Slowly along the service road, then left into High Street, and left again at the roundabout, giving way to a red Maserati.

Challis said, "Do you know the difference between a cactus and a Maserati?"

Murphy said, "With a Maserati the pricks are on the inside—but the usual reference is to Porsches, boss."

"Thanks for ruining my joke, Detective Constable Murphy."

"You're welcome."

She settled back, warmed by the sun streaming in, and said dreamily, "The thing about a Maserati is, it's a fuck-*off* car. It says, 'Don't get the idea you're equal to me.' Your four-wheel drive, on the other hand, is a fuck-*you* car. It says, 'Get out of the way, I'm coming through.'"

"And my ten-year-old BMW?"

"That's just sad," Murphy said. "With the greatest respect."

Murphy had keyed Colin Hauser's address into the GPS and checked it now, murmuring, "Right into Coolart Road . . ."

Challis said, "One day that thing will send you into a quarry."

"Boss, if I can't push buttons on a device, I'm nothing."

Challis snorted. He let her take the route suggested by the GPS. He knew short cuts the gadget didn't know, but he kept his mouth shut and looked out, mildly sedated by the morning sun, onto a familiar vista. Inland of the little Westernport towns, the Peninsula was a patchwork of paddocks—variously overgrown, cropped for hay, home to cattle or alpacas or striped with orderly rows of vines— stitched together by tree-lined roads. Here and there in the distance were dense stands of the kind of timber that might trap an unwary driver in bushfire conditions. Closer to, there might be a winery-cum-restaurant, an unlovely old weatherboard farmhouse or a set of massive stone gate-posts at the head of a driveway leading to an eye-searing starter castle on a hill. It was a pattern all across the Peninsula.

He ruminated on many things. The murder, ice crimes, what to get Ellen for Christmas. That led inevitably to thoughts of Serena Coolidge, the drug-squad senior sergeant, her quicksilver changes of demeanor. Alone with him, she was animated, leaning a little too close, sometimes touching. He supposed he knew what it was about. Ellen— his late wife, too—had ribbed him about being attractive but oblivious. But so what? Were they saying he had to act on it if a woman showed interest?

Challis wasn't able to run far with the idea. His thoughts drifted to Angela, his dead wife. He realized, with some surprise, that he rarely thought about her anymore. That was a good thing. Time and Ellen Destry had been the cure.

Time—years, in fact—had passed; he was with Ellen Destry and there was no hole inside him anymore. He didn't want to live with Ellen, necessarily, nor she with him, and they didn't need to spend every night together, but nor did they want to be with anyone else.

How to convey that to the vivid Serena Coolidge?

THEN MURPHY WAS SLOWING the CIU car and turning into a farmhouse driveway, where a uniformed constable took their details and waved them in.

A house came into view, a hundred meters along a track lined with pines and agapanthus. Coated in decades of road dust and mold, it needed a good scrubbing. Grass spouted in the gutters, paint had peeled away from the veranda posts and no one had tended to the lawn or garden beds for a long time. If there was money here, it had all gone on sheds, Challis thought. He counted six of them, one old and five new, in a cleared paddock some distance the other side of a creaky windmill and a newly strung cyclone fence.

Murphy parked between the crime-scene van and a small white Hyundai. They got out, greeted by the half-hearted barking of a pair of kenneled dogs, and Challis spotted a woman's jacket on the passenger seat of the Hyundai. Freya Berg, he thought. She's in there, examining the body.

He joined Murphy at the rear doors of the van, where Scobie Sutton and one of his technicians were pulling on crime-scene overshoes, suits and caps. Inside the van were metal shelves holding plastic tubs of various sizes that slid out like drawers. The larger held spanners, screwdrivers, hammers, saws, wire cutters and flex-claw pick-ups; the medium held evidence kits and collection bags; and the smaller held brushes, tongs, scissors and tweezers. Sizeable items like ropes, pulleys, vacuum cleaners, video equipment and spare crime-scene clothing sat in large open floor tubs.

"Scobie."

"Sir," Sutton said. "Pam."

"Keeping busy," Challis said, stating the obvious.

Sutton didn't smile. He said, "If you're going in, I need you to tog up."

"Certainly. Doctor Berg's with the body?"

"Yes."

Drawing on overshoes, Challis said, "How do you want to run this, Scobie?"

Sutton glanced along the driveway to the road. "No media yet, so that's a plus."

Challis nodded. Police at crime scenes were preternaturally wary of the probing lenses of cameras, the proximity of microphones.

"For now, let's consider the whole house a crime scene," Sutton continued. "At least until I know the entry and exit points, which could become secondary scenes."

Challis nodded as Sutton yawned suddenly, stretching his back. "Sorry, not had much sleep since the fire."

Then he turned abruptly and stepped through a crooked garden gate and headed toward the house. Challis followed, expecting Sutton to enter by the front door, but soon saw why he continued down the side of the house to the kitchen door. The front door hadn't been touched in years. This was a house in rural Australia. No one used the front door. Everything happened in the kitchen.

~

THE AIR, STALE AND close, held traces of old cigarettes and recent blood and decomposition. Flies buzzed sluggishly. Challis, taking in the grimy sink and hallway cobwebs, a drooping curtain here, a torn blind there, thought: the home of a single man. No love felt or given here for a long time.

Sutton led them to the end of the hallway. On one side was a bedroom, dirty crumpled sheets, and opposite was a small study. Here the smell was at its most acute.

"Please stay by the door for the moment," Sutton said.

At the sound of his voice, a head popped into view beyond a desk that had once been a dining table. Dark hair capped inexpertly by a paper bonnet, a clever, elastic face, eyes filled with humor. "The cavalry," she said.

"Freya," Challis said, breathing shallowly. "You know Constable Murphy?"

"Of course. Hiya, Pam."

"Doctor Berg."

Berg smiled at Sutton. "It's all yours, Scobie." She began to remove her gloves.

But she wasn't following strict protocol, and Sutton made a series of tiny steps on the spot. "Your ruling?"

"Well," Freya Berg said, "he's dead. Kaput."

She came out from behind the desk and Sutton took her place, uttering a faint sound that could have indicated disapproval. She ignored him. "Two gunshot wounds, one to the mid-torso, the other to the head. Heavy caliber, and either would have killed him."

"Not self-inflicted."

Berg shook her head. "No, and no weapon."

"When?"

"I knew you were going to ask me that. The flies, the

daytime heat, rigor has come and gone, decomposition is evident . . . I'd say several days. Friday, Saturday . . ."

Challis glanced around the room: partly from instinct, looking for a way out if he needed it, and partly as a detective, trying to understand the killer's movements. The window looked painted shut. A fringe of cobwebs hung over the upper half. Apart from the desk, the room held a chair, a filing cabinet, no other furniture. The desk was crowded: a bulky old computer, a cheap inkjet printer, a telephone, an in-tray crammed with opened and unopened mail, a desk diary.

"Shot from the doorway?" he said.

"The first shot, yes, that would be my guess. Hit in the torso and flung against the wall, then he slid to the floor."

Challis had yet to view the body. "And the killer came around the desk and shot him a second time?"

"Looks like it. Fired straight down into the forehead."

Scobie Sutton expressed another harrumph, as if to say that Berg was guessing. The truth wouldn't be fully known until he'd run the evidence.

"And it is the man who lives here? Colin Hauser?"

"According to his wallet, which is on the floor, yes."

Sutton, crouched with his back to them, said, "Doctor Berg, please."

"It's okay, Scobie," Berg said, "I didn't touch it. As you can see, it's lying there open, displaying his drivers license photo."

She winked at Challis, mouthed the words "I opened it."

Challis cocked an eyebrow. He didn't suppose it mattered.

"My work here is done," Berg said.

On the way out she said, "Haven't seen you for a while."

"Haven't had a suspicious death for a while. It's all ice overdoses and stolen tractors these days."

"How's Ellen?"

"Busy."

Berg turned solemn, gave Challis a pat on the chest and was gone, saying, "Give her my best."

"Will do," Challis murmured. Right now all he wanted to do was view the body. "Scobie . . ."

"Just give me a few minutes to work the floor between here and the desk, okay?"

"Okay."

CHALLIS EXPLORED THE REST of the house with Murphy, starting with the kitchen.

The laminex benches were worn and sticky. A cane basket beside a dusty, empty fruit bowl held car keys, a massive ring of other keys, sunglasses, a few coins and bills. The keys were to a Subaru; glancing out a side window, he saw a Forester parked behind a water tank.

Meanwhile every drawer in the room had been pulled out and the pantry door stood ajar. "They were looking for something?"

Murphy shrugged. "But what?"

Sitting room, bedrooms, laundry, bathroom. Again, drawers had been left pulled out or dumped on the floor, and cupboard doors left open. It occurred to Challis that the havoc was staged. Sure, it might look as though burglars had turned the place over but not as if they'd really been looking for anything. No mattresses displaced, no seat cushions sliced open or pockets turned out.

He was sure of it when he found a Longines wristwatch in a drawer of the bedside cupboard, partly concealed by a packet of antacids. A proper burglar would have found and pocketed it.

He told Murphy his theory. She blew a strand of hair out of her face. "So, not a stranger."

"Too early to tell, but I am floating the idea."

Murphy glanced around the room. "Not houseproud, our Mr. Hauser."

Challis nodded. The house and the life lived there depressed him. Dusty, stale, an odor of unwashed clothing under the stink of decomposition. No photographs, no books, one magazine, *American Rifleman*. Stained bathtub and toilet. Big-screen TV and a collection of DVDs: porn, *National Geographic* documentaries and live country-and-western concerts.

"Let's see if Scobie's ready for us."

SUTTON WAS ON HIS hands and knees, lifting dust, dirt and fibers with tape. He glanced up. "You can view the body."

"Finding anything?"

"A lot of tracked-in dirt and vegetable matter."

"Recent?"

"Some of it."

"Okay."

Challis and Murphy crossed to the desk and looked into the gap behind it. The murdered man lay splay-legged on his back, his head at the base of the wall. A massive wound to the belly, another in his forehead. Blood and other matter streaked the wall and his chest and lap were dark with blood. So much blood, and some of it on his hands. Had he grabbed at his stomach in pain? Had he held up his palms in supplication?

"Defensive wounds, Scobie?"

"You'll have to speak to Doctor Berg about that."

"Scobie," Challis said, using his patient, slightly irritated CIU boss voice, "I'm not asking you to put anything down in writing, I just need your opinion."

"Farmer's hands," Sutton said, flushing a little. "Old cuts and scrapes, that's all."

"Thank you."

Sutton sat back on his heels. "We found a badly mangled bullet under his head. From the size of it, a rifle bullet."

"It didn't go through the floor?"

Sutton shook his head. "There's a concrete slab under the carpet. But the first shot went right through the wall, it's just plaster and weatherboard. Good luck finding it. It'll be out there somewhere . . ."

Challis glanced through the window, at the dusty paddocks stretching to the horizon.

"Incidentally," Sutton said, "no match on the prints found in the drug lab."

Challis shrugged. If the cooks were students, they might not have been caught and fingerprinted for anything yet.

Sutton rocked forward again, peering down. "If you'll excuse me, I'd better carry on."

CHALLIS AND MURPHY LEFT the house carrying the keyring from the kitchen, the desk diary, the contents of the in-tray and the handful of files in the cabinet. "Get all this to Janine Quine for collation."

"Boss."

Challis, leafing through a manila folder, said, "We have a divorce here." He leafed some more. "Dated 2011. The ex-wife lives in Cranbourne. We'd better talk to her."

He stowed the paperwork in the car, waggled the keys at Murphy. "The sheds, do you think?"

"Worth a try."

To the music of a windmill rattling in the breeze, they crossed the broad dirt yard to a gate in the cyclone fence and headed for the nearest shed. It was large, the size of a tennis court, its double doors fastened with a padlock and chain. Challis peered into the gap while Murphy searched for a key that fitted. He could see dim shapes, that was all. Large shapes.

"Bingo," Murphy said and the chain rattled to the ground.

Inside were three aluminum motorboats on trailers. "Stating the obvious," Challis said, "who needs three boats?"

"Hauser and two of his friends?"

"I think I'd be looking at recent thefts, Constable Murphy."

"Tossing all possibilities into the ring, boss."

One shed was open to the elements, a legitimate back-road farming shed: hay bales and room for a Mazda Ute and an old Massey Ferguson tractor. The remaining four sheds were like the first: locked. One contained earthmoving machines: two Bobcats, a small Caterpillar grader. The second housed half-a-dozen ride-on mowers, the third two tractors and a vineyard spray machine, the fourth a small Isuzu truck and a collection of chainsaws and brush cutters.

"Either it's his way of preparing for the apocalypse," Murphy said, "or he's a thief."

"Maybe the man who discovered the body has some idea."

11

LEAVING CHALLIS TO PHOTOGRAPH the contents of the sheds, run serial numbers and coordinate with the crime-scene unit, Pam Murphy walked across the vast dry yard to the CIU car. The wind had picked up, a constant sad moan through the pine trees, quadrophonic in effect as different tree clumps took up the chorus, behind her, ahead, to her left, to her right. Not spooky, exactly, but depressing, and she was reminded of how dry the land was, how open to another fire.

She drove out of the yard and down the driveway to the constable on duty at the front gate. His name was Wollman. She'd seen him around the station. "You the responding officer?"

He nodded. He was about her age, thirty, and also a constable, so not readily impressed with an officer in plain clothes. "I was told to stay on and monitor comings and goings."

He hates it, she thought. Thinks it's a job for a probationary constable. She said, "You took a statement from the man who found the body?"

Wollman took out his notebook. "Name of Michael Traill," he said, and he stopped at that point, giving Pam a look.

She picked up on it. "Traill. I know that name."

"So you should. He's the bloke who king-hit Dave Booker."

Pam's eyes gleamed. Her pleasure was almost reverent. "Ah."

Then her gaze narrowed. "And you let him go home?"

Wollman wasn't going to be intimidated. "His car hit a roo, no phone signal, so he walked here to ask if he could call a tow truck, and found the body. That part of it checks out, I saw the car, it's a mess. Plus, he was dead on his feet, night shift at a servo up on the Moorooduc Highway."

"How was he getting home?"

Wollman shrugged. "No idea."

"Got his address?"

In reply, Wollman displayed a page of his notebook. Pam keyed the information into her phone. "Thanks."

"Watch for his right hook," Wollman said lazily, as though he hoped she wouldn't.

PAM FOUND THE WRECKED car and dead kangaroo, then doubled back, deeper into a network of dirt side roads through tilled and untilled farmland. Slowing for a hand-painted DUST PLEASE SLOW DOWN sign, she reached a crossroads, the road ahead a laneway blocked to all but local farm traffic. She turned right, taking her to Black Stump Road, where she turned left, following the GPS commands. She was in a region of dead grass, distant pine thickets marking farmhouses, lost wheel trims gleaming dully here and there, shaken loose by the road corrugations. Only the blackberry canes displayed any vigor, green and powerful under a patina of dust.

But she barely took it in, her thoughts racing. She needed to move house by Christmas. Her mother wanted to spend Sunday with her. And she was about to question a man reviled by millions. Thousands, anyway. Hundreds.

For Pam Murphy was a cricket tragic. Going back years, she could name the members of long-forgotten test teams, remember scores, tell you if X was a left- or right-hander, Y a better slips catcher than Z. She'd been half in love with David Booker when she was in her teens. A leg spinner who'd played international cricket for five years, a tall, dark, good-looking, lazily grinning man, always in trouble on tour for some larrikin escapade. Then, as he got older, he captained the Victorian team for a few years, and until his death was a selector and coach. Still remembered, still adored.

He went to dinner with friends one evening in March 2013, the dining room of an up-market hotel on the Melbourne waterfront. He drank, his friends drank, he grew funny and noisy and more and more people came up to shake his hand, clap him on the back, be photographed with him.

Later, on the footpath outside, amid a dozen or so people trying to come and go, there was some good-natured pushing, shoving, and fondling, some arguing over who'd had most to drink, who should drive, where was the car, and how about you come back to my place. They were loved and admired. They were loud. There was a complaint.

Michael Traill, the pub's security manager with a black belt in karate, emerged from the pub to ask them to move along, keep the noise down. A moment later, Booker was dead. Traill's defense: he'd used reasonable force—Booker, an aggressive loudmouth, had thrown the first punch. But no one corroborated this version of events. What's more, several of Booker's friends and acquaintances claimed that Traill had thrown the first punch, and Booker had thrown none.

The media attention was rabid, all through the investigation, inquest, arraignment and trial. Traill was acquitted. He dropped out of sight.

Now here he was . . .

THE AIR WAS MIASMIC at Everard Eggs, a collection of long, gleaming sheds and delivery vehicles in a hollow behind windbreak cypress trees. The Everard family lived in a small red-brick house behind the sheds, and a gruff man there pointed out a dusty white caravan a hundred meters further back.

"That's where he lives."

"Is he at home?"

Everard nodded.

"How did he get here?"

"He called, I picked him up."

"I was told he had no phone signal."

"Told me he climbed a windmill. And I believe him."

"What can you tell me about him?"

"A better question," Everard said, a burly poultry man with a face full of feathery whiskers, "is are you going to hassle him? He told me about Hauser. He didn't do it."

"Can you tell me anything about Mr. Hauser?"

"Keeps—kept—to himself," Everard said. He pointed back the way she'd come. "Plus he's not exactly next door to me." He paused. "A lot of traffic, but."

"What kind of traffic?"

"I'd go past on my way to Waterloo. Often saw trucks coming and going."

He couldn't tell her more than that. Pam nodded, returned to the car—Everard shouting, "Don't hassle the guy, all right?"—and bumped across the yard to the caravan.

It was weather-beaten, tethered to the earth by dead grass and a canvas annex, and utterly silent. Pam checked her watch: 11 A.M., meaning Traill had had very little sleep. That could be to her advantage. He'd be bleary, vulnerable . . .

She knocked and he was immediately there, the door swinging open and Traill at the head of the steps watching her. A moment later he was out and standing right in front of her. She took a step back, and another, keeping him at greater than arm's length.

"Mr. Traill?"

"You know it is."

"My name is Constable Murphy, Waterloo Crime Investigation Unit," Pam said, showing her ID. "I'd like to ask you a few questions."

He looked deeply fatigued, but had showered and shaved sometime in the past three or four hours. His hair was neat. He hasn't been to bed yet, Murphy thought. Expecting to give another statement, so he'd freshened up and sat down to wait. But he'd been working all night, he'd smashed his car, he'd walked some distance, and to top it all had discovered a murdered man in a house. He was entitled to be fatigued.

HE WAS ABOUT HER age, trim, sinewy, unsmiling, contained—super wary. Dressed in soft faded shorts and a vivid white T-shirt. Short dark hair, a faintly off-center nose. Slender brown legs, strong, bony bare feet and, to Pam's surprise, small, shapely hands. A man who'd king-hit and killed another should surely have frying pans on the ends of his arms?

"Please come in," he said.

A clear voice, polite. Rising and falling melodically; not sounding particularly aggrieved.

She followed him into the cramped dining area and sat at a chrome-legged table. There was more interior space than she expected, but a caravan is still a caravan, and she could see almost all parts of his living quarters from her vinyl bench seat. No mess and few possessions. A book, a news magazine, a radio, a photograph of a middle-aged couple. His parents? Apparently they'd attended every day of the inquest, committal hearing and trial. A small TV set, a pair of moccasins in one corner.

He continued to stand. He waggled a shiny steel percolator at her. "Coffee?"

"Please. White."

She watched him tip in the water and the grounds and ignite the gas flame. He poured milk into a frother, set it over a low flame. All of his movements were adaptive—the space was too small for large gestures—but also innately economical and precise.

Did he still work out? Lift weights, punch out his frustrations?

The coffee underway, he sat opposite her. "Please ask your questions."

She had a subtle sense of being managed. "You were coming home from work this morning . . ."

"I work the night shift at the BP up on the highway. I left work soon after six and on the way here hit a big kangaroo and wrecked my car. I tried to call a tow truck, but had no reception, so I walked to the nearest house."

A neat, pat, uninflected delivery. He's been rehearsing, Murphy thought.

"Did you know Mr. Hauser?"

"If the dead man was the man named on the front gate, no."

"He didn't fill up with petrol at any time?"

"He might have. All I saw was a dead man and a lot of blood. I didn't pay attention to his face."

"What were you doing late last week?"

He studied her. "You don't know exactly when he died. The smell was awful, so I guess he'd been dead a while."

She repeated, "What were you doing late last week?"

"I worked the night shift Thursday, Friday and Saturday. I have Sundays and Mondays off."

"You drove to and from work each time?"

"And didn't see a single kangaroo."

"You've never had business dealings with Mr. Hauser?"

He didn't blink at the change in direction. "No."

"You didn't call on him at any time prior to this morning?"

"This morning was the first time. I presume you checked that there is a car registered to me near the scene with its nose crumpled against a gum tree and a dead kangaroo in the ditch?"

"Were you coming or going from Mr. Hauser's residence when you hit the roo?"

"Oh, a trick question. I was going toward his house with the intention of passing it on my way home."

"Do you own a rifle, Mr. Traill?"

A faint sad smile on Traill's face, barely creeping into his eyes. "Is this where I ask for a lawyer?"

"I don't know. Do you *need* a lawyer, Mr. Traill?"

A cheap gambit, one she'd used a hundred times before. But she couldn't help it, he was the guy who king-hit David Booker.

And he said, sadly, "Please don't. You can do better."

Pam felt a misstep coming. She forced down whatever it was she might have said and wondered if her discomposure showed.

She was saved by a hiss from the milk frother.

"Oh, shit," he said, and darted to the stove.

Just then the percolator burbled, too, and Murphy took advantage of the reprieve to regroup. She reminded herself that Traill had found the body, which made him a legitimate first line of inquiry even if he hadn't once killed a man.

She waited for him to pour and carry the mugs to the table. The caravan interior, warm but fresh rather than stale, now smelled of coffee. Disarming, but Pam was done with being on the back foot.

"Mr. Traill," she said.

"Michael."

"Mr. Traill, you found the body."

"Yes."

"Then you'll understand why we must eliminate you from our inquiries ahead of anyone else."

"Yes."

She sipped, said, "Good coffee," before she could help herself.

"Thank you."

"What time do you start work?"

"Ten at night."

"Until six each morning?"

"Yes."

"Long hours."

He said nothing.

"What do you do between arriving home after six in the morning and driving to work each evening?"

"I eat something, go to bed and sleep until about two in the afternoon."

She said lightly, "And between 2 P.M. and 10 P.M.? Do you go for a drive, go shopping, visit friends?"

"Generally not."

"So what do you do?"

"In consideration for a reduced rent on this salubrious residence I do some yard work for my landlord."

"Such as?"

"I wash his trucks, do a bit of gardening, rake manure."

Pam had seen bags of fowl manure at the gate, two dollars a bag, a tin can nearby for the money.

"And these duties fill every afternoon?"

"No."

"So, what do you do?"

"I don't go around shooting the neighbors."

"Mr. Traill, what do you do?"

"I write."

She blinked. "Write what? Poems?"

She'd disappointed him again, with her sourness and flippancy. "Stuff."

Still sour, feeling defensive, she said, "A heartbreaking travesty-of-justice story, I suppose."

He looked at her levelly. "Pretty much. And as it seems to have become an ongoing story, I'm happy to put you in it."

THERE'D BEEN A LITTLE snarl in his voice. Pam Murphy was thinking of it as she retraced her route along the back roads, vexed and discomfited. The feeling was slow to ebb, and only vanished when she saw a listing Corolla the color of teabags ahead of her, slowing at Foxeys Hangout for the turn onto Balnarring Road. The driver, a woman, signaled left, but made to turn right, and at the last moment shot ahead into Tubbarubba Road. She planted her foot, the little car jerking forwards across the white line and back again, over-correcting, exhaust belching.

Pam recognized car and driver. She grabbed her radio, called it in: number plate, make and model, description, location, direction of travel, two heads on board.

One head was Christine Penford, the other her son, Troy, his little head showing above the strapped-in car seat behind her. No sign of the daughter. No sign of Owen Valentine—unless he'd ducked and was crouching there with a stolen rifle.

As she watched, the Corolla left the road, first sidewinding as though to dodge rock slides then ramming head-on into a gate post. The little car bounced, settled, and the driver's door opened. Pam braked and pulled over just as Penford fell out, swayed a moment and limped across the road.

Pam reported the accident, unbuckled and ran to the car. The child in the car seat was screaming his head off but seemed unhurt, more outraged than in pain. At his feet, behind the front seats, were a small TV, an Xbox, pristine Converse trainers and an iPad.

Pam soothed the boy, then turned away to chase down his mother. Penford had climbed the nearest fence—fallen through it, really—and was stumbling across dead and dying grass toward a stand of trees.

Fuck it. Pam put her hands on her hips, tilted her chin and yelled across the slowly widening gap, "Give it up, Christine. You can get bitten by snakes if you want to, but I've got a life to live, thanks."

Penford stumbled a couple more steps, froze and looked down at her feet. She began a panicky dance. "Where?" she shrieked.

"Everywhere."

Penford streaked back to the fence line, her hair flying, eyes wild. She's high, thought Pam. We won't get any sense out of her for a day at least.

She arranged for a divisional van to collect Christine, then called Christine's mother.

"Irene, I'd rather not involve children's services if you can look after your grandson until things are sorted."

There was a pause. A hitch, thought Pam. I'll have to bring in children's services after all and that'll take forever.

But Irene Penford said, "Of course I'll take him." Another pause. "No sign of Clover?"

Now we're getting to it, Pam thought. "Only Troy. You still haven't seen your granddaughter?"

"No one has. Not for days."

12

ON THURSDAY MORNING ELLEN Destry crept in the dim dawn light from Challis's bed to his bathroom and showered, the water pounding her head and shoulders. Too late, she remembered the bucket.

She toweled vigorously and crept back to the bedroom to find the blind up and sunlight striping the carpet and bed, Challis propped up against his pillow, talking on her phone. "She's just here," he said, taking the phone from his ear and proffering it with a grin.

She swarmed against him briefly, pink and damp, planting a kiss, before taking the phone. His hand went to her breasts. She slapped it away. "Destry."

"Sarge," Pam Murphy said, "you wanted to be informed about any burglaries or assaults or other types of incidents that might be related to the Tyabb assault?"

"Go on."

"I found three. I've emailed the details. One's a rape going back six months, the others fit into the might-have-been category." She paused. "Sorry to call so early."

"Best time to get me," Ellen said.

She hitched the towel around her and got comfortable, absently stroking Hal's leg under the covers. He needed a new quilt cover, she thought idly. Christmas present. "Give me a brief run-down."

"The rape victim's name is Jess Guthrie. Lives between Mornington and Mt. Martha. The burglary seemed to be an afterthought, so it was reported as a rape."

"The others?"

"A woman from Bittern came home from work and something stopped her from entering further than her hallway."

"Something?"

"Two things: she had a feeling her TV had just been switched off, and there was a smell."

"Bad smell, human smell?"

"Yes."

Ellen crossed to Challis's window and looked out at his quince tree without seeing it. "She called the police?"

"Got into her car and drove somewhere first."

"And by the time uniforms got there he was gone?"

"In a nutshell."

"Anything taken?"

"A camera and some jewelry."

Behind Ellen, Challis was swinging out of bed and padding in bare feet to the bathroom. "And the other case?"

"A woman in Somerville. Her boyfriend had just returned after two weeks away, so she stayed the night at his place. When she got home in the morning, she discovered her house had been broken into."

Ellen said, "But it wasn't a simple burglary."

"No, Sarge. Some small items stolen, but she also found her kitchen knife and a pair of tights on the floor just inside her sitting-room door—which is the first room on the left as you come through her front door."

"He was waiting for her."

"Yes, Sarge. And the thing is, what if that's part of his MO, he uses materials to hand?"

Ellen said nothing for a couple of beats; reflected that she wouldn't mind Murphy on her team. "Anything else?"

"She remembers seeing crumbs on the kitchen bench, the TV was tuned to a channel she never watches and the sitting-room cushions were untidy. "'I'm a neat freak,' she told me."

BREAKFAST WAS MUESLI WITH berries and yogurt at a rickety table on Challis's deck, the sun slanting in through the trees along the back fence. Strong coffee, the 7 A.M. ABC news. The *Age* and a story about yet more white-collar bastardry.

"How come," Ellen said, "you never hear of a banker or a financial adviser going to jail?"

It was rhetorical. She got a distracted smile for her pains, Challis's finely shaped head bent over yesterday's cryptic crossword. His hair, mainly dark, streaked with grey, was shaggy, beginning to curl. It needed cutting. His face was thinner, with new smile and tension lines at his mouth. Sometimes she just wanted to watch him for a while.

She said, "I'm pregnant."

No reaction.

"I'm taking up a position as head of security at Crown Casino."

Nothing.

"I'm thinking of moving in with you permanently."

He grinned and put the paper aside, sipped his coffee.

"I knew you were listening."

He set his coffee mug back on the table. He'd probably knot a tie around his collar later, but right now she could see his warm, tanned throat. She wanted him badly.

"You don't think it's working, separate houses, slightly separate lives?" he asked.

"I don't know," she said, "what do you think?"

"I think I'd have to meet my other women elsewhere if we moved in together."

"Like Serena Coolidge?"

He threw a hunk of toast at her.

She laughed. "Sorry, couldn't resist."

He'd introduced Coolidge into the conversation last night, in a roundabout way that had made her instantly suspicious. It helped that she'd been at the police academy with Coolidge, and remembered her vividly: a woman who played and studied hard. She wasn't surprised that Coolidge had tried it on with Hal.

But, moving on . . .

"Pam Murphy's good value."

Challis looked at her levelly. "Yes."

"Wouldn't mind having her on my team."

"Forget it."

The conversation drifted: work, her maybe-serial rapist, his new murder case and stolen farm machinery and ice crimes. Always ice crimes. Ellen watched Challis's mouth as he talked, the tiredness and intelligence in him. Presently the conversation lapsed again and they returned to their breakfasts as the early sun warmed them and the wind picked up.

LATER THAT DAY SHE interviewed Jess Guthrie, who requested they meet in the sex-crimes building.

"I don't want it brought into my home again," she said on the phone. "Anyway, I work in Waterloo."

The first thing she said was, "You're new to the unit."

"Yes."

"I dealt with Detective Judd before."

She said it with a *tone*, and Ellen guessed he'd got her back up in some way. "He's working on another case at the moment."

Guthrie was sleek, educated, articulate: qualities that Ian Judd would have found off-putting. Now she gave Ellen a little smile, a gleam of canny humor that said she knew all about personnel management and individual employee styles and the problem of stolid minds butting up against sharp ones. It also said: if you listen and let me speak—don't judge—we'll get along fine.

"Let's go in here," Ellen said.

A room designed to calm and disarm women, children and men who'd been sexually assaulted. Armchairs, flowers in vases, a coffee table piled with magazines, a TV, biscuits in a farmhouse tin, a bar fridge stacked with soft drinks. The lighting was muted, the colors pastelly, and the paintings on the walls more interesting and offbeat than the usual run of still lifes and puppies.

Right now Guthrie, leaning back in one of the armchairs, was frowning at a caricature behind Ellen's head. Her face cleared. "Jack Kerouac."

Jack Kerouac depicted in bare feet with his belongings hanging from a pole on his shoulder. "Yes."

"Tried to read *On the Road*," Guthrie said, "and didn't get very far. All that spontaneous prose, drove me mental."

Ellen glanced at her notes, compiled by Ian Judd. Guthrie was thirty-five, owned a new house on a street back from the beach between Mornington and Mt. Martha, and ran an IT consultancy in Waterloo. Computer science and business studies degrees. Divorced, no children.

Now she glanced at the woman in the chair. A nervy thinness, a bony face, hair cropped more for convenience than fashion, dangly amethyst earrings, a slim, black-faced watch. Bright lipstick, a bruising eye shadow, slacks, sleeveless cotton top, expensive strappy sandals.

"Finished?" Guthrie said, amused.

Ellen grinned. "You got me."

"So let's get started."

Ellen realized that Guthrie was unlikely to become emotional or evasive. She'd be matter-of-fact; she might even enjoy the puzzle-solving aspects. She might be a godsend, but Ellen couldn't ever be entirely sure. She'd known women who showered away the evidence and failed or delayed reporting to police, women who burned their clothing, bedding and towels afterward, women who sold up and moved far away, women who were too frightened to close their eyes at night.

"He was waiting—"

Ellen held up her hand. "Ms. Guthrie, I'll come to the details in a minute. First, we think this man has struck several times. We need to work out how he selects his victims."

Guthrie cocked her head and thought. "Are they like me?"

"Let me throw that back at you," Ellen said. "How would you describe yourself?"

"Live alone, youngish, reasonably well off."

"The others are not entirely like you, in that case," Ellen said. "They live alone, more or less, they are youngish, but one of our other victims works from home, another is a shop assistant."

"Houses or flats?"

"Flats, but why do you ask?"

Guthrie stared into space. "There are small blocks of flats all around where I live, and according to the local grapevine a few were broken into in the lead-up to my attack. What if he was in the area again, scouting around, and took a chance on my place, even though it's a house?"

"The investigating officers didn't connect your case to the break-ins at the time?"

"No. I thought *I* was the intended target, not my belongings. So did Judd."

Because the other break-ins had been simple burglaries, thought Ellen. But if the householder had been a young woman, home alone at the time . . .

"Were you able to compile that list I asked for?"

"Sure," Guthrie said, taking a sheet of A4 typing paper from her bag.

Ellen scanned it: shops, gym, pubs, cafes and restaurants that Guthrie frequented; her medical clinic, dentist, chiropractor, physio-therapist; sporting clubs . . .

"You didn't have a sensation of being watched or followed before the attack?"

"Not that I recall, but we're talking six months ago. Now I feel it all the time."

Ellen winced.

"No approaches by strangers? Strange phone calls? Men recently met who came on too strongly or wouldn't take no for an answer?"

"No."

"Had you called in a tradie to fix your wiring or paint a room or cut down a tree?"

"Nothing like that."

Ellen said, "If you're able, may we move on to the assault itself?"

"You mean the rape? Sure."

"It was mid-afternoon, and you were at home . . ."

"Normally I'd be at work, but I was home asleep after a marathon session at the dentist."

"And?"

"I heard a noise. I'd taken strong painkillers and I didn't really register the noise at first. Turns out what I heard was probably him prising open the glass sliding door that leads from my sunroom to the deck at the back of the house."

"You investigated."

"Not immediately. I was woozy. Then I wandered through from my bedroom and he grabbed me."

"From behind?"

"Yes."

"Did you ever see his face?"

"He wore a bandana."

"Not a balaclava?"

"No."

"So he grabbed you from behind . . ."

"A strong guy, solid, taller than me. Is this what you're after?"

Ellen, scribbling, said, "Go on."

"He had a knife."

"A kitchen knife? A knife belonging to you?"

"No. A Swiss Army knife, but I wasn't going to argue with it."

"Did he say anything?"

"Not at the time."

"We'll come to that. He grabbed you. Then what did he do?"

"Took me to the bedroom and threw me down on the bed."

"On your back? Face?"

"On my face, and then he pulled my hands behind my back and taped them together."

"Where did the tape come from?"

"It wasn't mine. It was a broad, silvery kind of tape. I have some of that thin electrical tape, but this was different."

It was all telling Ellen that the rapist used items he'd carried with him. If the same man had later raped Wreidt and Sligo, he'd evolved, he'd learned to use materials at hand.

"Did you struggle?"

"Was I supposed to?"

Ellen shook her head. "I was wondering about the possibility of evidence transfer or cuts and bruises."

Guthrie laughed. "No such luck. I froze."

Back in her CIU days, Ellen had interviewed a woman who'd been digitally raped on the beach at Balnarring. Summer, crowds of swimmers and sunbathers, and the woman had frozen. "I couldn't move!" she said anxiously, as if she thought she should have shouted, screamed, kicked and punched like a normal person.

"He raped you from behind?"

"Tried to, but then he turned me over."

"Tried to."

"I'd been in bed, wearing knickers and a T-shirt. He pulled off my knickers and tried to rape me and when that didn't work he turned me over."

"That's when you saw him."

"Solid, taller than me, in a black T-shirt, blue jeans and a bandana. Well, a rag of some kind. And he had a bag."

"What kind of bag? Tradesman's?"

"Adidas gym bag."

"Anything else about him?"

"White, brownish hair, average length, knocked-about hands, like he did manual labor, no tatts or birthmarks that I could see."

"You saw his hands?"

"He wore gloves to break in, took them off to handle me."

"A particular kind of shampoo or shaving lotion or—"

"He stank a bit. His clothes. BO."

"And the rape?"

Guthrie curled her lip. "A complete fiasco, if you can call it that. He couldn't get an erection, so he forced me to . . . fellate him, I believe that's the polite term. When that didn't work, he got riled and I thought he was going to stab me.

Instead, he got the knife and started slicing off my T-shirt and then he stood back and kind of stared and tugged on himself, like he needed the visual stimulation. Then he tried again and was partly successful."

"He ejaculated?"

"Yes."

Ellen knew he had. She'd read the report: DNA had been extracted from the bedclothes. No match in the system, though.

"After the rape, what did he do?"

"He made me take a shower. He even reached in and washed me, which was somehow creepier than anything else he did."

"And then?"

Guthrie scowled a little, glancing at Ellen's notebook and folders. "You know all this, right?"

Ellen shrugged. "True. Sometimes people recall new details."

"Suit yourself. So he took me to the kitchen, all chatty, and made me a cup of tea."

"Still wearing his bandana?"

"And his gloves."

"What did you chat about?"

"He lectured me. How I needed to be more careful, a woman living alone. How I needed to be more security conscious, how this wouldn't have happened if I'd been more alert." Guthrie paused. "He thinks about security matters because he's a burglar."

Burglar who has grafted rape onto his MO, Ellen thought.

Guthrie stared miserably at the floor. She raised damp eyes to Ellen. "The next day I got a text from him: *We should do it again.*"

"How did he get your number?"

"When I was trying to drink my tea he looked through my bag."

"Did you keep the text?"

"This was six months ago, Sergeant Destry. I was appalled. I felt dirty. So I changed my number, changed the locks, put in a top-of-the-line alarm system. My house . . . sometimes it's just that—a house, not a home."

13

CHALLIS AND MURPHY BEGAN the day with a tense exchange.

Pam, pleased with her arrest of Christine Penford, went on to tell Challis about her interview with Michael Traill, expecting him to share her outrage. But it was as if he didn't hear what there was to be outraged about. All he said was, "Okay, rule him out."

"But he killed a man."

"And the courts let him go. Was there any indication he knew Hauser? Any reason he'd go back there if he did kill the man?"

"No, but I think he's a danger. I think—"

His voice steely, Challis said, "Michael Traill was found guilty by the media and a small section of the general public. The outrage went on for weeks, months. The Pope could die and receive less attention. It was unseemly. Every time I opened a daily newspaper there was another few pages and photographs devoted to the story. *What* story? Booker was an obnoxious drunk who did nothing for the nation but hit a ball around, and then died a stupid death. And I'm sorry to tell you this, but I'd never even heard of David Booker. Most of the population would never have heard of him. The level of media and public handwringing was disgusting."

"But—"

"If you have reason to believe Mr. Traill is guilty of something, follow it up. If not, leave him alone."

THE STIFFNESS DIDN'T EASE until they'd thrown themselves into the life and times of Colin Hauser.

Hauser had a record for minor white-collar offenses and an ex-wife living in Cranbourne. The ex-wife had been questioned by two detectives on Challis's team, who reported that she had a compelling and easily verified alibi: she'd been in hospital when her ex-husband was murdered. But she might have commissioned the murder. Or, given that her ex-husband's dishonesty seemed to be an ongoing thing, she might have had a role in it, or something more to tell them about it.

But the farm first. Murphy, driving them across country, said tersely, "Do you think we'll find anything we didn't find yesterday?"

She's still disgruntled, Challis thought. "There's always inspiration."

She snorted.

Challis sighed, tuned her out, pondered the nature and extent of Colin Hauser's operation. A check of serial numbers against theft reports had established that most of the vehicles and farm machinery stored in the man's sheds had been stolen from various properties over the past six months. But Hauser was an ex-accountant jailed for dishonesty offenses. How would such a man know that a particular item of farm or winery equipment was worth stealing, let alone know where it was located, and how it might be spirited away and who might want to buy it?

"Could you start a diesel tractor, Murph?"

"Nope."

"Could you fit a weed sprayer to a towbar?"

"Maybe with some help."

"Could you drive a heavy transport truck?"

"I could steer it, but that's about all," Murphy said.

"Exactly."

Reaching the farm, they parked at the rotting house fence and got out.

"The dogs aren't here."

"RSPCA," Challis said.

He watched Pam swivel in the dirt, taking in the whole property. "Miserable place."

"That it is."

She was less frosty now. "What if it's simply a staging post for a larger operation? Hauser supplied the location, the sheds, but didn't do any of the stealing."

"I knew there was a reason I asked you to drive me around today."

She snorted. "You asked me to drive you around so you wouldn't have to."

"No, it's your brain I want," Challis said, striding toward the nearest shed.

The yard was still a dust bowl; today it looked churned up. Challis put that fact together with a mental note he'd made to get the stolen goods moved to the impound yard and said, "Oh shit."

Murphy, too, was examining the dirt. "Great minds think alike, boss."

Too late.

Each shed had been broken into. Standing in the talc-like dust at the entrance to the first one, Challis took out his phone, called up the stored photos and scrolled through them. He pointed. "There was a Kubota tractor in that corner, a couple of mowers over in that corner."

Leaving a rusted-out trailer and bare dirt spotted with oil.

The story was repeated at the other sheds: a second tractor missing, a Bobcat, a road grader, each of the motorboats and the Isuzu truck.

"Clearly they came back last night, but . . . how did they know? The murder wasn't on the news till this morning."

"Watching us?" Pam Murphy guessed. "Or they saw it online."

"How did they know to look for it? Either way it's a headache: questions to be asked, et cetera."

"Where did they take it all?"

"And how, whoever they are?" Challis said. "We need to hit wrecking yards, used-car yards . . ."

"Gumtree and eBay and used-vehicle websites . . ."

"Christ," Challis muttered. He glanced back at the crouching house uneasily.

Murphy followed his glance. "Anything wrong? You think we've got company?"

"No, but if they were here at the sheds, they would have been at the house, too."

WHICH HAD BEEN TRASHED inside. In addition to the earlier underlay of dishevelment and violation, more drawers had been upended, mattresses and cushions slit open, tins and boxes of biscuits, rice, pasta and laundry powder tipped onto the floors.

Murphy got out her phone and compared the latest damage with the previous morning's.

"Boss, yesterday they went through the motions. This time they were clearly looking for something. Files? Drugs? Cash?"

"We have all Hauser's paperwork at the station. Janine Quine logged it in."

"Janine," snorted Murphy. "There's a sad case."

Challis shrugged, having no interest in Janine Quine. He gestured at the mess. "The question is, a few days ago someone shot Hauser and rummaged around in his drawers and cupboards, then last night someone did all this. The same person or people? Why not search thoroughly in the first place?"

The question was partly answered when he called the crime-scene office. "Scobie, I need you back at the Hauser farm. We had visitors last night."

"I was going to call you about that, actually," Sutton said, and stopped.

Challis was accustomed to Sutton. Information had to be dragged from the man. "Oh?"

"I've heard back from the lab."

"Scobie, I'm not getting any younger."

"The rifle found in that burnt Mercedes . . . It could be the Hauser murder weapon."

Trailed by Murphy, Challis stepped out into the early summer heat, escaping the stale air and disorder of the Hauser farmhouse.

"Boss?"

"Scobie thinks Hauser was shot with the rifle found in that burnt-out car last Friday."

Murphy gazed with him into the distance. "They murdered Hauser for some reason, drove off and took a wrong turning. Or felt guilt-stricken and committed suicide."

"Both of them? In such an awful way? No. We need to know their relationship with Hauser, and with whoever was here last night."

"So, a large outfit."

"Possibly."

"Someone came back last night to finish off what the two fire victims failed to finish."

"But why leave it so long?"

Challis sighed. Just then the wind rose around them, another hot northerly, the treetops swinging violently, colliding and scraping, sounds of acute stress along with the mournful wind-rush of the tossing pines. He looked up, expecting to see limbs fall. Looked away.

"Let's visit the ex-wife," he said.

LOUISE HAUSNER HAD FLED the marriage but hadn't fled far. Cranbourne was about forty minutes' drive from the murder scene.

In other respects, she'd moved a long way from the miserable house with its collection of sheds behind a windbreak of untidy pines. Her new place was less than a year old, in a housing tract on the western edge of the town. Clean, pale brick, tiles and glass, a cropped lawn, modest back and side fences but no front fence, a spotless car in the driveway, and the pattern was repeated from house to house, street to street. And not easy to find, every street curving, doubling back or dead-ending without logic. Even with GPS Pam Murphy swore in frustration.

The woman who answered their knock scowled, as if another disappointment had been delivered to her doorstep. "Whatever it is, I'm not interested."

"We're the police," Challis said, showing his ID. "Are you Mrs. Hauser, Louise Hauser?"

"Not anymore. I reverted to Wignall."

She was aged in her mid-forties, a solid woman with widely set eyes under one eyebrow, dark hair and a thrusting jaw. She wore faded yellow shorts, pale blue Crocs and a loose white T-shirt. She was leaning on a hospital crutch.

Before Challis could speak she went on: "I've already

spoken to the police. I was in hospital most of last week, didn't get out till a couple of days ago. Knee surgery."

Challis knew his smiles could be off-putting. He willed his voice to be pleasant, introducing himself, then Murphy, and saying, "A couple of things have come up and we wondered if you could help us?"

She took them to a sitting room furnished in a fat black leather lounge suite, a pale green carpet and a vast TV set. Monet's waterlilies on one wall, family photographs on another—and on many of the available shelves, cabinets and other flat surfaces. An ugly herringbone pleated blind dimmed the vast window, allowing a few centimeters of sunlight to show at the bottom. A lifestyle magazine and *TV Week* on the coffee table, neatly lined up between a remote and a shallow glass bowl.

"You have two children, I believe?"

A woman of perpetual anger, Wignall said heatedly, "They're at school. I don't want them bothered."

"How old?"

"Ten and eight. So, no, they did not get into my car and drive to the farm and kill my ex-husband."

"We won't intrude on their grief, Ms. Wignall," Challis said.

"Grief! They were barely out of nappies when we left Colin. They see him once a year, if that. He wasn't interested in them, and *that* was the thing that caused them grief."

"They know he's dead?"

"They do. They're sad about it, but they'll cope."

Murphy said, "Who looked after them while you were in hospital?"

"My parents," Wignall said, addressing Challis. "And no, they didn't kill Colin either. Why would they? He was long out of the picture. No money issues, except the occasional late child-support payment."

She continued to stare at Challis as if Murphy didn't exist. Challis was a man, Challis was the boss. He saw that she didn't want to flirt or impress, or expect some kind of chivalry. She simply didn't rate women.

"Colin was an accountant when you married him?"

"An accountant with sticky fingers. Surely you know all this?"

"Do you know any of the people he dealt with back then, Ms. Wignall?"

"Call me Louise. He dealt, if that's what you want to call it, with family and friends mostly—and he siphoned their savings away. If you're asking whether any of them would've liked to kill him—maybe, at the time. But that was years ago and he paid it all back—with help from his father, I might add. So no one's still suffering."

She paused and added, "Plus he was a drunk. A pathetic one at that."

Challis glanced at the toothy children displayed on the mantelpiece, a girl in fancy dress, some kind of book or film character, he supposed, and a boy wearing football gear. The world was awash with similar photographs.

Dragging his gaze back to the disgruntled mother, he said, "Did Colin ever do business with any . . . ah, questionable types?"

Wignall looked affronted, as if the question reflected badly on her and the life she'd tried to lead back then. "What do you mean?"

"Well, criminal types. People who made you feel uneasy, people he tried to keep you from meeting. Was he given to secretive phone conversations or assignations? That kind of thing."

"He was not having an affair. I would have known."

"Not an affair," Pam said. "Anything business- or money-related that made you uncomfortable, suspicious."

Wignall continued to ignore her. "Nothing like that." Her face softened. "He was just a sad case, really. Lost. A loser."

"And in the years since the divorce?"

"How the hell should I know? I didn't have anything to do with him."

Challis said, "What can you tell us about his farm?"

"Farm! That's a joke. He grew up on a big property out in Gippsland, went to Scotch College, liked to think of himself as landed gentry, but he was hopeless, even his father said so. He's dead now, in case you think he did it."

"So Colin didn't go back on the land, he trained as an accountant?"

"And made a hash of that, too."

"Where did he get the money to buy the farm?"

Challis knew that Hauser had been heavily mortgaged; wanted to hear Wignall's take on the situation.

"Who knows? You sure he wasn't deeply in debt? Maybe his father helped him, or he inherited the money when the old fool died."

"Have you ever been to the farm?"

"Once, when he first bought it. He wanted to show the kids. We didn't stay long."

"Could you describe what you saw?"

"What do you mean? A run-down house, a crappy old shed; trees, paddocks. God knows what he was going to farm there. I didn't stay long enough to hear about it."

"Just one shed?"

She narrowed her gaze. "We're getting to the heart of things, aren't we? Yes, just one shed."

"There are now several sheds, newish ones," Murphy said.

Wignall said to Challis, "I wouldn't know anything about that."

"Full of farm vehicles and other heavy vehicles and equipment," Murphy said sharply.

Wignall gleamed at Challis as if he'd spoken. "What, he was a dealer? Dealer in stolen goods, more like."

"We believe so," he said. "And some of it disappeared before we could secure the property."

She didn't blanch but looked delighted. "Got caught out, did you? That wouldn't have gone over too well at head office."

Challis gave a cold smile. "So you don't know who he had dealings with in recent times?"

"No, I do not," Wignall said emphatically. "And just to be clear, not only do I have a buggered knee, I wouldn't know the first thing about driving some farm vehicle. And where would I put it?"

She didn't have to elaborate: she lived in a treeless satellite town of postage-stamp house blocks and clear lines of sight in all directions. "Sorry I can't be of further help to you," she said, hauling herself to her feet, moving to the hallway and the front door. Challis half-expected her to advise him against letting the door hit his arse on the way out.

"You notice she barely looked at me?" Murphy said.

She was driving. Challis, eyes closed in the passenger seat, warmed by the sun, said, "You have to admit you lack presence, Murph."

"Funny. It's like when I was growing up. It's like things now, whenever I see uncles and aunts and family friends: no one asks *my* opinion, they say things like, 'And what do your brothers think?'"

Challis sensed that this was important. He cast back to the things she'd been saying in conversation in the past few weeks. "Are you having a family do this Christmas?"

"It won't be the same," she said sadly, "Mum's in aged

care, my brothers can't decide what they're doing. Meanwhile I'm trying to find a new place to live."

Challis had promised to keep his eyes open. "I haven't heard of anything."

She sighed. "There isn't anything."

"Can your brothers help out with a loan?"

She shot him a look. "So I can afford to look at more expensive places, you mean? I daren't ask. I can just hear them. There will be this big pause and they'll look down on me from their lofty heights and stroke their weak professorial chins and say, 'Well, I don't know, Pam,' and then offer me maybe a hundred bucks and tie it up with all kinds of conditions and guilt."

Challis laughed. Murphy, fleetingly offended, laughed with him.

"What will you do for Christmas?"

"Spend it with Ellen."

"Will her daughter be there?"

"Possibly. Probably."

"You get on with her now, right?"

"I seem to have passed some kind of test."

"You seem to have saved her life last year, boss. That might have something to do with it."

"Not my personality?"

"God, no."

Challis's phone rang. He listened at length, then said, "Thank you, John, we'll be there in twenty," and closed the call.

Looked at Murphy and said, "Tank was on the front desk today. Had a couple of interesting visitors."

14

THE MAIN DISADVANTAGES OF working the front desk, John Tankard believed, were boredom and contact with the public.

And today had started like all the others. First, he waited for something to happen. He stood at the chest-high counter amid spare pens, phones, logbooks and computer screens, and forms and documents the public might need in their dealings with the police and other government bureaucracies. Wire racks of brochures were screwed to the wall at each end, and the whole lot faced a small foyer fitted with leatherette bench seats and a coffee table stacked with *Police Life*. Along a short corridor were the toilets, and an inner door to the main part of the station, keypad access only.

Sliding glass doors opened onto the street, and the sunlight out there was vivid today, promising heat, sleeveless dresses, bare legs. But there was one good thing about desk duty: it took place indoors. Tank suffered in the sun, his fair skin burned, perspiration broke out all over him.

When nothing happened during the first hour he logged on to the station's Facebook pages, hoping for a few minutes of peace before some old geezer came in with a noise complaint or a shopkeeper with a burglary report or a kid to say somebody had pinched his skateboard.

Bored, bored, bored.

But Facebook was always good for a laugh; sometimes even a bit of crime fighting.

There were CCTV cameras along High Street now, and last week they'd caught a mugging, two kids in hoodies shoving the Cafe Laconic night manager to and fro before snatching her iPhone. The uniforms hadn't been able to identify the kids, so Tank had posted the clip and dozens had viewed it. No ID yet, but Dixichik666 believed there should be police patrols along High Street 24/7 and RaZr argued that the night manager should have been watching where she was going instead of texting like she was addicted to her phone.

"And you're not addicted to yours, fuckwit?" Tank muttered.

The sliding doors opened and the first visitor of the day entered, a bland-looking woman who asked him to witness her signature on a stat dec. Then back to Facebook. Shoplifting posts, hoon burnouts near the skate park, rubbish dumping at the charity bins in the Coles car park . . .

Tank paused: a respondent had posted a link to a non-police Facebook page. He clicked on it, and Facebook gold: two idiots bragging about drag racing near the skate park and film to prove it.

Tank called his sergeant and sent him the link. Got a pat on the back.

An hour passed, and another. He read through the incident reports for the past few days. A child's clothing found at an abandoned meth lab; a burglary at Tyabb referred to the sex-crimes unit; a shotgun reported stolen by an orchardist in Merricks North; number plates stolen from a Mazda outside the Willow Creek pub; a woman arrested with a carload of stolen electrical items . . . He scanned down the list, coming to a follow-up to a call a week ago, in which two constables new to uniform had attended at a disturbance on the Seaview Estate. No one home. They left a calling card and drove off like the morons they were, unaware the householder was lying unconscious in a pool of blood at his back door. He was a part-time dealer, so no one was shedding tears, but the fact was that the attending uniforms should've checked around the back. That was the big difference between your beginner and your old hand like John Tankard. Tank always satisfied himself nothing was amiss before he left a scene.

THEN THE MANAGER OF a Stumpy Gully Road vineyard came in, wanting to know if the police had found his stolen tractor.

"We're still investigating, sir," Tank muttered, pulling out the requisite form and scanning the details. "We've had a rash of stolen farm machinery."

"You say that with some indifference," the man said. "Farm machinery, as you put it, can cost hundreds of thousands of dollars. And you don't shove it into a backpack in the dead of night. Surely someone's seen this stuff being driven about the countryside?"

After that, two kids came in, girls of seventeen, all glossy hair and nervy giggles, filling the foyer with light and life, and Tank soared a little inside.

"Help you?"

"We're worried about our friend," one said.

"He's out of control," said the other, tears splashing from the limpid eyes.

"Out of control?" said Tank.

"Drugs. Ice," said the first girl.

"He's like super paranoid," the second said.

"Unpredictable."

"He thinks we're out to get him."

"He steals from us."

"He hit me."

"We don't want him arrested . . ."

". . . we just want him to get straight. Like normal."

"Yeah."

Tank took their names, the boy's name. "Do you know who his dealer is?"

They shut down in front of him, glancing at each other, the floor and the walls. "No," they whispered.

Their dealer's a friend, or they're using themselves, Tank thought. He'd pass it on to CIU.

"We'll have a word with him."

"But don't arrest him."

"Don't tell him it was us who told you."

THEN JANINE QUINE CAME back from lunch, carrying a large shoulder bag. She scurried through, as if the bag held loot, and Tank stopped her, saying, "Janine, you got a minute?"

The civilian clerk took her hand from the keypad and stood at the counter mutely, waiting for him to speak. She was a plain woman, her face damp from walking in the sun and pink with what Tank guessed was shame or embarrassment.

He said, "How's Jeff?"

"Okay," she muttered, staring at the floor.

"No more tailing the school bus?"

"No."

"The driver's still upset, being yelled at like that in front of the kids."

"But he was speeding over the speed bumps!"

"Jan, how likely is that? Isn't it more likely that Jeff has too much time on his hands and he's obsessing over trivial things?"

"S'pose," Quine muttered.

"Has he been applying for jobs?"

"Yes."

"Something'll turn up," Tank said brightly.

TONY SLATTER WALKED IN, looking for justice.

"I want to take my complaint to a whole new level."

"And you are?" said Tank.

The name was familiar, but Tank didn't recognize the man on the other side of the counter. About sixty, wearing shorts, sandals, a T-shirt. Knobbly knees, a hint of old bruising around the eyes, a fresh scratch on one cheek.

Slatter ignored him. "I know I withdrew the original complaint but since then I've been to a specialist for shocking headaches and a feeling like my jaw's dislocated. He says I'm up for thousands of dollars' worth of dental work."

He part-opened his mouth in proof. "Not to mention visits to the doctor."

"This was an accident, sir?"

"Oh, for fuck's sake."

"Sir, I must ask you—"

"What's wrong with you people? Last week, in Moonta, I knock on someone's door and get smacked in the face and kicked in the ribs."

A lightbulb moment for John Tankard. The Moonta Moth. The guy who, after a skinful of booze, liked to knock on people's doors and invite himself in for a chat or, if he was lucky, more booze.

"I remember," Tank said.

"Will wonders never cease," Slatter said.

Tank also remembered that Slatter was a nicer guy drunk than sober. "It's all in hand, sir."

"That's what you think. Yesterday I went around intending to ask the guy to cover the extra cost and his girlfriend does this to me." Slatter inclined his cheek to display the scratch. "She was high on something."

Tank went very still. "Excuse me, sir, but you attempted to make contact with your assailant?"

"Assailant? Fancy name for a meth head. And for your information I did not talk to him, he's not there, according to his girlfriend—*who did this to me.*"

"Sir, I must advise you against further attempts to approach this man or anyone he lives with. It could be dangerous for you and interfere with our efforts to investigate or make an arrest. Let the law take its course."

"Unbelievable," Slatter said.

Tank said nothing.

"And when you do find him, what then? Some Mickey Mouse charge, affray or whatever you call it? And meanwhile he pays me reparation that barely skims the surface of what my real costs will be."

Little winds gusted from Slatter's mouth, old booze and bad food. Tank recoiled. "He paid you money?"

"Not enough, hence I went around to ask for more. Aren't you listening?"

"Sir—"

"I've got specialist reports here," Slatter said. "Dental, medical . . ."

He took a wad of paper from his back pocket. Warm from his backside, even a tad moist, it didn't bear touching. Wincing, Tank said, "I'll see to it that Constable Murphy gets these, sir."

"Her! Jesus."

"She's a very competent officer."

"I bet," Slatter said, "but she took long enough to get off her fat arse and investigate the original complaint, so I'm not holding out much hope this time around, not if the guy's disappeared."

And Slatter went out, muttering, "Hopeless, absolutely hopeless," to an old geezer who'd come in to wait, a government form in his hands ready for signature.

Tank signed, said goodbye, logged on, found Slatter's original report in the system. Date, time, brief narrative, assailant's name—Owen Valentine—and the address where the attack took place.

What caught Tank's eye was the address. He'd been there. He'd attended a noise complaint there, the day of the fire, on his way back to the station after dealing with Janine Quine's idiot husband at the primary school.

"Fuck!"

"I beg your pardon?"

An elderly woman stood waiting and Tank managed a huge smile. "Yes, madam, what can I do for you?"

She was tall, thin, stooped and grey, wearing cotton pants with an elastic waistband, a shirt and cardigan. Her fingers were veiny and twisted, holding tight to a handbag.

"You lot arrested my daughter yesterday. Christine Penford?"

Tank remembered. He'd watched her brought to the station. High as a kite. Then Pam had come steaming in to arrange a state-wide lookout for Penford's daughter.

He said, "Ma'am, I'm afraid she hasn't been interviewed yet."

The woman waved that aside. "Just now I was around her house to fetch clothes and toys and I found a gun."

15

LATE AFTERNOON NOW.

After discussing the Guthrie interview with Judd in the light of his original investigation, Ellen Destry briefed the others, and finished her work day with a tricky phone call to a specialist officer at Force Command in Melbourne. It concerned a pedophile, in jail for the sexual abuse of young boys, who'd been selling copies of his trial transcript to other pedophiles—in prison and out. She suspected the involvement of his lawyer and/or prison officers, but hadn't the means or experience to take it any further.

That done, she locked up and walked to her car. Unable to find a park outside the sex-crimes house that morning, she'd left the car behind the police station, and was pressing the unlock button on her keys when Sergeant Cleavage, sorry, Coolidge emerged from the building.

"Ellen."

"Serena."

They looked at each other, faintly challenging, bringing back old academy memories to Ellen but probably nothing at all to Coolidge.

"Haven't seen you for ages. You're sex crimes now," Coolidge said, as if that were a side path to nowhere in policing terms.

"And you're drugs," Ellen said.

Coolidge gave her a slow-burning smile and Ellen wondered at the intent: to tease me, unsettle me. She returned the smile, a quick hard nastiness in it, and opened the door of the car. "Good luck," she said, and got in and drove out of there. Not much of a victory—not much of anything—but why get bogged down fighting the woman?

ON HER WAY HOME she called a house in Merricks Beach. A big house, raised to the glory of its architect, it sat with other palaces on a headland above the sea, and was home to a husband and wife, both doctors, their seventeen-year-old son and a fifteen-year-old daughter. During the year they'd hosted a Spanish exchange student named Francesca Arena, who, two weeks into her stay, had flown back to Spain. A hint rather than a direct allegation of sexual molestation had come from the Spanish headquarters of the exchange program. The host father? Someone at the school? Family friend or gardener or male visitor?

Within five minutes of her arrival, Ellen knew it was the son, a huge but soft-looking boy, shifty, sullen, frightened, spoiled. The mother was dismayed, the father confused, and Ellen went away feeling that blame would be flying around the family kitchen and no one would look at the boy in quite the same way again.

AT HOME ON HER deck, the late sun angling in from across Port Phillip Bay, she sipped a glass of wine, demolished half-a-dozen crackers loaded with small slabs of mousetrap cheese and called Hal Challis.

"Had my first delicate staffing issue today." Her iPhone to her ear, feet propped on the deck table, she told him about the Guthrie interview, and comparing notes with Judd afterward. "I had to tread carefully, so he wouldn't think I was double-checking his work."

"Which you weren't."

"I know. I was reinterviewing her in the light of new information."

"Did he accept that?"

"I think so. It's not easy being a boss."

"Now you know what I went through when you were on my team."

"I wasn't a handful, was I?"

"You were a bolshie nightmare," Challis said.

"Somehow I wish Judd was a bolshie nightmare," Ellen said. "Someone with imagination. Instead, he's a stubborn, by-the-book, old-style kind of copper."

They chatted. The light softened to an evening dimness. Challis said, "How's your sister?"

Ellen glanced at her phone—6:48. "I'll soon know," she said. Pausing, she added, "You don't mind that I didn't invite you around tonight?"

Challis laughed. "I'd be in the way."

"Normally you wouldn't be, but we have things to discuss."

Ellen thought of Allie's bright, easily hurt—or hostile or offended—dark eyes. Feeling tentative and disadvantaged, she said, "Do you ever think about your wife?"

A pause. "Sometimes. What brought that on?"

"Nothing."

"It's history," Challis said in her ear. "But it's my history, so inevitably I think about it sometimes."

He said it firmly, almost sharply, an air of finality, and Ellen said, "I'm just being silly."

Not that silly. Her own marriage had ended in divorce, her ex-husband remarrying. And Allie had a very patchy love history. In the old days, husbands and wives stayed together.

Then again, many of them probably shouldn't have. These days, with a third of all marriages ending in divorce, why bother?

Her thoughts were all over the place and then there was a horn tooting down on her driveway and Allie was parking on the lawn. "They're here, I'd better go."

"Take care. Love you," Challis said, and it occurred to her that he didn't often say it. He displayed love, she felt loved, but he didn't often voice it.

"ELLIS," SAID ALLIE, "I'D like you to meet Clive. Clive Mieckle."

The photographs hadn't lied, Mieckle was a burly, compact man with cropped hair and a face full of experiences. But what experiences? wondered Ellen, as he stepped forward, his hand extended, his expression guarded. The handshake was firm, dry, a brief tough squeeze.

And the first words out of his mouth: "Allie told me on the way over here you're in the police force."

Ellen glanced questioningly at her sister, then gave Mieckle an off-hand smile. "For my sins."

"I have a great deal of respect for the police," Mieckle said, washing his hands together, as if to reassure her. "I'm ex-army myself—SAS—so I know something about matters of law and order. Hot spots overseas, that kind of thing."

Then Allie was hooking his arm in hers, melding her flank with his. "Clive's very tight-lipped about his experiences."

He shot her a look. "Well, I have to be, love. Secret work, a lot of it."

A fond tone, but a hint of steel, too. Bad memories? A warning not to pry?

They couldn't just stand about on the deck in the

GARRY DISHER ～ 146

dwindling light, so Ellen said, "Come in. Would you like a pre-dinner drink, Clive? Beer? Wine? Something stronger?"

He shook his head, about to answer, when Allie pulled him tight against her again. "Clive's not a drinker," she said, as if the virtue were somehow hers.

Ellen showed them to the sitting room, poured wine for Allie, water for Mieckle, and perched on the edge of her armchair. "How did you two meet?"

"Something smells good," Mieckle said.

Allie rode over him. "Frankston Art and Craft Expo," she gushed. "We bonded over a shared interest in photography."

To Ellen's knowledge, Allie didn't own a camera. "Photography?"

"Especially cats."

"Cats."

"I'm more into black-and-white photography than Allie," Mieckle said.

"You should see his work, Ells, it's truly beautiful. Not cutesy. Kind of moody. Expressive."

Mieckle shrugged. "Black and white allows for a degree of mystery."

Ellen found her mind drifting. She brought herself back to the room and her sister and the boyfriend. Especially the boyfriend. "Quite a change from army life. Are you a full-time photographer?"

"One day I hope to be. License my work for greeting cards and calendars, that kind of thing. Right now I'm trying to center myself."

Jesus Christ, thought Ellen, who was trying to get an answer to the question, *Do you earn a living or are you a grafter?*

Allie, no fool sometimes, narrowed her eyes. "Clive received compensation from the Army."

For what? Ellen didn't find out, for Clive bumped

shoulders with Allie fondly and dug her with his elbow. A startled flicker crossed Allie's face.

A warning not to shoot her mouth off? And then the timer sounded in the kitchen and Ellen got to her feet, saying, "Timing is crucial, especially when I'm the cook."

Mieckle laughed. Allie laughed, a little shrill.

"I hope you like spicy food, Clive. We're having a curry."

"Oh, Clive's well-traveled, don't you worry about that, Ells," Allie said, as if she didn't know when to shut up.

AN HOUR LATER THEY were slouched around the dining table. Ellen and Allie, mildly sloshed, were swapping stories of childhood while Clive Mieckle sat listening, wearing a smile. A fond smile, or was he concentrating?

"Remember that holiday house we'd spend summers at on Phillip Island?" Allie said. "Clive spent his summers on the island, too! Talk about ships passing in the night, if only, et cetera, et cetera."

Mieckle gave a pained smile.

"We've discovered heaps of parallels," Allie continued. "Holidays on Phillip Island. Walks on the beach. Photography. Cats . . ."

Mieckle did not look relaxed.

"Clive thinks we should buy an investment property on Phillip Island," Allie burbled on. "He says prices are favorable and in a few weeks from now places will start to come onto the market. People finishing their holidays and going back to work."

An off-handed gesture from Mieckle. "Oh, it was just a thought. Daydreaming aloud."

His voice was tinged with tension, but Allie didn't hear it. "No, like you said, darling, we should act rather than feel sorry later, when it's too late."

Ellen laughed immoderately, as if she were a carefree, slightly drunken and envious older sister. "Lucky things, I wish I could afford to buy a holiday house somewhere."

Allie said with kind concern, "One day you will, Ells. Anyway, I can always help out."

Somehow not the kind of information Ellen wanted her sister to be broadcasting this soon in a relationship.

16

ONE YEAR ON, CHALLIS'S ten-year-old secondhand BMW had become a headache. It was less gutsy than he'd thought a European sporting saloon should be, but mainly it was full of touchy and expensive mechanical and electrical parts. Sensors, for example, that stopped sensing and forced the car into limp-home mode.

Challis might have quipped that he knew all about limp-home mode; he'd been in it for much of his working life, at the tail end of twelve-hour days viewing murder scenes, attending autopsies, briefing the troops, grilling suspects and witnesses. But fucked if he felt like laughing this morning, Friday, the car losing power halfway to Waterloo and creeping onto the forecourt of Waterloo Automotive.

Bernie Joske sauntered out. The head mechanic, he was also one of Challis's informants.

"Not this shit-heap again. What's the problem?"

Challis told him, and Joske plugged a laptop into the electrics, ran a diagnostic check and said, "It's your mass air flow sensor."

"Whatever that is," Challis said.

"Mate, what can I tell you?" the mechanic said sadly. "European, over-engineered to buggery. Plus, you live on a dirt road, right? Dust? Corrugated to hell? Plus the car's ten years old."

"Yeah, yeah."

"Thing'll just keep going wrong. Buy Japanese, mate."

Challis glanced at his watch: Friday, 7:35 and he was late for the briefing. "Can you get me going again?"

"I'll get the part overnighted from Sydney and have you on the road sometime tomorrow."

"And keep your eyes open for a decent car for me?"

"Not a problem."

Challis thanked him and turned to go. Turned back and said, "Let me know if you hear of anyone unloading farm vehicles and machinery."

Joske saluted. "Count on it."

Challis gave him a nod, headed back onto the main road and walked to work.

TWO DEVELOPMENTS: SCOBIE SUTTON'S investigation into the burnt-out Mercedes had raised a red flag with the New South Wales drug squad, and John Tankard claimed to have seen that car, and its occupants, at the house of Owen Valentine and Christine Penford. Serena Coolidge demanded an immediate sit-down involving her squad, CIU, Sutton and Tankard, but Challis overrode her, insisting they interview Christine Penford first. "We need to know what she can tell us about Valentine's activities and likely location."

"Please yourself."

THE DOCTOR HAD PASSED Penford as fit to be questioned, but Challis was doubtful. She entered the interview room doubled over as if in pain, and sat cradling her head in her hands as though afraid it would drop from her shoulders to the pitted surface of the rickety plastic table. Or perhaps it was the air. The room was a hot, stale cave deep inside the police station and had never witnessed anything but lies and hopelessness.

He began, saying, "My name is Challis, the Crime Investigation Unit inspector for the Westernport region, and also present in the room are . . ."

"Sergeant Coolidge, drug squad."

"Constable Murphy, CIU."

Penford raised her head and looked blankly at the three officers. Gaunt, her hair hanging in limp strings to her shoulders, wearing loose-fitting pants and a T-shirt, she twitched and picked at her forearms. Challis could see sores near her nose and mouth, but her teeth looked okay.

"Before we begin, is there anything we can get you? Tea, coffee, water, something to eat?"

Penford shook her head violently. "You'll put a truth drug in it."

"Would you like a lawyer? We did advise you that you're entitled to free legal representation, Christine."

Pam Murphy leaned forward to add, "And your mother said she'd pay for a lawyer of your choosing."

"Her!" Penford said.

Challis leaned back, folded his arms. "To be clear, you are refusing legal representation at this time?"

An abbreviated nod.

Challis said, "Let it be noted that Ms. Penford has indicated she is not seeking legal representation. All right, Christine, let's begin. First, I advise you that this interview is being recorded for your protection as much as ours, okay?"

No response, so Challis went on: "On Wednesday you were arrested and charged on suspicion of burglary and possession of stolen goods. Is there anything you wish to say in regard to these matters?"

"No."

"I should advise you that we also intend to question you on other perhaps more serious matters, do you understand?"

Penford folded and unfolded her arms, as if to stop her hands from their tormenting ways. "Don't sweat it."

Challis nodded to Murphy, who said, "Christine, on Monday afternoon I visited you at your house to ask the whereabouts of your partner, Owen Valentine, is that correct? Do you remember?"

"I can't remember shit," Penford said.

"You told me he'd packed up and left you, taking his dog and some of his things with him, do you remember?"

"He run off on me," Penford muttered.

"Has he tried to contact you since then?"

"Why? He run off."

"Do you know why he did? Had you two been fighting, arguing? Had he been hassled by other people about anything? Was he frightened or in trouble?"

Too many questions in one go, thought Challis, and heard Penford alight on the last question. Staring as if astonished at Pam's naivety, Penford said, "You lot were going to arrest him."

"Do you happen to know the reason for that, Christine?"

"He bashed this guy up."

Then she seemed to sober suddenly. Stabbed herself in the chest with a gnawed forefinger. "You think *I* got rid of him or something? You mad?"

"So you didn't harm Owen or ask others to harm him in any way?"

"We were in love."

"Yet he left."

"He was scared of going to prison."

"That wouldn't necessarily have happened, first offense."

Penford hung her head and for a long moment was

still and silent. "We were doing okay till a few months ago. Clean and that."

Challis saw Coolidge glance impatiently at her watch. She wanted information from Penford and wanted it now. Her tone barbed, she said, "Cut the crap. You both got hooked on ice."

Penford bristled. "Go fuck yourself."

"Tell us who your dealer is."

"What?"

Murphy cut in. "So Owen was scared he'd go to jail for hitting Mr. Slatter."

Penford spread her palms, pleading. "But he'd paid him off. Talk about greedy."

Pam murmured to Challis, "I spoke to Slatter on Monday. He told me he didn't want to go ahead with police or court action." To Penford she said, "Owen paid Tony Slatter not to press charges?"

"That's what I said."

"When was this?"

"I don't know, a few days ago."

"Where did he get the money?"

Penford's gaze slid to the corners of the room. "How would I know?"

"He sold Clover's bike to a secondhand shop."

Penford shrugged. "It was too big for her."

"What did he get for the bike? Fifty dollars? Not enough to pay someone off."

"Nothing to do with me. All I know is, he paid the guy and the guy comes back wanting more."

"Mr. Slatter came to your house demanding more money?"

"That's what I said."

"And you attacked him."

"I never."

Challis said, "Don't worry about anything Mr. Slatter says. We've had a firm word with him, and he won't be pressing charges. But he confirmed that Owen gave him five thousand dollars in return for his silence. Now, how did Owen obtain that money? Did he borrow it? If so, who from?"

Christine Penford's gaze slid away again and altered, morphing from resistance to shame and anguish, each emotion passing quickly across her face and failing to settle. Her eyes teared up and she swiped at her face and whispered, "Clover."

Challis and Murphy seemed to deflate, tension leaking away. They had their opening. But Coolidge looked pointedly at her watch. Trying to ignore her, Challis said, "Christine, where is Clover?"

Penford stared at the scarred tabletop as though every cut and scratch writhed to get at her.

Harder now: "Where's your daughter, Christine?"

Penford tore her gaze from the table and stared at her hands.

"We found an abandoned meth lab on Monday. The bushfire came right up to the back fence and presumably scared away whoever was in it at the time. Do you know anything about that lab or the people who operated it, Christine?"

Presently Christine Penford shook her head, but minutely, little more than an ice twitch.

"We found a young child's clothing in the lab. What can you tell us about that, Christine?"

No response.

Coolidge was thrumming with tension, leaning forward as if to grab Penford by the throat. Challis, curling his lip at her warningly, took a photograph from a binder and slapped it down under Penford's gaze. "Here's a photo of the clothing we found. Do you recognize it, Christine?"

"Bearing in mind you're a meth head," Coolidge said.

"Shut your mouth, bitch."

Challis felt his jaw tighten. He said, "We fear for Clover's life, Christine. Where is she?"

"Is she dead, in other words," Coolidge said.

Penford lifted her wet face to them. "I don't know!"

"What happened, Christine?" Murphy said gently.

"Like I said, we needed money. Owen needed money."

"To pay off Mr. Slatter."

"Yeah, him."

"You asked the meth cooks for money?"

"Not me, *Owen.*"

"Can we move this along?" Coolidge demanded. "I want names."

"I don't know their names. Owen used to hang with them."

"Who do they cook for?"

"I dunno."

"One of the bikie gangs?"

"I said I dunno."

Coolidge opened her laptop, tapped keys, turned the screen to Penford. "Do you know these men?"

"No."

"Have you ever seen them before?"

"No."

"Do the names Pym and Lovelock mean anything to you?"

"No."

"To your knowledge did Owen ever meet with or talk about any person from Sydney associated with the trade in ice or other drugs?"

Penford was astounded. "What? No."

"Just to be clear, Owen did not meet with or talk to these two men in relation to borrowing money to pay off the man he attacked at the front door of your house a couple of weeks ago?"

"Fucking hell. I said, *no.*"

Coolidge subsided. Challis said, "So he asked two lab cooks for money. Why them?"

"Aren't you listening? He done some stuff for them before."

"Did they give him money, to your knowledge?"

Penford was pale and shaking. "Dunno. Must of. He give them Clover."

Challis said gently, "Why, Christine?"

"She was, like, collateral."

"You'd get her back when he repaid the loan?" Challis asked.

"Wasn't my idea. I never had nothing to do with it."

"Why didn't you go to the police?"

Christine Penford's gaze slid away. She shrugged, and Challis thought, of course not. She had drugs and stolen goods in her possession; she was probably afraid child protection would get involved.

He said, "So Owen paid off Mr. Slatter . . ."

She muttered, "Yeah, must of. I thought he'd kept the money and run off, especially when that guy come around."

"Mr. Slatter, wanting more money?"

"Yes." Her face streaked with misery, Penford said, "I don't know what's going on. I go to work, I take care of my kids, I—"

"So Owen's gone, and the only way you could ensure Clover's return is raise the money to buy her back, hence your little run of house-breaking?"

"Isn't that what I've been saying?"

"No, you've been lying and evading," Coolidge said.

Murphy leaned over the table as if to shield Penford from

the drug-squad officer. With great gentleness she said, "Is Owen the children's father, Christine?"

"He's Troy's dad, not Clover's."

"How was he with Clover? Was he ever mean to her?"

"She'd go, 'You're not my dad,' and you could tell it pissed him off."

Coolidge snarled, "Forget about that. Tell me about your boyfriend's drug dealing."

"He never dealt," sniffed Penford.

"So he was mates with a couple of ice cooks, nothing more, is that it?"

With a trace of miserable pride, Penford said, "He used to be their best cook."

"Jesus," muttered Coolidge. "Here on the Peninsula?"

Penford shook her head. "Out in Gippsland somewhere."

"So have they been cooking long on the Peninsula?"

Penford shook her head. "Owen only hooked up with them again a couple of weeks ago."

Pam Murphy cut in. "Christine, I need you to concentrate on what's important here. When I look at you, I see someone who's made some mistakes and wants to get her life back on track. It wasn't your decision to put up your daughter as collateral on a loan from drug dealers, and you did your best to get her back."

Penford straightened her spine and tried to stare unflinchingly at the world. She failed. She slumped and sniffed, swiping the back of her hand across her face and eyes.

"Christine, we're very worried about Clover," Murphy said.

"So am I."

"We need to find her before something terrible happens, do you understand? We need to know everything you know, now. Any first name you can give us, last name, nickname.

Descriptions, times, dates. Any trips you went on or that Owen went on. Anything at all."

"Where's Troy?"

"Your mother's looking after him."

Challis expected Penford to explode again, but all she did was struggle feebly with the revelation and slump. "Okay."

She began a confused and halting account of trying ice and ice taking over her life, but gave no hard facts, despite Coolidge firing sharp questions at her. Then Coolidge took a call on her mobile, gathered her notes and laptop, said, "That's it, got to go, get what you can from her," and left the room.

Challis said, "For the benefit of the tape, Senior Sergeant Coolidge has left the room."

Her priority, he thought, is unlikely to be finding Clover Penford. He leaned in. "Christine, when Owen's pals don't get their money, what do you think they'll do?"

"I dunno."

"They'll think of ways to use her, if they haven't already."

"Boss," warned Murphy.

Fear suffused Penford's sallow face. "It's not like that. It's just money."

"They will share her around. They will sell her to men who will film her being raped by them. They will sell these films via the Internet."

"Boss . . ."

At once, Challis dropped the harshness and aridity. He clasped Penford's forearm. "But we will do everything to get her back before that happens, so you need to talk to us."

"The department'll take her off me."

"Persuade us," Murphy said. "Tell us about Owen and how you met and how things fell apart."

The story emerged in fits of misery, sweet memories and

pathetic pride. Unhappy at school, miserable at home, Christine had hooked up with Owen Valentine at the Westernport Festival the year she turned fifteen. He was nineteen, and unlike anyone she'd met before.

"His room had all these posters everywhere, like Bob Marley and Jim Beam and a skull and crossbones. It was like a den with the windows covered over and that. We'd sit in there and watch DVDs and listen to music and do dope."

"Did your parents object to him?"

Penford shrugged.

"What did Owen do for a job? You said everything went wrong a few months ago, but it sounds like you and Owen had a settled life for several years. Were you managing the habit? Did you start injecting recently?"

She shrugged.

"Did Owen have a job? Did you?"

"He was a welder. He'd go off for months on pipeline jobs." She shrugged. "We lost touch for a few years."

"You had Clover with someone else?"

"So?"

"Then Owen came back?"

"Beginning of last year. We hooked up again, all right?"

"He was still employed as a welder?"

Penford shook his head. "He was cooking meth for these guys."

"In Gippsland."

"Shipping containers, empty houses, sometimes these sheds they'd put up and pull down again. Once even in the back of a truck."

Sometimes he'd cook for days at a time, producing an ounce a day, then go home and crash for a week. She shook her head in amazement. "He'd go four days without sleep."

"Not hard if you're using while you're cooking," Murphy said.

"Shut your mouth, bitch."

"A wonder he didn't blow himself up."

"He was good at it, all right," shrieked Penford.

The loyalty, thought Challis. Amazing. He said, "He cooked an ounce a day—how many hits did that work out to be?"

Penford sneered. "*Points*, not hits."

"Okay, how many points?"

"Up to 280."

"Worth?"

"Twenty-eight grand."

There was that pride again. "And you helped."

"No. I had the kids."

"And Owen? He was using, growing violent and unpredictable?"

"A bit."

"Why did you stay?"

"I was in love," Penford said. "We had Troy together."

"Who gave Owen the precursor chemicals, the pipettes and the rest of the gear . . . ?"

"I told you, these Bandidos."

"He first hooked up with them when he was away for that extended period, welding?"

"That's what I said."

"They stopped using him when he became unreliable?"

"So?"

"Christine, is it possible these men saw Owen as a liability? Is it possible they did something to him?"

She stared down the months and years of her life and didn't speak. Challis thought she'd drifted away from them, from the room and her misery. He saw the memories behind her eyes.

She shook her head. "He run off," she said sadly.

"Do you know anything about the movement of ice on the Peninsula, Christine? I don't mean bikie labs, I mean ice that's coming into the area from outside."

She shrugged. "It's everywhere, I know that much."

"Who did you and Owen buy from?"

"Wasn't me, Owen did all that."

"You both doing break-ins to feed your habits?"

"Owen did."

"Christine, your mother went to your house to collect toys and clothing for your son and found a gun hidden on top of a wardrobe."

"Nosy cow."

"Did Owen specialize in stealing firearms from farms in the area?"

Penford shrugged. "Sounds like him." She paused and with miserable pride said, "I have a job. Part time."

Then she looked squarely at them in turn. "Tell me now, will I do jail time? Will I lose the kids? I told you everything I know. Wasn't me what sold Clover."

"That's possible. It's up to the DPP. But if in the meantime we find Owen and he tells us a different story . . ."

"Wasn't me!"

Her misery was naked, unchecked, tears splashing onto the table. "I done me best. I'm an addict, but I can turn around."

17

NOW COOLIDGE COULD HAVE her briefing.

As the others filed into the conference room, she muttered to Challis, "I don't intend to waste any more time on Christine Penford or that ice lab. I've got bigger fish to fry."

"Serena, we've got a kid in peril."

"*Your* case," she said, tapping him lightly on the chest.

CHALLIS BEGAN THE BRIEFING:

"Certain information has come to our attention that seems to link apparently unrelated incidents and crimes. First, when Senior Constable Tankard manned the front desk yesterday, two visitors made reports related to a man named Owen Valentine. John checked Valentine's address and realized that he'd attended a disturbance there a week ago today. John?"

Tankard, his large frame overheated, lumbered to his feet as though a teacher had put him on the spot. "Yeah, 5 Banksia Court in Moonta. Noise complaint. Bad language and shouting. An old woman over the back fence called it in."

Challis said, "Sit, John, no need to stand. Tell us what you saw when you arrived."

"Two guys were there, standing around in the car shed at the side of the house. They told me they were doing some

DIY house painting and did a bit of shouting and swearing when they spilled a tin of white on the floor."

"What else did you see?"

John Tankard struggled with that, and then his face cleared. "Black Mercedes, backed into the car shed."

Challis inclined her head to Pam Murphy, who slid a photograph across the table. "Was this one of the men?"

Tankard leaned over the table and peered at it, eyes narrowing in his pouchy face. "Nope."

Murphy slid copies of the photograph to the others, tapped the face of her own. "This is Owen Valentine. He resides at that Banksia Court address, along with his girlfriend, Christine Penford, and Christine's two children. I called there early this week to speak to him about an assault complaint, since withdrawn, and was told by Christine that she'd come home the previous Friday—the day John was called to the house—to find that he'd left her. She seemed genuinely bewildered and upset."

Murphy glanced at Challis, nodding to say she'd finished.

He said, "It doesn't end there. It's probable that Owen did a bit of breaking and entering, targeting firearms from farmhouses which he then sold to drug dealers. Keep that in mind a few minutes from now, when you hear from our crime-scene expert. Meanwhile, Owen was facing an assault charge. Fearing it would mean jail time, he paid off his victim to the tune of five thousand dollars. To raise the money, he put up Christine's six-year-old daughter, Clover, as collateral."

A soft, anguished moan from Scobie Sutton. Casting him a sympathetic smile, Challis went on: "We believe the clothing found at the ice lab on the outskirts of Waterloo early this week belongs to Clover Penford. We have yet to find her or the men who'd been cooking ice there. Needless to say, it doesn't look good."

He glanced at Sutton. "That's one avenue of inquiry stemming from Owen Valentine. Now let's hear about another. Scobie?"

Scobie Sutton had set out his reports in neat piles. "Preliminary findings," he said, his cadaverous face troubled, as though he hated to disappoint.

"That's fine, Scobie."

"Last Friday's bushfire, two men burnt to death in a car," he said, and stopped.

"Go on."

"We also found a high-powered rifle and animal remains—a small dog."

Pam angled the photo of Owen Valentine, holding Cluedo the dog. "Could this be the dog?"

"Impossible to say, but the size is right."

Challis said, "Can you match DNA from the dog, if there is any, with DNA from the house—from a toy or food bowl or rubber bone, for example?"

"A long shot."

"Have you been able to work up DNA profiles for the two men?"

"Still working on it," Sutton said. He looked at everyone in turn. "If we can retrieve viable DNA, and if one of the men is Owen Valentine, then we can compare with DNA from his little boy or from a comb or toothbrush from the Banksia Courthouse."

Pam Murphy said, "He took all that with him, but how about an ice pipe?"

"That would work."

Sutton lapsed into silence.

Challis said, "Scobie, the rifle and the car."

Sutton coughed. "Yes, of course. Along with the remains of two men and a dog, we found some interesting items in the boot of the car: a set of molten but readable New South Wales number plates, a shovel head, and what's left of an aluminum gun case containing a rifle. The case protected the rifle from more extreme damage, enabling me to test-fire it." He paused. "I don't want to go out on a limb, but I think it's the Hauser murder weapon. I can't match the bullet fired through his head to rifling on the test-fire bullet because it was badly deformed when it hit the concrete slab under the carpet, but the metallurgical analysis shows a match, and the firing-pin marks on the test cartridges are a match to those on the two cartridge cases left at the scene. Incidentally, we found prints on the cases but they're not in the system. Now for the car itself: it was carrying plates stolen from a station wagon in Bega late last week, but the VIN number, and the plates in the boot, belong to an S-Class Mercedes owned by a car hire firm in Sydney."

This was all carefully orchestrated by Challis. Now he turned to Coolidge. "The drug squad has more on this angle."

Coolidge had been attending to the briefing with a faint smile, not yet bored or impatient, but getting there. Folders, files, notebooks and an iPad were heaped untidily before her and she was tapping at the keyboard, apparently ignoring him.

She waited a beat before aiming her gaze at Sutton. "Good work, Senior Constable Sutton," she said, barely meaning it. Glancing around at the others, she continued: "According to my New South Wales contacts, the car was hired by a couple of syndicate enforcers working for a man named Kaye, who's very big-time, sources his crystal meth from China at seven thousand dollars a kilo and sells it on at a huge mark-up. Why he sent his boys down here, I don't know. We know he supplies dealers here, but not exactly who. I mean, Owen Valentine's a loser, not a drug kingpin. Maybe the answer lies with Colin Hauser, or the people behind him."

Challis looked at her with interest. She's not going to leave me any cases to run, he thought. "Are these men known to use firearms?"

"Not really. Knives, fists, blunt instruments." She tapped at her iPad and swung it around in a slow semicircle. "Their mugshots."

She finished at John Tankard, who took a moment before saying, "That's them."

"To be clear: these are the two men you saw at the house in Moonta last Friday?"

"Yes."

She swung the screen back to Pam Murphy. "And neither man is Owen Valentine?"

"Correct."

Coolidge turned to Sutton. "Their names are Stephen Pym and Elliot Lovelock. Their DNA is on file, so we need the profiles from the dead men as soon as possible to see if there's a match."

Pam Murphy said, "Scobie, you didn't find a body in the boot of the car by any faint chance?"

"No."

She said to the room, "A lot of unanswered questions. If Owen Valentine isn't one of the dead men, we still need to find him. And where does Hauser fit in? Were our heroes hired to kill both of them?"

"I'm strongly inclined to take over both investigations," Coolidge said, "but my team is stretched enough as it is and we have a big surveillance operation this weekend, so for now I suggest we continue to run parallel investigations: the drug angle from our end, the murder et cetera from your end."

No promise that she would share information, Challis noticed. He said, "Meanwhile we don't know that these men did anything to Valentine. He might already have cleared out when they arrived. After all, they killed Hauser at his house and left his body there, so why not Valentine?"

"We need a thorough search of that house," Coolidge said. "Senior Constable Tankard, describe exactly what you saw when you answered the disturbance call."

Tank inclined his head at Coolidge's iPad. "I saw those two men, Pym and Lovelock, in the garage at the side of the house."

"And their car was there? The Mercedes?"

"Yes."

"Did you search the car?"

Still uncomfortable and looking around the room for assistance, John Tankard said, "There was no reason to."

"Nothing that you could see inside the car? Nothing in the boot?"

"The boot was closed. Tinted windows, but I wasn't really looking, sorry."

Coolidge's look scorched him. "What were the men doing?"

"Like I said, it looked like they'd spilled some paint. I got the impression it was a do-it-yourself gone wrong, hence the yelling and swearing the neighbor complained about."

Challis said, "Which neighbor?"

"Forgotten her name. Elderly, from Melbourne, comes down most weekends. Her house backs onto Valentine's."

"So she wouldn't have seen anything, just heard shouting?"

Tankard shrugged.

Challis was decisive. "We get a warrant and search the house, the shed, the yard and any vehicle from top to bottom. We want anything that will tell us more about the whereabouts of Owen Valentine, but bear in mind that we also need to find Christine Penford's daughter. He turned to Sutton. "Scobie, concentrate on the garage, and if possible obtain DNA for the dog, the missing girl and Owen Valentine."

"The girl?" said Sutton, appalled.

Challis didn't have time for his feelings. "DNA, fingerprints and/or photographs."

"You think . . ." said Sutton.

Coolidge leaned forward to stare at him pityingly. "He thinks she's dead, okay?"

Then she stood, gathering her files. "I'll meet you at the house."

18

TOLD THAT THE WARRANT would be ready by mid-morning, Pam Murphy clattered downstairs, signed out the ring of car and house keys in the possession of Christine Penford at the time of the arrest, then grabbed coffee and an apple from the canteen, and returned to CIU. Passing Challis's office, she saw Coolidge there, leaning toward him, animated and sparkling, Challis leaning back from her, hands laced behind his head. A half-smile on his face, but Pam read strain in it. "Don't like your chances, Serena," she sang, unheard by anybody.

She caught up on emails, wrote some notes and an action list based on the briefing, and then Serena Coolidge was standing before her desk, some kind of tension under the cynicism and amusement. "When you're ready, Constable."

"We have our warrant?"

"We do," Coolidge said. "Lead the way. My team will follow."

PAM SIGNED FOR THE CIU car and walked past John Tankard and Janine Quine outside the door leading to the car park, surrounded by cigarette butts. Snatching a lungful, Tank was saying, "Jan, he needs counseling."

"I know," Quine replied, jetting smoke from her slash of a mouth as if she had seconds to live.

Tank took another drag. "He's got to get his act together."

"I know," Quine muttered.

Pam looked around for the CIU car, which was never parked in its allotted space. She could see Scobie Sutton and his assistant waiting beside the crime-scene van and Coolidge and a drug-squad senior constable heading for their unmarked Commodore as though they had countries to invade. She pressed the unlock button on the ignition key. A chirping sound came from the hidden side of a rubbish skip. It all seemed to sum up her day.

MURPHY LED THE LITTLE police cavalcade out of Waterloo and north-east around Westernport Bay toward Moonta and its huddled dwellings. Only the Penford–Valentine house was out of place, with its parched lawn, dead pot plants and peeling paint. The car shed door yawned open, further adding to the sense of desertion and desolation.

Murphy parked, the drug-squad car pulling in to the curb behind her, the crime-scene van into the driveway. When they'd assembled and dragged on crime-scene suits and footwear, Coolidge marched across the miserable grass and onto the concrete front step. She hammered on the door.

Waste of time, thought Pam. Penford's in the lockup, Valentine's in the wind. She jangled the keys. "Senior Sergeant? Keys?"

That earned her a scowl. Coolidge stepped back onto the lawn, strode toward Murphy and grabbed the keys. Then she was letting herself into the house and Sutton was calling after her, "Please don't touch anything."

Coolidge's voice floated back, "I know my job."

Sutton muttered, "And so do I."

He was overheard by Coolidge's offsider, who sauntered after his boss, giving them an apologetic shrug.

Pam touched Sutton's sleeve. "I'll keep an eye on them, Scobie. Maybe you could start with the garage?"

They walked in and eyed the paint spill, thick, white, puckered. Sutton's assistant said, "It doesn't look like anyone tried to clean it up."

"True, and you have to ask what use a tin of paint would be to two hit-men who've driven here all the way from Sydney."

Pam crouched at the spill, keeping half a meter back from the ragged edges. It seemed to her that very little of the original floor showed after years of tracked-in beach sand, oil and grease spills, dust and dirt, drifts of dead leaves and pine needles, old wood and iron shavings . . . And now spilt—or poured—paint. A few more days, she thought, and the paint spill would have grown its own patina of filth and not have warranted anyone's attention.

"Covering evidence is one logical answer."

Sutton crouched with her, poked experimentally at the paint spill with a gloved finger, then looked up at his crime-scene technician. "Kristen, I'll deal with this. I want you to find anything that will give us DNA for the dog, Owen Valentine and a six-year-old girl."

"Boss."

Pam followed the technician into the house. Ignoring the drug-squad officers, who were sifting through bills, letters and receipts in the kitchen and the sitting room, she did a quick walk-through. The house seemed unchanged from her earlier visit, but with an overlay of desperation that she couldn't identify. It was the house of people who'd struggled and failed.

The children's bedroom contained two single beds, one blue, one pink, each with a little bedside cupboard, and a thin wardrobe crammed with dresses, jeans and T-shirts. Footwear on the bottom, one tiny pair of blue trainers, a larger pair of pink; tiny blue gumboots, slightly larger pink gumboots. Kristen the crime-scene tech was there, a crackly, plump shape in her forensic suit, slipping a hairbrush into an evidence bag. "The girl's?" Pam said.

"In this drawer," the woman replied, pointing to a little cupboard beside the pink bed.

"Toothbrush?"

"I'll look, don't worry."

"Sorry, you know your job."

The woman smiled. "That's okay. I used to be in CIU too, same as Scobie. It's impatience. You're on the scent."

Pam returned the smile. "I'll see if I can find any photos."

She wandered through to the main bedroom. The covers had been carelessly pulled over the bottom sheet and pillows. She flung them back, seeing grimy cotton flecked with blood and what she guessed was semen. She'd seen it before, blood on bedding. Addicts injecting their inner thighs. Or scratching at tormented arms and legs.

Nothing under the mattress or the pillows. Nothing of note in the wardrobe or bedside cupboards.

Coolidge was in the doorway, her trademark silent materialization. "Find anything?"

"Not yet. You?"

"We found a little dope in a freezer bag."

Pam nodded. "The thing is, would an addict who decided to go on the run leave anything behind?"

"My thoughts exactly."

Pam turned for a final glance around the room. A shelf had been bolted to the wall above the terrible bed. It was crammed with tiny framed photographs, brightly painted dishes the size of doll-set saucers, a couple of cheap glass necklaces piled untidily with ribbons and hair scrunchies. She reached behind the worst of the clutter and retrieved a photograph. It showed a small girl, a big grin and a missing tooth.

She proffered it to Coolidge. "If I'm not mistaken, she's wearing the clothes we found at the meth lab."

An expression passed over Coolidge's face. Pity? Anger? Anguish? It was there and gone and Coolidge said, "Well, good luck finding her."

Then Kristen called, "Got something."

They found her in the bathroom, sealing toothbrushes in separate evidence bags. She pointed to the floor, showing that she'd removed the cheap patterned vinyl bath surround. Nestled into the cavity under the bath's curved underside were two shotguns.

Coolidge rounded on Pam. "What do you really know about Valentine. You sure he doesn't go armed?"

Pam flushed. "He doesn't have a record. Until he assaulted a local man several days ago, he hadn't come to our attention at all."

Coolidge scowled at the guns. "Maybe he's made a career change."

"Maybe, but I think he's just a junkie burglar with a sideline, stealing firearms from rural properties."

Coolidge glared at her, glared at the shotguns. "Let's hope you're right."

"Ma'am," Pam said.

When Coolidge had wandered off, she noted the serial numbers before slipping each shotgun into an evidence bag. Logged them into evidence and went outside to breathe the briny air briefly before following up on possible sightings of Christine Penford's daughter.

19

AT FRIDAY MORNING'S SEX-CRIMES briefing, Ellen Destry said, "This is what we know so far," and wrote *average height* on the board. Turning back to her crew she said, "What else?"

They fed her the identifiers one by one and she listed them:

Slim build
Manual laborer?
Age—30s
Balaclava
Jeans, T-shirt, dirty running shoes
Uses material to hand
Graduated from burglary?

That done, she said, "Not much to go on, but I think a picture is emerging. We've found a rape and burglary victim case from six months ago in which the attacker supplied his own tape and knife from a bag that probably contained break-and-enter tools. If the same man was responsible for the rapes of Wreidt and Sligo, then he seems to have evolved, no longer bringing a weapon or tape with him but threatening his victims with their own kitchen knives and binding them with their own scarves or tights."

Katsoulas put up her hand. "Convenience, or he doesn't want to explain a knife and gaffer tape if he gets pulled over by the police."

Ellen shrugged. "Or both."

"But he's still a burglar; he does steal from these women."

"Yes, small items."

"So he goes equipped with burglary tools."

"But not necessarily specialist burglary tools. No one's going to view an ordinary pry bar in a toolbox in the back of a work vehicle as suspicious."

They pondered that, trying to picture the man. Judd said, "He *is* evolving, though. The rape has become the primary objective, not the thieving."

Ellen nodded. "I imagine he still gets a kick out of breaking in and stealing, but now there's the waiting, the anticipation, and finally the rape itself."

"And the stalking, if that's what he's doing," Judd said.

"Good point."

Ellen told them more about Jess Guthrie. "There may be earlier victims, or others around the same time, but in this case the victim was home alone one workday afternoon recovering from a dental procedure, and was woken by a sound that she believes was her attacker prising open a sliding glass door at the back of the house. She was groggy, she was easily overcome. We have the DNA profile, but as yet there's no match in the system."

"Normally she would have been at work?" said Rykert.

"Yes."

"So, an opportunistic rape. He was there to burgle the house."

"I believe so."

"He got a kick out of it and wanted to do it again."

"If it's the same man, yes. And in the more recent attacks,

and might-have-been incidents, we have him *waiting inside for the victim to come home.* And threatening her with her own kitchen knife and tying her up with her own clothing."

"Or it's not the same man," Rykert said.

Ellen nodded. "Naturally we have to consider that. But I haven't finished detailing the similarities."

She turned to the whiteboard and added:

Bad smell

Bathed the victims

Cosy chat

"Body odor?" said Katsoulas.

"Bad breath."

"Washing away his DNA?"

"Yes, but it also goes further than that, as if he thinks he's showing care and consideration. Similarly with the chat afterward. One victim said he warned her to be more careful in future, another that he suggested they could meet up again."

Ellen turned to the whiteboard and added:

Fantasies about a relationship

Her writing hand fell to her thigh as if weighed by a brick. "But don't be fooled by the nurturing. He's still aware that he's done something wrong and could be caught for it."

Returning to the board she wrote:

"Count to one hundred after I leave"

They were scribbling down their own versions of her list, and she watched them, their bent heads, almost with fondness. "Now, his MO," she said. "He seems to have perfected this method: break in, bag up a few valuables, wait in hiding for his victim to come home, grab her from behind, threaten her with a knife, bind and gag her, cut off her clothes, rape or attempt to rape her."

Judd cocked his head. "Attempt?"

"It's possible he has difficulty obtaining or keeping an erection."

Katsoulas said, "Heroin user?"

"Could be."

"One day," Katsoulas said, "his failure to perform will turn him vicious. He'll hit or stab someone, maybe even kill them."

"Which could become a new thrill on top of the old one," Ellen said.

Judd had been sitting there with his arms folded. "That's all well and good, but what we need to know is not what drives him, but how he chooses his victims. Whether or not they have anything or anyone in common. So far all we have is a handful of actual and might-have-been incidents over a six-month period. It's not enough to go on with."

Katsoulas snorted. "Knowing what drives him is important, surely?"

Judd dismissed the objection with a brief, indifferent glance at her over his glasses, perched on the end of his nose. He turned his attention back to Ellen. "Look, we're police, not shrinks. We detect, we find evidence, we do trace and elimination work."

"Policing has moved on a little since your day, Ian," Katsoulas said.

Ellen stepped in, her hand up. "You're both right. We have to keep in mind what kind of man this guy is, and we also need to know how he operates on a practical level. So, we look at local traffic and parking infringements around the time of each attack. We continue to look—*with some tact*—at burglaries where the victim is a young or youngish woman living alone.

"Which leads me to the victims," she added, turning to the whiteboard and scrawling a heading: *Victimology*.

"Single, female, young," suggested Katsoulas.

Ellen listed these. "What else?"

"Home at a certain time of the day," Judd said.

Ellen went very still. "I hadn't thought of that. Mid- to late-afternoon."

"Meaning if he has a job, he's either not at work then, or his job gives him the freedom to act then."

Ellen summarized this. "Anything else?"

Judd continued to prove that experience and old-style thinking mattered. "I've been visiting each location, and studying the maps. These women all live in quiet locations. Suburban, but with easy access to escape routes like the Nepean Highway or Frankston-Flinders Road. Wreidt, and the woman who got spooked and didn't go in, and the woman who found signs someone had made himself at home—they all lived in ground-floor flats backing onto laneways."

Katsoulas gave him a grudging acknowledgment. "Creepy. I live in a block of six flats and four of them are occupied by single women."

"His hunting ground," Judd said. "Places with easy access and suitable victims."

"His burglary experience coming in handy," Rykert said.

"He could have been at it for some time."

"But never arrested or charged—no DNA on record."

"Luck, then," Katsoulas said, "if he's on heroin."

"And he's a traveler, to a limited degree," Judd said.

Ellen nodded, added it to the list. "Explain?"

"We have attacks in Tyabb, Somerville, Balnarring, Mornington. Not a huge distance apart, but it does involve some travel. Guthrie's one of the earliest—she lives between Mornington and Mt. Martha. Maybe he lives near there, and started operating further afield after that."

Katsoulas said, "So we look at early break-ins in and around there."

"Time," Rykert said.

Ellen looked at him encouragingly. "Yes?"

"He attacks mid- to late-afternoon, but he might have broken in a lot earlier than that."

"True, but psychologically speaking, can he tolerate a very long wait?" Katsoulas said, throwing a look at Judd, expecting him to roll his eyes.

Instead he said, "Maybe he works at night. Work-roughened hands, supermarket storeman or similar."

"He doesn't wear gloves?" Rykert said doubtfully.

"He does," Ellen said. "Takes them off for the sexual attack, then bathes the victim."

"Getting back to victimology," Katsoulas said. "We need to look at gym memberships, clubs and societies, sporting activities." She paused. "Hair color?"

"So far, a blonde, two mousy browns," Judd said. He asked Ellen, "Souvenirs? Lock of hair, underwear?"

"Not that I'm aware of."

Katsoulas said, "Where do these women shop? Do they visit the same hairdresser, petrol station, fast-food joints, cafes . . . ?"

"Or," said Judd, "he cruises around, looking for the right location—quiet, good escape routes, easy access—and then watches and waits."

"Not a very efficient way to go about it," snorted Katsoulas.

"Why not? Plenty of pickings."

"Look—"

"Enough, both of you," Ellen said. "This is not about your ways of thinking, it's about catching a dangerous creep, okay?"

Katsoulas stared at the table, her jaw working. "Boss."

But Judd merely watched Ellen calmly. Presently he said, "Understood."

Ellen left it at that. "This is what we do now. We talk to the victims again to see if there's any overlap in terms of movements, places and people. We look for further incidents. We see what else the evidence might show about this man's movements and actions in the cases we know about and in cases where he might have been involved. We look again at known rapists and burglars: maybe our man is a brother, father or cousin. We look at crime-scene history: who's visited recently and why. Friends, family, tradespeople, neighbors, cold callers."

Rykert threw down his pen. "Last year I worked on a case where we ended up with two hundred potential suspects and witnesses."

"If that's how it is, that's how it is," Ellen said flatly.

She bent to tidy her folders, wondering what he'd take from her voice. Life's not a holiday? Wake up to yourself?

He was young, had a lot to learn, and she had a mentoring role. "Slow and steady gets the job done," she said, feeling like an idiot.

20

JANINE QUINE SAID THAT morning, as she'd said every morning this week, "Stay home, Jeff. No following the school bus."

Her husband twitched. Three weeks since his last ten-day stint at the rehab clinic and claiming he was clean, but Janine could see the vestiges in his nerve synapses, on his skin, in his ruined mouth. The traces of paranoia.

"Promise?" she said.

"Promise."

"The kids are quite safe. He's a good driver."

Jeff snarled, "He was going too fast over the speed bumps."

Janine pushed aside her toast and tea, went around the kitchen table to where her husband sat full of tics and demons. She pulled his shoulder against her thigh, his head into her stomach, held him like that, saying, "Hush now, hush now."

Three weeks clean and he wasn't roaming at night. In the bad old days she sometimes woke at midnight or 2 A.M. to find herself alone, his side of the bed cold. She'd call him, text him, no reply. Then, around breakfast time when she was trying to get the kids ready for school, he'd return.

"Just driving around," he'd say. "Helps to clear my head."

Except one morning he confessed: he'd gone to meet his dealer. So she confiscated his keys, told him she was leaving,

GARRY DISHER ～ 182

taking the kids with her, if he didn't get straight. Off he
went to rehab again. Came out full of confidence, eyes
clear, only to bust again. She'd wake to find the bed cold,
again, but neither car missing. So the idiot was *walking* to
meet his dealer.

Weeks of mounting violence and paranoia followed,
Jeff increasingly fucked up in mind and body, the police
knocking on the door, called by the neighbors. She contacted a lawyer to find out about restraining orders, custody
of the children: meanwhile Jeff had used her credit card
to get cash, and one of the dear, sweet, gorgeous, infinitely
understanding banks had pre-approved him for a twenty-
thousand-dollar personal loan. She managed to put a stop
to that, but Jeff continued to apply for credit, for cards, for
an extension on existing credit limits.

He raided the kids' savings accounts.

Then, miraculously, he entered rehab—*again*—and came
out determined to keep her and the kids, keep whatever job
came his way.

That job was IT for Raymond Loeb. Janine had known
Ray at school, Mornington Secondary College; watched
him enter and eventually inherit his father's auction-
eering, property maintenance and conveyancing firm.
She'd stayed in touch, even used him to handle a clearing
sale when her grandfather died on his asparagus farm near
Longwarry.

Fat, slow-moving Ray Loeb had always seemed keen on
her, and she'd seen no harm in flirting a little, even though
he was married with kids, knowing she might need him
one day. So with Jeff announcing that he'd turned his life
around, Janine went to Ray, asking if he had any work for
her husband.

"He's good with figures, computers."

"I've got an accountant, Jan," Loeb said. "My secretary does all the computing I need."

"I know, but maybe he could drive you around, help out at auctions, sweep floors . . ."

After an agonizing half-minute, Ray said curtly, "I can give him some menial data entry work, very part time," not appearing quite so fat, slow and amiable when it came to business.

"Done," Janine said.

WORST MISTAKE OF HER life—after marrying Jeff Quine.

At least marrying Jeff had led to two beautiful children, but Jeff working for Raymond Loeb had led to anger, fear and panic.

"Jeff said you sacked him."

Loeb had almost screamed at her. "Sacked him? I'll say I fucking sacked him. He stole from me."

Janine closed her eyes. Jeff was using again, buying drugs again. "I'll make it up to you, Ray, I swear. I'll pay back every cent."

"Pay back twenty thousand dollars? When? How?"

She'd wondered where the money for their new TV had come from. "Please let me make it up to you."

"If I press charges, he could go to jail, Jan."

"Please, can I just pay you back in stages?"

YES, SHE COULD PAY him back, but not in the way she'd hoped.

"You work in the Waterloo cop shop, right?"

"Yes," she said, her heart sinking.

"Filing stuff, filling out forms, clerical duties?"

"Yes."

"You'd have access to files."

"Yes," she said miserably.

"I need you to be my eyes and ears."

"Why? How?"

He ignored the questions. "For example, people going away on holiday or overseas, they can register their properties with you, right? The police keep an eye on their houses while they're away?"

"Yes," she whispered.

What he wanted her to do was feed him that kind of information. Names, dates, addresses. Plus intel regarding ongoing police operations that targeted burglaries and vehicle theft.

"If you break into any of these places, they'll eventually trace it to me!" she told him, scared out of her mind.

"No they won't. I'll be selective. Not every property, not even most of them."

That part of his response to her doubts was delivered with a buoyant smile. The next part wasn't. He grabbed a swatch of her hair, jerked her face close to his and snarled, his breath reeking. Cigarettes, some intestinal rottenness. "If you cross me, Jan, your kids die, understand? If you want me off your back, if you want to repay your useless husband's debts, you'll get me the information I need when I need it, as I need it. Understood?"

"Yes."

He shoved her away, no longer a joke figure, and straightened his lapels, brushed his hands through his carefully barbered hair.

"Good. Settled, then."

AT FIRST, THEY COMMUNICATED via cryptic text messages on stolen mobile phones, a new phone every week. Then, for a while, emails on stolen phones. But Janine knew how the police worked, how they traced and intercepted texts and emails, and was worried sick.

Until she thought of Annette Tranh's phone. Annette, the office manager, was away sick, and Janine was the one who dealt with all her calls. No one would question it if she made and answered calls in Annette's office.

But then Colin Hauser was found murdered, and the next morning Loeb demanded information on every step of the police investigation. Shoulders hunched in Annette Tranh's office, as if the clerks in the main room could hear her, Janine whispered, "It's too dangerous! It's a murder!"

His voice crackled sharply in her ear. "In particular, I need copies of any paperwork from Hauser's study."

"I can't."

"Bullshit you can't. Letters, desk diary, invoices. Anything."

"Was it you who shot him?"

He was genuinely astounded. "What? No."

"But you had something going with him?"

"Not your concern. I need information, I need documents, and I need them now."

"Haven't I paid you back enough?"

"Not even close, Jan. Haven't you heard of compound interest?"

She could visualize him, a solid, smirking, dampish and dangerous shape in the driver's seat of his Lexus.

"You think Mr. Hauser left something incriminating," she said, feeling she had a slight upper hand here.

A pause while he gauged that. He said, "Look, if you do this one thing for me, I'll consider clearing the debt, okay? So, is there much paperwork?"

"I've collated most of it. Invoices, letters, contracts . . ."

"What about on his desk? Diary? Calendar? Address book?"

"Are you asking me to destroy evidence? It's been entered on the computer."

"Well, un-enter it, get me copies, destroy the originals."

"Then we're even, Ray. If I take a fall, you'll take a much harder one."

"Yeah, yeah," Raymond Loeb said.

Janine had tried to believe him. Truth be told, she didn't love Jeff anymore, he was pathetic. Big changes were needed. This one last thing for Loeb and then she was leaving with the kids.

NO OPPORTUNITY PRESENTED ITSELF at any time on Thursday, but now, Friday at noon, Janine headed out of the station and down High Street as though to buy lunch, the Colin Hauser desk diary and other material in a Kmart shopping bag. Past Blockbuster, the post office, Telstra, a discount chemist, the Port Authority, a pub, then across the road and down to the library. She paused on the steps. Out across the mangrove flats and the waters of the bay a pair of smokestacks shimmered, strong orange flames licking the sky.

She went in, asked to use the photocopier. She'd used it before.

The librarian smiled at her from behind the front desk. "Don't tell me, the police force is broke again."

Janine shrugged. "What can I say?"

With the approval of the senior sergeant in charge of the station, Janine had used the library's photocopier on police business once last month and twice the month before. The station's monthly budget didn't extend very far. Officers were forever supplying their own torch batteries, envelopes and postage stamps, even their own vehicles. Whenever the station's photocopiers ran out of paper or toner, it was down to the library for Janine.

She waited a few minutes for the machine to be free. A passing parade as usual: young mothers with little kids, retirees piling books into wire baskets, students tapping into the free wi-fi, battlers using the computers, a reading circle discussing a novel in the far corner. Janine had seen them before, had even lingered for a brief while, wanting to join in, but had anyone, anywhere, at any time in her life, asked for or welcomed her opinion on anything? No.

She waited, chatting to the librarian. An old man elbowed in, reciting the plot of a novel he wanted to borrow but couldn't remember the title of. Someone else had a genealogy inquiry. Another person wanted to dispute a two-dollar fine. Meanwhile the young woman using the copier was reproducing pages from a nursing mothers magazine one by one, at an agonizing pace. Read a page, frown. Align it carefully on the scanning glass, close the lid, press the button, gaze into space . . .

A woman from one of the estates, thought Janine sourly. Narrow, hunted-looking; and she'd been stupid enough to let someone impregnate her.

Janine caught herself. What's wrong with me?

The Kmart bag was heavy. She set it at her feet, rolled her shoulders, hoped there was plenty of A4 paper in the machine, plenty of coins in her purse.

It occurred to her that she was getting nothing out of her relationship with Raymond Loeb. She didn't have to do this to help Jeff anymore. She was getting nothing out of either man; in fact they were costing her.

21

CARL BOWIE OF BOWIE Bakehouses, outlets in Waterloo, Mt. Eliza and Mornington, spent Friday lunchtime in his main office, the Mornington branch, totting up figures: wages, payments in and out, projections. True, mince pies and plum puddings were flying off the shelves in the lead-up to Christmas, but he'd had to hire more staff and buy more ingredients. So he wasn't getting rich quickly selling baked goods.

Just as well he had a supplementary business model.

Business model. At the Grow Your Own Prosperity seminar on the Gold Coast last weekend (it was important that he had an alibi for the Friday) the term had been bandied about by everyone. Along with *Hesitate—too late* and *Failing to prepare is preparing to fail* and *Never let good-enough be enough.*

He'd taken it all in. He'd always taken that kind of stuff in, and applied it, and his success was a consequence.

Another one: *It's not your fault—but it is your responsibility.* A way of saying be prepared. So later that afternoon he locked his office door and switched his attention to the three screens placed edge to edge on the left-hand side of his desk. They showed live CCTV feed from each of the bakeries. Meanwhile his laptop was set up to receive the feed via wi-fi, split-screen so he could follow the action at all of his bakeries if he happened to be out shopping, lunching, sitting in his car or fucking Chloe Minchin.

The Waterloo outlet first. No customers at the moment, so that little bitch Tiffany thought she'd slip off to the toilet. Carl watched her hoist her skirt to her waist. A quick tinkle, a quick wipe, pants up, skirt smoothed down, hands washed—thank God—and back behind the cash register.

Where *three* customers were waiting.

Carl reached for the phone.

He watched Tiffany snatch it up, wedge it between ear and shoulder, freeing her hands to shove a baguette into a paper bag, take money, make change from the cash register, her voice in his ear saying, "Bowie Bakehouse, how may I help you?"

"Tiffany, I never want to see you leave the shop unattended again."

"But—"

Carl closed the call, switched to the Mt. Eliza store, where Lisa was sitting on a plastic delivery crate in the corridor at the rear of the shop, drinking a Coke while Roisin served customers.

He reached for the phone.

"Bowie Bakehouse, how may I help you?"

"Roisin."

"Yes, Mr. Bowie."

"What's Lisa think she's doing? Can she be seen by customers?"

The voice was weak and thready. "I don't think so, Mr. Bowie."

"Either way, it's not a good look. She can go out the back if she's on a break."

Roisin shot a quick, frightened look at the CCTV camera and scurried through the archway leading to the corridor, apparently said something to Lisa, hurried back behind the counter.

A moment later, Lisa joined her, meek as a mouse. Carl watched her serve, wipe crumbs away, sweep the floor, trying to look busy. A student, she was easily replaced, but students were a headache to employ, with their lecture and exam timetables, their meltdowns over boyfriends, the way they blithely switched shifts to attend music festivals. Carl was betting the people who ran grow-your-wealth seminars had never employed students.

He turned his attention to Mornington.

Meters from where he was sitting, Emily and Trina were busy, busy, busy. No customers at the moment, so they were wiping tables, sweeping, cleaning the display cabinets. It gave Carl Bowie immense satisfaction, seeing the fear, the diligence. He watched Emily for a while. Sixteen, still at school and this was the third day of her after-school trial period, 3:30 to 5:30 p.m. shift. He'd needed her to help with the general Christmas rush, but he wouldn't be calling her back. He hadn't paid her. He wouldn't pay her. Her parents might get pissy but fuck them, he wasn't a charity. She was on trial and hadn't passed the trial; suck it up.

Plenty of kids out there wanting a trial.

He fished a disposable mobile from his bottom drawer and called a woman who worked at the Somerville Pharmacy. Without preamble he said, "It's about your cousin, Nick."

"What?"

"Tell him if he doesn't come up with the nine grand he owes me by Sunday, *your* car will be torched."

"*Who? What?*"

He made another call, reaching a scratchy old voice. "You're Sophie's grandfather?"

"Who is this?"

"Tell Sophie she does not simply walk away. The cost for doing so is thirty-five thousand dollars, you got that?"

"I beg your pardon?"

A KEY ASPECT OF Carl's business model, the employment of cleanskins.

People like Chloe, Sophie and Nick were from respectable families and had never come to the attention of the police. Also, Carl kept them at a far remove, just as Chloe kept her runners at a far remove.

And if anyone stepped out of line, he didn't threaten *them* but their families.

A sound business model also involved sound intelligence. Carl opened his laptop and logged on to a news service. He liked to follow any story that impinged on him in some way—like the Waterloo meth lab. Unfortunately, that story had made way for others pretty quickly. Today's main story was a road-rage incident out near Bacchus Marsh, a guy crossing four lanes of traffic and crashing head-on into a station wagon driven by a pregnant schoolteacher. Then he'd piled out of his car and attacked the station wagon with a tire lever. Pulled the woman out of the car and punched her in the stomach before other motorists managed to grab him and throw him to the ground.

Carl sighed. Dirty drug, ice. But that was none of his concern. He was a supplier, not a social worker. If an individual couldn't control himself, was Carl to blame? Besides, the road-rage incident had occurred out west of Melbourne. Nowhere near his patch.

But he wished the meth-lab story hadn't vanished. They *had* been on his patch, muscling in.

TIME TO GO HOME. He did a quick final check of the monitors, satisfied himself that everyone was bright and perky,
and walked out to his car, a black Audi, 1BAKE on the number plate.

However, the car took him not home but down the coast
to Chloe's house, a brick, steel and glass cube overlooking
Safety Beach. Finding her topless on a banana lounge
beside her pool, the water shimmeringly blue, a hard glitter
in the afternoon sun, he stopped. Drinking in her olive skin,
gleaming with coconut oil.

"Hi," he said huskily, crouching beside her chair.

She lifted her sunglasses, gave him a sleepy smile that
altered as he watched, languor dissolving into need. Her
lips were large, moist, her eyes vivid. Even her nipples stared
at him hungrily, and he couldn't stand it.

Cleared his throat. "You all set for tomorrow?"

Tomorrow she was making the run to the border. "I'm all
set for *now*," she said, and, in one fluid articulation of her
legs, waist and torso, was out of the chair and dragging him
toward the house.

"Wait one second," she said, after they'd crossed the cool
living-area tiles and entered her bedroom.

His mouth dry, Carl watched her open a drawer and take
out a sweet puff. She dropped a couple of rocks into the
bowl, thumbed a lighter, heated the bowl, sucked deeply on
the pipe.

"Jesus, Chloe."

She drew again, held it in, slowly released. "Want some?"

"How long you been using?"

"Come on, couple of puffs won't hurt, the sex will be
amazing."

How did she know that? Other men? Women? Had she
been high the other times he'd been with her and he

hadn't noticed? Was she high when she made her runs up north?

Not part of his business model. "I thought you understood, no using."

"No, Carl, *you* understood that, I didn't."

"It's not good business sense, Chloe. I need my management team fully on the ball. Please, put the pipe away. Chuck it in the bin."

She gave him a look full of conniving glee. "You don't know what you're missing, Carl."

"I need you to have a clear head tomorrow."

"Tomorrow's tomorrow. This is now. Chill out. Have a puff, then have me."

She peeled off her bikini pants. Her body seemed to alter, open up, pull him in. He swallowed.

But Carl hadn't got where he'd got in business by taking his eye off the ball.

"Later," he said, turning his back on all that and walking out to the car.

HIS WIFE'S CAR, a white Mercedes coupe, 2BAKE, was parked in the driveway when he reached home, high on a ridge in Mt. Eliza. He was the first to admit it was a hideous house, a starter palace designed by his wife's architect and decorated with a dominant motif of self-indulgence. What he particularly loathed was the mahogany chess set in the hallway, each piece the size of a wine bottle, set out on a thick base of polished, crosshatched steel.

No one in the fucking family even played chess.

Not for the first time, Carl reflected that he'd married down. Bowie was an old Peninsula name, there'd been Bowie bakeries since the 1940s, when his grandfather started the business in Rosebud. Carl's father inherited, and added the

Waterloo bakery, then died when Carl was five. It all very nearly ended there. His mother started drinking and married an alcoholic; together they got cracking on drinking away the Bowie fortune and dying of alcoholism.

What they hadn't drunk away was the modest trust set up for Carl by his father. His education was expensive—Geelong Grammar—and at the age of twenty-one he'd cut all ties with his mother, stepfather and half-brother and begun buying back the bakeries. He wasn't interested in baking, really, he just wanted to make a point.

Guys he'd gone to school with were CEOs, bankers, top QCs, army officers and diplomats. Well, he had a bakery empire. But back before he had a business model he'd let his dick guide him.

"Honey, I'm home," he called, sending up the phrase as he sauntered in, tossed his keys on the hall table.

And there was his wife, blonde, gym-toned like all her friends, skin stretched to splitting point over her cheekbones, holding out the phone. "It's for you. Didn't say his name."

Didn't have to say his name to Carl. Carl recognized the voice. Hector Kaye. Up in Sydney, wanting to know where the hell his boys were.

22

ALLIE HAD WOKEN TO a dozen texts from Clive on Friday morning: *You light my way; The girl of my dreams; Without you I'd be nothing; She walks in beauty; I'll never tire of looking at you.* Stuff like that.

Never *tire*? It couldn't be auto-correct; it wouldn't have put in a British spelling.

Her gorgeous man had sent a couple of risqué texts, too, that made her a little fluttery inside: *I want to taste you* and *I long to be inside you.*

They had made love, once, a few days ago. It hadn't been earth-shattering but she was quite enthusiastic about the prospect of doing it again. Practice makes perfect and all that.

Except he always had things to do, places to be, people to meet, and he'd tap the side of his nose in that old gesture— making her complicit in whatever plans he'd made.

Something photography-related? Was he taking moody nude shots of eighteen-year-olds? Or some other lover?

Now it was late Friday afternoon and she was in her first-floor sitting room on the Esplanade in Mornington, looking out over the sea. Heat beat in at her from the other side of the vast glass wall; she was fighting it with a gin and tonic in a tall, frosted glass. Ice and a twist of lemon. Norah Jones singing in the background. Having a man in her life should have been the cure for her nagging dissatisfaction, but Clive wasn't exactly *in* her life, not with all of his comings, goings and secrecy. Flooding her with texts, emails and presents was all very well, but she wanted old-fashioned attention and a warm body in her bed.

The front door buzzer sounded. She clopped downstairs in her sandals and there was Clive with a huge grin, a huge bunch of red roses and a huge wad of travel brochures. Her heart turned over and she planted a smacking kiss.

"I wasn't expecting you."

She stood back to let him in, half-listening to his patter as they climbed the stairs. Been busy . . . Missing her . . . Thought he'd surprise her . . . Did he need a reason to drop in on his lovely?

Turned to face him when they reached the sitting room, kissed him again and smacked her forehead, saying, "What am I thinking? I'll get a vase," and clattered downstairs again. She returned in a more orderly fashion, gathering herself as she arranged the roses, finally joining him at the feature window where the waters of the bay were laid out like a pane of blue glass. He put his arm around her. She molded herself against his solid, reassuring shape.

"Allie," he said, "there's something I have to tell you."

She froze, pulling away from him, but his arm was as stiff and binding as a cable around her. "It's not what you think," he said.

"You're married, aren't you? You want to break it off."

"No, never." He let her go, turned her to face him, his hands on her upper arms. "I love you, you know that."

"Do you?"

"You know I do. But sweetheart, I need to tell you something serious. It's to do with my work. It's a national security matter."

"Your work?" she said, reeling a little.

"I need you to promise me you won't repeat what I'm about to tell you."

"How can I promise that when—"

"Like I said, it's a national security matter."

The words sank in. Now a lot of things made sense, his unexplained absences and secrecy. He leaned his rugged face to her until they were nose to nose. "Promise?"

"Promise," she said.

"About leaving the Army—that was a cover story. I'm in fact on active duty, national intelligence with the cooperation of Homeland Security in the United States."

"Okay," she said, feeling light-headed.

"Sometimes I have to fly overseas, secret work, risky situations."

"God." She didn't know what else to say.

"I couldn't tell you before. I needed to be sure of you."

"This is all a bit unreal, Clive," she said. "I mean, it's like a movie. Are you about to go on one of these . . . these . . . missions?"

He eyed her searchingly. "Short answer, yes."

"And the long answer? You're not coming back?"

He waved that away. "Of course I am, I can't live without you, can't you see that? Dear, dear Allie."

He gestured at the travel brochures, which he'd piled on the coffee table. "When this is all over, I want you to come away with me, somewhere exotic and romantic."

She could see the islands of Tahiti. Angkor Wat. A white sail and blue waters in the Bahamas. Lovely . . .

She glued herself to his solid chest. "Don't leave me," she said, her voice muffled, partly wanting him to hear her say it, partly conscious of sounding pathetic.

His voice rumbled, a deep bass sound in his powerful

chest. "The thing is, I can't be a hundred per cent certain my cover hasn't been blown."

Allie pulled away from him in dismay. "Pardon?"

"My cover may have been blown."

"You're in danger?"

"Could be. My handlers"—he shook his head—"well, you don't want to know."

She was caught up in the implied threat from powerful hidden forces. "You don't trust them?"

"Allie, the thing is, if I'm in danger, *you're* in danger."

"What? How?"

"If my cover has been blown, then certain people will know of my relationship to you. I'm sorry, but you could be vulnerable. And I need to keep you safe."

"But how?"

"There are ways of making you invisible to these people but everyone leaves a paper record. If we were to put this house, your car, your finances and so on in someone else's name, that would make it all that much harder for you to be found. It's not something we can delay," he said, looking at her in a way that laid bare the depths of his regret and heartbreak.

She pursed her lips, thinking of the hoops she'd have to jump through. "It might take a while. The car's easy. But my money's kind of tied up and this house isn't mine, I rent it."

He stiffened against her. "Rent it?"

"When I divorced Rick, I thought it'd be best to put it all in superannuation."

A complicated expression crossed his face and she was, for the briefest moment, frightened. But then his face cleared. "You did the right thing. I can't tell you how glad I am."

Relieved, she snuggled against him, her cheek on his

hard chest, drawing in a mix of Clive smell and talc. "But the car should be easy."

He squeezed her. "We'll start there."

FRIDAY AFTERNOON WAS PAM Murphy's first opportunity to run a more thorough background check on Michael Traill. Here it was, after 5 P.M., and she was logged on to the force's LEAP system, reading all she could find on the killing of David Booker before she crossed town for her appointment at Mervyn White Realty.

She was steamed up before she even began. It was bad enough that Challis hadn't taken her side, but she was also cross with herself for letting Michael Traill—the man rather than the news story—unsettle her. He'd looked tired when she visited him, sad. He'd carried himself with a measure of dignity when another man might have bitched, moaned and sulked.

All an act, she thought sourly.

Yet there was that contradictory pull inside her. When she'd left Traill on Wednesday, pocketed her notebook and nodded a curt goodbye, she'd felt a completely contradictory impulse. To step closer to him, into his orbit.

What was that about?

She read through the notes on file, including witness statements. David Booker had been in an exuberant mood, said some witnesses. In an obnoxious mood, said others. He'd shouted the bar; he'd been grinning and boisterous all evening. But three witnesses had seen him clamp his hands around a young woman's upper arm, leaving vivid bruises. He'd hissed something at her, they said, his face contorted in rage. When called to the stand, the woman said she had no memory of the incident. Meanwhile bar staff had several times asked Booker's party to keep the noise down and been abused by him. There was another young woman, a drinks waitress, first week in a new job. "I stood too close to him," she told the court, "and he felt my . . . my rear." The prosecution hammered her, getting her to admit that in the hurly-burly of a busy bar, she could expect a carelessly flung hand or arm to make fleeting contact with intimate parts of the body from time to time.

No wonder women don't report sexual assaults, Pam thought.

And why hadn't the media reported this side of the story? Why had they concentrated on Traill and his fatal punch? Because everyone thought Booker was God? She certainly had.

Now she didn't know what to think. She read on. One conclusion was unmistakable: Booker wasn't God. If he'd been drinking, he could be the devil.

She logged out, checked her emails. One from Ellen Destry: "Sincere thanks, your tip was sound, we have a pattern emerging. If you hear of any other questionable burglaries, let me know ASAP."

An email from Scobie Sutton. The Colt AR15 found in the burnt-out Mercedes had yielded a serial number. It was registered to a Merricks North orchardist named Arnold Coxhell. He'd reported it stolen six weeks earlier.

She debated visiting Coxhell, called him instead. If he hadn't reported the theft, then she would have gone in with backup. "We've found your rifle, Mr. Coxhell. Unfortunately it was involved in a crime and has been damaged."

He asked the right questions. "A crime? Hell. Was anyone hurt?"

"I can't comment on that at this stage."

He subsided on the end of the line. "Oh, right, sorry."

"Mr. Coxhell, do you know a man named Colin Hauser?"

"Colin? Sure. It's terrible what—Wait, are you saying he was shot with my gun?"

"How do you know him?"

"Westernport Sporting Shooters," Coxhell said, an edge of hysteria in his voice. "Look, did he—"

Pam was regretting the call. "Mr. Coxhell, we're investigating a string of gun thefts from rural properties in the past several months."

Coxhell said, "Well yeah, of course, we've heard stories."

"Have these stories pointed in any particular direction? Any names bandied about?"

"No."

"Do you know a man named Owen Valentine?"

"Nope, can't say I do."

Then Murphy's mother called.

"Are we all set for Sunday, dear?"

"All set."

"I know you can be called away at a moment's notice . . ."

"Not this time," Pam said warmly. "I've squared it away with my boss. I thought we'd walk on the Flinders pier, have lunch at a winery . . ."

"Oh, I know exactly where I want to go, dear."

Pam checked her watch, panicked, said goodbye to her mother and raced down the stairs. Threaded her way through the bottleneck in the main corridor, men and women gossiping, sipping cups of water from the cooler, discussing weekend plans. Happened to glance into the large room at the end, near the door to the car park. The domain of the civilian staff, clerks, typists, intelligence collators, it had emptied of everyone except Janine Quine, who was standing helplessly at a desk piled with material Pam recognized as coming from the Hauser murder scene.

She stepped in. "Everything okay, Jan?"

Quine jumped violently, her hand going to her throat. "You frightened me."

"Sorry," Pam said, not feeling sorry. She disliked Quine. The dislike had been immediate and powerful the very first day she met Quine, earlier in the year. "Anything wrong?" she repeated.

"I'm just collating the paperwork belonging to that man who was shot."

"It shouldn't be left out in the open like this, Janine. It's sensitive material, relating to a murder. We're still gathering evidence and some of this paperwork could be crucial."

"I'm working as fast as I can."

"Glad to hear it," Pam said. "When it's all itemized, please lock it away."

"I will."

Pam turned on her heel, feeling faintly ashamed, and went out to her car.

FIVE MINUTES LATER SHE was in the office of Mervyn White Real Estate, White himself confirming that the figure was correct. "That's what the landlord's asking."

He said it apologetically, a man with silvery hair, a somber suit, a garish tie, a calm, scraped-clean man on the other side of a vast desk. "Sorry, Ms. Murphy," he added.

Pam spluttered, "But two days ago he was asking fifty dollars a week *less*."

Not that it mattered: she was too late, the little Balnarring house already rented.

The agent looked at her sadly. "For what it's worth, our firm handles a third of the residential property market on the Peninsula, and that house was the first vacant one we'd had in two months. Vacancy rates are at an all-time low."

"So landlords can charge what they like."

"Pretty much."

"I'll never find a place as good as the one I'm in now."

"Pity your landlord wants to sell. Look, you might have to try further afield. Gippsland. Dandenong. The Latrobe Valley."

"I need to be close to work. I can't live ninety minutes away."

"People do it."

"People aren't on call at a moment's notice."

He shrugged.

She gnawed her bottom lip. "I'm on a reasonable salary. How do the battlers manage?"

"Food parcels," the agent said.

Pam shot him a look. Was he being snide? No. If anything, he looked troubled.

"We have a one-bedroom unit in Waterloo available in the next few weeks."

Pam shook her head. "Rule of thumb, Merv, if you're police you don't live among your clients."

He gave her a quick grin. "Clients."

"Repeat clients, a lot of them," Pam said.

She drove desultorily, not wanting to go home just yet. For a while she steered in and around Tyabb, Somerville and Baxter, as if a FOR RENT sign might appear, hammered into the front lawn of some gorgeous little house.

She could take out a mortgage, but her financial history was patchy, her prior decisions skewed in unwise directions.

Shook herself and headed back across the Peninsula toward home, taking back roads. Maybe a cute farmhouse would announce itself.

What announced itself was the poultry farm gate, the glimpse of the poultry sheds and Michael Traill's caravan parked at the rear.

WTF? Cross with herself, dismayed and embarrassed, she sped past.

23

ON SATURDAY MORNING, TENSE as he always was when Chloe made a run to the border, Carl Bowie flicked around his CCTV monitors. In the Waterloo bakery, Liv stood slack-jawed behind the counter, staring into space. No customers right at that moment, but Carl saw clearly the dirty cups and crumpled napkins on one of the tables. *Get off your arse, Olivia.* Every now and then her jaw made chewing motions—her mouth open—as if recalling that a wad of gum was still lodged there.

He called the store, watching as she snapped awake and glanced fearfully at one of the cameras. "Bowie Bakehouse, Liv speaking, how may I help you?"

"Olivia, what I want of you, what I simply expect of all my staff, is a fair day's work for a fair day's pay and a pleasant, professional demeanor. You with me?"

"Yes, Mr. Bowie."

"So be a good girl and spit out that chewing gum, all right?"

"Yes, Mr. Bowie."

"And if you really want me to be a happy chappie, *clean the fucking mess off that table.*" Having no wish to hear her say, "Yes, Mr. Bowie, sorry, Mr. Bowie," he cut the connection. He wiped a fleck of spittle from the monitor.

Then he checked his watch. Chloe should be at the motel by now. He called her, using one of his disposable mobiles.

"Carl, I'm still in the car."

"All good?"

"All good."

"Where are you?"

"Just coming into Mildura now. Carl, I have to go."

The line went dead. Carl sat back and watched the monitors gloomily and thought of the call from Hector Kaye yesterday, wanting to know where Lovelock and Pym had got to.

"Haven't seen them," he'd said.

"*No word for a fucking week*," Kaye said.

"Look, Hector, they texted to say the job was done, I paid you. That's all I know."

Since that call, Carl had put two and two together. What he got was last Friday's bushfire, flames engulfing a Mercedes. He agonized. Maybe he should call Hector back, say something like: "Now that you mention it, we had a couple of guys die here when their car got caught in a bushfire."

He tried to think through the ramifications if the dead men *were* Hector's boys. Had they been identified yet? Identified but not linked to Hector? Identified, and linked to Hector, but the cops were biding their time? But what would the police do when the time came? How would Hector account for Lovelock and Pym's actions south of the border? If Hector goes down, Carl thought, what are the implications for me? And right then, Carl felt a creepy inversion, the CCTV cameras watching *him*, the walls closing in, the shadowy corners deepening all around him. He knew what Kaye was capable of. The guy had a tattoo for each man he'd killed, for fuck's sake.

Carl rubbed his face to clear a tic that had developed beside his right eye. His knee jiggling, he texted Chloe: *All good?*

Minutes passed, then his phone beeped, incoming: *Same as five minutes ago.*

Bitch.

FEELING NOT ENTIRELY SURE that his kingdom was intact, Bowie drove to the gym. Early afternoon, a quiet time. He could work out in peace, not feel crowded and looked at by dozens of men and women gasping and sweating around him. A sign in the foyer said YOUR BODY IS A TEMPLE, and Carl muttered, as he always did, "Or a moderately well-run Presbyterian youth center." He'd heard it on a comedy show a long time ago.

Not so funny anymore.

God, he felt jittery.

Some stretching, weights, an aerobics routine; finish with a few laps of the pool. The exercise cleared the immediate brain fog, but didn't answer any of his more pressing questions.

Say for a moment it wasn't Lovelock and Pym in the burnt-out car but a pair of ordinary luckless civilians . . . What if their text, *It's done,* had been intended to lull him into a false sense of security? What if Hector Kaye had briefed Lovelock and Pym to team up with Owen as the start of a move against him? Or what if Lovelock and Pym, acting alone, had teamed up with Owen? Or what if Owen had got the better of Lovelock and Pym?

He should call Hector. Stress again that as soon as he'd got word the job was done, he'd transferred the rest of the fee, upheld his side of the bargain. If Lovelock and Pym got killed accidentally, it wasn't his fault.

Surely?

Turning under the change room shower, Carl wondered if outsourcing the hit on Owen instead of doing it himself had gone *against* notions of a good business model.

~

HE WAS ALMOST TEMPTED to sample his own product.

But look what it had done to Owen.

So he drove home and hit the scotch, "accidentally" knocking over a rook with his briefcase as he passed the chess set. His wife was off playing tennis, the kids were God knows where, so he had the place to himself and he sat and paced and thought until deep into the afternoon.

A part of him said: pull the plug, get out while you're ahead. He had millions tucked away where no one could get it. Let this be Chloe's last trip. She was a cleanskin, nothing traced back to her. Ditto her runners. They knew her, but not where she lived or her real name, and they certainly didn't know him.

But what if Hector didn't like that idea?

What if *Chloe* was moving against him? She was getting cocky.

He tried to count his reasons for staying in the game. Fear of Sydney: got that, let's not think about that. The money was good. He was at arm's length from his operations. Business was booming, and according to Chloe, who'd heard it from her runners, new market opportunities were opening up out in the Yarra Valley and closer to the Belgrave–Monbulk area.

Would she let him know things like that if she was moving against him? He texted her: *All good?*

The reply came back a long time later. *Fucking good, all right?*

New territories would mean more dealers, more clients, greater managerial responsibilities. There was always someone who paid late, or not at all, or not the full price.

Always someone who wanted to pull out, or start their own operation. Always someone who might be working for the cops or the opposition.

He didn't think he could stand that. And now he tasted blood. He'd bitten the inside of his mouth.

24

IN THE BAD OLD days, sexual assault victims were questioned first by uniformed officers, usually male, then by detectives, usually male, and then—if they were unlucky, or the paperwork was mislaid or inaccurate, or the detectives were transferred or took leave—by even more detectives, one after the other. These detectives would be busy, distracted, working car theft, burglary and other cases. Some of them didn't much like women, others had no empathy, or tended to victim-blaming, and a handful were themselves given to exploiting their authority to commit sexual assaults. That left a small number of detectives who had the nous, sensitivity and experience to be good sex-crimes investigators.

Meanwhile, in the absence of single points of contact, specialists to act in their best interests, or clear avenues for counseling, the victims were further traumatized. Then, in court, defense barristers would go all-out to discredit them:

"How many sexual partners have you had?"

"What were you wearing?"

"How intoxicated were you?"

"You were carrying condoms in your purse, were you not?"

"I put it to you that you were flirting with the accused."

The old days . . .

At least specialist detectives handled each incident from start to finish now, taking victim statements, referring victims to counselors from the Center Against Sexual Assault, investigating and arresting offenders, and following the case through the court system. Trials had become less traumatic. Victims were more prepared to come forward.

But Ellen Destry knew that vestiges of the old system remained. The majority of sexual assaults continued to go unreported, and there were still uniformed police, detectives, lawyers, magistrates and judges who paid no more than lip service to the reforms. In action, speech, body language and legal rulings it was clear they saw fault in the victim, excused many assaults as male high spirits, and didn't understand the short- and long-term impacts on victims.

Was Ian Judd one of these men?

He'd been a good thief catcher before moving to sex crimes. He was proving to be a good sex-crimes investigator. But a couple of victims had found him to be—in the words of one of them—"stiff, reproving."

And so, after dropping Hal at Waterloo Automotive on her way to work, Ellen called Judd into her office and began a slow, careful assessment of what made him tick.

"OUR MAN'S CLEARLY A commuter," she said.

Judd nodded. She could see him thinking. He cocked his head and said, "Uh huh," wondering where she was going.

"Remember that conference earlier in the year, the four categories . . . ?"

Hosted by the Criminology Department of the University of Melbourne, attended by sex-crimes detectives, lawyers, counselors, academics and postgrad students, four sessions a day, lectures and workshops. A keynote address by an FBI profiler who spoke about four types of violent sexual attacks: power–reassurance, power–assertion, anger–retaliation, anger–excitement.

"I remember," Judd said, pushing his glasses back on his nose.

"How would you rate our man?"

"May I ask why?"

"Humor me, Ian."

She knew he had a prodigious memory and an analytical mind. She saw the mind at work in his eyes, saw his long unseeing stare as he began to sort, order and select.

"He could be after reassurance. Let's say he has doubts about his sexuality: he's attacking women to prove he's not gay. Meanwhile, his inability to achieve and maintain an erection *feeds* this doubt, so he keeps raping, or trying to rape."

"Or he's a heroin addict and can't get it up," Ellen said, "or can't get a woman in the normal social sense because he stinks."

A tightness in Judd's face. He didn't like to be interrupted. "According to the FBI profiler, the power–reassurance rapist is a careful planner and not overly violent—which seems to fit our guy."

"Grabbing a woman?" said Ellen. "Tying her up, gagging her, cutting off her clothes . . . ?"

Judd shook his head. "I'm not downplaying that, Ellen. What I mean is, he doesn't punch or kick or stab or torture."

"Okay. So does he fit the power–assertive category?"

Judd was emphatic. "No."

"Explain."

"For a start, he doesn't know these women."

"As far as we know."

"As far as we know he hadn't met any of them beforehand. He hadn't had a date with them, made sexual advances to them at a party . . . He hadn't met them, hadn't been rebuffed by them, so there's no indication that these rapes were revenge attacks for being rebuffed."

"Unless," Ellen said, "there was an early assault we don't know about, and he decided he liked the experience."

She watched Judd consider that, his frowning concentration, the rapid mental testing and sifting, as if the exercise were academic and there were no real-life victims.

Perhaps that was part of the problem with Judd—if there was one. It wasn't that he was hostile or unsympathetic to women—he was first and foremost a man who saw the world in analytical, not emotional, terms.

Finally he gave his answer. "I don't buy that, frankly. He's a planner. The first assault might have been spur of the moment, committed during a burglary, but the burglaries, and the subsequent rapes, show planning. I'm not discounting hate, even rage, but it's controlled."

"Okay, anger–retaliation?"

She watched Judd put his mind to it. Time passed.

"Possibly," he said. "There is an element of humiliation in his treatment of his victims. Does he feel anger toward all women? Maybe. He's clearly not targeting a specific physical type. But, again, he's a planner and not overly violent. Identifying the target, scouting her house and her street, breaking in, waiting, then the orchestrated attack—each one's an important stage in a process."

Ellen found herself thinking not about Judd's apparent shortcomings as a victim interviewer but their shared concern, catching a rapist. She said, "You're right. He needs all of these elements. He's not impulsive."

"Apart from that first attack."

"Yes."

"That leaves us with the anger–excitement rapist," Judd said, as if taking charge.

But he waited, eyeing Ellen. She looked at the ceiling, trying to remember the definition of the anger–excitement rapist. "Some of the elements are there," she said presently. "Location, tools, method—all carefully worked out. And he probably gets a thrill out of seeing fear in his victims."

"But he's not sadistic in the sense of inflicting great pain," Judd said. "No torture."

Ellen nodded glumly. "Maybe in a sick way he's looking for love. Makes them a cup of tea, stays for a chat, says he's worried about their security. Imagines a relationship, almost."

"I don't think so. I think it's cheek. He's having a laugh."

Ellen saw something in that. She shivered. "A cruel laugh."

"Yes," Judd said, and he was watching her again.

"Ellen," he said, "trying to find a category for this bloke is a waste of time, in my opinion. Let the shrinks come up with the category after we've caught him. It's police work that'll catch him, not pontificating."

"It's good to understand him, Ian."

"No, it isn't," Judd said, and he was unshakeable.

"Ian," Ellen said gently, "I've been talking to Robin Lincoln."

The Lincoln case dated back some time and was just now limping through the system. Judd was the investigating officer.

"And?"

"Since the rape, she's moved house three times."

He gazed at her levelly. She had no idea what he was thinking.

"She used to like living alone, now she needs others around her. Then if they're careless about security, she has to look for others to live with. Mentally, she's in a terrible state. Apparently her friends confiscated her car keys, worried she'd do something stupid like kill herself or kill others."

"I know that," Judd said flatly.

"All I'm asking is, go easy on her."

Meaning, go easy on every victim.

He blinked, genuinely baffled. "What do you mean? I'm understanding. I'm sympathetic. But we have to cut through the dross sometimes."

Ellen hated this. She liked Judd, she realized. He was an unmovable block of wood, that's all. "A smile, a nod," she said. "Listen, be understanding, don't interrupt, don't judge."

"I don't judge. Never that," Judd said. He paused. "I judge the pricks who do it, though. You can count on that."

MEANWHILE CHALLIS STOOD ON the forecourt of Waterloo Automotive, viewing his car. Parked at the side of the building, freshly washed, all of the road dust sluiced away, the little BMW looked sleek and desirable, and he was torn.

Bernie Joske sauntered out, as always wiping his hands on a grimy rag. "Good to go, mate."

"The damage?"

"Parts plus labor, four twenty-five."

"Christ."

Joske made a gesture of appeal. "Mate, what can I say."

"Yeah, yeah," Challis said. Then he made a slight inquiring motion with his head.

Joske read it. "Come inside and we'll settle the bill."

Joske's office was at the side of the building, his daughter, who handled his invoices, in a smaller adjoining office. "Got some car options to discuss, love," he said, and shut the door, sealing him in with Challis.

Challis glanced through the half-glass wall to the service bays, the hoists, tools and mechanics busy in their overalls. "Someone moving farm vehicles and machinery, earth-moving equipment . . . Any joy?"

Joske gave him a humorless smile. Shifting in his chair he said comfortably, "One of me nephews has the sheriff after him."

"Let me guess, unpaid fines."

"Four grand's worth, the little idiot," said Joske. He paused. "My sister's boy. Not the sharpest knife in the drawer. I told him, Darren, that slip of paper stuck to your windscreen means something, it's a parking fine, not a Christmas decoration. It means you overstayed at the meter, it means you parked on a yellow line." Joske shook his head. "But everything I say goes in one ear and out the other. It's like, if he ignores it, it'll go away. But he's my sister's youngest, she's a single mum, and I try to help out where I can, you know?"

"Sounds like he needs some tough love," Challis said.

Joske grimaced. "Well said. You're a king among men. But he's family, Hal."

"I can't make the fines disappear."

"But . . ."

"A payment plan, maybe. Say, a hundred a week. Or a reassessment of the total."

"We can live with that," Joske said.

But could Challis? It would mean asking a favor of someone else, and favors tended to pile onto favors . . .

"So, is anyone moving farm and winery and earthmoving gear?"

Bernie Joske said, "I'm still sniffing around, but there's a whisper about an operation down the coast, maybe Inverloch. But I don't know who or exactly where. Yet."

A strange relationship, policeman and informant. What motivates a snitch? Bernie was on the books as a registered informant, he was always paid, but money didn't drive him; he earned a comfortable living mending cars. Perhaps the money and the favors owed made him feel better about his treacheries. And Challis was certain Bernie was selective in the information he passed on. Avoiding potential trouble for himself, damaging competitors or avenging some slight. He'd once steered Challis to a mechanic dealing in rebirthed chassis, Challis learning later the mechanic had outbid Joske at a car auction.

Not that Challis didn't have other informants. Policing couldn't occur without them. But he disliked the dependency, the reciprocity. And he knew never to sink all of his hopes in a man like Bernie J. It was impossible to know how long Bernie would go on giving useful information, or stay a step ahead of the law himself, or even stay alive. And Challis could never be sure there wasn't a forestalling or diverting factor behind it, with Bernie pointing him in one direction and pulling something shady in the opposite direction.

One thing was for sure, Challis would never let himself be spotted in public with the man. He'd risk being tagged as Bernie's tame copper, a policeman on the take.

"Let me know as soon as you hear anything definite."

"Will do."

25

ALLIE'S VOICE ON THE phone was tense, trembling with excitement.

"I have to see you."

Ellen had been passing the Dromana drive-in cinemas, heading for home, but pulled over to take the call. Traffic streamed south on the freeway overpass, the sun was low, she was tired. "I'll be home in a tick."

"Are you in the car? Turn around and come to my place. Please? It's important."

Ellen grumbled, said goodbye, called Challis. "Did you get your car back okay?"

"Yep."

"Good. I'll be a bit late. Allie wants to see me about something."

"She okay?"

"Just another drama."

Ellen pulled out and took the up-ramp north, and on to the Craigie Road exit and down to the beach and from there to the Esplanade in Mornington.

SHE STOOD AT ALLIE'S vast upstairs window, drawn, as ever, to the view of the bay. A container ship was steaming for Port Phillip Heads. But she was thinking about the travel brochures spilled across the coffee table and guessed the nature of her sister's news.

Then Allie was entering behind her, carrying chunky glass tumblers of gin and tonic, ice, a slice of lemon. Condensation beaded the glass. Ellen itched to grab her drink and sink it, a balm for a difficult day, but said, "Light on the gin?"

"I know you have to drive, Ells," Allie said. She was flushed, eyes sparkling, as she handed Ellen one of the glasses.

Cool and moist and more tonic than gin. Ellen sank, relieved, into an armchair, sipped again and placed the glass on a coaster. It was right beside a brochure for Tahiti.

"Going on a trip?"

A blaze in her sister's eyes. "Yes!"

"With Clive?"

"Yep," Allie said, a slight challenge in her jaw.

"That's nice," Ellen said, peering at the brochures. "Where, exactly?"

Allie put her head on one side, the other, as if tossing up. "I haven't decided yet. Clive sprung it on me."

Ellen wanted to tread carefully, but in the end said baldly, "He's paying?"

"Why does everything have to be about money with you?"

Mainly because I don't have much of it, thought Ellen. But at least she'd found out where the money was coming from. Side-stepping, she said, "Sounds like fun. When are you going?"

"Soon."

Ellen frowned. "You'll be here for Christmas though?"

"Sure."

Christmas. They both sat and stared vacantly at the walls. A year earlier, their parents had sold up and moved to a small home unit in a retirement village.

"But you're not *old*," Ellen had protested.

"Of course we're not," her mother said.

"It's a *retirement* village," her father said, "not an aged-care place."

Ellen remembered that first Christmas in her parents' new home. Everything about the day seemed wrong: the tiny rooms, nothing familiar, the spirit of family somehow diminished. Her parents' old home—her family home— had absorbed the love and goodwill of scores of Christmases and birthdays and always seemed to give it back. Their new home, their little *box*, was arid.

But the daughters were expected. The dutiful daughters.

"So when is your trip?"

"As soon as Clive gets back. Sometime in the new year."

"Where's he gone?"

Allie's gaze slid to a corner of the room. "Away on business."

Ellen said tightly, "Are you bringing him for Christmas?"

Allie studied another corner of the room. "Probably not."

Ellen left it. "What do you want for Christmas?"

Allie extended a sleek leg and waggled a shapely foot. "There are some strappy sandals I've had my eye on."

"Okay."

"Late night shopping, I could show them to you."

"Now?"

"Sure. Why not?"

"Could we go in separate cars? I'm a bit stuck for time."

Allie examined the coffee table. "Actually, Clive borrowed my car."

Damn, thought Ellen. She just wanted to get home and go out for a meal with Challis. "Oh. Okay."

"It won't take long, honest."

Ellen sighed. "Sure."

"I'll get my things."

Allie slipped from the room, light as a fairy. There are no half measures with my sister, Ellen thought. Either she's floating on air or she's a stone around our necks.

Listening out for returning footsteps, she used her car keys to slide two of the travel brochures into her bag.

THEY CHATTED ABOUT THIS and that as Ellen headed along the Esplanade and right onto Main Street, scanning left and right for a parking spot. Late Saturday afternoon, two weeks until Christmas, she didn't like her chances.

"Will Clive be away for long?"

"Not sure."

"Where's he gone?"

"Oh, just business."

"I haven't told you what *I* want for Christmas," Ellen said. And you haven't asked me. You never do—you always buy me a last-minute thing I don't like or need.

"What?"

"One of those French cast-iron cooking pots. Pale blue."

"Aren't they expensive?"

Always aim high first, Ellen thought. "Or a full set of *House of Cards* DVDs."

"Okay."

"The American series. If it's not too expensive."

"No, that's okay."

Ellen swung the car left, down toward the car park beside Target. It was crammed. She drove up and down, peering. "Allie, if you're short of cash, it doesn't matter."

"It's all right, I said."

"I mean, if you need money for the trip, or you've given Clive a loan or something, I quite understand."

"Everything's fine, he'll pay me back," Allie said, folding her arms, upright in her seat.

Ellen slowed and steered carefully into a narrow space between a Mazda and an Audi—which was parked over the line, of course, as though it deserved two spaces. "How much?" she asked, careful not to glance at her sister.

Allie said, "He had some hospital bills to pay," and, from her voice, Ellen pictured her sister's face, mulish, stubborn and righteous, the face she wore when accused of something, caught in a lie or burdened by some request or demand.

Her usual face.

"He's ill?" Ellen asked.

"His niece, if you must know. His sister's girl. They're treating her for leukemia."

"Poor child, that's awful," Ellen said neutrally.

"They've all had a rough trot, his family."

"What are they like?"

"I'll meet them, hopefully, after Christmas," Allie said.

Ellen pulled on the handbrake, switched off. People were clumping between the parked cars, laden with groceries and Christmas shopping. No one looked happy. They didn't look unhappy, just burdened.

"Allie, be careful."

"What do you mean?"

"For example, if Clive suggests you set up joint bank accounts. Just be careful."

"You think I'm that stupid?" Allie demanded, but her voice gave something away, some tiny seed of doubt.

"No, I don't think you're stupid at all."

"Well, you think I've been stupid in love," Allie said.

Meaning her past marriages. "We all make mistakes," Ellen said.

She opened her door, careful not to bang the Audi, then thinking to hell with the Audi. "Let's go and spend my hard-earned money."

But then she caught the expression on her sister's face, a look of misery glimpsed across the roof of her car. "Joke, Alls, sorry. I'd love to get you your sandals."

Allie opened her mouth, closed it again and turned away, hoisting the strap of her bag over her slender brown shoulder. About to tell me all, Ellen guessed, and had second thoughts.

26

SUNDAY, 7 A.M., A weak surf running at Point Leo.

Pam Murphy bobbed on her board, idly paddling, looking back over her shoulder in expectation of a good break. Nothing doing. The waves coming in this morning merely lifted and lowered her gently, or broke falsely or too late, full of fat, swelling promise but no payoff.

Still, sitting out here on the water was a nice punctuation to her day, her week. Surfing grounded her—so to speak. The air was clear, the water clean and vivid further out, where the December sun struck it. Summer's here, she thought, and Christmas is coming.

Presents for her brothers and their wives and kids. A present for her mother, the inspector, a couple of friends.

What friends? Almost no one in the police force.

Pam bobbed on the water, lost to dreams. A shout and a curse and a guy unfamiliar to her was gliding past and she was in his way. "Fucking beginners," he shouted. But she wasn't a beginner. She was an experienced surfer bobbing in a slow swell, that's all. She watched the guy ride it out, barely making it to shore, and paddle back again. A couple of the other regulars, early-birders like her, bailed him up, leaning intently on their boards, muttering to him. Then they let him through and he paddled past Pam uneasily, half-sulky, half-chastised. They'd stuck up for her. Pretty tribal, she thought, out here on the water.

SHOWERED, WEARING LIGHTWEIGHT CARGO pants, a sleeveless top and sandals, she breakfasted on coffee, muesli and a croissant in Red Hill before cutting down to the freeway and onto Peninsula Link and EastLink. Suburban main roads and side streets after that, through the leafy eastern suburbs of Melbourne. Leafy, but saturated with traffic exhaust.

Her mother lived in Capel Gardens Lodge in Hawthorn, not far from where Pam had grown up. The place was two hectares of shrubs, paths and cottages at the end of a driveway set with speed bumps. Finding a park, Pam switched off and checked her watch. Ten minutes early.

She made her way along a now-familiar route, nodding hello to one old woman, one young staff member. She dodged a garden sprinkler, stopped to smell a rose and realized that she felt buoyant for the first time in days, her skin tight on her bones, her senses tingling. It was the mild sun, the break from work, the promise of an adventure. Normally when she visited her mother, all she did was sit and talk and drink tea and meet other old ladies.

She found her mother waiting on a garden chair in the sun, ready to go, her cottage door locked, curtains drawn. Pam leaned in and kissed a creased, papery cheek. "Not late, am I?"

"Early, dear," Harriet Murphy said, putting weight on her stick, a bony shoulder pointing skywards, then levering herself upright. She wore stockings, a blue woolen skirt, a blouse and a cardigan. There'd been a rug on her lap. It fell to the grass.

"Whoops, forgot that was there."

"I'll get it," Pam said, swooping down.

Then a familiar claw was hooking onto her arm and they walked to the car, a slow march, only a faint hum of distant traffic in the air, the hiss of lawn sprinklers, birds rustling. Pam encountered no one this time. It was as if she were removing her mother from a deserted hamlet, the last of her kind.

"This is fun."

Pam laughed. "We haven't even reached the car yet."

"Trust me, dear, this is fun."

FIRST TAKING HER MOTHER past the old family home two streets away, Pam made a fast trip back to the Peninsula, exiting at Frankston, where she wound through to the coast road. Up over Oliver's Hill, then down into Mt. Eliza, directed by her mother.

At the end of Canadian Bay Road, she said, "Where on earth are you taking me?"

"Hold your horses, dear. You were always the impatient one."

Was I? thought Pam. She compared herself to her older brothers. Neither had ever struck her as fast or furious or indeed active at all, with their propensity for elliptical put-downs of their athletic police officer sister. She supposed she must have been the impatient one.

But I am mellowing, aren't I? I'm not feeling impatient right this very moment. I just want to know where you're taking me.

"There!" her mother exclaimed.

It was a Mt. Eliza gin palace, a massive block of pale stone set amid severely groomed lawns, a Lexus four-wheel drive and a BMW convertible glimpsed between the bars of a metal gate.

"Are you sure?"

Harriet Murphy nodded. "When your father and I lived here it was a little run-down house in a patch of bushland, not that monstrosity."

"When you were first married?"

"Yes."

They sat for a while. The house offering nothing, the street unrecognizable, Harriet said, "Okay, that's enough, take me down to the water, dear."

They parked at the end, got out, Pam clasping her mother's elbow, letting the older woman feel her way down over the tricky surfaces: pavement, steps, sand.

They stood and for five minutes sniffed the wind and watched it feather the water. Then Harriet said, "That's enough," for a second time.

"Early lunch?"

"Excellent idea."

Lunch on the pier at Mornington, Harriet picking at a salad, sipping a glass of mineral water. She'd reapplied her lipstick in the ladies, thick, hectic stripes, and now her lips were imprinted on the rim of the glass. The room was drenched by sunlight and Pam thought: she's getting old.

She reached across the table to clasp a veined hand. "It's a lovely idea, spending a day with you like this."

A rueful smile. "There might not be many more opportunities."

"Don't say that."

"Just being realistic, dear."

They chatted about old friends, vague family connections and history, Pam's brothers.

"It wouldn't hurt them to come home for Christmas."

"They have their own lives, dear."

And I don't?

No, I guess I don't.

The thing was, Pam's brothers were listened to, admired, talked about. Pam didn't doubt that she'd been loved by her parents, was still loved by her mother now, but she'd been born years after her brothers—an afterthought, someone once said. A girl; sporty, not academic. No one had ambitions for her. No one asked what drove her, or encouraged it. Generally, it was expected that Pam would marry and have children. Expected in a vague, distracted way, if at all.

Perhaps her anger flicked across her face; her mother was watching closely. "Darling," she said, the word a warning of some kind.

"What?"

"I love you. Always loved you, always will."

Tears pricked Pam's eyes. "I know. I love you, too."

"Shall we go? The music's terrible."

Pam hadn't been aware of the music. Now she listened: pan pipes. God, was that coming back into fashion?

AT THE PIRATE SHIP playground, her mother said, "Turn left, dear."

Then another turn, into a little side street that ran past St. Macartan's Catholic Church, where her mother said, "Stop."

Pam pulled in to the curb. "I'm guessing the church has significance?"

"It's where we were married."

"It is?"

Pam looked out at the reddish bricks, faintly perturbed. She'd seen the wedding photographs, had always assumed her parents had been married in Melbourne somewhere. She'd been on the Peninsula for a few years now, and had walked past this church several times; attended one wedding and a funeral there.

"Was it a big wedding?"

"Yes and no," Harriet Murphy said. Her eyes blinked. "My father refused to attend."

Revelation upon revelation. "Why on earth not?"

"Because I married a Catholic."

Pam felt mildly outraged. "You're kidding."

"Water under the bridge. Not important."

"Of course it's important," Pam said, thinking of emptiness and hard grudges and her mother's hurt, all those years ago. "Did he come around in the end?"

"Eventually. Your father wasn't exactly a Papist, and I didn't produce ten little Catholics."

Pam couldn't recall attending church at all when she was growing up. "What other bombshells have you got for me?"

"Was that a bombshell, dear?"

NEXT PAM HEADED ACROSS to the Moorooduc Highway and then the freeway to the Red Hill exit. Passing the BP station where Michael Traill worked, she felt her shoulders tense, her hands tighten on the wheel.

"Everything all right, dear?"

Her mother, the detective. "Fine."

"Any boyfriends on the horizon? Girlfriends?"

Her mother, the witch. "Far over the horizon, where they can't be seen."

"Patience."

"How old were you when you met Dad?"

"Twenty-two."

"I'm thirty," Pam said, as if to underline a point. What point, she couldn't say.

"But Dad wasn't the first," her mother said.

"If you were playing fast and loose, mother, I don't think I want to hear about it."

"You young ones think you invented fun," Harriet Murphy said.

Getting the expression slightly wrong: we're supposed to have invented *sex*, Pam thought. She thought about the fun in her life: an early morning surf, taking her aged mother around in the car. That was about it.

"So who were these other boyfriends of yours?"

"One was a pilot," her mother said. "Another had a fishing boat on Westernport."

Active, outdoors men. And she'd married a professor.

"So how did you meet Dad? He didn't grow up here?"

"He came apple picking."

Harriet had grown up on a Red Hill orchard. "And you saw him with his shirt off . . ."

Harriet laughed. "Something like that."

Pam could only go so far, conjuring up her parents' sex life. "Is that where we're going now? The orchard?"

"If you don't mind."

"We're doing a reverse run of your life," Pam said. "I collect you where you're spending your declining years, then we have a squiz at where you spent the bulk of your married years, then your early married years, then the church where you were married, and now where you grew up."

"Yes, I suppose you're right, dear," her mother said vaguely.

THE OLD ORCHARD WAS a winery and restaurant now, a twee-looking place overlooking vines, expensive German cars nose-up to a rail beside the main building. Pam pulled into the shade of a pine windbreak and they looked over the hillside folds, smoothly rolling and intertwining like the limbs and trunks of lovers.

"I just adored growing up here. A few houses and farms, that was about it."

"Does it bring back memories, even though it's all altered?"

"Memory isn't just visual, dear. Smells, sounds . . ."

"How long did Dad work for your father?"

"Not long," Harriet said. She paused. "We got caught."

Pam opened her mouth, shut it again. She saw the hot sun, the dappled shade and the bare skin. "You wicked girl."

"My father's exact words."

"Mother, do I really know you?"

Harriet touched her forearm. "What you see is what you get, dear."

NEXT STOP, AFTERNOON TEA at the Merricks General Store, where there was more German car flesh. That's what you get for driving around the Peninsula on a Sunday, Pam thought.

They sat on the deck, shaded, drinking iced tea and eating scones and cream.

"I used to go horse-riding near here."

"See? We're going back and back in time. We've reached your childhood. Next you'll be showing me where you were conceived."

Her mother patted her lips with a napkin. "An event I've never been able to visualize."

The people next to them were listening. A man, a woman, a second woman, aged about fifty. They grinned at Pam. Pam shrugged, grinned back. She was enjoying herself.

"Where next?"

Harriet looked at her watch. "We've just time to pop in at Shoreham, and then perhaps you can take me home?"

"That's where you were conceived?"

"That's where my best friend lived."

THE OLD PART OF Shoreham: the highest point, where old houses lurked with new ones behind dense stands of trees.

Pam parked where the road ran out at the cliff top and said, "Here?"

Harriet craned to look through her side window. "It's still there, the old house."

"Who was your friend?"

"Hazel Carlyle."

"Harriet and Hazel, the terrible twins."

"Yes, it was a bit like that. We were inseparable—when we could be together, that is."

"Is she still alive?"

There was a tear on the pouchy cheek. "Mum, are you okay?"

"Just memories, dear."

"Good? Bad?"

"Hazel. She drowned when I was nine."

They sat there, mother and daughter, staring back along the years, and it occurred to Pam what today was all about. Her mother was dying. She was saying goodbye.

LATE AFTERNOON NOW, PAM heading back after taking her mother home, the sun low on Peninsula Link. Traffic was light in her direction, with heavy outbound traffic, week-end tourists returning to the suburbs. Meanwhile a strange, bleak elation had settled in her, a feeling she couldn't name. It was composed of grief, loneliness, love for her mother and her childhood memories, a sense of privilege in that she, not her brothers or anyone else, had been entrusted with the purpose of the day. The pilgrimage. Up and down and sideways, that's what she felt. She felt unmoored.

But the stream of traffic in the outbound lanes rooted her in the mundane again. Traffic, petrol. Her thoughts drifted to Michael Traill and to another set of feelings she couldn't properly name.

She checked the time, after 6 P.M., so at the Balnarring Road exit she circled back onto the Moorooduc Highway and up toward the BP station. He wasn't there. "He doesn't work Sundays," the man at the cash register said. Iranian, Afghani, Iraqi . . . maybe a doctor or an engineer trying to make a new start in a shit job.

Like Michael Traill.

AND SO HER CAR found its way to the poultry farm, the driveway that curved around the owner's house and through the scattered sheds and feed silos to the caravan at the rear.

"A few more questions, Mr. Traill."

He glanced at his watch. "You work long days."

Then he seemed to shake himself. "Sorry, forgetting my manners. Please come in."

He wore faded jeans, a grey T-shirt, scuffed trainers—knocking-around gear, but he looked fresh, trim. Pam, conscious of her hours behind the wheel, felt grainy and scattered.

"Tea? Coffee?"

"Water's fine."

They sat at his little foldout table. He watched her expectantly. She matched his gaze, and then couldn't match it. She didn't know what she was doing here.

So she glanced around at the interior. Crammed, tidy, clean. A monastic man lives here, she thought—habits that a man on remand might learn. But had he spent time in jail? She couldn't remember.

"Questions?" he prompted her.

"Were you ever aware of large vehicles coming and going from Mr. Hauser's property?"

"No. But his place is a few kilometers away, and I'm usually asleep during the day."

"Any local gossip about the man?"

His gaze was still calm and she formed the impression of a keen mind whirring away.

"Would you like me to ask?"

She smiled, shook her head. "We'll do that."

"What do you suspect him of doing?"

That was taking a liberty. She needed to put him in his place. "What makes you think we suspect him of something, Mr. Traill?"

"Have I heard rumors? Have I seen heavy vehicles coming and going?"

She twitched her mouth left and right glumly. "Fair enough."

She should leave, but didn't want to. With one punch he'd killed a man she'd idolized, and he thought he could just sit there calmly as if he hadn't altered the world in a fundamental way. Or was Inspector Challis right in saying he'd been given a rough trot?

"How do you like living in a caravan?" she asked, as if that might remind him of who he was and how he'd been brought down.

"Beggars can't be choosers."

She snorted, ready to scorn him further, but something stopped her. The slight tilt of his chin as he regarded her. The knowledge that he wasn't seeking favors or forgiveness. His air of composure. Her absolute sense that he expected something better of her than an attempt to wound him.

She felt small, suddenly. Mean.

He looked down. Played with a ring of water from his drinking glass, a slender forefinger tracing shapes on the tabletop. Why did she want to reach across and stop the movement?

She found herself talking. Telling him her housing woes:

her lease lapsing, the owner selling. Missing out on the only rental place she could find in her price range. Her fear that she'd be forced to rent some crummy place far from work.

He looked up. Said, "That's bad luck," and meant it. Nothing trite in the words or their intent.

As Pam held his gaze a current of understanding passed between them. They both blinked, a moment of shared astonishment.

Traill remained composed, but it had slipped a little. She thought he seemed to float toward her, although of course he hadn't moved.

"If I hear of anything . . ." he offered.

She felt a surge of grief—about nothing, about everything; the lost certainties of her life—and reached, finally, across the table. His hand stiffened in hers. He might have drawn breath, a tiny sound. But he didn't pull away and the warmth deepened and spread, from him, from her, seeking a kind of equilibrium.

27

THE DRUG SQUAD'S MOVE against Chloe Minchin that weekend had its genesis in a scared kid spilling to his parents.

The kid, Josh Saville, twenty years old and the son of jewelers in Somerville, had been selling ice and ecstasy since he was in Year 12 at Peninsula School. Small amounts to friends, later branching into pubs and clubs, the Between the Bays music festival, the Westernport Festival, even at football and cricket matches. He was a bright, vaguely motivated kid, his motivations growing more focused as he witnessed the dedication and apparent healing power of the physical therapists who treated injuries among his footballer friends. So when he was accepted into a mid-year physiotherapy intake at La Trobe University's Bendigo campus, he told his supplier he was quitting.

"I've lined up a share house," he told the guy in late June, "filled the tank, pumped up the tires, and kissed the oldies goodbye. I'm out of here."

Well, not immediately: the course didn't start until July. So he was still residing in his parents' house in Somerville when, later that week, his girlfriend's car was torched. His supplier, Andy Molnar, who'd been a year ahead of him at school, said, with a note of apology, "Mate, you don't just walk out on the boss, you negotiate."

Who the boss was Josh didn't know. But he was scared enough to keep selling gear for another couple of weeks, then begged, "Please, I'm going away to uni, I need to quit. Can I talk to the boss?"

He waited for his car to be torched or a Molotov cocktail to come flying through his parents' shop window, but his supplier came back and said, "Here's the deal: when someone pulls out of the syndicate, it fucks with the business model. There are costs involved. The boss wants thirty-five grand."

Josh had thirty-five thousand, but not a dollar more. He said, "Who's the boss?"

"Fucked if I know," Molnar said. "He uses this chick. So, you got the dosh?"

Josh fell in a heap. If he paid up, he'd never be able to afford uni fees or living and accommodation costs. So he told his parents, who looked at him sideways and told the drug squad, who passed it on to Senior Sergeant Serena Coolidge.

Who'd been thinking of mounting an operation on the Peninsula, and here was her way in. But it would take time. Using all her powers of persuasion and threat, she arranged for Josh to pay the money and clear off to Bendigo with one year's financial support from his parents.

She and her team began to watch Molnar. One Sunday in October he climbed into his mother's Subaru and drove to Albury-Wodonga, on the border with New South Wales. Two cars tailed him and watched as he entered a room in the Travelodge on the Wodonga side of the border. He remained inside for thirty minutes.

When he emerged he was carrying a cheap nylon daypack, which he stowed in the rear of the Subaru. Telling two of her detectives to keep watching the motel, Coolidge and a third drug-squad detective followed Molnar back to his parents' house in Mornington.

Meanwhile in Wodonga, three more young people, a woman and two men, visited the motel room at staggered intervals and left carrying daypacks. They were photographed and their plates were run against the DMV database. Coolidge's detectives kept watching the room. They needed to eyeball and tail the occupant who, according to the motel clerk, was a woman named Melanie Higgins.

Melanie Higgins proved to be a sleek blonde aged about thirty, who climbed into a rented Mitsubishi and led the drug-squad car to the Hertz agency in Mornington, where she swapped to a taxi that took her to a flash-looking house in Safety Beach. An Audi TT sat in the driveway. They ran the plates. They ran the address. Car and house belonged to Chloe Minchin.

CHLOE MINCHIN RAN A travel agency in Waterloo. She earned good money but the house, car, investments, lifestyle and lack of debt pointed to a higher income than her tax returns showed. She had boyfriends—a fitness instructor, a surfboard manufacturer, the owner of a bakery chain who was cheating on his wife—but preliminary checks of their phone and financial records yielded no red flags.

Late one afternoon after Minchin had left work for the day, Serena Coolidge wandered into the travel agency and discussed a few cruise-ship holidays with one of the other agents. In her experience, people liked to be asked about their jobs; mostly they felt overlooked and unappreciated by the public. Bit by bit she elicited the information that, yes, travel agents did get to view holiday destinations first hand, and that Minchin's specialization was local, taking her every couple of months to motels, hotels, resorts, wineries, tourist attractions and restaurants around Victoria. The woman Coolidge spoke to specialized in Pacific locations, so they spent a while discussing these, to take her mind off Minchin.

Coolidge believed that Minchin was using these trips to take delivery of ice, speed and ecstasy. Instead of driving back with the drugs, she got her dealers to come to her. They then returned to their territories and started distributing to a lower rung of dealers, people like Josh. The fact that the October distribution had occurred on the New South Wales border pointed to the drugs coming down from Sydney.

She broached her suspicions with her New South Wales counterparts. Working from times, dates, toll-road records and CCTV footage, together with some firm suspicions, they confirmed that the drop-offs had probably been made by a couple of drivers for a Sydney parcel-delivery firm. Digging around in a thicket of company records, they uncovered the name of a woman who was the sister-in-law of a major drug importer named Hector Kaye.

MEANWHILE, ON THE FRIDAY morning when Coolidge was ascertaining that two of Kaye's enforcers were possibly involved in the disappearance of a local addict and low-level dealer, the watch on Chloe Minchin paid off. Minchin booked a Saturday morning pickup from the Hertz agency in Frankston, a Toyota Camry, and a room at the Colonial Motor Inn in Mildura for Saturday night. An innocent tourist-amenities scouting trip? Coolidge doubted it. She saw significance in the different car rental agency and location: by varying the pattern, Minchin was less likely to draw attention to herself.

In the short time available to her, Coolidge arranged for cameras and microphones to be installed in the Camry and the motel room. Her first instinct had been to shirtfront the managers of both businesses, but wisdom prevailed—her senior constable's "Softly, softly, boss."

"You're not serious."

"Boss, if you appeal to their crime-fighting and cloak-and-dagger instincts, they'll be only too glad to help."

Diplomacy was foreign to Coolidge, but it seemed to work. That, and the promise to pay for damages and absolve each business of legal consequences.

CHLOE WOKE AT SEVEN on Saturday morning, collected her hire car and set off, heading northwest across the city and out the other side, a tiresome trek, only to be followed by another kind of tiresomeness, the flat, dry, hot monotony of rural Australia. She hated these trips for Carl. The hours passed: great! A town! And then it was gone in an eye blink. Another car! And it was gone.

She could write a road song, the things she saw and felt when she made these trips. A song about love and the road and dreams, dreaming. The road unrolled and the hours passed and here was another call from Carl. "All good?"

"Carl, for the thousandth time, everything's fine," she told him. The idiot wanted constant reassurance. You wouldn't want to spend a lifetime with someone that insecure, no matter how good the sex was. She hoped like hell he was using an untraceable phone.

"CARL? CARL BOWIE?" COOLIDGE asked.

She was in the mobile command vehicle, a boxy white department-store delivery van fitted with recording equipment, monitor screens, headphones, seats and two detectives beside herself and the driver. The team was also running an unmarked sedan today; it kept pace a hundred meters behind.

The AV guy checked his screens. "If so, he's not on his mobile, house or office phone."

Until today, they'd had nothing on him, except that he liked to sneak visits to Minchin once or twice a week. He was wealthy, but he'd inherited a string of bakeries and the business was prospering. And he was, well, a man who baked bread and cakes for a living. Short hair, wife, two kids in private school.

"She sounds pissed off with him," the AV guy said.

"And he sounds tense," Coolidge said. "So, first thing Monday, we dig a little deeper."

She settled back in her seat, breathed shallowly of the stale air. Still, she'd rather be here, doing something, than back in Waterloo, sitting through another mind-numbing briefing with the local plod. She chewed the inside of her cheek in glum concentration. She'd liked the look of Challis the moment she first saw him; he had a kind of lean, quiet, patient menace. But he was a disappointment. She'd given him plenty of cues, but he'd ignored them, and it wasn't that he was thick, or slow. He didn't want her. And then she'd seen him in the company of that tedious Destry cow, and someone had said they were an item—which was normally no deterrent to Coolidge, but Challis gave her no opening whatsoever.

Fuck him.

She said, "What phone is Chloe using?"

The AV guy shrugged. "It's not tied to her work or personal accounts."

THEN THE CAVALCADE WAS drawing into Mildura, Chloe in her rented Camry, followed by a semitrailer and a couple of dusty rural sedans, and finally the drug-squad surveillance van. The Camry turned right, toward the southern bank of the Murray River.

"The motel's down this way, right?"

"Yes, boss."

Coolidge advised the drug-squad sedan, which was already at the motel, and settled back tensely to watch the Camry. She saw the turning light blink, and then it was nosing into the forecourt of the Colonial Motor Inn.

"Drive past," she said. "Circle the block."

Passing the motel entrance, she saw Chloe Minchin lock the Camry and turn toward the main entrance. "She's picking up her key. Let's hope the reservations clerk doesn't blow it."

Then they were half a block down the street, adjacent to the unmarked drug-squad Holden. A lazy hand lifted as they passed.

They made a series of turns and came in from the south again, drawing in to the curb a block short of the motel. Coolidge called the Holden: "Did she go to her assigned room?"

"Yes, boss."

Coolidge sat in nervy concentration, one leg jiggling, one hand washing the other. The AV technician fiddled and one of the monitors flared with light: Chloe, dumping her bag on her bed.

But she didn't stay. She made for the door and disappeared, and the radio crackled, "She's coming out again."

All Coolidge wanted to do after hours of sitting was get out, stretch her back and hamstrings, walk around the block. She rolled her shoulders, peered at the screens, at the back of Chloe's head, at the wheel of the Camry. Then Chloe was looking back through the rear window as she reversed, and fifteen seconds later she was out on the street, heading away from the river. The driver ducked his head as she passed the van; they all tensed.

~

CHLOE LED BOTH DRUG-SQUAD vehicles to a McDonald's. She parked in full view of the dining windows, got out and walked away from the building.

"Did she lock it? Anyone see the lights flash?"

"No, boss."

Wanting the Holden ready for any possible high-speed pursuit, Coolidge ordered one of her officers to leave the van and follow Chloe on foot. "See where she goes, what she does, who she talks to—if anyone. I think the exchange is about to go down, and she's supposed to keep her distance."

"Boss."

TWO MINUTES LATER, A man sauntered out of the McDonald's. He was young, short-haired, wiry, carrying a gym bag and dressed for weekend sport in a polo shirt, white shorts and Adidas running shoes. He strolled to the Camry, lifted the boot lid and leaned in.

"He's counting the money," Coolidge said.

Apparently satisfied, the man stowed his gym bag and walked around to the driver's door.

"She left the key for him," Coolidge said. "Get ready to follow."

She supposed it was smart. A curious person hoeing into a hamburger in the McDonald's window would be less curious about a customer stowing his bag, getting behind the wheel and driving away than a customer *not* getting behind the wheel but walking away, only for a woman to take his place.

The driver led them down the main street to a Coles supermarket and pulled into a slot in the far corner of the vast car park. He got out, walked around to the rear, removed a different gym bag and sauntered out onto the street.

"The exchange has taken place," Coolidge said. "We need a clear shot of his face."

"On it, boss."

The camera clicked but before they could tail the man, a BMW with New South Wales plates swerved in to the curb. The man climbed into the passenger seat. The car shot away.

"You got the plates?"

"Boss."

"Send them to Sydney."

"Boss."

Then they waited. Presently Chloe wandered in from the street. She strolled around the car park, her gaze pausing at any vehicle that might have been an unmarked police car, her gaze passing over the surveillance van. She was followed a short time later by the detective who'd been tailing her. Coolidge tensed, half-expecting the detective to knock on the van for admittance, but she entered the supermarket and watched through the plate glass, and only hurried to the van when Chloe finally lifted the Camry's boot lid and leaned in.

"She's checking she has the drugs," Coolidge said.

She turned to the detective. "What did she do?"

"Window-shopped."

"Talk to anyone? Calls, texts?"

"One call. I heard her say, 'Carl, chill, okay?'"

Coolidge was forming a picture of Carl Bowie: a micromanager, a fusspot. But potentially dangerous. Access to dangerous people, anyway.

THEN IT GOT BORING.

They tailed Chloe to the motel and switched to the room cameras and microphones and saw her shower, change, pour a drink and watch the tail end of a Saturday afternoon sports telecast, golf somewhere on the other side of the world.

She's done this a dozen times before, Coolidge thought. When she's ready, she'll parcel up the drugs and deal with her runners.

CHLOE MINCHIN WASN'T READY until Sunday morning. Saturday night she stayed in, eating a room-service club sandwich and watching two pay movies, soft porn, to which she masturbated. Coolidge's detectives were stiffly silent. They might have offered some kind of commentary, but Coolidge unnerved them.

Then Chloe slept.

Coolidge and the others took shifts, four hours on, four off, dividing their time between the stale air of the van and the chemical air of a room in a budget motel across the street from the Colonial Inn.

At 8 A.M. on Sunday, the cameras showed Chloe stirring. She sat on the edge of the bed, looking dazed, then hauled herself upright and attempted a few half-hearted stretches before scuffing her way to the bathroom. She came out with wet hair, a towel around her torso, and dressed, packed her bag and ate a room-service breakfast. The show proper started when she unzipped the gym bag and spread the contents on the bench under the wall-mounted TV set.

"What is that?" Hoddle said, peering at the screens.

"Definitely ice. The pills probably ecstasy."

"And a set of scales," Coolidge noted.

They watched Chloe divide the drugs into four, a pill at a time and the ice by weight.

"Now what?"

Chloe was fishing a series of flat, square, cellophane-wrapped packets from her case. She tore off the cellophane from one packet, shook out the contents.

"Looks like a little daypack."

Four cheap nylon daypacks. Chloe stuffed each one with ice crystals and pills. She sat back to wait. Coolidge alerted the local police, who would carry out today's arrests, and sat back to wait with her.

THE FIRST RUNNER WAS a woman, aged about thirty, driving a bright yellow VW. She wore torn black leggings, a torn black skirt, plenty of piercings, tattoos on each bare shoulder, and black eye makeup under black and purple birds-nest hair. She stayed talking strategy and marketing with Chloe, revealing that she serviced the southern Peninsula district. Twenty minutes later, she left with her little pack of drugs.

Meanwhile Coolidge had checked the VW's plates and matched the owner's license photo with the goth. Never arrested, not even a speeding fine. She muttered, "And the winner of this year's Miss Junior Chamber of Commerce is . . ." and called the lead pursuit cars with the plate number and description of the VW.

"You know the drill, stop her some distance out of town, don't let her make a single phone call."

Twenty minutes later, the call came back: the goth had been pulled over and arrested on possession and suspicion of trafficking charges.

At noon a young man arrived in a silver Holden Ute. Short hair, beige slacks and a white short-sleeved shirt—he could have come straight from church. He stayed, talked business with Chloe, and left with his drugs. His area was Cranbourne, apparently. Coolidge called the drug-squad car. "He's all yours; get cracking."

She was starting to see the planning involved. Like the goth, the driver of the silver utility was clean. So, she realized, was Molnar, the dealer who'd supplied Josh Saville.

This time she waited thirty minutes for news of the arrest. Apparently the young man with his boy-next-door clothes and haircut had threatened the arresting officers with a knife and had to be subdued with capsicum spray.

Molnar was Chloe's next visitor. He stayed to talk shop with Chloe, but appeared jumpy.

"Anything wrong?"

"I'm good."

"You seem nervous."

"It's just, I've had this feeling like I'm being followed."

Coolidge said, "Fuck," and Chloe said, very sharply, "Today?"

Molnar shook his head. "Not today, just in general."

"How long for?"

Molnar gestured and twitched and hemmed and hawed as if flummoxed by the question. "Few weeks, maybe?"

"Few weeks?" hissed Chloe. "Fuck."

"Yeah, fuck," Coolidge muttered. "Get ready, she could wrap this up and try to run."

They watched intently. Almost at once, Chloe twitched aside the curtains. She seemed to focus on the van and ducked away.

"This is it," Coolidge said.

SHE SENT TWO DETECTIVES in the drug-squad unmarked after Chloe Minchin, following more sedately in the van. The passenger kept her informed: Chloe was heading west, toward South Australia, across flat red-dirt country where the main roads are long, straight and built for speed.

"She's going like a bat out of hell, boss."

"Keep up, that's all I'm asking. I've arranged for pursuit cars to take over."

That would take time. Meanwhile Chloe was streaking

across the flats. The Camry had the capacity for some speed, but it was a family car, after all, one of the most common vehicles on the road, and not built for outrunning the police. It was a wallowing box on wheels with a terrible oversteer, and a far cry from Chloe's regular ride, her nippy Audi sports. But she expected the same handling and performance going into a sixty-degree bend at a hundred and twenty k's. The car rolled, rammed the only roadside gum tree on that stretch of the highway and split in two.

The monitors in Coolidge's van showed snowy conditions, out there on the red dirt plain.

28

FIRST THING MONDAY MORNING, Carl Bowie was sitting at his table in the yard behind his Mornington bakery, an expression of concentrated harassment on his face.

Chloe, dead. He felt a strange, stubborn truculence. He wanted to lash out. But: *A cool head prevails*, according to the keynote speaker at Grow Your Own Prosperity. He'd written it down and underscored it twice. A cool head. Prevailing. They were his defining characteristics, when you thought about it.

He fought to recover his equilibrium. Bit by bit then, sounds, smells and other sensations returned to him. He could hear birds squabbling in the trees, a woman walking down the laneway. He could smell baking from his own ovens, feel the sun on his forearms.

But Carl had developed a seasoned instinct for nuances, for the unspoken and the unconscious, and knew that forces were at work against him. The jitters returned. He bit the inside of his cheek; a tightness came swamping over him. *Chloe was dead.* Mid-afternoon yesterday she'd texted him on one of his disposable mobile phones: *Cops im running*, then silence. He'd immediately destroyed the phone and sim card, and then, after sitting and thinking, had begun to move money, burn paperwork and ditch the remaining phones.

After some agonizing, he'd gone to a 7-Eleven and notified Hector Kaye.

"So, mate, I'm out of the game. Finished. Finito."

"Bullshit you're out," Kaye said.

"I've transferred one point five million into your Caymans account. Call it a cancellation fee."

Then he'd spent the rest of yesterday monitoring the news, radio, TV and on-line services. At 6 P.M., channels seven and nine had stories with film of a high-speed car chase west of Mildura, resulting in a fatality. In a separate story, three drivers had been stopped, searched and arrested on possession and trafficking charges south of Mildura. They'd shown film of one of the drivers, a woman with purple hair who snarled at the camera. Chloe had said one of her best runners was a goth from south Frankston.

Carl thought about Chloe and almost wept for a moment. He'd miss her. Not just her body, her air of riskiness. But as the seminar leader had said, *There is risk and there is risk.* She might have pulled him down in the end, just as Owen might have.

Well, he was dead.

And Hector's heavies were dead. Probably.

Carl examined himself for twinges of guilt or grief. Nothing, really. Just that momentary lapse when he'd thought of Chloe.

THAT SAME MONDAY, JOHN Tankard was working the front desk again. So far, no drama. Nothing to trip him up, only a lost wallet, car keys handed in, a stat dec witnessed.

But mid-afternoon a wry, twinkling woman with cropped hair walked through the door and headed straight for the counter. She wore dark pants and a pale blue shirt bearing the shire logo and was vaguely familiar. "Yes, madam?"

"I work in the library."

Ah. Tank placed her now; some guy trying to access porn on a library computer a few years ago. "Help you?"

She had a huge bag over one shoulder and began to dig around in it. "Someone from here used our photocopier late last week and left a sheet of paper in the machine."

Not the crime of the century, then, Tank thought. Just another day in purgatory. "Do you know who it was?"

"Janine Something," the librarian said. "I know she works here, but she's not police. Office staff, maybe? Anyhow, she's used our copier before, when you've had a paper crisis."

She grinned as she said it. Paper crisis, as if Victoria Police had been brought to its knees. Well, it was an ongoing process. He'd had to bring in a couple of biros from home for his shift . . .

"I'll see she gets it."

The librarian was still scrabbling around in her bag. "It's amazing the stuff people leave in the copier. Birth certificates, passports, receipts, house plans, bank statements, garage sale notices, contracts, CVs . . ."

"Really?" said Tank.

In the little back room of his personality, impatience was stirring. He wanted to shake the woman and her damn bag.

"Here we are," the librarian said.

She plonked it on the counter, a slip of paper, handwritten words scrawled in a kind of list. Tank scanned the items. Halfway down, he went very still.

And the woman said, "I would have returned it sooner, but one of our juniors found it in the copier and simply dumped it with the rest of the material that people leave behind. I take it upon myself to go through it periodically, trying to trace ownership, and when I read *this*"—she tapped the paper scrap—"about two men and a rifle, I remembered

Janine coming in and thought I'd better bring it back straight away in case it's important."

ELLEN DESTRY WAS IN the sex-crimes cottage, briefing Katsoulas and Rykert.

"You all set for tomorrow?"

"Yes, Sarge."

The playground stakeout. Ellen's unit had been asked to assist Mornington police catch a guy described as "creepy" and given to watching, photographing and approaching children. Nothing more definite than that and no clear descriptions.

"The agreement is, they can have you for two to three hours. After that, it's back here."

"Boss."

She dismissed them, and before going home herself, cleaned up her emails. There was a new one from Scobie Sutton. The travel brochures she'd scooped into her bag from Allie's coffee table had been handled by four persons not in the system and one who was.

She logged on, keyed in the name Wayne Hall and found herself staring at a mug shot of the man calling himself Clive Mieckle.

Hall had a history of dishonesty offenses going back almost twenty years. In the late 1990s he'd been charged with receiving unemployment benefits while working, operating as an unlicensed private investigator and obtaining loans using false names and addresses. In 2001, and again in 2007, he'd obtained bank loans to set up fake churches using forged divinity degrees and a letterhead stolen from a judge of the Family Court. Meanwhile he'd also been charged with cashing valueless checks and claiming insurance for fires at his furniture renovation and computer-repair businesses.

Then he disappeared for several years after marrying a widow and cleaning out her savings.

Ellen made a phone call. The widow had since died.

So he thinks it's safe to come back?

Ellen made further calls, and reached the widow's daughter, an Adelaide nurse named Tina Cannon.

"That bastard!" Cannon said. "He killed my mother."

Ellen went very still. "You mean—"

"I mean he ruined her life. He stole all her savings and left her with nothing. She fell into a deep depression and eventually she wouldn't even leave the house." Cannon paused. "I think she died of low self-esteem and a broken heart. She never recovered from the blow, the hurt."

"He disappeared after stealing from her?"

"That's right. He spun her this story of working for the American government, the Australian agent of Homeland Security, can you believe it. My mother did, unfortunately. Anyway, he swore her to secrecy, something about his identity had been compromised and his life was in danger from Muslim extremists and he'd better leave the country for a while. He said he'd call for her to meet him overseas but of course he never did."

"Did you inform the police?"

"I did, Mum wouldn't."

"Any hard evidence?"

"They said they'd prosecute if he ever cropped up again but they weren't going to bust a gut looking for him."

"Any letters, emails, postcards . . . ?"

"Not much. Listen, has he come back?"

"Possibly."

"Just get him. I don't care how, just get him."

"Forgive me for asking this, but did your mother ever say anything about her, ah, intimate relations with him?"

"You mean sex, right? He kept telling her he'd been wounded in Afghanistan and any strain on his back could cripple him. He looked all right to me. But now you mention it, I don't think they had sex at all."

"Did he ever mention family?"

According to the records, Hall's parents were dead and he had no siblings. "He talked about a sister," Cannon said.

"You didn't meet her?"

"No. Nor did Mum. She lived in Brisbane and couldn't get away because her kid had leukemia."

Ellen said carefully, "Did your mother help with the doctor's or hospital bills, by any chance?"

"Sure," Cannon said, "that was my mother all over. Are you going to find him through the sister?" And then she groaned. "Wait. That was part of the con, right? To squeeze money out of my mother?"

"I'm afraid so."

"Mum *cried* to think of this little kid with leukemia. You *really* have to get this guy."

Ellen muttered the usual things and finished the call.

She thought she might find Mieckle/Hall by finding Allie's car.

Then the phone rang and it was Ian Judd, saying they had another rape victim. "She's in hospital, boss. Can't talk to her until tomorrow."

29

ON TUESDAY MORNING, CHALLIS slid a copy of Colin Hauser's scribbled notes across Serena Coolidge's desk. "I think the men he's describing are Lovelock and Pym."

The drug-squad senior sergeant seemed bright, forceful, her color high—a complicated look, Challis thought, as if she was still interested in him and commensurately cranky because he'd rebuffed her. She pulled the note closer to her and placed her head in her hands to read it.

She looked up. "Where's the original?"

"At the lab."

"How did you come by it?"

"He'd slipped it among the paperwork on his desk," Challis said. Coolidge didn't need to know about Janine Quine.

"Your theory is . . . ?"

He settled back in the visitor's chair and crossed his legs. "If we assume it's Lovelock and Pym—and I think we can, given the descriptions, the plate number, the rifle—Hauser saw them at the entrance to a laneway leading through farmland to Devilbend Reservoir. Anyone on foot or horseback can use the track, but vehicles are barred by a locked gate."

"The local farmers have keys?"

"Yes. Now, Hauser walked there every day. He'd know the type of people who typically use the lane and the types of vehicles they drive. Something about Lovelock and Pym—well, *every*thing about them—aroused his suspicions so he raced home and wrote it all down. They realized he was a witness, so they followed and shot him."

"Witness to what? Are we thinking they buried something?"

Challis made a gesture that said the supposition was reasonable. "Drugs? Owen Valentine's body? Anyhow, I've ordered a handler and a couple of cadaver dogs. They're coming down from Melbourne, won't get here till sometime this afternoon. And it's a longish stretch between the road and the reservoir, so the search itself could take a while."

"You didn't think to consult me first?"

Coolidge's color was higher now, and Challis hunted around for a way to make things right. That was his habit. But could every little thing be made right?

His tone harder, a chilly politeness, he said, "I'm consulting you now. Look, I only received the note this morning. I needed to check the location and Mr. Hauser's reason for being there. Cadaver dogs and trained handlers are not thick on the ground, so I had to move fast. Remember, I'm investigating a murder and a suspicious disappearance. I'm having trouble seeing either as drug-related. Hauser was in the wrong place at the wrong time. And Owen Valentine? Small fry. So who would bring in experienced outsiders, and why? Have your Sydney colleagues questioned Hector Kaye about what his men were up to?"

Coolidge grimaced. "Lawyered up. He denies even knowing Lovelock and Pym, let alone what they were doing down here."

"I don't see Christine Penford hiring them—although she'd have a motive for killing Valentine. He sold her daughter to drug dealers, after all."

Coolidge snorted. "She'd do it herself with a kitchen knife."

"Slatter also had a motive, but not much of one. And I can't see him doing anything about it."

Coolidge was looking shifty. "It's a mystery."

"Unless he's your ice king."

Coolidge's smile was like a cat's. "No."

ANXIOUS NOW TO MOVE on the Hauser note, Challis headed downstairs to the general office.

Before he reached the door, Janine Quine and two of her colleagues emerged, heading for the canteen, so Challis lingered a while in the corridor, ostensibly browsing the flyers and FOR SALE notices pinned to a long corkboard between the rear doors and the staff pigeonholes stuffed with unwanted and unnecessary mail. When he was satisfied, he poked his head in. The office was empty but for Lily, one of the collators. Annette Tranh's small corner office was dark behind the glass door.

At once Lily said to him, "Yes, I'm busy; no, I won't drop everything."

He'd known her for years. "I don't ask you to do that, do I?"

She grinned. "You and everyone else around here."

"Just thought I'd say hello."

"I'll bet."

"Where is everybody?"

"Morning tea. I should be so lucky."

He glanced at the pair of photocopiers in the corner. "Lily, how often do you run out of paper and toner?"

"Hardly ever."

"The last time?"

"Oh, weeks ago."

"When it does happen, do you take the material down to the library at the end of High Street?"

"Well, a couple of times, but never anything sensitive."

Challis tried a disarming smile. It didn't work. Lily cocked her head. "What's going on?"

"I thought I'd put in a request for more funding for you."

"Bullshit, excuse my French."

At that moment the phone rang in the darkened corner office. Lily gave him an apologetic look, crossed the room to the glassed-in cubicle, flicked on the light and lifted the handset. He saw her speak, scribble a note, hang up.

She returned, saying, "Sorry about that. Now, where were we? Oh yes, you're up to something."

"So Annette's still away?"

"She's due back at work next week."

"You've had to field all her calls?"

"Jan Quine usually does that. She seems to spend half her time answering Annette's phone."

Challis glanced around the office as if to locate Quine. "She's at morning tea?"

"And so should I be, except someone has to keep this show on the road."

"You're a trooper," Challis said, "a role model and an inspiration to us all."

"What do you want?"

"I want to swear you to secrecy," Challis said.

THAT DONE, HE WENT upstairs to his office, propped his feet on an open desk drawer, and began to plot.

His phone rang. He was needed at the hospital in Mornington.

30

PETER MOORE, THIRTY-TWO, STAY-AT-HOME dad, divided his time between editing (actually, totally rewriting) technical manuals at his desk (actually, the dining-room table) and looking after his son, Jack, who was three. Jack's morning needs were simple: breakfast, then the pirate ship playground at the beach end of Main Street, Mornington. It was a laid-back life, which might explain why Moore sometimes went a day or two without shaving and slopped around in tattered jeans and T-shirts.

This Tuesday morning he sat on a bench, his face to the sun. Behind him, at the base of the cliff, the beach curved in one direction to the pier, boatsheds, and a couple of cafes; up to Mt. Eliza in the other. On his left was the pirate ship, on his right a massive gnarled tree with a huge canopy, and ranged before him, on an area of bark chips and grass, were swings, slides and small bucking creatures on stiff springs. Over on the grass, a pink plastic sandal. Moore didn't think he'd ever been to a playground where kids' shoes hadn't been left behind.

He closed his eyes, letting the sun seep in. Sometimes when he did this a client's clunky sentence would pop into his head and he'd recast it until it was elegant and precise. Then he'd open his eyes, fish out his notebook and scribble it down. He felt left and right with his foot: the backpack was there, crammed with his notebook and Jack's water bottle, snacks and change of clothes.

He opened his eyes, flicked his gaze around until he'd isolated his son, closed them again. A gentle warm sun today. He was very tired. He'd got up to Jack during the night—Maddie slept through everything—and was wide awake until dawn. Then Maddie had gone to work and Jack was shaking his arm, "Daddy, wake up." He'd bathed, dressed and fed Jack, built Lego towers with him, snatched a few minutes here and there to correct some engineer's grammatical howlers. Then the ride to the playground, Jack in a basket seat over the back wheel of Moore's ancient bicycle.

He opened his eyes again and groaned inwardly. Jack seemed interested in climbing onto the pirate ship, which would require a bit of supervision, and Moore just didn't have the energy today. But a moment later Jack was crouching in that effortless elastic way of kids beside a girl who was sitting sullenly on the ground, a doll in one hand, throwing bark chips at the seagulls with the other. Jack reached out a pudgy hand and patted the girl. He put his arms around her and planted a kiss. Then he led her by the hand to one of the slides. It was an odd sight, the three-year-old boy leading the girl, who looked to be twice his age. They climbed the slide, slid one after the other down it, raced around to the steps and repeated the action.

She wasn't wearing underpants. Moore shrugged, none of his business, and closed his eyes again.

A faint movement of the bench seat and a woman was sitting beside him, gazing at him with an odd, smiling fixation. No warmth in it, only intensity. A mother. The world was full of mothers at playgrounds and sometimes they were perplexed by him, as if the world hadn't moved on but was stuck in the era where dads went out to work and mums stayed home with the kids.

Moore managed a weak smile, located Jack—in one of the sandpits now—and ran his gaze over the other kids, trying to guess which one belonged to the woman. At least a dozen kids this morning, and across the way were other mothers and one other father on bench seats, a couple of mothers on a blanket on the grass, a woman approaching with a toddler in a stroller. The air was still and sweetly scented. Squeals and laughter and the distant murmur of the sea. It all lulled Moore into another dozing state.

And the woman beside him said, "Let's make this easy, shall we?"

Some kind of pick-up line? Moore didn't consider himself much of a catch, but the woman had shuffled closer to him and suddenly he didn't have room to move.

"Sorry?"

"Let's just walk out of here without a fuss and across the road to the police station for a little chat, shall we? Or we can make it dramatic. Your choice."

An attractive woman with strong Mediterranean features, black hair and dark, unappeasable eyes. She wore black pants and a tan linen jacket over a white top and now she was showing him her ID. "My name is Constable Katsoulas of the sex-crimes unit and I should advise you that here and there in the immediate area are other plain-clothed officers, so please don't run or make a scene."

Badly frightened, Moore shot to his feet, yelling, "Jack! Jack!"

His voice communicated the panic. Jack, about to mount one of the slides with his friend, froze and said, "Dadda?"

Then he was running for his father, trailed by the little girl, emitting brutal, explosive sobs.

Everyone looked up, everyone froze, apart from Moore's son and the little girl, who herself began sobbing wretchedly.

And apart from the man on a bench on the other side of the slides and swings. He stood, turned, and scurried away across the grass, heading for the Esplanade and the houses on the other side. "Scurried" was the word that popped into Moore's head. Words did that to him. This one was apt. It denoted guilt.

The woman named Katsoulas said, "Oh, bugger," and murmured into a lapel microphone. The women on the blanket leapt to their feet and began to chase the fleeing man.

Katsoulas turned to Moore, touched his forearm briefly, unconsciously, and said, "My apologies, sir, but we've had reports of a man paying untoward attention to the children who play here."

She began to edge away, one eye on Moore, the other on the hunters and the hunted at the other side of the park.

"Go," Moore urged her. "I understand. I'm fine. No complaints."

She flashed him a smile and then was running. He watched her. A fast sprinter, her figure diminishing across the grass and out onto the street.

Something to tell Maddie tonight. Something other than bowel movements and scraped knees and the price of avocados, which for some reason Jack loved eating, mashed on toast.

Moore glanced down at his son, who was clasping his legs tightly, a child sensitive to everything around him and whose instinct was to make things better. Moore did feel better in the grip of those tight little arms, and ruffled his son's hair.

The girl was gazing at them solemnly. She was filthy, Moore realized. Clutching a little plastic-faced doll, she looked dazed, deeply fatigued and quite lost and abandoned. And no pants on.

Moore searched wildly for her mother, but the women

nearby were occupied with gossip and keeping an eagle eye on their kids, so he crouched and said, "Hello, what's your name?"

This close, she shied away, but recovered enough to say, "Clover."

"Is your mum here—or your dad?"

The question seemed beyond the child. She sat abruptly, all energy spent, and Moore gathered her with his son and walked the short distance out of the park and up Main Street to the police station.

31

ELLEN DESTRY AND IAN Judd had driven to a pocket of side streets running off the Nepean Highway between Mornington and the industrial estate. The housing here dated from the 1960s, modest brick-veneer places with tiled roofs and a handful of eight-unit apartment blocks, two up, two down, four facing the street, four at the rear. It was outside one of these that Judd stopped the car.

"Ground level, rear?"

"Yep."

"Forensics?"

"Been and gone. Nothing useable."

Ellen didn't get out. She could see well enough from the car. A high fence and dense shrubbery shielded the flats from the houses on either side and behind it. And if disturbed, their rapist had his choice of escape routes: the highway, a tangle of side streets and a road leading east to the Peninsula Link freeway.

"Let's go."

Judd accelerated wordlessly out of the street and back to the highway, turning north to Frankston.

KAREN ROBARDS HAD BEEN admitted to the Frankston Hospital and kept overnight. Destry and Judd found her dressed and sitting on a chair beside her bed in a small ward on the first floor. Eight beds, either empty or occupied by women who appeared to be asleep.

Making the introductions, Ellen said, "They're letting you leave?"

"My mum's picking me up in an hour."

Robards was a wisp: short, slender, with thin brown hair, her bones hard knobs and ridges under the skin. She wore jeans and a T-shirt. Her right arm was in a sling across her chest, a plaster around her wrist, which had been broken during the attack.

"I asked the hospital to let you know we'd be coming in to talk to you . . ."

Robards shook her head. "No one told me nothing."

A public hospital's like a police station, Ellen thought. Everyone racing around like crazy, messages delayed or lost. "Are you up to talking to us, Karen?"

Robards looked panicked and gazed at the other beds. "Not here."

Securing the permission of a ward sister, they settled in a snug room beside the chapel. Ellen eased into the interview with a series of bland questions. She learned that Robards was twenty-six, lived alone, sold CDs and DVDs at a chain outlet in Somerville. No current boyfriend. Her mother lived in Cranbourne and Karen would live with her until she found another home. "No way I'm going back to that flat." A hysterical edge.

Ellen tried to sound soothing. "I don't blame you."

Gathering herself visibly, Robards said, "What do you need to know?"

"Let's start from the beginning. You came home from work . . ."

"Uh huh."

"What time was this?"

"I finish at four, so about four-twenty."

"And the man who raped you was—"

"Didn't rape me."

Ellen trod carefully. "Okay, the man who assaulted—"

"No, he would've raped me but it went wrong."

"I understand. You got home . . . then what happened? Not the fine detail, just the broad stages."

"I walked in and he grabbed me and took me to the bedroom."

"He was already in the flat?"

"Yes. He got in through the bathroom window, knocked all my bits and pieces flying."

"Did you see his face at any stage?"

"Depends what you mean. He had this thing over his face, balaclava."

"Did he speak?"

"When he grabbed me he said he had a knife. I saw it. It was one of mine." Robards shuddered. "I don't want nothing from my flat. The landlord can have the lot."

"So he took you to the bedroom . . ."

"And he pushed me onto the bed and fell on top of me."

"Pushed you onto your front or your back?"

Robards looked at Ellen as if she were dense. "Onto my front. Then he landed on top of me. That's how come I broke my wrist. I put my hand down and he fell on top of me and my wrist snapped." She winced, remembering.

"Just to be clear, he tried to force himself on you from behind?"

"No. Listen. The rug slipped and he fell on me."

Ellen had it now. Robards was tiny, the rapist a sudden heavy weight slamming her down. "That must have hurt."

"It was . . . unbearable. I just lay there. I couldn't think. I think I must've fainted."

"Then what happened?"

"He said sorry. Then he looked at his arm and rushed to the bathroom. Told me to shut up and not move."

A squeamish rapist? Heard the bone snap and was overcome with nausea?

"Do you know why he went to the bathroom?"

"Cut himself."

The forensics team hadn't found blood. "Badly?"

Robards shrugged. "Dunno. Took a heap of my Band-Aids."

"He accidentally cut himself?"

Again, Ellen seemed dense to the young woman. "Well, yeah."

"Which part of his arm?"

Robards indicated an area of Ellen's forearm near the wrist.

"Then what happened?"

"He come back with some Band-Aids on and started waving the knife around and I thought that's it, I'm a goner, I couldn't stop crying either, the pain was killing me, and his phone rang."

"You're joking. Did he answer it?"

"Yep. Then he just did himself up and left."

"When he talked on the phone, did he mention a person or a place by name?"

Robards shook her head. Her flashes of spirit had disappeared and now she simply looked depleted.

"He listened a bit, then he said, 'That would be QF, right?' Don't ask me what it means."

"'That would be QF, right?'"

"Something like that."

THEN ROBARDS' MOTHER ARRIVED and Destry and Judd left the hospital.

"QF: mean anything to you?"

"Qantas," Judd said. "Flight number prefix."

He was a still, competent, expressionless presence at the wheel of the car, and Ellen knew at once that he was right. "Confirming for himself? Meeting someone?"

"I'd say meeting someone, wouldn't you? If he booked a flight for himself, why would someone call him with the flight number?"

Ellen saw it then, the rapist's mobility, his familiarity with the towns and streets of the Peninsula. "He's a taxi driver."

Judd nodded. "Yep."

"But no one reported seeing a taxi."

"Who sees taxis? But I don't think that's the issue. I think our guy drives for someone, the night shift, leaving the daytime free."

"For rape and burglary," Ellen said.

Her phone buzzed. She fished it out, read the text.

Clover Penford had been found.

32

CHALLIS PARKED IN THE hospital grounds and went looking for Ellen.

He found Lois Katsoulas in a ward corridor. "Boss not here yet?"

Katsoulas eyed him with open curiosity, fully aware of his relationship with Destry. "On her way, sir."

She paused. "This relates to one of your cases?"

Challis nodded. "We have her mother in custody. The mother's partner is currently missing, but she says he gave the kid to ice cooks as collateral on a loan. I have to admit, I thought we'd find her dead."

A flicker on Katsoulas's face, Challis reading it as rage. "Poor little kid. She didn't say much. She was in a house with two men for a couple of days and then a fire came so they went to another house. She said they didn't hurt her but they did take pictures of her. With her clothes off."

"They just dropped her at the playground?"

"Apparently. Told her to run and play with the other children and her mother would be along to collect her shortly."

"Any cameras down there?"

"No."

"Witnesses?"

"No."

"Could she name or describe the men?"

"Only very vaguely."

Just then a door opened, a doctor emerged, and through the gap Challis saw Clover Penford, in a tiny gown, sitting on her grandmother's lap. The doctor gave a confused glance, Katsoulas to Challis, and finally settled on Katsoulas. "Her clothing."

A dress, in an evidence bag.

"Thank you."

"To set your mind at rest, there are no obvious signs of sexual assault or interference. No bruising or tearing."

All of Katsoulas's energy drained away. "Thank God for that."

"She said they took photos of her."

"I know."

The doctor watched her with a mix of pity and fatigue. "Good luck," she said, returning to the room and shutting the door.

CHALLIS LINGERED LONG ENOUGH to greet Ellen, then raced back to Waterloo, finding Pam Murphy in the main CIU office, leafing through a file marked *Hauser*.

"Is it intact?"

"According to the inventory, which means nothing, given it was Janine that drew up the inventory," Murphy said. She paused. "Boss, was it Clover Penford?"

Challis nodded. "She's okay—more or less. Hungry, thirsty, possibly sedated. They took nude shots of her."

"Bastards."

Challis said, "Have you seen Janine yet?"

"I kept out of her way in case my face revealed our suspicions."

"Your notorious poker face," Challis said. He swung a chair around, straddled it and said, "I spoke to Lily earlier.

She said the photocopiers have been fine. She *also* said that while Annette's away, Janine's been handling her calls."

A silence settled and Challis watched Murphy's famously transparent face register the dawning thoughts.

Gleeful. Murphy in hunting mode. "That's how she makes contact."

"I think so," Challis said. "It would be worth checking calls in and out—especially out."

"I'm right across it," Murphy said, reaching for her desk phone.

He stopped her. "In a moment. It's not enough to know who she was calling, we need to know the substance of the calls. If we challenge her, she could ask for a lawyer and refuse to cooperate."

"So we tap the line."

"That will take time to arrange. We need to act now."

"Okay, so we bug the room. Plant a recorder somewhere."

"And wait days for her to contact whoever it is she contacts?" Challis shook his head. "We also need to give her a push."

WAITING FOR JANINE QUINE to head out for lunch, Challis and Murphy installed a voice-activated recorder in Annette Tranh's office and returned to CIU, discussing Quine.

"It's not as if she has access to sensitive material," Murphy said. "She doesn't see witness statements, case notes, interview transcripts or forensic reports."

"But she is in charge of the unoccupied dwellings register."

"So her contact's a housebreaker?"

"Or someone running an operation that includes housebreaking. Someone who fences stolen farm machinery, for example."

"This someone was scared Hauser had incriminating information at his house, and asked Janine to copy any paperwork we found."

Murphy glanced at the Hauser inventory again. "Nothing incriminating that I can see, unless she destroyed it. But what I don't get is why she didn't inventory the note she left in the photocopier."

They mused on that. Challis said, "If Hauser is suspicious enough to make a note describing two men and what they were carrying and what they were driving, would he leave it in plain sight if those same men followed him to his house? He'd hide it. Tuck it away in the back of his desk diary, for example."

"Meaning Janine didn't know it was there. It fell out when she was at the library."

THE AFTERNOON WORE ON and they worked on a narrative, Challis glancing at his watch occasionally, willing the cadaver-dog handler to call.

"We need her to think Annette's coming back sooner than next week," he said. "We need to panic her a little."

"Why don't we just let slip that we're close to making an arrest?"

"Not specific enough. I suggest you take all of the Hauser material back for refiling, tell her thank you, we had an unexpected break after viewing aerial photographs from a police drone and matching these to downloaded GPS coordinates for the stolen vehicles."

Murphy snorted. "Is that even possible?"

"I dunno. Sounds good."

"Should ramp up the tension, anyway," Murphy said. She piled the folders and loose sheets together and got to her feet. "Wish me luck."

~

IT WAS EARLY EVENING before the dog handler called. Unavoidable delays, wouldn't be able to start the sweep until first light.

33

WEDNESDAY, SUNRISE, CHALLIS IN his kitchen, agitated, wondering if he should join the dog handler or wait for news.

He waited. To siphon off the tension, he dragged out the vacuum cleaner. Five minutes into the job, he decided he felt about vacuum cleaners as he did whipper-snippers: he doubted the men who designed them had actually used them. He'd had several different whipper-snippers over the years. With all of them he'd had to stop the machine regularly to dismantle the head and manually extend the cutting line. And his vacuum cleaner—German, top of the range—always tipped onto its back if he looked at it sideways, locked hard against furniture legs rather than slide past and displayed the bag-full indicator after about one pass of his sitting room.

So he caught up on his post. Half of it was from *charities donating to him*—pens, envelopes, Christmas cards, address labels . . . He gave up.

By 7 A.M. he was sitting in the sun, sipping coffee, reading the paper without concentration. Into the mild spill of sunlight coming over the tall pines at the rear of the house came two protective ducks, seven ducklings. He watched, the ducks watched him, and then they were across the yard and down through the grass to the dam, and all the time he was waiting for his phone to ring.

At 8:05, it did. He immediately called for a crime-scene unit.

THE DOG HANDLER WAS at the entrance to Lintermans Lane, loading the dogs into a van.

Shutting the cage door, he told Challis, "For the first half an hour the dogs weren't picking up anything, which makes me think our victim was already dead and they carried him in."

"Uh huh."

"And I'd been concentrating on the paddocks on either side, which took time. It wasn't until I reached the gate at the end that the dogs got excited. It's possible they dumped the body or tipped it over the top bar of the gate, leaving a trace. After that it didn't take us long to find the grave."

Challis thanked the man and watched him leave, just as Pam Murphy arrived from Waterloo driving the CIU car. She wore pants and a sleeveless top with walking shoes, her hair pulled back in a ponytail, so no different from any other day, but her . . . aura was different; Challis couldn't think of a better word.

"Your aura is different, Constable Murphy."

She went pink and evasive. "My aura?"

"Anyone would think you'd had a pleasant night."

The pinkness deepened. "Well, there's a euphemism for you," she said. Then she pointed down the track. "We good to go? Sir? Boss?"

"Okay, change of subject," Challis said, and they set out on foot.

THE GOING WAS EASY, in dappled light between the gums on either side, the only sounds a few warbling galahs and the soft swishing of their shoes on the trampled grass. Here and there yellow evidence markers indicated where the crime-scene techs had already made quick-setting plaster casts of full and partial shoeprints.

While they walked they talked. "Your cunning plan paid off," Pam said. "Janine made an anxious call to one Raymond Loeb, of Loeb Property Management."

Challis filed that away. He'd run the name past Bernie Joske. "Does Loeb have a record?"

"No. And the business is legitimate, mainly rural: conveyancing, property auctions, clearing sales, permit applications."

"Anyone working there would have sound reasons for poking around farms and wineries."

"Yes."

"What exactly did she say?"

"She tried explaining about the drone photographs and GPS coordinates, and then she listened for half a minute, and then got a bit panicky, saying, 'I can't do that. I wouldn't know where to look.'"

"He asked her to get copies."

"I think so."

"We'll hit her hard after lunch," Challis said.

Then he froze, shot his hand out to stop Murphy as a snake flicked at the corner of his vision, slipping unhurriedly into longer grass at the fence line.

"You scared me!"

"Scared myself," he said.

"We should get danger money."

"This government?" Challis said. "We're lucky to get anything."

They walked on, thinking of death around them and the dead man at the end of the track.

~

THEY CAME TO A gate, a hint of muddy, reedy water in the air. Challis couldn't see the reservoir but heard voices downslope of the gate, beyond a screen of scrub and blackberry thickets. The gate had been padlocked but Sutton's crew, or the dog handler, had used bolt cutters and dragged it open.

They walked through to the water's edge. It was mostly choked with reeds but here and there were small cliffs, rocky outcrops and muddy clearings. In one such clearing Scobie Sutton's team was at work disinterring a body and searching the area around the grave as well as between the grave and the track leading back to the gate. Metal stepping plates led to the body, a dark, mud-caked shape in a shallow depression. Yellow markers had been distributed around the site, and Sutton was taking a cast of another shoeprint.

Good luck with that, Challis thought. The footwear worn by Lovelock and Pym had been reduced to ash. At that moment, as if to echo him, kookaburras laughed in the encircling gum trees.

Hearing voices, he turned around. Two men with a stretcher, and Freya Berg, dressed in a white forensic suit and rubber overshoes.

Reaching them she nodded hello. "Hal, Pam."

"Freya."

"Doctor Berg."

She heaved a sigh: "Duty calls," and carried on down to the body.

Pam turned to the stretcher bearers. "You might have a wait."

"Story of our lives," one of them said and they strolled to the nearest shade, where they sat with their backs to a tree.

Eventually Scobie Sutton labored up the slope, saying, "The dogs found him at first light."

Challis nodded. "I talked to the handler. Is it Owen Valentine?"

"Hard to say. The body's been there for a week and a half. There's decomposition, but less than if he'd been left in the open. The general size and shape is a match."

"Clothing?"

"Jeans, T-shirt and trainers. I haven't looked in the pockets yet."

"Is his face intact?"

Sutton shook his head. "A mess. Some decomp, but mainly he's been beaten. His nose is broken, teeth are missing and his cheekbones and eye sockets are damaged."

"I'll need a rush on his DNA."

Sutton nodded. "I found blood under that paint spill in Valentine's garage. I'll see if it matches DNA from the body."

"That won't prove conclusively that it's Owen Valentine, only that the dead man was at the house."

"I know that," Sutton said testily. "I'm also running the DNA I found inside the bedroom."

THIRTY MINUTES LATER, FREYA Berg climbed to where they waited.

"It's all yours, Mr. Sutton."

He thanked her, called to the stretcher bearers and returned to the grave.

Challis, watching the men maneuver the body, asked the pathologist for her preliminary conclusions.

"White male," Berg said, "undernourished, possibly an addict, aged in his late twenties."

"Murdered?"

"I won't know cause of death for sure until I perform the autopsy, but he wasn't shot or stabbed. Took a severe beating, though, and there are shallow cuts all over his face."

"Knife?"

"Or a razor."

"No big sign around his neck saying, 'My name is Owen Valentine?'"

"Something just as good," Berg said. She took out her iPhone, swiped her finger across the screen, showed them a photograph.

A muddy blue amateurish tattoo, saying "Owen and Chrissie 4 ever."

Challis sighed, fished out his phone, walked in circles until he got a signal, and called Serena Coolidge.

34

WEDNESDAY'S SEX-CRIMES BRIEFING BEGAN with the strangest and most uncomfortable few minutes of Ellen Destry's working life. She'd set a plate of pastries on the table, brewed the coffee and greeted her officers, when Serena Coolidge entered the room as if she'd conquered a nation and intended to address its citizens. Ellen remembered the body language from the police academy and from the more recent encounter in the main police station car park, when Coolidge had shot her a look that suggested she was trying to remember what it was about Ellen that irritated her so much.

And here it was again.

"Sergeant Destry."

"Serena," Ellen said, earning herself another look.

"I need," said Coolidge, "a brief word with everyone."

"Be my guest."

An intense figure at the head of the room, Coolidge announced her name, her squad, and said: "Yesterday's stakeout. Which one of you found the girl?"

Katsoulas, bristling a little, raised her hand and said, "To be strictly accurate, a parent took her to the police station just as I was bringing in a prisoner."

This time the body language said *whatever*. Coolidge gestured indifference with the long, predatory fingers of her right hand. Perfect polished nails, Ellen noticed.

"The point is, there's a drugs connection," Coolidge said.

Ellen stirred. "We're aware of that, but there's also a sex-crimes connection. The girl, whose name is Clover Penford, was made to pose naked for photographs and videos."

Coolidge stared at the room, then turned her head slowly to Ellen. Nothing was said but all noise was stilled, the hush premonitory, and Coolidge's face tightened.

"*Sergeant* Destry, I'm afraid my investigation trumps yours. The kid—"

"Her name is Clover," Katsoulas said.

"—is tied up in an ongoing case with far-reaching ramifications and involving a range of very dangerous people. You will have access to her in due course, and press sex-crimes charges as warranted, *after* we've made arrests on manufacturing and trafficking charges."

Ian Judd was disgusted. He'd been chewing the end of a ballpoint pen. He threw it down in front of him.

"Is there a problem?" Coolidge said acidly.

Judd shrugged.

Coolidge tried for appeasement. "Look, I'm happy for you to throw the book at these pricks for whatever sex crime you can hang around their necks, but not until we have them on drug offenses. We think the little girl's stepfather was murdered by syndicate members from New South Wales, so we need to look hard at anyone and everyone involved with him."

Ellen wondered if something had shifted. In Hal's pithy view, expressed last night, "diminished resolve" pretty much summed up Coolidge's approach to investigating Clover Penford and the ice-lab cooks, and Ellen knew all about diminished resolve, senior officers backing down or failing to pursue investigations and prosecutions.

But now Coolidge was muscling in. Scouting around for another coup?

Before Ellen could say anything, Coolidge left the room.

Rubbing her chin, Ellen said, "That was . . ."

"Enlightening."

"Fulfilling."

"Inspirational."

"Help yourselves to coffee and pastries," Ellen said.

Stepping back from the scramble, she texted Challis: *You found Valentine's body?*

And back came the text: *Yes.*

So that explained Coolidge.

WHEN JUDD, KATSOULAS AND Rykert were settled she briefed them on the Robards attack.

"Assuming he's a taxi driver, how does that fit our rough profile?"

Rykert: "He's familiar with the streets and towns of the Peninsula."

Katsoulas: "He's probably an owner-driver's *night* driver, meaning he's free during the day. What time did Ms. Robards say he received the phone call?"

"About five-thirty."

"The call could have come from the day driver. Five-thirty in the afternoon would be getting close to his or her knock-off time, so a three-hour round trip to the airport would not be welcome. They'd give it to the night driver."

Judd: "We're assuming he started with burglary and graduated to rape? In any event, he spotted target buildings while driving at night and returned to them in daylight."

Katsoulas: "It's also possible one or more of his victims had been passengers."

Rykert: "But for all we know he lives up near Melbourne

and just has the occasional fare down here. In which case we'll never find him. The city's crawling with taxi drivers."

Judd: "I think there's a better than fifty per cent chance he's local. The city firms are allowed to drop passengers here, but not tout for fares. They'd not hang around, they'd head straight back to the city, where the work is."

"But a Peninsula cab is allowed to drop off and pick up at the airport?"

"Any taxi's permitted to take passengers to the airport, but only taxis from the metropolitan region are allowed to stay there and join the rank. If you're a Peninsula resident and want a Peninsula cab to collect you at the airport, you have to book in advance."

Katsoulas: "So we don't know if our guy was being asked to take someone there or drive there to collect someone?"

"Correct."

Ellen: "The taxi companies are pretty obliging. They're very sensitive to issues involving drivers."

Judd: "So long as we don't alert our guy."

Rykert: "What if the phone call referred not to a Monday night airport run but some other night?"

Ellen shrugged. "We have to start somewhere. And it's not as if the Peninsula cabs are making an airport run every ten minutes. It's an expensive trip from here, and most people drive themselves or take the airport bus. Some cabbies can go days without an airport run." She paused. "And even if we end up with a couple of dozen drivers, we're looking at a male, tall, fit and youngish, and he cut himself on Monday afternoon, so look for someone wearing a bandage or at least a deep scratch on his left forearm."

Katsoulas quivered. "DNA, boss."

Ellen shook her head. "He didn't leave any at the scene, unfortunately. And even if we find him and can legally test him, we can only compare his DNA to that one early rape."

BY EARLY AFTERNOON EMAILS from the local cab companies revealed that four taxis had made an airport run on Monday evening. All four were made by owner-drivers, two middle-aged men, two women, and all four trips were regular Monday bookings: three drop-offs and one pick-up.

Ellen was about to ask for details of the Tuesday evening runs when a notation from Coolart Cabs caught her eye: the pick-up passenger, a Sydney woman who flew down for a three-day period each week, consulting on a Peninsula golf course development, had called to say her usual 3 P.M. Qantas flight had been canceled and she'd be getting the 6 P.M. flight, getting in at 7:30 P.M. Her regular cabbie was an owner-driver named Posie Laing.

So would Laing have made the evening run?

LAING WAS SIXTY, A short, barely woman with cropped grey hair and a face full of scowling eyebrows, and Destry and Judd found her in the lead cab at a rank beside the ANZ bank in Waterloo. She got out of her taxi, propped her rump against the passenger door and folded her ample arms. "Will this take long?"

"Mrs. Laing, you regularly collect a Ms. Weatherby from the three o'clock flight from Sydney every Monday afternoon?"

"Yeah, so?"

"Did you collect her this Monday?"

The cabbie seemed to test the question for tricks and hidden meanings. Time passed, and she said, "No. Her flight was canceled."

Before they knew it an elderly woman laden with shopping

bags had slipped into the back of the cab. Laing beamed, hurried around to the driver's door and yanked it open.

Judd slammed it before she could get in. She lost the smile. "Hey! My passenger!"

"In a moment," he said. "Just a couple more questions."

Doors opened on two of the waiting cabs, the drivers calling, "Posie, you okay?"

Ellen showed her ID. They retreated, muttering, and Laing parked her rump against the taxi again. "I need to get Mrs. Richards home with her shopping," she grumbled, and started to cough, a wet smoker's cough that Ellen thought might lead to palliative care at any moment.

They waited. Laing recovered. "So what's this about?"

"You didn't collect Ms. Weatherby from the airport on Monday."

"I told ya, her flight was canceled."

"She came in on a later flight."

Laing's eyes slid sideways, hunting for a way out. "Yeah, I remember now."

"She told us a man collected her."

"Me other driver. I usually knock off around six."

"His name?"

"Look, did she make a complaint? I explained I couldn't make the trip and me other driver would pick her up and she seemed okay with that. I mean, I've used Mitch for years."

"Mitch who?"

"Pyne. Did he do something wrong?"

She's going to contact him, Ellen thought. A part of her will want to warn him, and another part will want reassurance, so she'll contact him and she'll try to read his tone.

So Ellen ran with her imagination. "There was an incident in the taxi waiting area at the airport. A Silver Cabs driver said he was assaulted by a driver he thought worked for one of the Peninsula firms. Is Mr. Pyne of Sri Lankan appearance, Mrs. Laing?"

Laing chortled, which set off another coughing fit. Recovering, she spat into a handkerchief and said, "Well, there you go, Mitch is as white as my backside."

Ellen tried and failed to quash the image. "Thank you, Mrs. Laing; you've cleared that up for us. We'll let our city colleagues know it's a dead end."

"You do that," Laing said, getting behind the wheel of her cab.

"Hope she buys it," Destry said.

They were in the car, heading for Crib Point, where Pyne lived. According to records, he was twenty-nine years old, no convictions, but at the age of eighteen he'd been suspected of handling stolen goods. No charge, no conviction, no DNA sample.

"That Sri Lankan reference was a nice touch," Judd said. "Distracted her and probably appealed to the racist in her too."

Ellen nodded. "With any luck it's enough to keep her off the phone to him."

"Now I guess we eyeball him for a while," Judd said.

Pyne lived in a rundown weatherboard house on a side street behind the Crib Point swimming pool. His car, a listing white Falcon with one grey primer-painted door, sat in the driveway, weeds brushing the underside of the chassis. Ellen checked the time: 2 p.m. Maybe Pyne felt spooked by Monday's failure, and would stay at home until it was time for his night-driving shift. Or maybe they'd get lucky and he'd go out to rape someone so they could catch him at it.

They got lucky in an unexpected way.

~

"TOWEL, BAG, HE'S GOING to the swimming pool," Judd said.

Pyne was tall, solid, with thick pelts of black hair on his arms and legs—as described by two of his victims. He looked faintly out-of-date to Ellen, in brief tight shorts, tight T-shirt and black hair styled in something like a mullet.

"Ugly bugger," Judd said.

They watched him to the end of the street, then started the car and followed, passing Pyne but eyeing his progress in the rear-view mirror as he turned into the sports complex and headed across the dust and dead grass to the pool entrance. Reaching the corner, Ellen turned left and immediately parked. She'd been to the gym that morning; she reached around for her Adidas bag. "Go in after him, Ian. Pretend you've come for a swim or to join, something like that."

"Boss."

"He might be a regular, or he might be meeting someone, like his fence."

"Got it."

Ellen watched him head for the swimming pool. A few minutes later, she did a U-turn and drove past the football ground to the pool, parking in the shade of a large gum tree. The air was sharp with summery eucalyptus smells and a fainter chlorine tang. She could see mothers and small children through the cyclone fence, hear the children cry out. She checked her watch: 2:20 P.M. Schools would be getting out soon. She got out of the super-heated car and at that moment was struck with a powerful image of bringing her daughter to this pool for an interschool swimming carnival. The mosquitoes had been hell.

Then Judd was back. He waggled his handkerchief at her. "I come bearing gifts."

He unwrapped the handkerchief, revealing a bloodied bandage.

"I sat in the change room pretending to unlace my shoes while he got into his togs, and saw him toss this into the bin."

35

CHALLIS DIDN'T WANT TO spook Quine. Keeping it low-key, the harried boss with lots on his plate, he poked his head into the general office, waved hello, encompassing everyone, and said, "Janine, sorry to interrupt, but could you bring me anything you've found on Owen Valentine?"

She wore her habitual face, a woman used to disappointment, and the expression deepened. "Yes, Inspector."

Challis didn't wait but bounded up to the first floor and into CIU. He jerked his head at Murphy. "She's on her way."

THREE MINUTES LATER, A timid knock, and Challis called, "Come in, Janine."

He was leaning back in his swivel chair, clutter spread over his desk. Quine eyed it disapprovingly, then sat on a visitor's chair next to Pam Murphy. Her gaze swiveled between Challis and Murphy; reading their smiles with suspicion, she tossed a manila folder across Challis's desk.

"I did some digging—he has a half-brother, Carl Bowie, but apparently they're estranged. The brother owns a few bakeries."

She was talking too fast.

"That's not why we're here, Janine," Challis said, his voice low and almost unmodulated.

He opened a drawer, pulled out a digital recorder and

touched a finger to the play button. "Yesterday afternoon you were observed going into Annette Tranh's office and using her desk phone. You were observed hanging up shortly afterward and returning to your desk. Five minutes later, Annette's phone rang and you left your desk to answer it. Here is your side of the conversation."

"Annette's phone . . . Ray, I hoped it was you . . . Look, they say they're about to make a series of arrests . . . No, not the murder, the stolen vehicles and equipment . . . That wasn't you, was it, the murder? I told you I wouldn't help you cover something like that up . . . Well, they said by calibrating GPS coordinates with aerial photographs from police drones they can track where . . . Ray, I don't know what it means, either. I'm no expert . . . It could be stored somewhere here, I suppose . . . I can't just destroy it, Ray . . . Look, I'll have a look and let you know, all right? And I think that clears Jeff's debt with you. It's getting too dangerous."

Challis pressed the stop button. "That was your voice, wasn't it, Janine?"

She stared at the desk, haggard and vacant.

"Raymond Loeb. Were he and Mr. Hauser partners?"

Nothing.

"What's *your* involvement in this?"

Nothing but a stirring of sulky anger as Quine shifted in her chair. She kept looking down. Darted a glance at Pam Murphy, who saw sadness, regret and guilt under the truculence.

"Raymond Loeb Property Services," Challis continued. "Valuations, property management, auctions and clearing sales, stock agent, specializing in farms and wineries."

Janine shrugged.

"He gets about, old Ray," Challis said. "Perfectly placed to spot a truck or a trailer or a weed sprayer or a ride-on mower that's not well secured."

Another shrug.

"What happens then? He sends in a team? One guy, like Colin Hauser? How does it work, Janine?"

He watched her for a moment, then went on. "I think he uses a team of people. I think Hauser's farm was a kind of way station while Mr. Loeb found a buyer. Or does he steal to order?"

Janine Quine looked thoroughly hunted now.

Pam Murphy said, "We've also had a run of house burglaries, Janine. Houses on the register administered by *you*. People on holiday or away on business, trusting the police to keep an eye on their properties, and what happens? *You* happen."

After a long pause, Quine lifted her face. She was depleted of hope. "Will I go to jail?"

"That's up to the Department of Public Prosecutions, but if there are mitigating circumstances, and you agree to help us, we are prepared to make recommendations for leniency," Challis said.

"*If* deserved," Murphy snapped. "A man was murdered, after all."

Janine Quine seemed to have only two expressions, defeated and sulky, but now her face flashed spiritedly. "I had nothing to do with that. Ray Loeb had nothing to do with that."

"Convince us," Challis said indifferently. He placed the Hauser photocopy on the desk between them. "You left this in the library photocopier a few days ago. In it Mr. Hauser describes two men, who probably shot him dead a short time later. We believe them to be from a major New South Wales drug ring. This is *huge*, Janine, and you're right in the middle of it."

She said wretchedly, "Nothing to do with me."

"You admit to using the library copier?"

"Ours was broken."

She was being true to form. She would admit, retract the admission, hint, deny, shift blame and generally downplay her role until the cows came home. Perhaps she thought they'd give up and let her go?

"*Stop lying.* Our photocopiers were not broken or out of paper or toner. You took the Colin Hauser murder case material out of the station and copied it for Raymond Loeb, correct?"

She looked at the floor. "Might have."

"Are you sleeping with him?"

She jerked in the chair. "What? No. Never."

Pam Murphy leaned forward. "So why are you helping him, Janine? Partners in crime? It didn't sound like a very equal partnership on the recording we just heard. It sounded like he was giving you orders."

Quine looked around wildly. "What do I get if I help you?"

"Satisfaction. A weight off your shoulders. Is Mr. Loeb threatening you? We can protect you."

Quine couldn't get comfortable in the chair. It was as if she still thought there might be a way out.

Challis said, "We've checked the call history on Mrs. Tranh's phone. You've been in almost daily touch with Loeb while she's been away. That shows a pattern of con-spiratorial behavior. We're not talking a one-off phone conversation, Janine."

An incident rose in Murphy's mind, chatting with John Tankard last week. "What's Raymond Loeb got on you, Jan? Is it your husband? We heard he's been acting erratically lately, yelling abuse at a school bus driver . . ."

Challis shot her a querying look, but nodded, giving her the okay.

"I understand Jeff's a gambler," Pam said. "Does he owe money to Mr. Loeb? Is that the threat?"

Quine whispered, "Jeff worked for Ray for a while last year. He stole from him, a few thousand dollars. Ray said he wouldn't turn him in if I fed him police information from time to time."

"It started with the register?"

"Yes."

"How does Colin Hauser fit in?"

"I never met him. All I know is Ray got very agitated when he heard about the murder and said I had to find out everything I could."

"You passed on information? Copies of documents?"

She whispered, "Yes."

"Is it your belief," Challis said, "that Mr. Loeb was not involved in the murder?"

"Yes! He sounded really upset and confused when he heard about it. Scared."

Challis didn't see that he needed to bring Coolidge into this. In his mind, he was dealing with an internal leak and the theft of farm vehicles and machinery. But he had to ask: "Is Loeb involved in drugs that you know of?"

"Never. He hates drugs. He wouldn't know a drug if he fell over it. He just steals stuff and sells it."

"When you pass documents on to Mr. Loeb, how do you do it?"

"We meet various places: down near the jetty, on the boardwalk through the wetlands, on one of the park benches near the coin barbecues."

"But he lives on the other side of the Peninsula."

"It's easier for him to come to me. Like you said, he's always out and about."

"So he comes by . . ."

"Walking his dog," Quine said.

"Do you speak, or simply hand over an envelope?"

"He stops and chats while I pretend to pat his dog."

"Here's what I want you to do, Janine," Challis said, and the steel was there in his voice, a sharkish glint as he smiled. "I want you to tell him you were able to make copies of the GPS readouts and aerial photographs relating to the movement of vehicles and machinery in and out of the Hauser farm over the past month. It's nonsense, but he'll want to know what it all means, okay?"

"I'm frightened."

"We'll be there," Challis said, "watching and listening."

36

NOW IT WAS TIME for the death knock.

Pam had done a few of these over the years, calling on people to say a family member had been found dead. It was a job for junior police. But this time Challis wanted to come with her. "I need to eyeball this half-brother."

She drove, of course, and, steering into Mornington, found herself falling silent, remembering last Sunday, lunch here with her mother. She might have told Challis about her mother and her fears, but she'd gone to see Michael Traill. Michael listening, a cool hand on her wrist. She might have told Challis that she thought her mother was dying, saying goodbye to the people and places that had made up her life, but she'd told a stranger. Then she'd made love to that stranger, a man she thought she hated.

And it had meant something.

She wasn't sure what, yet. But her life, for so long defined by her job, suddenly had a private dimension of some substance. She didn't question her decision to keep it all from Challis. It was instinctive and right.

Finding a park opposite the library, they got out and walked up Main Street to a side street and the Bowie Bakehouse. Nothing in the windows, but the timeless comfort of baking smells inside. Half-a-dozen tiny tables and chairs spaced along one wall, leaving a narrow aisle for customers.

Cakes and pastries in glass display cases, breads in wire racks on the wall behind the shop staff.

Two young women were serving, dressed in tight black skirts and black T-shirts with *BB* embroidered on the left breast. They were attending to a woman with small children and an elderly man, so Pam took a moment to scope out the shop. There was an open archway at the far end, leading to a corridor. The ovens would be down there somewhere, she thought. The office, a loo, a storeroom. She spotted three CCTV cameras, which she thought seemed a bit excessive: one was trained on the front door, one along the corridor, the third on the young women behind the counter. And it was making them tense, she realized. They were hurrying about their business, dodging one another in the cramped space, wiping wisps of hair from their foreheads with the backs of their wrists.

Otherwise it was a pleasant place, with gleaming wood and chrome, terracotta tiles, and that lovely smell. Finally Challis and Murphy were asked, "How may I help you?"

Her name was Alicia, about twenty years old, tall but with an unformed face and an awkward manner. Challis said gently, "We're from the police, Alicia. Nothing to worry about, but we'd like to see Mr. Bowie."

Alicia looked stricken. "That was you on the phone, asking where Mr. Bowie was working today?"

It was, but Challis said, "I don't know anything about that. May we see him?"

Alicia's gaze darted to the camera watching her and then across at the corridor at the end of the shop. "I'm not sure. I mean . . ."

"Perhaps you could let him know we're here?"

That amplified rather than eased her burden. She whispered to the other girl, who seemed stronger and more calculating, casting the detectives a glance almost of anticipation before turning away and disappearing in the direction of the rear of the business. "Trina's getting him now," Alicia said.

She turned to a new customer, messed up the order and darted anxious glances at the yawning archway. Then Trina was back, saying, "He's out in the yard. He said to come through."

TRINA LED THEM DOWN the corridor, the kitchen on the left, heat and baking smells rolling out from the bank of ovens and racks of cooling loaves, past three closed doors, to a door that opened onto a small paved courtyard. Potted plants, a small bottlebrush growing in one corner, jasmine growing along the laneway fence at the rear. A garden table and chairs under a huge canvas umbrella. A man at the table, working on an iPad, a mug of coffee and a croissant at his elbow.

He was about forty, slim. When he stood and came around to meet them with an outstretched hand, of average height. Short, sandy hair and a pleasant, narrow face. But he was wearing a bemused frown and under that Pam sensed a man wrapped up in private resentments, and the police coming to his place of business was yet another one. He wore dark grey trousers, a darker shirt, sleeves rolled in precise folds to the mid-point of each tanned forearm. There was a complicated lump of chrome on his wrist. Pam guessed Rolex and spent part of the visit trying to eye the watch face so she could confirm that.

They shook hands and Bowie offered coffee, which Challis declined.

"Water?"

To shut down this line of dialogue, Pam smiled. "Yes, thanks."

Bowie snapped an order at Trina, manner faintly malevolent, then turned with smiles to his guests and gestured at the empty chairs. "Please."

They sat and contemplated each other. Bowie's knee jiggled. Challis said, "I'm afraid we're here with bad news, Mr. Bowie. Concerning your brother, Owen." Pause. "His body was found this morning."

Pam saw Bowie try for the right expression: bewilderment, shock, grief . . . He spluttered. "Sorry? He's dead? Overdose?"

Pam said, "Why would you say that, Mr. Bowie?"

An unwarranted question, her tone almost rude, but she didn't like the man. And he flushed a little, his face tightening.

"I'd have thought that was obvious: he's a crackhead."

"Were you close?" she asked, knowing the answer.

"Haven't set eyes on him for years. I ask again, was it an overdose?"

Challis said, "We believe he was murdered, Mr. Bowie. He was found buried in a shallow grave."

Bowie swallowed. He reached for and gulped his coffee. "He owed money to the wrong people."

"Do you know that for a fact, Mr. Bowie?"

"Stands to reason."

"But you don't know for certain?"

"No."

"Do you know anything about his life in recent months?"

"No."

"Not aware of anyone making threats?"

"Look, I didn't want him in my life, all right? Junkie loser." He paused. "Are you sure it's him?"

"Judging by his clothing and general size and shape, and his wallet, then yes, I'm afraid so," Challis said.

Pam said, "But DNA will confirm it."

She saw Bowie search for the words. "DNA? Why not dental?"

"His teeth are a mess from the drugs. We have a DNA profile from material found at his house and once that's compared with DNA from the body, we'll know for certain."

"If there's any doubt," Challis said, "we'll compare it to your DNA."

"But we have different fathers."

"Doesn't matter," Pam said.

With his pinned-back ears and face suffused with strong, hard-to-read feelings, Bowie looked sleek and dangerous briefly, belying the neatness, the pampered hands.

Challis, gentler, smiled and said, "But that's for later. Right now, is there anyone we can inform for you? Anyone who can be with you?"

Bowie shook his head a little wildly. "No, I'm fine. I'm sorry he's dead, but he was a lot younger than me and he was on drugs since he was fifteen. We had very little to do with each other. I haven't seen him for years. *Years.* Our mother's dead, his father's dead, my father's dead. There's nobody. Wait, I think he had a girlfriend."

"Christine Penford?"

"If that's the one he had at school, then yeah. Otherwise I can't help you, sorry." He paused. "I mean, I'll pay for the funeral. The least I can do."

They gave him empty smiles. Challis stood, handing the man his card. "If we can help in any way, please call."

"Sure," Bowie said, as if that were quite unlikely.

THEY ENCOUNTERED TRINA ON their way out. Flustered, she offered Pam the glass of water, her gaze darting past their shoulders to the garden door and the splash of sunshine out there. Pam wanted to say, "Your boss, bit of a bastard, is he?" but didn't. Instead, she said, "Thank you," and gulped the water down and followed Challis out onto the street.

They were strolling toward the car park across from the library and the shire offices when a voice said, "What the fuck do you think you're doing?"

Senior Sergeant Coolidge, steaming along the footpath.

MEANWHILE ELLEN DESTRY HAD lodged Mitch Pyne's bandage for a DNA profile, and arranged for Judd and Rykert to shadow him. She'd take the evening shift with Katsoulas.

But now, late afternoon, she had Allie in her car, heading north along the Nepean Highway. "You're being very mysterious," Allie said, arms folded, staring out, refusing to look at her.

There wasn't much to see, only a strip of houses on one side and the Seaford foreshore reserve and occasional glimpses of the bay at the drainage outlets on the other. "Not much of a surprise," Allie went on.

Oh, it will be, Ellen thought, darting a look at her sister. Allie was in full obdurate mode, her skin tight over her cheekbones, her mouth a thin grimace. She'd agreed to this journey, "Only to shut you up, Ells."

"Be patient," Ellen said.

Allie folded her arms under her breasts. Nice breasts, Ellen thought, better shaped than mine. And then: strange how envy works. I've envied her figure, she's envied me my apparent stability, even while she's sneered at it.

"You know what I think? I think this has something to do with Clive."

"What makes you say that?"

"I know you, Ellen. You want to teach me a lesson of some kind. You're pretty predictable."

Got me there. Ellen bit her lip.

Allie went on, "I think you're jealous."

"I have Hal."

"Who you rarely see. Why you don't just move in together, I don't know—unless you're holding back because you know it's not going anywhere."

Ellen said nothing. Denial seemed to be Allie's default state. By the same token, it was significant that she'd agreed to come on this excursion. She knows something's not right, Ellen thought. She wants reassurance. But she'll keep sniping and chipping away because to admit her own foolishness would be more than she could bear.

And I'm about to hit her over the head with what a fool she's been.

They came to Seaford railway station, Ellen signaling a turn inland of the sea, the road taking her over the railway line and into a region of small houses on quiet streets. The house she wanted was huddled behind a meagre patch of lawn, pale yellow bricks cringing under a mossy tile roof. Apt enough, Ellen thought, parking on the opposite side of the road and half a block short of the yellow house, giving them a clear view of it through the windscreen.

"So?" said Allie, staring around grumpily.

It was warm in the car. Ellen had been racing around like a mad thing all day and needed a shower. Her sister, on the other hand, was fresh and crisp, just the way she'd gone through life.

Ellen wound down the window, leaned her forearm on the sill, just as Allie stiffened. "That's my car!"

"Yes."

"What's it doing there?"

"Allie, that's where Clive lives."

"He does not. He has an apartment in Southbank. He took me there once, a gorgeous place."

A detail that Ellen filed away. Whose apartment? An accomplice? Another victim, conveniently not at home that day?

"Believe me, Allie, Clive lives in that house."

"Probably a friend's house," Allie said. "Anyway, have you been following him?"

"He's not who he says he is."

Allie gnawed at her bottom lip. "You're lying. You're jealous, you always have been."

She stared out mulishly, building on her story. "Egg on your face if you find he's looking after a friend's place or asked a friend if he could park his car there while he's overseas."

"*Your* car, the one you signed over to him."

"I told you the reason for that."

"Not much of a reason, and I have to ask, what else have you signed over to him?"

"Don't know what you mean, and I don't think it's any of your business, people's private arrangements."

"Have you given him shares, for example. Property deeds. Valuables. Cash loans. Have you set up a joint account? I could go on."

"Please don't, it's boring."

"He told you he's going overseas, right? Did you give him the money for his ticket? First class, perhaps?"

Allie wouldn't look at her.

"What was his story?"

Allie bristled. "He swore me to secrecy, okay? You're in the police, you should know some matters have to fly under the radar."

"He's away on a mission, maybe? Dangerous one?"

Allie said stiffly, "It's related to his work, that's all I can say."

"Did he tell you he's an operative of an American intelligence organization, by any chance? CIA? Homeland Security?"

Allie's jaw dropped. "Have you been *questioning* him? Have you arrested him or something? Tell me."

"He's going overseas because he fears for his life, right? Extremists are after him?"

Allie turned away huffily. "If you know so much, why are you asking me?"

"He told the same story to a widow in 2011. He married this one, so at least you were spared that. He took her life savings, then vanished overseas. So I'm asking you, how much did you give him?"

Allie wriggled around and probably considered not replying. She whispered, "Only the car."

"Thank God for that."

Allie chewed her bottom lip. "Where did he go overseas?"

"We're still looking into that. But he was probably monitoring the situation here, and when he heard that the widow had died, he came back to try again. This time, you were his target."

"I don't believe you. Who would believe a story like that?"

"His real name is Wayne Hall. He has a string of arrests and convictions for dishonesty offenses going back many years. There are currently two arrest warrants out for him, one for fleecing that woman of her savings, and the other for falsifying loan documents in Adelaide. He gets around, old Clive. Sorry, Wayne."

Allie shrank, starting to believe.

"Furthermore," Ellen said, "he doesn't have a sister. There is no niece with leukemia."

Allie stared at her car in the driveway of the yellow house.

"I can't believe it. Why are you doing this to me?" Then she stiffened. "What's happening?"

A patrol car had pulled up outside the yellow house, then an unmarked car, uniformed and plain-clothed police piling out. Two uniforms ran to the rear of the property, one stood in the driveway, one on the lawn, and two detectives pounded on the door.

No result. They knocked again. Unseen by them, at the side of the house a window slid open and a young guy slipped out. Tanned, gleaming and gym-toned in tight shorts and a tighter singlet top. He was Chinese, tall, with glossy black hair to his shoulders. A lithe, fast-looking kid who touched the ground and began to sprint.

Stopped dead when he saw the uniforms at the front of the house. Put his hands up in surrender.

"Clive's boyfriend," Ellen murmured.

Carefully looking past Allie, Ellen nevertheless sensed the pain and confusion on Allie's face. Then Allie was shaking her head, her hair whipping about. "No, it's not true."

"Allie, didn't you ever ask yourself why Clive didn't want to have sex with you?"

"I don't believe it, it's a lie."

Ellen let the news sit and stew. She watched the action at the door. It opened. The detectives forced their way in.

"Ellen, tell me the truth. That boy's a housemate or something."

This was all taking too long. Ellen got out of the car and crossed the road. She marched past Allie's car and onto the veranda, just as the detectives emerged, holding Clive by the elbows.

"Found him under the bed, sneezing in the dust," said one of the men holding him.

"That'd be right," Ellen said. "He is a bottom feeder."

They laughed. Clive, dressed in shiny blue tracksuit pants and a paunchy white singlet, like a 1980s Mafia hood, looked full of sulks. He spotted Ellen.

"What are you doing here?"

"Hello, Wayne."

"You have no right. This is a conflict of interest."

"Shut up, Wayne."

Allie came running up. Clive brightened. "Allie, tell them, love."

Allie spat on him.

37

STILL AWESTRUCK BY COOLIDGE'S meltdown—"You came *this close* to jeopardizing a major investigation"— Challis and Murphy spent the next morning bugging the Loeb–Quine rendezvous site.

Loeb had stipulated a park bench some distance from the jetty, barbecue shelter and skateboard ramps in Waterloo. Overlooking a belt of mangroves and the Westernport tidal flats, it was set in a copse of casuarinas, one of them so close its leaves brushed the back of the bench. Knowing from Quine that Loeb would pat her down and check the bench for a wire, they'd installed microphones and tiny video cameras in the casuarinas and a nearby rubbish bin, and a member of the surveillance crew was concealed under a weather tarp in one of the little rowboats and motorboats anchored offshore, aiming a camera with a telephoto lens and video function.

With Janine settled on the bench by noon, Pam Murphy began walking the path behind the bench with a friend on maternity leave from the new police station at Somerville. Murphy pushed the woman's toddler in a stroller while two CIU detectives tossed a Frisbee back and forth on the grass between the path and the main road. Challis was sitting with Ellen Destry on a picnic rug scattered with plastic cups and a cane basket. Now all they could do was wait. According to bayside police, Loeb was yet to leave his office.

Challis, stretched out on the rug and warmed by the sun, thought he could almost forget he was a policeman. The air was mild, tangy with the smells of salt water and barbecued onions. Hovering gulls watching him for crumbs or sliding down the channels in the sky. The sea sucking around the exposed roots of the mangroves and crabs popping in the mud. He didn't even mind the refinery smokestacks giving him the finger, beyond the stretches of tidal flats and bay waters.

He went through the details of the operation once more. The cane basket contained recording equipment, pre-tested for range and clarity. When he had enough on tape, he'd call in the others for the arrest, mostly using hand gestures and mobile phone communication. If Loeb was paranoid about bugging equipment, he'd be doubly conscious of men and women wearing earpieces.

Then the call came: Loeb was on the move. Challis got to his feet, crossed the grass to the park bench, crouched with Quine and squeezed her forearm reassuringly.

"Twenty minutes, Janine, okay?"

She looked pale and tense, but then she probably always did, meeting the man who had such a hold over her. He squeezed again. "Okay?"

"Okay," she croaked.

TWENTY MINUTES LATER, ANOTHER call, this one from the shadow car as it peeled away after reporting that Loeb had arrived. "Black Range Rover, parked by the barbecue shelter."

Challis called Murphy. "Black Range Rover. Do you have eyes?"

Above the wheel-squeak of her baby stroller, he heard her reply, "He's just sitting. Wait, he's getting out. He's clearly jumpy. Looking around, giving everyone the evil eye."

Challis murmured, "Look and smile at your friend as you speak."

"I know how to do it, boss."

They were all tense.

Then, "He's on the move, heading your way."

"Dog?"

"Affirmative. Some little yappy-looking thing on a lead."

CHALLIS HAD BEEN AWARE of a low ambient rattle in the air. His subconscious told him the sound was a small petrol motor, a mower, perhaps. After all, there were houses on the other side of the approach road, two hundred meters away. And the park itself was half a kilometer long, stretching from the skateboard jumps at one end to a bait shop, a motel and a handful of small engineering businesses at the other.

It was background noise, that's all. Meanwhile the audio on Quine was crisp and clear. He could hear the crepitation of her clothing as she moved and breathed, hear her clear her throat, hear the gentle tidal pull of the water.

Until the mower came into range, drowning out all sound but the rattle of the engine and the churning whip of its blades in the grass and tiny stones and fallen tree debris. Challis, looking past Ellen's shoulder, saw a shire worker in a yellow safety vest, astride a huge ride-on mower, appear from behind a stand of spindly young gum trees. His intention was clear: mow the broad stretch of grass where the Frisbee players stood. A twenty-minute job, at least.

Challis glanced wildly toward the barbecue shelter. Loeb was not yet in view, but that would change in a matter of seconds. And he could see that he and Ellen were closer than Murphy and the Frisbee players. Leaning in to murmur in Ellen's ear, he said, "Get him out of here. Nicely. Show him your badge."

"Putty in my hands," she said.

The noise was deafening now. Ellen stood, a graceful articulation of legs and waist, and strolled across the grass, heading the man off. She stopped him with her hand up and when he cut the motor to a low idle, she stepped close to the machine, a friendly grin splitting her face. Challis saw her palm her ID quickly, then play-act for Loeb's benefit, although he hadn't yet come into view. She looked in one direction, pointed dramatically, said something, repeated the action in the other direction. The driver tipped back his head and laughed. He pointed. Then he grinned and waved and revved his motor and headed back the way he'd come.

Blessed silence.

Ellen flopped onto the blanket, nuzzling and kissing Challis, murmuring that she'd told the guy he could come back in thirty minutes.

"You seemed quite animated, the pair of you."

"People say I'm an ice queen, but it's a filthy lie," she said, tweaking his nose.

A few more seconds of proving it a lie, and then Challis heard a crackling voice from the interior of the cane basket: "Hello, Ray."

THE WORLD CARRIED ON around them but, to Challis, time seemed suspended. He half-expected Loeb to flee, or attack Quine, or spot the watchers or the spy gear.

Then, "Breathe," murmured Ellen, and it did the trick. He relaxed.

Stretched out on the rug on the grass, he drew her against him so that her head was propped on his cocked hip. He stroked her hair, and listened, and watched from the corner of his eye.

Loeb was suspicious, jumpy. He crouched a moment to

peer under the bench seat, his dog licking his face. Then he eyed the moored boats, the shoreline in each direction, before turning to face inland, his gaze passing over Challis and Destry, over Murphy walking with her baby and best friend, over the Frisbee players, just then mock-wrestling for possession of their toy.

Apparently satisfied, he sat with Quine. He patted her down, a swift, asexual exploration of her neck, shoulders, breasts, stomach and upper legs.

"You have it?"

Challis watched the bugging equipment inside the basket. The green recording indicator swelled, receded, as the dog panted and Loeb and Quine talked and were silent.

Then it picked up different sounds, Quine fetching a sheaf of papers from her bag. The paper rustled, crackled as Loeb took it from her.

Then papery flicks and scrapes as he flipped through the material, sheet by sheet. He was puzzled. "These are aerial shots around Baxter. Look, there's Peninsula Link, the Moorooduc Highway. I thought you said they had shots of Colin's farm?"

"I don't know anything about this kind of thing. It's double-Dutch to me," Quine said. "You asked me to get the file, that's the file."

More wordless sifting. "Even the dates are wrong."

Loeb was a soft, heavy man, losing his hair, losing his looks to flab, but Challis could hear a gravelly rasp as his voice hardened. "Are you sure this is the right file?"

More rustling noises as Janine Quine apparently leaned in. "Look at the label, *Hauser, surveillance monitoring*."

"And these GPS coordinates," Loeb said. "It's not Inverloch. I've been fishing down there enough times to know the GPS coordinates. I don't understand, Janine."

GARRY DISHER ❦ 310

Inverloch. It was a coastal town south-east of Phillip Island, but where had Challis heard it mentioned recently? Ah: Bernie Joske.

Perhaps the cameraman under the tarp moved then, or a passing boat set off a line of wavelets, Challis didn't know, but Loeb saw something out on the water, a lens flash perhaps, for he stiffened, snarled, "You bitch," and slammed his fist into the side of Janine Quine's head.

She toppled onto the ground, uttering a soft moan of pain, but by then Loeb was running, leaving the dog. He seemed to know to avoid Challis and the others. He ran along the path away from where he'd left his Range Rover and toward a thicket of trees that bordered a small industrial estate—where Challis had not thought to base backup police. And for a flabby man, he was fast and light enough on his feet, and he had a head start.

A moment later, the dog was streaking after him, lead bouncing on the grass.

Then the mower appeared. The driver had been watching from a screen of trees, he told Challis later. His was an uneventful life, he said, the same every day, so he got a real kick out of watching a police operation. And then he got to be a part of it! He saw the guy hit the woman—"What a cunt act"—and could see he might get away, so he'd climbed aboard and come rattling and screaming into view, cutting the guy off.

Loeb, startled, dodged one way and then the other. He backpedaled, tripped over the dog, fell heavily onto the footpath.

Murphy and the Frisbee players fell on him.

Ellen thanked the driver.

Challis, amused, called Lily in the general office and asked her to find out what linked Raymond Loeb to Inverloch.

38

ON FRIDAY, WORD CAME from South Gippsland police: Loeb's brother-in-law was in custody for possession of stolen farm vehicles, machinery and equipment, with many of the serial and other identification numbers matching the list supplied by Challis. The brother-in-law, Lance Merchant, reportedly belligerent and abusive, had also been charged with resisting arrest.

After securing the okay to take part in the interrogation, Challis and Murphy made a fast trip around the northern part of Westernport Bay and down the coast to Inverloch. By the time they arrived, Merchant was calmer, aware that he was facing jail time.

"Ray called me in a panic, said he had the tax man on his back and would I help out by storing some gear for him."

"Some gear," Challis said.

Merchant shook his head in disgust. "Turned out he meant tractors, Utes and trailers . . . I had to send all me spare drivers and low-loaders to collect it all. Two return trips."

"You didn't think it odd he had so much stuff stored on another man's farm?"

"I didn't know it wasn't his place! I thought he got in too deep, one of his deals, and needed some breathing space."

Merchant owned a farm-supply business, a sprawl outside

of town. Sheds, offices, baled hay and grain sacks undercover; tractors, ploughs and combine harvesters in a dusty
yard fronting the highway. Challis said, "I put it to you that
you have been on-selling vehicles and machinery for Raymond Loeb from the very start."

Merchant shook his head adamantly. "One-off favor, mate."

Challis said, "Lance Merchant, you are still under caution
and not obliged to say anything, but I am further charging
you with accessory to murder and—"

A cheap trick, but it worked, Merchant falling over himself to sell his brother-in-law down the river and weasel his
way out of further trouble.

SATURDAY AND SUNDAY CHALLIS spent at Dromana, providing moral support for Ellen, who was looking after her
sister. Allie spent the weekend ricocheting between self-
loathing, weepiness, sibling grievance and hatred of men.

It was exhausting and almost unrelenting, but occasionally Allie would storm off, leaving them in an edgy kind of
peace, which they tried to lighten with gardening and nonsense conversations.

"A heavy enameled cooking pot, French, would be a very
thoughtful Christmas present," Ellen said.

"I'm happy with my old pots and pans," Challis said.

She threw a clod of dirt at him. "Meanwhile, what would
you like?"

Challis had never had a clear notion of material objects
he lacked, or desired. "A new car."

"Anything else?"

"Book voucher."

She threw another clod. "I am *not* getting you a book
voucher. You need new pants, new shirts, a new jacket . . ."

Challis winced. Dread settled in him.

On Sunday morning, with Ellen and Allie sniping in the kitchen, he did the laundry. Badly, it seemed: discovering that none of the women's garments had a clearly defined top, bottom, neckline, waist or hem, he'd apparently pegged them out all wrong.

Better to be elsewhere. He wandered down to the beach and stared out at the tones of pink and grey in the sea and the sky. Felt himself relax. Life was in fact pretty good, notwithstanding his fucked-up car and his partner's fucked-up sister.

When he got back, he found Ellen emerging from the house with her keys. "Hop in."

"Where are we going?"

Ellen grinned. "We're going to get lost."

"From Allie?"

"Lost, lost."

She meant the Arthurs Seat maze. Speeding up the hill to Arthurs Seat and down to the maze, she explained that her senior constable, Ian Judd, had been watching their rape suspect, Mitchell Pyne.

"Pyne doesn't set foot outside his house all weekend, then suddenly gets in his car and comes here."

Challis looked around him doubtfully as she pulled into the car park. "People do visit mazes, Ells."

"I don't think Mitch is a maze kind of guy," she replied. "And who comes to a maze alone?"

She found Judd's white Skoda, and Judd emerged as she parked alongside. She was amused to see her detective in cargo pants, T-shirt and sandals. His glasses, scratched and filmy, caught the sun.

"Our boy's bought his ticket, but all he's done so far is enjoy the view."

They went in and paused a while, staring across at the main arena, a vividly green maze stretching across a hillside slope on the other side of a depression. People were streaming in, swallowed up then occasionally glimpsed within, their voices calling hollow in the still air.

Meanwhile Pyne, wearing a two-day stubble and jeans, runners and a khaki shirt with multiple pockets, stood downslope from Judd, Destry and Challis. At a glance, he was just another tourist, but Challis sensed he was tightly wound. He wasn't there for the entertainment.

"Waiting for someone?"

"I'd say so," Judd said.

They strolled downhill, passing close to Pyne. Feeling the man's suspiciousness, Ellen tucked her arm tightly around Challis's waist and leaned her cheek on his upper arm, while Judd, trailing them, blew his nose, trumpeting into a handkerchief.

They went on, in all their ordinariness, hoping Pyne wouldn't pay them a second look.

He stayed put so they watched him from below, screened by trees and other people, their faces and bodies in dappled light. Twenty minutes passed. Pyne was nervily vigilant, scanning every adult who passed him. Then, shortly after 1 p.m., a young family drew near him, the mother fussing over two small children, the father carrying a blanket and a picnic basket. The father did a double-take. "Mitch?" he seemed to say. Pyne mirrored the double-take. Challis, Judd and Destry saw him shake the other's hand and clap him on the back. Then Pyne was introduced to the woman and the children; hands were shaken.

The pantomime continued, Ellen providing dialogue and voices: "Mitch, mate, fancy meeting you here! Have you met the wife? Mitch, Celica. Celica, Mitch. And this young man is my son, Camry, and this is my daughter, Corolla. Hey, you had lunch yet? Care to join us?"

Challis snorted, dug her with his elbow, and even Judd cracked a smile before turning serious again. "Do we know who he is? Or who she is?"

Challis said no, Ellen shook her head.

"I'll follow them out, get a plate number," Judd said.

"Let's hope they're not here for hours, then."

Now the other man was asking Pyne to carry the cane basket while he scooped up one of the children, and the little group walked on, to a patch of shaded grass.

Ellen said, "Keep a close eye on Pyne and the basket."

They watched as the adults and the children settled onto the blanket. Pyne, sprawling on the outer edge, began removing plates, cups, a Thermos and packaged sandwiches from the cane basket, his hand dipping in and out, in and out.

Ellen saying tensely: "Did you see that?"

They nodded. Pyne, coordinating his movements seamlessly with unpacking the picnic basket, had fished a small, rectangular object from his breast pocket and slipped it into the basket. A few seconds later, his hand brought out an envelope, which vanished into the same pocket.

Judd said, "Cash?"

"Could be."

"In return for Karen Robards' iPhone? The only thing stolen, and it was a new one: worth a bit."

"Can we prove it's her phone?" Ellen said. "No doubt Pyne did a reset."

"We could match the IMEI number."

Ellen shook her head. "Karen didn't keep the box or the receipt."

"Question everyone," Challis said. "Account for this phone. Account for this cash."

"But what if it wasn't a phone? What if it wasn't cash in the envelope? We have no grounds to question or search."

THEY WATCHED FOR A further five minutes, until Pyne stood and stared at his watch face in a pantomime of regret, shook hands and took his leave.

"Sorry, guys, time got away from me, got to run," Ellen muttered. "Lovely to see you again, mate, but I better rush. Catch you later, all right?"

Pyne drifted back up the hill and out to the car park. Ellen said, "Ian, can you take Pyne? Hal and I will tail the father of the year."

"Got it," Judd said.

"What now?" Challis said, when they were alone.

Ellen glanced at Pyne's friends, still munching on their sandwiches, and snuggled against him. "Wanna fool around?"

"Is that allowed?"

THE FATHER OF THE year packed his family into a Honda Odyssey at 3 P.M. and led Challis and Destry to a narrow cul-de-sac in South Frankston and a small 1980s house of burnished-turd bricks and mossy terracotta tiles. Parked in the open carport was a Falcon Ute, and on the lawn a Green Thumbs franchise trailer.

The house of a man who might not want to attract attention to himself, Ellen thought, and ran both sets of number plates. She was looking at the home and vehicles of Clay and Anita Bernard. Ellen smiled in satisfaction. She recognized Clay Bernard's name from the Mitchell Pyne file. Two convictions for the handling and possession of stolen goods, and back when Pyne was nineteen, he'd been questioned in relation to his association with Bernard.

Old dogs, new tricks, she thought. Mitchell Pyne was using the same fence, all these years later.

What other tricks hadn't he changed?

39

MONDAY MORNING, ELLEN WAS in her office finalizing the briefing agenda when Scobie Sutton called.

"I've just given Inspector Challis *good* DNA news, but I'm afraid your DNA news is inconclusive—sorry, Ellen."

She waited. She'd had years of experience, gleaning information from Sutton one crumb at a time.

And years of experience giving up the wait and prodding him. "What news is that, Scobie?"

If Sutton heard the hard vibration in her voice he didn't bow to it. "Ellen, I tested that bandage as a favor. No job number, and you say it was fished out of a rubbish bin . . . ?"

"Sorry Scobie. Just tell me what you found."

"Give me a clean, legal sample, no contaminants, no soap or ointment, no secondary transfer from other people, and I'll give you a result that will stand up in court."

"Scobie," she said.

"Sorry, yes, a partial match."

"A partial match to *who*?"

"An unsolved rape from earlier in the year," said Sutton hurriedly, and read her the case number. Jess Guthrie.

"I *could* run a low-copy-number analysis," he went on, "but that takes time and I'd probably have to send it off to a specialist lab, and for something that's inadmissible anyway . . ."

"Thanks Scobie, let's leave it as it is then. You've been a great help," Ellen said, and headed for the briefing room.

SHE BEGAN WITH THE DNA results.

"Pyne's our man but we can't pick him up yet. We need a clean arrest."

She saw a cops' kind of disappointment on their faces. It said that nothing surprised them and setbacks were to be borne and the system was fucked, but they'd just roll up their sleeves and start again.

"Meanwhile," she went on, "something interesting happened yesterday. Pyne was observed meeting with a known receiver of stolen goods."

She described Judd's tailing of Pyne and the events at the Arthurs Seat maze.

Katsoulas brightened. "Okay, so we get him on burglary, obtain his DNA, charge him with rape."

Rykert curled his lip. "Like bring in a CIU burglary team to get all the glory."

"Shut up, Jared."

"Children, children," Ellen said, "just do your jobs—which will include looking closely at Pyne's friends and family and acquaintances. Ian's done some checking."

Judd read from a sheet of paper, head tilted back to focus his glasses. "Pyne's thirty-one, lives alone, never been married. No hint of girlfriends in recent times, according to his landlord and his neighbors—who don't particularly like him and were happy to talk. He's been a part-time taxi driver for the past five years, a courier driver before that, so he knows his way around the Peninsula. Never been arrested, but he was questioned in relation to a handling and receiving investigation when he was nineteen." He looked up. "At the time of Clay Bernard's first arrest."

"Go on," Ellen said.

"Other than that, he was expelled from school when he was sixteen for spying on the girls' toilets."

"That's where it all began," Katsoulas said with satisfaction. "Next step, burglary and rape. What about friends and family?"

"Still a few holes in my knowledge," Judd said, "but his father died in a car smash when he was ten. His mother lives in Pakenham, but he rarely sees her, and he has a married sister over in Perth and a brother in the navy. Essentially, he's a loner."

"People know to steer clear of him," Katsoulas said, a nasty gleam in her eye.

"Here's what we do," Ellen said. "Shadow Pyne around the clock, look more closely into his past, look more closely into his present, and dig into his recent association with Clay Bernard."

"But without DNA . . ." Rykert said.

"Without DNA we need to catch Pyne in the act. Or get him on something else and hope he coughs," Ellen said.

THE TASKS ASSIGNED—JUDD ON deeper research, Katsoulas and Rykert on surveillance—Ellen drove to the Bernard home in South Frankston. Parked across the road and down from his house, she settled into the back seat with a pair of binoculars. The Green Thumbs trailer had not moved from its position on the front lawn and the Falcon Ute was still in the carport; the Honda people-mover was missing. She didn't know what that meant. The whole family was out? The wife was out with the kids? The husband ditto? Two children under five: did they go to kindergarten? Day care?

A partial answer to her musings: Clay Bernard emerged from the carport half an hour later, unshaven, tousled, wearing only shorts, as if he'd just got out of bed. Yawning, scratching his balls and carrying a five-liter fuel can, he walked around to the rear of the trailer. Now he was partly invisible to Ellen, but then she saw the wire gate swing open and guessed he was refueling something, a lawnmower or leaf blower. A short time later, he closed the gate and shuffled, as though deeply fatigued, back through the carport and into the house.

Ellen thought about the mowing job. People would see the Green Thumbs trailer and think nothing of it. There were Green Thumbs mowing and garden maintenance franchisees all over the suburbs of the city. No one would question their presence. Good way to collect or deliver stolen goods, too.

Anita Bernard returned in the Honda and parked it in the driveway rather than in the carport, as though she intended to go out again. She was alone. Ellen watched her get out, walk around to the rear of the car and grab a couple of supermarket bags. Groceries, by the looks of it: the leafy heads of celery stalks, the end of a baguette. And the bags were heavy. Ellen could see tension in the woman's arms, tendons and muscles clenched under the skin. A pretty woman, her skin softly golden, as though she spent time outdoors. It seemed likely: apart from the battered gardening franchise trailer, everything else at the front of the house, lawns, shrubs and garden beds, was neat but busy with spills of color: green, red, yellow, blue.

But what really caught Ellen's eye was not a plant or an item of shopping or even a shapely, sun-golden arm. It was a Pandora bracelet very like Marilyn Sligo's.

Then the woman was disappearing into the carport—maybe there was a side door to the kitchen. Ellen left the car swiftly and crossed the road, full of tension. Passing the Honda, she saw more shopping bags on the back seat.

Just then, Bernard's wife reappeared, stepping into the carport and heading toward Ellen. But she didn't see Ellen. Her husband was behind her and she was sniping at him. "Not my fault. I had to drop the kids off and do a shop and the traffic was hell, okay? So get off my case, Clay, all right?"

She came on, into the sunlight, and froze. "Who are you?"

But Ellen was watching Clay Bernard, still back in the shadows. Homing in on his wife with a look of sulky determination, he saw Ellen and faltered. Opened and closed his mouth.

Wondering if she should have brought backup, Ellen held up her ID. Still watching Clay Bernard, she said to Anita, "Nice bracelet."

The husband closed his eyes and seemed to crumple. Ellen relaxed minutely. She doubted she'd need backup.

Anita Bernard seemed confused. She peered at the bracelet. "What?"

"Did your husband give you that bracelet, Mrs. Bernard?"

Anita went very still. Looking older, tireder, she turned to her husband. "You bastard. You promised me."

"Anita, wait—"

"I can't hack it anymore, Clay. I warned you."

Her husband stared at her miserably, marriage, fatherhood and his cushy bent life unraveling. "Please, love—"

"Don't you 'love' me, you dickhead."

Then Anita was turning back to Ellen. "Tell me."

"I can show you pictures if you don't believe me, but your bracelet is an exact match for one belonging to a woman in Somerville."

Anita turned to her husband, wailing, "You said you got it specially for our anniversary."

"I did, love. The business was struggling, that's all. You mean everything to me."

There were emotional sub-tones to their voices that Ellen didn't like. They'll start forgiving each other in a minute, she thought.

"*Mrs. Bernard.*"

Anita jumped. She turned back to Ellen. "What?"

"The bracelet was stolen in the commission of a serious sexual assault, a rape, and now it's on the end of your arm."

That tipped the balance. Anita flew at her husband. "Rape? You raped someone?"

He went white, put up a forearm protectively. "What? No. Never. You know me."

"We're finished, *finished.*"

"Sweetheart, I swear, I don't do rape."

"That is *so* not the point. You betrayed me. You're handling again, for someone who *does* do rape."

"I didn't know—I swear I didn't know," Bernard said.

Ellen waited. She let the drama play out.

"Tell this policewoman who it is," stormed Anita.

"Pardon?"

Anita started tearing off the bracelet as though it were noxious. "*Who gave you this?*"

Finally: "Mitch Pyne."

Anita turned to Ellen triumphantly. "There, satisfied? I knew nothing about it. I am not involved in *anything* my husband's involved in. I thought he was going straight. Now I know he's going straight to jail, and I'm glad."

"Anita, please."

"Our sixth wedding anniversary," the woman told Ellen. "September the nineteenth."

Clay moved toward his wife. Reached out an arm, completely failing to read her anger, and she kneed him in the groin.

40

MEANWHILE SCOBIE SUTTON HAD called Challis with the good-news DNA result.

"I'll email you the details, but the dead man's DNA is tied to an unsolved murder dating back almost twenty years."

Challis was in his office with Murphy and Coolidge, explaining the nature of the Loeb–Hauser operation, Coolidge wanting to be absolutely sure drugs weren't involved. The sun streamed in, warming his back. With a half-consumed croissant and mug of coffee at his elbow, all was right with the world. But then Sutton called with his bombshell and he came alive, tilting back in his chair, propping his feet on his open bottom drawer, his thinking pose.

"Twenty years ago? Owen was barely a teenager."

"I'm not saying he committed the murder," Sutton said.

"But he was there?"

Fat lot of good that was, if he was dead.

Sutton said, "No, he wasn't there."

"Scobie, so help me, I'll wring your neck."

Sutton heard the snarl and said hurriedly, "What I mean is, the DNA isn't a perfect match, it's a familial match."

Challis took his feet off the bottom drawer and sat forward, his elbows on his desk, staring at Coolidge. She stared back, her green eyes searching. Full of intelligence, irony and a hint of scorn. No more sleepy, ambiguous looks. Of late, her expression seemed to say that his rejection of her was his loss.

Echoing Sutton, he said, "A familial match."

"Mitochondrial DNA," Sutton said. "Owen Valentine and the murderer are related by blood. Half-brothers, maybe?"

Challis locked eyes with Coolidge again. "Half-brothers."

He saw a shift in her then, her mind marshaling and ordering her thoughts and intentions to stay a step ahead of him. "Hang on, Scobie," he said, "I'm putting you on speaker."

He glanced at Pam Murphy as he did so. She looked suddenly more alert, aware of the undercurrents in the room.

"Done," he told Sutton. "Now, tell us about the murder."

Sutton's words sounded tinny and distant:

"A strangulation murder dating from 1998. Annika Watanabe, aged nineteen, a New Zealander here on a working holiday. Four months pregnant, she was found strangled on the back beach at Rye. The DNA source was found under her fingernails: she scratched him."

"And the fetal DNA?"

"Same as the killer's," Sutton said.

Challis thanked him and started to end the call when Sutton stopped him: "Wait, wait . . ."

"Yes?"

"You remember we didn't find any useable prints at the ice lab?"

"Yes."

"It occurred to me to test Clover Penford's doll."

Sensing Challis's impatience, he raced on. A partial print, matching a Monash University chemistry dropout arrested for possession in 2013 and still living with his parents in an inner Melbourne suburb. "I passed it on to the child exploitation team."

"Thanks, Scobie," Challis said, ending the call.

He shot a look at Serena Coolidge, knowing she'd wanted first shot at Clover Penford's abusers. "Senior Sergeant?"

Coolidge shrugged. "Win some, lose some."

Challis shook himself, irritated. "On that note," he said, "I intend to do Carl Bowie for murder. Now. Today."

Coolidge whipped her head back and forth. "No. Bowie's ours. He's central to a large-scale and ongoing drug-squad operation. As I said before, I want you two to back off."

"Three linked murders trumps that," Challis said, his tone hardening.

"Three? What three?"

Pam Murphy answered, deadly calm. "*Four* deaths, if you want to get technical. The New Zealand girl and her unborn child, murdered by Carl Bowie. Owen Valentine, murdered on Carl Bowie's orders. Colin Hauser, murdered by the men hired by Carl Bowie. The link? Carl Bowie. What's so hard to understand about that?"

Coolidge sat, coiled and dangerous, ignoring her. "Motive?"

Challis rocked back in his chair, propped his feet on the bottom drawer again. "Annika Watanabe was pregnant. Perhaps she wanted to marry him, or meet his parents. Perhaps she wanted an abortion and that was an affront to him."

Murphy leaned forward to strengthen the case. "He got away with it and felt safe, but at the back of his mind was the DNA."

"If he kept his nose clean," Challis said, "he'd be okay forever. What he didn't count on was his half-brother."

Watching Coolidge stew on it, he added, "Owen didn't have an arrest record. Carl would have been okay so long as Owen kept his nose clean. But Owen got hooked on ice and started dealing, breaking and entering. Meaning it was only a matter of time before he was arrested and his DNA made it onto the record."

"Why didn't he get rid of Owen years ago?"

Murphy said, "Perhaps he didn't have the resources. Probably he didn't know there was such a thing as mitochondrial DNA."

"Why use heavy hitters from Sydney?"

Challis shrugged. "Didn't want to get his hands dirty, didn't know the right people here."

"Or didn't want tongues wagging if he used a local," Murphy added.

Coolidge didn't like any of this. Challis leaned forward again. "Think about it: we arrest Carl right now. Not only does his little empire crumble even further—and we have to assume he might be about to do a runner—but we clear the murders and stop more from happening. Meanwhile, he might look to do a deal. My team puts him away for murder, *you* get to mop up a big operation here and feed information to your Sydney colleagues."

He watched her, the peculiar intensity of her frown and lowered eyes. Then her expression cleared and she looked up.

"I have people watching him, so I'll know if he does do a runner. Meanwhile—"

Challis interrupted: "Where is he?"

"At home. Meanwhile, this is what I want. One, a quiet arrest. Two, I want to be there. Three, in addition to the arrest warrant we secure warrants to search his house, all vehicles and all business premises. Four, simultaneous with the arrest, we shut down his wife and kids and all employees, in case they're involved and try to send word to each other. Five, I tell Sydney right now where we're at."

Challis grinned. "Done."

She left. Murphy stayed to start the paperwork, and Challis organized the uniformed backup.

They were interrupted a few minutes later: Coolidge returning, her expression tense. "We might have a problem. Apparently Bowie's fallen out of favor. There's a price on his head."

GRIPPED BY A KIND of paralysis, Carl Bowie spent most of Monday morning in his armchair.

Last week and all weekend he'd been charging around like a man possessed, putting his affairs in order. Thursday he'd contacted a real estate agent to find buyers for all but one of the bakehouses—one as a kind of fallback in case everything turned out all right. After that, he'd let most of the staff go, knowing not to call it "sacking" or "retrenching" or "terminating" or "downsizing" but "*right*sizing," as Grow Your Own Prosperity advised. And he'd been careful not to be a prick about it. No emails, no texts, but face to face. Telling each of them, gently gruff: "You will bounce back bigger and better, and that is a positive for you." But were they grateful? Like fuck. He just didn't get the workings of the casual-staff mind.

Friday and Saturday he'd gone on-line to liquidate the rest of his assets. Which turned out to be a fucking fire sale. Most of his spare cash was tied up in bitcoins, currently trading at five hundred dollars, down from his 2013 purchase price of eleven hundred. Sacrilege, getting rid of them at that price. He tried auctioning small parcels at a time on US and European wholesale markets, to soften the blow, but it didn't work.

Then Sunday he sent the wife and kids to his mother-in-law's. Lois wanted to know what he was up to, her hands planted firmly on her skinny hips: "Are you in trouble?"

Trouble? You dozy cow. He'd snarled at her, she'd snarled back, feet were stamped and doors slammed.

Now, Monday, he still hadn't finished liquidating. All he wanted to do was run, but he felt too tense for that. Tense and curiously sluggish. It was as if he was waiting for the knock on the door. Fucking mad. The hours passed, he checked the auctions, he sat, he paced, he sat again . . .

He had a little Beretta pistol, licensed, and took it out, held it in his lap as he thought, or tried to think. He stalked through the house now and then, glancing at his image in the mirrors. Tanned, slim—with the pistol, he had a certain aura. Sleeves casually rolled, the Rolex gleaming on his left wrist, the crispness of his shirt. A striking portrait; a frisson of danger around him. That aura must have been present when those detectives visited the bakehouse to tell him about Owen. They didn't seem to notice, but then they were cops. Occasionally the phone rang. He let the answering machine monitor the messages. Lois rang, several times. His father-in-law. The respective managers of the bakehouses.

"Just deal with it," he'd shout at the machine. "*I* am."

Then Tiffany, with her whining up-talk: "Mr. Bowie? Andrew called in sick and we have a big Red Hill Pantry order?"

A blinding red rage ejected him from the chair. He screamed down the line, "Tell them sorry, tell them fuck off, and why don't *you* fuck off while you're about it?"

He should have sacked her, too.

He waited for the red veil to fade from his eyes and Lois was on the answering machine again, saying, "Carl, we need to talk about the kids' Christmas presents. I don't know what's going on with you, but I want you to put it to one side *and consider your kids*. Bree needs a new bike and I think it's time we got Yazzie an iPhone."

Carl thought about his daughters, tears pricking his eyes.

He'd worked bloody hard to bring the Bowie bakery empire back from the brink. Meanwhile his loser half-brother smoked a lot of dope, left school early and shacked up with the high-school slag. Christine Penford. Carl was surprised they'd stayed together.

Then a few weeks ago, high on ice (ironic if it was *my* ice, Carl thought), the idiot smacked some guy—hard enough that he'd be charged and maybe do jail time. And Carl wouldn't have known about it if Owen hadn't come crawling to him after a gap of years, twitching and paranoid, wanting to borrow five grand.

"Why?"

"Pay this guy off," Owen said, his breath giving off waves of chemical rot.

"What guy? Why?"

Owen's gaze slid away. "I might have, you know, given him a belting."

"You mean he's pressing charges and you want him to shut up."

"Something like that."

"What the hell happened to you, Owen?"

"Fuck off, Carl. You going to help me or not?"

Owen was family, so Carl gave him five grand. Of course the prick spent it on drugs or whatever and was back the next day, wanting another five.

"Mate, the guy laughed in my face."

"So you want to offer him *more* money."

"Well, yeah."

"You showed him the five?"

Owen's gaze slid away. "Yeah. Course."

Carl told him to fuck off.

And the very next day, when watching one of those dumb

CSI shows, Carl learned about mitochondrial DNA. It didn't matter that he and Owen had different fathers: they had the same mother, and their DNA would show that.

And if the police ran Owen's DNA . . .

So Carl called Hector. Asked if he could do a mate a favor.

MEANWHILE, IN WATERLOO, SERENA Coolidge looked up from her iPad. "Bowie is licensed to own a pistol."

Challis nodded. He'd already checked. "Beretta nine mil."

"What was your impression of him? Is he the type to use a gun against police?"

Challis shrugged. "His empire's collapsing. He's facing arrest. I called for an armed response team."

Coolidge's face tightened. "Without consulting?"

Challis said flatly, "Serena, there are houses all around him. He's armed. We have no choice."

"How long's it going to take armed response to get down here? Couple of hours? And that's *after* we jump through all the bureaucratic hoops."

Challis felt his temper rise. He stared at her expressionlessly, about to retort. Then Pam Murphy touched his arm. "Boss? She's right."

All of his tension vanished. Serena Coolidge *was* right. Clearly the situation warranted an armed presence, but there was no time for a risk assessment briefing that could take three or four hours to complete. Everything would be measured in "parameters," with reference to a psychological profile. Was the subject armed? Did he or she have a record for violence or armed violence? How should the "solution" be structured (the type and placement of strike corridors; the possible evacuation of neighboring houses; the dangers and benefits of a rapid entry; the deployment of flash-bang

grenades)? What was the likelihood of third-party compli-
cations (the presence, or arrival, of friend, family member,
neighbor, domestic servant or henchman)?

And on top of that, the operation had to pass several
levels of permission, from an assistant commissioner to
the area commander to the superintendent down to lowly
Inspector Challis.

He nodded finally.

"We go in now, but we take what armed backup we can
muster to breach Bowie's house, block the street, manage
traffic and warn the neighbors."

He paused. "We all wear vests."

They rolled shortly after that. They were two minutes
from their destination when the radio chatter reported
shots fired.

CARL HEARD GLASS BREAKING somewhere at the rear of
the house, a sharply perilous noise, as if the entire picture
window had been breached. He sat incredulous for a couple
of beats. He hadn't really thought it would happen. Didn't
the police at least knock first? Didn't they come through the
front door?

In that short delay a man clearly not police came
swarming at him from the hallway and Carl shot him.
A gut shot. Carl stared at his hand as if it, not he, controlled events. The wounded man, meanwhile, was clichéd
muscle: bald, tattooed, enormous. But piteous in the way
he tossed and squealed, reeling off invective amid pleas for
an ambulance.

Carl stepped over him and into the hallway. A flicker of
movement down at the end where the light poured in from
the back garden. A second man, ducking out into the yard.

"Come in and get me," Carl screamed.

He didn't move and the second man didn't move and Carl wondered how something like this might play out.

For something to do, he dragged the wounded man down the hallway and dumped him onto the broken glass. Then, as fire was returned—from the yard this time—he let off three rapid shots into the lawn and raced back to the sitting room and behind the main sofa.

41

WOORALLA DRIVE WAS FLAT for the first couple of kilometers, passing a sports ground, then crossing the little tourist railway line with its Hogwarts train, dipping for Balcombe Creek and finally climbing steeply to one of the highest points on the Peninsula. Stunning south-easterly views over farmland and westerly views over the bay, Challis noted, before assessing the location for a siege situation or shootout. The road was narrow where it passed Bowie's house, before broadening for the downslope to the Nepean Highway and the Mt. Eliza shops.

Bowie lived on the upslope a short distance before the Mountain View Road roundabout, his house set back from the road and amid trees, a low fence on either side separating him from his neighbors. Challis counted a dozen cars nearby, in driveways and carports and two wheels up on the grassy strips on either side of the road. He didn't like it: through traffic from the highway to the shops, neighbors, trees, the narrowness of the road here, and no clear line of sight. And the neighbors were starting to gather and point.

Pam Murphy was driving, hard on Coolidge's tail, with uniformed officers in two cars close behind them. Then Coolidge was slowing to a crawl and pulling in behind the drug squad's surveillance car, its passenger side wheels up on the street's narrow grass verge. Coolidge parked, but there was no room for the Challis and Murphy unmarked car or the police cars.

"Go past," Challis said, "into Manna Court."

She complied, the police car following. They all piled out and Challis gave a series of terse commands to the uniforms: block traffic in both directions, usher the neighbors back inside and tell them to lock their doors. Then he ran with Murphy back onto Wooralla Drive and joined Coolidge at the drug-squad car. She gestured tensely at Bowie's house. "Two men, two minutes ago."

Challis gazed across at Bowie's house, a split-level glass and white-painted concrete nightmare. All quiet now. "How many shots?"

"Two, a couple of minutes apart," a drug-squad detective said. "I've notified armed response and asked Mornington and Frankston to attend."

"Good. These men: did Bowie let them in?"

"Not that we could see. They split up and headed down each side of the house to the rear."

"Didn't knock on the front door first?"

"No."

Coolidge felt she was being left out. "Car?"

"They came in that," the detective said, pointing to a Toyota Camry parked twenty meters downhill from Bowie's house. Hertz sticker, noted Challis. He said, "Can we disable it?"

Coolidge stiffened. Challis was talking to *her* officer. "Dave, you carry a pocketknife."

The man grinned. "Done," he said. He ran at a crouch to the Camry and punctured the two driver's side tires. Then stiffened. Crouched closer to the road. There was another shot.

~

THREE MORE SHOTS, MUFFLED. Two guns, Challis thought, noting the differences in tone.

But mostly, like the others, he was frozen in a half-crouch, shoulders hunched, a natural first instinct. No one knew what movement to make. Much of their training had faded in the years of paperwork and drudgery so that, right now, they were motionless for a moment, hands on the butts of their service pistols.

Then they flew into movement, ducking behind the drug-squad car and Coolidge's unmarked Holden. Further up the hill, the uniforms were going door to door; one constable stood exposed in the roadway to stop traffic. Another stood exposed downhill from Bowie's house, also to stop traffic. They looked vulnerable to Challis, but were some distance away, risky pistol shots away, and they were needed to stop drivers who would otherwise sail blithely through and maybe collect a stray bullet.

Their sergeant came running down the footpath from the direction of the roundabout. Puffing, he crouched with Challis. "My men are exposed."

"I know, I'm sorry," Challis said, "but there would be hell to pay if a civilian got shot."

"Yeah, yeah," the sergeant said, and readied himself to run back uphill when Pam Murphy shouted, "Someone's coming out."

NOT BOWIE. THE TWO gunmen.

Serena Coolidge stepped instinctively out onto the road as they came bursting from the shadowy side garden, a narrow space between the downhill wall of Bowie's house and the fence dividing it from the neighbor's. One man supported the other, who was clawing at his bloodied waist. The first man seemed astonished to see police there—but he was less dithery than the police. Raising his pistol, he snapped off three shots, the sounds sharp and waspish now, no longer muffled by walls and windows.

Coolidge was his first target simply because she was the closest. She said, "Oh," softly, and fell without grace onto the hard road surface. One of the uniforms was hit then, spotted by the gunman stepping out of one driveway to enter another. He spun around, holding his thigh. He tottered a couple of steps and went down on one knee, then onto his hip and finally onto his back.

Everyone was screaming now, at each other and into their radios. Challis sent one of the drug-squad detectives to pull the wounded constable back behind the nearest car and the others to vantage points up- and downhill from Bowie. That left Coolidge exposed, out on the edge of the road and between her car and the drug-squad car. The gunman fired again, aiming at Coolidge, and Challis saw her pants dimple and flex, her leg jerk, and there was a hole, blood seeping. He couldn't see where the first bullet had struck, but guessed her waist or hip. Seeing the gunman duck behind a car, he darted across to Coolidge and stretched out on the road to shield her.

She turned her head, registered him, and in a creaky voice said, "One way to get intimate."

He barked an uncomfortable laugh. "Save your strength."

Pam Murphy, where was Pam? Challis risked lifting his head from the road and saw her, on the grass and mostly shielded by the drug-squad car, white faced, holding her shoulder.

His head still raised, Challis swung his gaze up and down the sloping road. The uniformed sergeant and the drug-squad detective were attending to the wounded man, the other officers were waving people back into their houses, taking cover, speaking wildly into their radios. He was dimly aware of distressed cries all around him, then wondered if he'd been contributing to it, a frightened kind of keening.

He rolled onto his left shoulder, feeling chips of pot-hole asphalt dig into his hip, and faced Bowie's house, his body still shielding Coolidge. His pistol was heavy in his hand. He'd barely passed his last firing-range test.

Sirens, there should be sirens by now. Or not. Frankston police, Mornington police, they were both ten minutes away. How long had it been, this shootout in the suburbs? Two minutes?

The gunman came out from cover, streaking down to the rental car, firing at Challis. One bullet punched him in the chest, the vest barely absorbing the impact, and another ricocheted near his head. He snapped a shot at the blurred figure, hit an ankle. Blind luck. The man stumbled full tilt onto the road, losing his gun.

He got to his hands and knees, head swiveling to locate the weapon. Challis couldn't risk another shot: downhill of the gunman was a uniformed constable controlling the uphill traffic and, beyond him, half-a-dozen cars.

The uniform saw what was happening. He stood frozen in the middle of the road, one hand out to hold the motorists, the other up to stop the gunman. Then he remembered his pistol. He took it out, shouted at the gunman: "Flat on the ground!"

The gunman had found his gun. He tried to stand, rocky now, aiming wildly, prompting Challis to make a crouched dash across the road and onto the gunman. They fell together, the pistol firing uselessly into the sky above the marooned cars, Challis punching, wrenching. Spotting the uniform, he said, "Help me, for fuck's sake."

The uniform seemed to come out of a trance. He ran to Challis, helped him wrestle the gunman to the road.

"Cuff him," Challis said, "then sit on him and don't be afraid to use your capsicum spray."

"Sir."

Pocketing the gunman's pistol, and feeling full of pounding pain now, all of his adrenaline drained away, Challis stumbled uphill to Bowie's house. Into the yard, down along the side wall, watching for the second gunman, every shrub and tree a potential trap.

He found the man on his back between a rosebush and the far corner of the wall. Panting, eyes glazed, no gun.

Crouching painfully, his whole torso feeling dented and bruised, Challis cuffed the man's ankles together and crept into the yard at the rear of Bowie's house. The back wall was mostly glass, leading onto a deck overlooking a pond and a scattering of bottlebrush and other small native trees. A brick had been thrown through the glass sliding door and blood had pooled on the tiles a short distance inside it. And there was the missing pistol, several meters in from the broken glass, on the floor beside a glass-topped bamboo table.

He called, "Mr. Bowie?"

Silence. He called again. "Police, Mr. Bowie. You're safe now, your intruders have been arrested."

Still no answer. "May I come in, Mr. Bowie?"

"Go away. Leave me alone."

A kind of shrieking panic in the voice. This is going to take a while, Challis thought. Negotiator. Armed response. Evacuation.

He could start the process. He could talk to Bowie, a

mild, soft-pedaling conversation that didn't accuse the man but rather built him up a little. But he felt so tired.

"Did Owen come to you for money, Mr. Bowie?"

There was no answer, and no answer with the passing of time, the gathering of armed response police, negotiators, gawking citizenry and TV vans, until, hours later, one muffled gunshot sounded somewhere deep in the house.

Prompting one policeman to mutter, "Another fucking cliché."

42

A WEEK BEFORE CHRISTMAS, and Pam Murphy said, "I can drive."

Michael Traill soon scotched that idea. "It might have escaped your notice, but your arm's in a sling."

"I can steer with my good hand and you change gears for me."

"And you an officer of the law," he said.

And so he drove, from her front door and across to Peninsula Link, then up EastLink and finally to the car park of the funeral home on Canterbury Road.

Pam was powerfully aware of him beside her, contained and unruffled, showing only a trace of the slow drip of disappointment and loneliness she'd first witnessed in him. She watched his capable hand on the gearstick of her car, and thought of her shot arm, the punching sensation of the bullet and the shock she felt afterward, how now the arm, in its sling across her breasts, was both comforting and being comforted by her.

Since the shooting, she'd been given to stupid fancies. If anything, Michael was the comfort. He'd been her comfort in hospital, and out, then at every fraught and tedious stage that had attended her mother's death.

"How's your book?"

He gestured. "Ah, I'm not going to write a book. I don't need to write a book."

She glanced at him uneasily. Was that a good thing? Had she been responsible? He seemed settled enough, and, as they drove, another idea grew in her mind. "Are we going to live together?"

She'd never lived with a partner. Hadn't had much of a love life, in fact. The usual adolescent fumbling, a mad few weeks with a young surfer, a madder week with a female sergeant . . .

He shot her a look. "It's not too soon?"

"As in, we barely know each other? No. It feels right."

"It does feel right," he said.

"Good."

"Of course, I'm universally loathed . . ."

He was sun-browned and slim and compact there beside her. "Not by me," she said.

He nodded. "Good to know."

"Two incomes, we can afford to rent a decent place."

"Okay," said Traill simply.

What Pam didn't say, and it stirred a touch of guilt in her, was that there would be some money from her mother's estate, sometime down the track.

AS IF TO ATONE for these thoughts, she contemplated the nature and existence of misery which, it turned out, resided everywhere. She should be glad to be alive, but her feelings, all of them, were scrambled. She would burst into tears at nothing. Life was short and risky. People lived in misery. The misery of Christine Penford, the misery of the children.

Pam only wanted to feel better.

She said, "Let's buy a bike."

~

CHRISTINE PENFORD'S MOTHER LIVED in a small brick house on a street that had never entertained hopes or expectations but merely endured. She answered Pam's knock with Troy Penford on her hip. Peering, frowning, she said, "I know you: you're that policewoman."

"Pam Murphy, Mrs. Penford."

The older woman looked past her. "Who's that?"

"That's Michael. My friend."

Her eyes narrowed, darted, her mind making rapid calculations and adjustments. She recognizes him, Pam thought, and readied herself—but for what? To give him a mouthful?

Mrs. Penford's gaze finally settled on the bike. It was pink, with purple grips and pedals. A white cane basket above the front wheel, pink and purple flowers woven into it, and a pink saddle.

Her eyes blinked. "I tried to get her old bike back but the fellow had already sold it."

Michael wheeled the bike past Pam, up onto the veranda. He flipped the stand with the toe of his shoe and propped it there. Pam said, "Will you give it to her now, or for Christmas?"

A decisive woman, but just then indecisive. Pam said, "We bought wrapping paper and ribbon, just in case."

And Michael said, "What's one week, in the scheme of things?"

That decided her. "I'll hide it in the shed."

MEANWHILE, IN A MENSWEAR department, Ellen Destry was saying, "And how was Sergeant Cleavage?"

Arguing with the nurses and doctors, the last time Challis

had seen her. Showing just a little cleavage. "Fighting fit," he said.

Ellen tucked her arm in his. "I don't mind if you visit her, you know."

"I know," Challis said.

She squeezed his arm, a simple gesture, but he saw complicated layers of meaning behind it. Ellen was glad that he hadn't been wounded. She was glad Coolidge hadn't died. She was glad Challis was hers, not Coolidge's. She, herself, would hate to be shot, and pitied Coolidge. And she acknowledged Coolidge's attraction and power.

She gave him an affectionate shake as they walked, but the movement wrenched his bruised rib cage and he smothered a gasp. She failed to notice, so intent was she now on the racks of shirts and trousers. After shopping for him, they would head up the escalators to search out a Christmas present for Ellen's daughter. Right now, it was his turn.

"I bet Sergeant Cleavage doesn't take her boyfriend clothes shopping."

Challis laughed, but the sweat was breaking out. Every item of clothing felt harsh on his skin, too pressed and starched to bear. A great many carried patterns and inscriptions. Some were woven from unusual but uniformly awful fabrics. He'd tried on a pair of chinos with a false back pocket, stitched shut! And the muzak lodged deep in his skull.

His jaw ached from clenching.

Then, with relief, he spotted a face he recognized. A big guy . . . assault? Armed robbery. Paroled only a couple of months ago. His interest quickened. Maybe the guy was here to rob the place. Or shoot me, he thought. He stiffened, wanting to pull away from Ellen and slip into cop mode, shadow the guy, anything but this . . . this . . .

A competent, stern-faced woman swung around to face the bruiser. She held a shirt to his chest. She eyed it for color and fit. And the hulking, tattooed giant reached out a hand and touched her cheek.

Maybe he endured the torture because he loved, and was loved, and it was Christmas. Like me, Challis thought.

"My love?" Ellen said then, her mind not on guns or thugs but some little thing of life.